Lesser Evils: An Animal Rights Novel

Zola Creech

Bazetta Press, LLC

Lesser Evils: An Animal Rights Novel is a work of fiction. The names, characters, businesses, organizations, places, and happenings are used fictitiously or are the product of the author's imagination. Any resemblance to actual events or persons (living or dead) is entirely coincidental and not intended by the author.

Published by Bazetta Press, LLC, Cortland, Ohio. For permissions, contact: BazettaP@gmail.com

eBook ISBN 979–8–9863720–0–6

Paperback ISBN 979–8–9863720–1–3

Cover photo by Michael Chacon on Unsplash

Library of Congress Control Number: 2022914828

Printed in the United States of America

DEDICATION

For my mother, a great lover of animals and dark, psychological thrillers.

CONTENTS

1: The Fall

Why did I burn that letter? Professor Mark Blackwell picked up the college newspaper without reading the headlines. He strolled down the hallway, smiling and nodding to passing colleagues as though it was any other Monday morning. He paused in front of his office, fumbling with his keys while glancing up and down the empty corridor. Upon entering, he exhaled and closed the door, flipping the lever to lock it. The overhead lights remained off, giving the impression no one was there. After popping a couple of chewable antacid tablets into his mouth, Blackwell turned on a desk lamp and sat down with the paper, bracing himself for the worst.

The headline read *Wittgenstein Cheerleader Falls to Her Death*. The half-page picture of Candy Rowan came from the college yearbook, showing her leaping high in the air at last year's game with Yale. Blackwell read the article, meticulously digesting every word. It had lots of condolences and kind observations from Candy's family and friends but little factual information. Surprisingly, the story said nothing about what might have happened. Was this good or bad? An autopsy would reveal she was pregnant—new headlines, a more serious investigation. It may take a while, but they would eventually have a DNA profile of the father. Detectives would put two and two together and get a court order to collect his DNA. Game over.

Should he admit the affair? His guilty conscience said yes, but that wouldn't bring Candy back, and it would be name staining napalm for his career. Yes, they had a ripping wrangle about terminating her pregnancy, but Mark never believed she would kill herself. Coming forward now would be a viable option if he had kept her suicide note. The damnable letter arrived the morning after she jumped, and he destroyed it on impulse, knowing it would cost him his job. This, however, was a dreadful blunder. He should have saved the handwritten document as proof of her suicide, his reserve parachute if things got ugly with the police.

Candy drew a tombstone at the bottom of the letter, displaying the numeral 3. What did that mean? She hadn't had an ultrasound and would have no way of knowing if she carried twins. Blackwell ceased speculating and went to the window, shutting his eyes as if that would make it all go away. *My God. Losing Candy, and now this. What a nasty welter of thorns.* He had made the mistake of being precipitous once. It wouldn't happen again. *Just wait and watch to see what happens.*

* * *

The following Thursday, Blackwell ran into a colleague in the men's room. The elderly professor told about attending Miss Rowan's funeral and asked how well Mark knew her. Blackwell said she was his best student and would be missed. The two men talked on, and Mark discovered that Candy's family blocked the autopsy. Her parents said the cause of death was eminently clear and unnecessary bodily intrusions violated their religious beliefs. Cremation would occur tomorrow morning, and her ashes would be deposited in the Atlantic Ocean. This was a lucky break. No autopsy meant no DNA analysis.

Blackwell went back to his office and sat down, calmer than he had been in days. The situation should be survivable because he and Candy were careful, but was that enough in a world filled with security cameras, picture taking cellphones, and prying eyes? Going on like nothing was wrong would give the safest impression. But that meant being on campus and running the risk that, in light of recent events, some student might recall seeing him and Candy together. Alternatively, taking an extended leave could also attract unwanted attention. Somehow he needed to stay off the radar screen of the police. He swiveled back and forth in his chair, trying to think of a good reason to be absent.

Mark sorted through a pile of old mail until he found a letter from the FBI. Assistant Director Patrick Greene had extended a personal invitation for a two-year faculty sabbatical with the Bureau. Blackwell had taught several criminal psychology seminars for Greene, had hosted a criminological soirée for the Behavioral Analysis Unit, and both men were on a first-name basis. The idea of relocating wasn't appealing, but the sacrifice seemed necessary under the circumstances.

Final exam week was here, followed by a long Christmas break. If things worked out well, no one at Wittgenstein would see him again for a long time. He reached for the phone but hesitated. He thought of his dead mother's favorite thunder-of-God expression: *Whatsoever a man soweth, that shall he also reap.* Mark punched in Greene's number, believing this was his best chance to thwart providence.

* * *

Over the next several days, Blackwell graded exams and performed end-of-semester chores. The tricky part was convincing Dean Shoemaker to approve his sabbatical on such short notice. Yet he was able to blend truth and fabrication into a narrative Shoemaker bought: grant him the sabbatical, and voilà, five high-quality journal articles would appear. Shoemaker would try to hold him to the agreement, but this problem could be solved later. Two years is a long time.

Friday morning was filled with anxious anticipation. Just turn in the grades, pick up his auxiliary supply of insulin and syringes, and he was gone. Blackwell met with his administrative assistant and gave her instructions about forwarding his mail and informing callers that he would be unavailable. He hurried toward his office, but slowed upon entering the hallway. Someone was knocking on his door. His immediate reaction was to flee, but the man had turned his way. *Keep walking. Stay calm. Be friendly.*

"Professor Blackwell?" the man asked.

Mark flashed an easy-going smile. "Yes."

"I'm Sergeant Miller from the Wittgenstein Police Department."

They shook hands. "You must be new here, Sergeant. I know all the officers personally. We are good friends."

"I was hired last month, coming over from the Boston police. Could I have a word with you?"

Blackwell maintained his confident grin. "Certainly, Sergeant. Please come inside." He held the door open and closed it behind Miller.

The police officer paused in the middle of the room. "What a marvelous office. It's much nicer than the others, every bit as grand as Dean Shoemaker's."

"It belongs to the holder of the Jensen Chair of Forensic Psychology, a position I currently have."

"I'll bet that job pays well, more than a normal professor's salary."

Mark nodded modestly. "A little more." Actually, it was a lot more, including a fifty percent reduction in teaching to afford time for research. However, he didn't want to dangle a possible motive for murder in front of a cop.

Miller approached Blackwell's vast assortment of degrees and awards. "You're a doctor, a real MD?"

"My original training was in psychiatry, but my love of exploratory investigation and writing led me to academia."

Miller took his time looking everything over, mutely admiring and acting impressed. But he wasn't fooling anyone—this was all police business. Mark waited with infinite patience, defensively positioned on mental tiptoes, smiling and giving little anecdotes to Miller's ostensibly innocent questions. This gray-haired cop was too old to be a sergeant. He was probably let go by the Boston police and was looking for an easy paycheck. When Miller finished browsing, Blackwell offered him a seat.

They sat down, Miller in the chair used by students, Blackwell behind his imposing oak desk. Miller's wandering eyes skimmed over every paperweight, pen, and picture, presumably looking for what shouldn't be there. Mark had, however, sanitized everything. *Look all you want, Sherlock. You won't find a damn thing.*

Miller finally looked up. "I wish this was merely a social visit, but I'm investigating the death of Candace Rowan, and I understand she was in your criminal psychology class."

"She was. It was a terrible tragedy. Do they know what happened? The newspapers said practically nothing."

"To tell you the truth, sir, I know very little. The forensics crew is still processing evidence, and the detectives on the scene haven't said much." Miller smiled with awkwardness. "Being the new guy, they've got me out talking to students and faculty, beating the bushes for leads." Miller pulled out a notepad and tawdry pen. "Did you notice anything unusual about Miss Rowan or see any recent changes in her behavior?"

"She was definitely high strung, always feeling the need to be first in the class, which she was. The intense pressure to be perfect might have been a contributing factor."

"Contributing factor to what, sir?"

"Her death." Blackwell tried to keep a straight face, taken aback by Miller's intellectual shallowness.

"Suicide?"

Mark nodded. "It seems like the only logical explanation, unless she was doing her cheerleading gymnastics on top of this building and accidentally slipped off, which is unlikely."

Miller meditatively rubbed his chin.

"You don't think so?" Blackwell asked incredulously.

"Well, sir, I don't have your credentials, but if I were going to kill myself by jumping off a tall building, I don't think I would remove all my clothes."

This was salt in an open wound, Candy's way of striking back after she was dead. Mark composed himself and raised a corrective finger. "You must understand that suicidal people are not in a normal frame of mind and sometimes do strange things." Blackwell opened a desk drawer and pulled out his most famous book. "I wrote this shortly after transitioning to academia." He extended the tome to Miller. "Take it with you."

Miller read the title out loud. *"The Psychological Autopsy*, by Mark Alan Blackwell, MD." He smiled. "I'll look this over and get it back to you as soon as possible."

"You may keep it. Consider it my welcome aboard gift."

"Oh, thank you." Miller sat silently thinking. "To the best of your knowledge, did Miss Rowan have a boyfriend?"

"She was always talking to guys. They found her irresistible, like wild honey to hungry bears."

"No, sir. I mean, was she involved in a romantic relationship?"

Mark shrugged. "I have no idea. Our association was strictly professor to student, as is required by the *Wittgenstein Code of Conduct.*"

"A talented girl like that must have had someone, but so far, this part of her life is a complete mystery."

"Maybe she didn't have anyone by choice, being busy with cheerleading and her academic studies." Blackwell peeked at his wristwatch. "Is there anything else? I have an appointment in the J. Edgar Hoover Building later today."

Miller got up from his chair. "No, sir. Thank you for your time and this interesting book. I'll be in touch if we have further questions."

"It will have to be by phone, unless you want to make a trip to Virginia. You see, I'm about to begin a two-year faculty sabbatical with the FBI."

Miller raised his bushy brows. "Boy, would I love to do something like that. What exactly is a faculty sabbatical?"

"I will work with the Behavioral Analysis Unit, observing and studying how they conduct investigations. They, in turn, will have the benefit of working with someone who does groundbreaking research in forensic psychology, an expert in the latest theories of criminal behavior."

Miller reached out and shook Blackwell's hand. "You live a fascinating life, sir."

Mark ushered Miller to the door. "Please call me if I can be of further assistance. Consider us unofficial partners in solving this tragic dilemma. But mark my words, it was a suicide. Miss Rowan was a compulsive overachiever, and she snapped under that pressure."

"I'll pass that along, sir. And good luck with your sabbatical."

Blackwell closed the door, uttering an elongated sigh of relief. That went exceptionally well. Miller never even asked him for an alibi.

2 The Museum

Blackwell rented a modest home on a wooded lot at the end of a quiet street, signing a two-year lease with an option to buy. Of course he had no intention of staying and would return to Boston when his sabbatical was over. He underwent an accelerated orientation on FBI organizational structure and procedures. It was naturally assumed that he would not be placed in harm's way, but they gave him basic firearms training and issued a 9 mm Glock pistol. After three weeks with no contact from Sergeant Miller, Mark assumed his endowed professorship was secure. After all, the Wittgenstein Police Department isn't Scotland Yard.

Much to Blackwell's surprise, his first official task was to conduct a security evaluation of a government data analyst. The issue concerned whether she was psychologically compatible with her top-secret clearance. This assignment undoubtedly arose from his insightful writings about FBI traitor Robert Hansen, a man responsible for the worst intelligence disaster in United States history. Mark had no idea who this woman was, but the request came directly from CIA Director Anthony Naples. Blackwell would pose as a member of the FBI's Behavioral Analysis Unit, responding to a report filed by her about a data anomaly. While working with her, he would evaluate her psychological fitness, and she would be unaware of his actual mission. The woman worked in the newly constructed underground intelligence facility known as the DDI, a place supposedly impervious to eavesdropping by foreign powers. Blackwell was given top-secret security clearance for this assignment, a necessity for completing the mission. The confusing paperwork increased the oddness of the situation. Naples made the request, but FBI Director Margaret Marshall assigned him to the case. Was he working for Naples or Marshall?

* * *

Security at the DDI entrance was tight. After having his fingerprints and retinas authenticated by a machine, Blackwell went through a body scanner. He had to surrender his firearm and everything in his pockets: cellphone, keys, wallet, even the Mensa ring on his finger. He retained his shoes, clothes, and his security badge. A guard pressed a concealed button, and the cylindrical door of the far-right elevator opened. Blackwell stepped inside and began a long descent.

The elevator door opened to a polished granite lobby, showing the emblem of the United States Intelligence Community. The words *Digital Data Interrogation* were engraved on the far wall, the first letters cut deep in the rock, forming the acronym DDI. Multiple corridors converged on the entrance, each labeled with a heading that only a technical geek could understand. He took several steps forward and stopped, remembering his subject had a split appointment between the FBI's Counter Terrorism Division and the CIA's Counterintelligence Group.

A gentleman of Asian descent, wearing a pistol, stepped out of a security station and approached. "May I help you?"

"I have a meeting with Valeriya Highland."

"Corridor A, take the first left, then go to the end of the hall."

Blackwell entered Corridor A and walked at a brisk pace, his footsteps creating a cascading echo in the stone tunnel. He passed two conference rooms and took the first left. The door had the words *Advanced Queries* etched in frosted glass. He went inside.

A receptionist talked on the phone while rolling a pen among his fingers. He glanced up and smiled. "I have to go," he said into the phone. He pressed a button on a console and extended his hand. "Professor Blackwell, I'm Richard Moore. This is a real honor. I wrote a term paper in college about your trilogy on personality disorders and their link to criminal behavior. You certainly have a flair for making complicated things easy to understand."

Mark accepted the handshake. "Thank you, Richard. I write with the presumption that difficult ideas can always be simplified to their inner essence."

The first of several metallic doors rolled open, and a woman wearing a white turtleneck sweater and dark slacks approached with haste. Mark recognized her as his subject.

"Professor Blackwell, I'm Valeriya Highland."

He shook her hand. "It's a pleasure to meet you."

She took a deep breath. "Something serious has come up, and it requires my immediate attention. It should be over within an hour. If you can wait, Richard will show you around and we can meet later."

"Perhaps I can be of some assistance. I've had quite a bit of experience in crisis management techniques."

"I don't think ..." She paused upon seeing his security badge, the three gold stars being the same as hers. "Normal DDI protocol says no, but your security clearance says yes," she said in a small voice, drawing out her last word as if still thinking. She gazed back at Richard, who was typing. Richard looked up and nodded. "I guess it's no longer need-to-know because everyone's going to know." She guardedly let fall a grin. "Come on in."

Valeriya proceeded to the metal door and placed her hand on a scanner. Locking bolts popped, and the heavy barrier slid open. Mark followed her inside, the door closing automatically behind him.

She moved to a sprawling desk covered by monitors, some of which were suspended from the ceiling. "I'm going to be busy for a while. Make yourself comfortable." She pointed to a small room in the corner. "There's fresh coffee over there."

Blackwell thanked her and perused the opulent surroundings. The room was about thirty feet wide and fifty feet long, loaded with computers and electronic equipment. Thick, emerald-green carpeting covered the floor, and the walls were overlaid with elegant walnut paneling. A weight-training machine, treadmill, and dumbbells were organized into a miniature gym. The overhead lighting was dim, and the temperature was cool, but not unpleasant if one had a jacket. The resounding feature, however, was the innumerable floor-to-ceiling shelves, each loaded with a sparkling menagerie of beautiful things. He hovered in the middle of the room, first believing these were mere decorations, like the charming little knickknacks you see in faculty offices. But as he got closer, this notion melted away.

Mark roamed hither and thither, making his way through a constellation of Bronze Age hatchet heads and a splendid assortment of ancient daggers. He studied white marble urns and examples of beautiful Grecian pottery showing dancing youths playing flutes and hurling spears. The gold coins were marvelous, most of them bearing the likeness of Roman and Byzantine emperors. There was a timeworn Aladdin's lamp bedecked with sparkling rubies and sapphires, an antiquarian masterwork engraved with flowing arabesque lines and swirls. The collection of rarities went on and on, everything appearing to be museum quality, an art collector's paradise, rich with the aroma of ancient things. The only "modern" piece was a Louis Quatorze clock encrusted with emeralds and onyxes, something that could have been displayed in the *Palace of Versailles*. Valeriya's Ph.D. in computer science from the University of Michigan hung next to the clock, along with a citation for being the high school valedictorian. Mark kept looking, flabbergasted by the wealth he was seeing.

A photo of Valeriya standing beside a twin-engine airplane grabbed his attention. Her personnel file showed she had a pilot's license with an instrument rating, but only now did things fall into place. Blackwell had questioned why Naples requested the review. That now seemed a little clearer. She could leave the country, with or without a passport, flying to Cuba or South America with significant amounts of classified material. Her mother was Russian, and she was fluent in that language. Both of her parents were dead, and she was unmarried, without children or close relatives, just an aunt who lives in St. Petersburg, someone she wires money to every month. If she defected to Russia, there were no family ties to worry about.

He turned to her, watching quietly as she worked. Unlike Candy, Valeriya wore no makeup or lipstick. She did have Candy's glossy brown hair, warm chestnut eyes, and prettily plump lips, the same milky-white skin, the same high cheekbones and graceful feline jaw. Both women stood about five-foot-eight and had the same athletic body—amorous, slender, and beautiful. Candy was prettier than Valeriya, but not by much, and they both had a similar sonorous voice, the intonation of someone who knew what they wanted.

Mark progressed by an exquisite gold candelabra and lingered around a glass display case protecting two figurines, both carved from cream-colored ivory. The winged effigies portrayed nude females in lecherous detail, one of them playing a lyre, the other brandishing a blade. He scrutinized the remarkable statues, stroking his fingers across the glass. Were these angels, demons, or golems?

Apart from a kitchenette, there was a bedroom with matching French armoires and a bathroom with a full shower. Someone could live down here. Two leathern lounge chairs and a color-coordinated sofa surrounded a walnut coffee table, an extravagant work of wood that had to be old and expensive. A large computer monitor hung on the wall next to a spectacular oil canvas, a copy of one of Raphael's famous frescoes. The voluminous picture was too large for most settings, although it fit well in the oversized room. Raphael's masterful patterns and symmetry were reproduced perfectly. Yet the vibrant colors in this replication went well beyond the original in a surprising and positive way, especially with the professional lighting from spotlights that brought out the most delicate details. One could see the individual brushstrokes cascading together in seamless harmony, the breadth of oils with their sumptuous loops and swirls, and the limpid eyes rich with wisdom.

Valeriya snapped up the phone and chided someone about a badly needed satellite connection. "I need it right fucking now!"

A few moments later, the blurred faces of three men appeared on the big monitor. She signaled to Blackwell, directing him to one of the leather armchairs. He sank into the comfortable seat and watched the unfolding drama.

A harsh, male voice came over the speaker: "Highland, we're here. Are you ready?"

Valeriya kicked off her shoes. "Yes."

She tapped the keyboard, and the monitor image became clear. Mark recognized Anthony Naples. He didn't know the other two men, one obese with blotchy skin, the other bald.

"Do you confirm encryption?" Naples asked.

"Audio and video are scrambled."

"Okay, what's up?"

"Seventy-three minutes ago the DDI CPU decoded a message from Chief Director Tigran Smyslov of the Russian Federal Security Service. Smyslov ordered their covert agents to enter our wiretap facility in Cairo. They are aware of the right building but not the exact location. They also know we have an escape tunnel, but they don't know where it is. Smyslov told their people to seize our code equipment and whatever intelligence they can find. Russian agents are en route and will have the building sealed off in less than forty-five minutes. Normal communications with the Cairo team have failed, but I can reach them via text message with a backup satellite. I've alerted the Mossad, and they have dispatched Israeli agents to facilitate the removal and transport of our people from the escape tunnel to a safe house. Mossad ETA is about fifteen minutes from now."

"Why isn't CIA Central handling this?" Naples asked.

"I don't know. They are not responding. We must act quickly, sir. The Russians might jam the one link we have."

"Tell them to demolish everything using the established procedures and then leave."

"Sir, there are two problems with that."

Naples' eyes narrowed. "What problems?"

"The code equipment does not have flash-destruction. That means it will delay their departure by thirty minutes, maybe longer. Their escape window under this scenario is going to be tight, too close to risk—"

"Company men know the risks, Highland. It comes with the job."

Valeriya frowned. "But this is different. All the equipment at that location is out of date. We shouldn't even be using it. The intelligence we would leave is just the recordings of their own embassy in Cairo, so it's useless to them. We need to tell our people to leave now."

Naples pulled himself closer. "You said two problems."

"Smyslov used their best encryption algorithm to send the message, something he reserves for special situations. If we sanitize everything, he is going to know we broke their code. We should—"

"Are you confused about who's in charge, Miss Highland?"

"No, sir. I'm just pointing out an alternative—"

Naples hammered the tabletop with his fist. "A stupid alternative! You want us to just leave our equipment so Smyslov won't know we cracked their goddamn code?"

Valeriya dug her bare feet into the thick carpet. "Yes. The hardware and intelligence are irrelevant. Our people must head for the escape tunnel ASAP."

"You are wasting precious time, Miss Highland," chimed the fat man.

The bald man nodded in agreement.

"Is there anything else?" Naples snarled.

"Just that this is a critical decision with long-term consequences."

Naples pursed his lips into a thin line. "Give us a minute."

Valeriya typed frantically at the terminal, face red, droplets of perspiration hanging from her brow. She finished just as Naples reappeared.

"Highland?"

Her hand hovered over the keyboard, index finger down. "I'm here."

"We've decided to follow the proper destruction protocol. Tell them to destroy everything and leave, but only when they have finished."

Her finger dropped onto a single key. "Message encrypted and sent," she said in a subdued voice. She stared at the monitor for a few seconds. "The message has been received and acknowledged. I've sent an update to the Mossad about what's happening."

"I'll dispatch company men to the Cairo site. We can take it from here. You may resume your regular duties."

"Yes, sir."

Naples loosened his tie. "I'm not pleased with your noncompliant attitude, Miss Highland, nor with your sluggish performance." The screen went dark.

Valeriya interlaced her fingers and placed them behind her neck, arching her head and stretching. Visible scars appeared at the neckline of her sweater. Mark recalled seeing the photos from her personnel file: turtleneck sweaters in every one—*she's hiding burn scars.*

"Sorry I couldn't help," Blackwell said. "I didn't know Naples was such a twit. Is it always this bad?"

Valeriya rose from her chair, wiping her moist face with a tissue. "Dealing with Naples is always arduous, but the past several months have been awful. It's like he's trying to make me quit my job."

"Any idea why?"

"Not a clue." She walked around the desk. "Oh, I've got such a terrible headache. May I get you a beverage, Professor Blackwell? I need some ibuprofen and strong coffee."

"Call me Mark, please," Blackwell replied in a soothing voice. "I would love a cup of coffee. I take it black."

"All right, Mark. Call me Val. Give me a few minutes to recuperate." She plodded into the bathroom and closed the door.

Mark pondered her tense encounter with Naples. She did advocate giving the code equipment to the Russians, but she had a reason—saving lives. He didn't have the proper background to know who was correct.

Valeriya emerged with a washed face and a different turtleneck sweater. She entered the kitchenette and returned with two cups of coffee on saucers.

Blackwell accepted the coffee. "Thank you."

Valeriya sat across from him and crossed her legs. She looked down and grimaced, apparently realizing she was barefoot and showing unsightly scars above her ankles. She stood up. "Sorry for my lack of office protocol. I don't get many visitors."

Her absence of etiquette was endearing, a refreshing departure from stuffy old Wittgenstein U. Mark eased off his shoes. "Don't concern yourself. How else can one appreciate this phenomenal carpeting?"

She sat back down, knees together, sliding both feet under the table where they couldn't be seen.

He took a sip of coffee. "Explain something to me. Why bug the Russian Embassy if we can decipher their coded transmissions?"

"Many important discussions are never transmitted by satellite or radio waves. We get more details with a real bug. Is the coffee too strong?"

"I like coffee with muscle. May I ask you a personal question?"

"Sure."

"What is this place? It looks like an art gallery."

"It's my office and private universe. Richard jokingly calls it the Bat Cave."

"You mean all these exquisite artifacts belong to you?"

She nodded. "Collecting is my passion, although I don't have the time to pursue it properly."

Blackwell thought for a bit, contemplating the absurdity of the circumstances. *This woman has serious money. Why is she working so hard and taking abuse from Naples?* He gestured to the glass display case. "Unusual angels."

"They're not angels. The one playing a lyre is a Siren from Homer's *Odyssey*, beckoning unsuspecting sailors to a watery grave. The other is a Ker, one of the daughters of Nyx in Greek mythology."

"Is that a dagger in her hand? She appears intimidating."

Val nodded. "She's the incarnation of painful death. They were once in Napoleon's Ottoman collection."

"Are you serious? Napoleon Bonaparte?"

She nodded again. "They're carved from elephant ivory. Carbon dating shows the elephants died in the second century BC. The ivory hunters of the time swiftly sold their spoils, so there is good reason to believe the statues were fashioned well before the time of Jesus. Napoleon obtained them along with my oil lamp during his campaigns in Egypt and Syria. Later on he gave them away as a wedding gift."

Mark eyed the Aladdin's lamp. "I didn't realize government service paid that well."

"My doctoral dissertation delved into increasing the speed of internet search engines. That led to a radical idea in chip design, inducing me to apply for a patent. But once the government realized what it was, they bought it outright to keep it a secret. I get royalty payments every month." Valeriya glanced around the room. "It would've been great to have had a little of this wealth while growing up."

"I'm amazed they let you bring all this down here."

"I spend considerable time in this room, so they get what they want. And this is the perfect storage place. A burglary is impossible, and the air is filtered for dust."

Mark thought about hitting on her, maybe dinner and a movie, but the current circumstances made that impossible. He looked up at the canvas. "It's a remarkable collection, particularly this gorgeous copy of Raphael's *School of Athens*. I've seen the original."

"You've been to the Vatican?"

"I had a tour of Europe as a college senior, and we went to Vatican City."

Blackwell rose and ambled over to the masterpiece. "The original fresco was beautiful, but not like this. Where on earth did you get it?"

Val followed him. "I was in Europe shopping for Greek artifacts. An old dealer who liked me and knew I had means told me about a fabulous copy of the fresco. The owner needed money but was reluctant to go through a public auction. I went to see it, fell in love, and bought it on the spot." She drew his attention to various figures. "There's Alexander the Great, Socrates, Pythagoras, Euclid, and many more. But above all, at the center, stands Plato and Aristotle having the greatest dialectic debate of all time—Plato pointing to the heavens and a better world, and then there's Aristotle, disagreeing and gesturing to this world."

Mark nodded. "And who do you agree with, Plato or Aristotle?"

"Plato's *Allegory of the Cave* is one of the greatest things ever written. Yet, Plato wrote about what he wanted to be true, true because it was beautiful. Aristotle composed what was true, based on keen observation. Truth can be brutally unpleasant. Accordingly, I stand with Aristotle."

"I couldn't agree more. Aristotle laid the groundwork for the scientific method, the cornerstone of Western civilization."

With sumptuous delight, Valeriya reached up and touched Aristotle's blue robe, her fingers gliding in lavish swirls. "If a magic genie appeared from my oil lamp and granted me three wishes, one of them would be to sit at the feet of Aristotle. There are a thousand questions I'd like to ask."

"Great minds think alike." He moved closer to her, but not too close. "Should your enchanted friend mystically materialize, will you promise to take me with you?"

She chuckled. "It's a deal. We'll hop on his magic carpet and fly back through time."

They exchanged genuine smiles—the ice had been broken.

Valeriya turned to a chirp from the workstation. She went to her desk and studied the largest monitor. "It's another data request from the CIA, something easy for a change. They want a list of every Syrian national who flew from Tehran to Moscow in the past six weeks, delivery within two hours." She picked up a manila file and went to the chairs. "I guess I'd better show you why you're here."

Mark sat across from her, playing his role as the assignment required.

Val gave him a sheet of paper. "I've discovered a strange pattern of deaths and disappearances. Here's the latest example, which occurred last week."

In a police report from McKinley County, Ohio, Blackwell read about a deceased man named Dewey Webster who had been torn limb from limb in a bizarre farm accident. The narrative stated that Webster had been running a dogfighting ring and was facing numerous felonies. Valeriya passed him two additional reports. The first discussed a man from Lexington, Kentucky, who died when he walked into an open elevator shaft. The man, free on bail at the time of his death, had been charged with animal cruelty when he threw his girlfriend's cat off an interstate bridge. Mark went to the third report, a narrative about a Detroit couple who drowned in Lake St. Clair in a boating accident. They were charged when they threw dozens of exotic birds, cage and all, into the same lake after their pet shop went bankrupt.

"Do you see the pattern?" Valeriya asked.

"I do. It's like the invisible hand of providence reaching down from the sky."

"Not providence. Here's thirty-eight more."

Mark elevated his brows. "Thirty-eight?"

She nodded. "Take a look."

He spent the next twenty minutes skimming the summary descriptions. "So, you've got forty-one deaths related to animal abuse."

"There are forty-one events, but some of them involve multiple deaths. We're at forty-six persons who are dead or missing."

Blackwell looked through the papers again. "All I'm seeing is accidental, accidental, accidental. How many were homicides?"

"None."

"None?" Mark echoed.

"The events span ten years and happened shortly after the individual was charged with animal cruelty."

"How many missing persons?"

"Fifteen missing and thirty-one dead in accidents."

"Could this be a statistical fluke?"

Val shook her head. "The interval between events is approximately the same. If these were random accidents we wouldn't see equal spacing in time. There is also a disproportionate cluster in the eastern half of the United States. It has to be serial murder."

"And you've double-checked all this for accuracy?"

"I've quadruple-checked it."

He nodded and sank into thought. Valeriya had to be mistaken. No one is clever enough to beat modern forensic science. It must be a numerical aberration. He couldn't say this, however, not with Val believing so firmly that it was true. He watched her with peripheral vision, sitting relaxed, legs crossed now, freely swinging her bare foot. Her clock chimed the bottom of the hour—she expected an answer. He put on his game face, a multi-layered expression blending Sigmund Freud with Albert Einstein.

"Well, Val, you've unquestionably found something interesting. I want to consult some of my research journals, delving deeper into the psychology of serial murder. This will help us identify potential suspects. It could take a few days to find the relevant material. How does that sound?"

"Sounds great to me. This means my job is done, and you can turn it over to the Behavioral Analysis Unit."

"I may need considerable help in convincing BAU that this statistical anomaly is murder. Will you work with me?"

Valeriya nodded. "Anything I can do."

"Marvelous." Blackwell slipped into his shoes and rose. "You can also further my badly neglected Aristotelian education."

She placed the police reports in the manila folder and gave it to him. "Nothing here is classified. The Dewey Webster story is the most detailed and the most interesting. It's a good place to start if you want to drill down into case details."

"Dewey Webster. I'll study it carefully."

Val escorted him to the door.

3 Dogfight (One Week Earlier)

A Thousand Dogs Slaughtered read the headline of the *Columbus Dispatch*. The bold print and italic font seemed to aggrandize what was, in all respects, the most trivial of situations, something that should have been relegated to the bottom of the last page, if mentioned at all. Dewey Webster chomped on a cigar as he read the unfair editorial, becoming angrier with each passing paragraph. He spat the ragged cigar butt onto the offensive newspaper and flung both into a wastebasket.

Webster approached a bay window overlooking the east side of town. The shadow of the McKinley County Courthouse loomed long in the morning sun, creeping steadily toward the county jail. People hustled along the street below, their breath visible in the bitter cold. The torrential rains from yesterday melted all the snow, leaving the sidewalks and streets washed clean of the salt and grime that comes with an Ohio winter. A major snowstorm was coming, and the tops of white clouds peered over the horizon like kids peeking above the high school stadium fence.

Webster looked back into the office of his old pal. Everything appeared clean and well-ordered, yet the furniture seemed old, not in an antiqueish way, more like the junk you see piled in the road when someone is evicted. The entire image of the workplace fell well below what he expected from a prosperous attorney. Dewey hoped he wasn't making a mistake.

A familiar voice spoke on the phone through a closed door. Webster tried to listen, but the conversation was too muffled to understand. He recognized a photo on the wall, yellowed with age, showing him holding a football just seconds before William Dean kicked the winning field goal in the championship game. Webster smiled and shook his head. *Those were the days.*

Soft footfalls grew louder, and the doorknob to the inner office turned with an annoying screech. William Dean entered the room carrying a stack of legal folders, not smiling or making eye contact. Both men sat at a conference table, Webster quickly and confidently, Dean more slowly, displaying the dignified movement of an attorney in court. Dean organized the folders, separating them according to whether they contained photographs or documents. Webster lit a fresh cigar, blowing a single smoke ring that floated through the air. His thoughts drifted to the possibility of a quick resolution with minimal expense and no time in jail. But Dean's outward demeanor seemed grim, like he was the bearer of dreadful news.

"Jesus Christ, Bill. You look like you're going to a goddamn funeral. Show me some optimism."

Dean's face remained worrying. "I got these 8 x 10 photographs from the assistant prosecutor." Dean picked up the first photo and showed it to Webster, an interior shot of Webster's barn, including the bleachers surrounding his rectangular section of chain-link fence. "What is this?"

"It's the arena."

"Arena?" Dean asked with a single nod of his head.

Webster planted both feet flat on the floor. "That's right, Bill. You can't hold dogfights without an arena."

Dean removed his eyeglasses and massaged the bridge of his nose. "Dewey, you have a successful automotive salvage business. How could you possibly get mixed up in something like this?"

Webster glared at him. "If I wanted a sermon, I'd go to a church. Are you a lawyer or a preacher?"

"I'm here to help you, but I need to understand what happened."

"You mean you don't know? It's all over the fuckin' newspapers."

"You aren't being tried in the press. We are going to court now, and the prosecutor will show all these photographs to a jury. I must know everything to prepare your defense. Fair enough?"

Dewey took a long drag from his cigar. "Fair enough. I guess I'm edgy this morning. But can you blame me?"

"Not at all." Dean showed the next photo. "And what is this?"

"A motorized treadmill. I tie my best fighters to it to build fitness and endurance. Makes the fight last longer. Longer fights mean more money."

"Money? Was your business in trouble? Is that why you did it?"

Webster shook his head, irritated by the inference. "It's not the cash. It's the game, the pleasure and excitement of seeing a good fight."

Dean held up a magnifying glass and continued to examine the photo. "What's on the wall? Looks like chains."

"It's an old trick of the trade. I wrap heavy logging chains around their neck to build upper body strength."

"And this photo of drug bottles and syringes?"

"Anabolic steroids to increase muscle size and aggressiveness. All the professionals use them."

Dean took the next photo, pulling his eyeglasses down and looking over the rims. "This is a bird. Why would they ..." The picture showed a sizable black bird sitting on a mound.

"That's the disposal field behind the barn. Today's *Dispatch* did a real hatchet job, like the ground was covered with human bones." Webster chuckled. "The fuckin' press is talking about me like I was John Wayne Gacy. Give me a break!"

Dean turned over photo after photo of rotting dog carcasses. "Are there really a thousand dogs in this field?"

Webster shrugged. "Yeah, probably. I never kept track."

"How can there be that many?"

"There are seven or eight fights a night. Half of those mutts will be taken out in the arena, and there's always one or two that need to be retired."

"Retired?"

"They're too chopped up to fight again. I pop them in the head with a silenced .22. The crowd never hears a thing."

"Did you ever seek medical treatment for any of the dogs?"

Dewey coughed out a laugh of cigar smoke. "Come on, Bill. You know I can't take them to a vet. The cops would be out there the same day. All I'd be doing is spending a lot of money for nothing. This is a practical business. I patch up the ones that can fight again and retire the rest."

"The newspapers say you fought all these dogs to the death."

"Didn't have a choice."

"Why?"

"When guys are betting big money on a single fight there has to be a clear winner. No one argues with the Grim Reaper."

Dean grabbed another photo and held it under a lamp. The wrinkles on his forehead deepened with an inward slant. "What about these little dogs in cages? They look too small to fight."

"They're bait dogs."

"I beg your pardon?"

"B-a-i-t dogs. It's another trick of the trade, a necessity if you want to be a professional."

"What's wrapped around their mouths?" Dean asked.

"Duct tape. They raided the place just before a training match."

"I don't understand."

"This business is about putting on a show for the crowd. I get a piece of the action, but there's got to be a real skirmish to whip up a betting frenzy. I can't put dogs out there that won't fight. So I use training matches to gauge aggressiveness and fighting ability. A practice event with real fighters will cut up the dogs. Using bait dogs solves the problem."

Dean blinked at the photo. "I'm still trying to grasp what you're doing. If the bait dogs have their mouths taped shut, they can't fight. Worse yet, they cannot even ..."

Dewey glanced out the window, trying to think of words that would work with his simple-minded friend. "Look, Bill, the fighters are kinda like gladiators from ancient Rome. They've gotta look good and feel great when they enter the arena. Even a little bait dog can inflict a nasty wound. Duct tape is the practical solution."

"Is there tape on the fighting dog's mouth as well?"

"Of course not! How could I measure aggressiveness?"

"So, the bait dogs are killed?"

Webster nodded and flicked cigar ashes into an ashtray. "It's a significant expense. The time and trouble to get them, and they only last a few minutes."

"And just where did you get all these animals?"

"That's the best part—animal shelters in Ohio and Indiana. I've saved the taxpayers the cost of housing or gassing these mutts and turned them into a way to make money, helping the local economy. Pretty smart, right? And yet those assholes at City Hall are rousting me around. Where's gratitude?"

"You had time to do all this and operate your junkyard?"

"My cousin did a lot of the heavy lifting."

Dean shuffled through the legal papers. "You're the only one charged."

Dewey pointed his finger at Dean. "And it's going to stay that way. I'll never give up my cousin. *Never ever!* We're like brothers."

"Naturally, the two of you didn't tell the animal shelters what you were going to do with the dogs?"

"Naturally."

The telephone rang in the inner office. Dean stood up. "I need to get this. Could be about your case."

Webster watched Dean scribble on a pad while bantering on the phone. This was going much worse than he expected.

Dean returned to the conference table, looking as gloomy as ever. "That call brought more bad news. It hasn't hit the papers yet, but they've found several dog carcasses with chip implants. One of them, a Yorkshire Terrier, has been traced to Councilman Lewis." Dean tapped a pen on the table. "I presume this was one of your bait dogs?"

Webster crushed out his cigar. "That's total bullshit. I never took nobody's pet. I ain't that stupid."

"And what about your dodgy cousin?"

"Absolutely not. He worked the out-of-town shelters, and that's it."

"The theft was caught on a surveillance camera. I'm told it shows the dog being taken from Councilman Lewis' front porch, dragged with a restraining pole and nearly hanged before being thrown into a black van."

A twitch tugged at Dewey's eye. "Maybe it was a dogcatcher. Maybe the mutt didn't have a license."

"The video isn't clear, but it seems to show the perpetrator as a white male in his twenties, about average height with a thin build and fair skin, short hair and a goatee, wearing a white T-shirt and a red baseball cap turned backward. The sheriff is going to release it to the news media in hopes of obtaining an identification. Should make the six o'clock news tonight."

Webster clamped his hands together. "It's got nothing to do with me."

"Do you think the jury will be that dimwitted? The dog carcass was found at your farm."

"So, make me a deal with Lewis. I'll buy him another pooch."

Dean stared at Webster, saying nothing.

"Come on, Bill. Find a way to pull some strings. There's plenty of dough to grease Lewis and City Hall. Show me some real lawyering."

"Lewis knows people in high places, and new charges will be filed. Income tax evasion, mail fraud, money laundering—serious felonies. The photographic evidence alone guarantees a conviction. We cannot go to trial and win."

Dewey yanked open his collar. "Okay, just cut all this legal crap and give me the bottom line."

"Well." Dean thought for a moment. "If we plead no contest and provide financial restitution, with good behavior you could be back on the street in three years, depending on the breaks."

"Am I hearing you right? Three years in the fuckin' slammer is the best you can do?"

"It's the best anyone can do under the circumstances. You've made some serious mistakes."

Dewey bolted up from his chair. "Mistakes, sure, lots and lots of mistakes. And the biggest howler of them all was choosing you." Webster reached for the folders on the table. "Is this everything, all the legal papers 'n shit?"

"Yes, but there's more coming."

"Mail me the rest. I'm outta here."

"It's not that bad, Dewey. Things could be worse."

"Worse?" Dewey cackled. "How could it possibly get any worse?" He put on his winter coat and trudged to the door, stopping and turning. "When we were kids we practiced together for years kicking field goals. I placed the ball perfectly every time and made you look good. You got the girls, the glory, and the college scholarship while I got nothing. I hope your conscience bothers you." He left, slamming the door.

* * *

Five dump trucks loaded with road salt ambled along Wagstaff Road. Webster floored his Bentley Continental to get around the slow-moving convoy, wondering where they were going. *Oh, shit—the snowstorm—and I haven't even hooked up the snowblower.* He turned on the radio, rotating the dial until he found the news. The weather forecast predicted eighteen to twenty inches of fresh snow in the Ohio Valley, made worse by high winds that would create impassable drifts. Many schools and businesses announced their closure for two days. Dewey checked his Rolex. *Still twelve hours before the heavy stuff starts—plenty of time to make preparations.*

Webster slowed as his roadside mailbox came into view. Some PETA protesters were there that morning, carrying signs and causing trouble. Fortunately, they were gone. He stopped the car and got out to get the mail. The line of threatening clouds was closer now, hanging low and churning like angry surf. Two of his neighbors talked to each other across the road, one of them shaking his head, the other listening with folded arms. Thinking he needed every friend he could get (possible character witnesses at his trial), Webster waived and called to them.

"They're saying the storm will be worse than expected. I've got a new snowblower, and I'd be happy to dig you out when it hits—free of charge."

Without giving the slightest acknowledgment, the two men kept yakking. "Assholes," Webster mumbled under his breath.

The steel gate protecting his drive chattered as Webster pushed it back. He drove through and closed it, locking out news reporters and PETA. The gravel drive was a good half-mile long, making the house and barn invisible from the road. That was the tragedy of it all. This was the perfect place to hold dogfights. Atop the massive barn stood a running horse weathervane, squeaking as the wind pushed it to and fro. An old weatherbeaten sign on the side of the building read *Harlan's Buggy Shop*.

Webster clicked the overhead remote, opening the attached garage door to his house. He continued down the driveway and stopped—the barn door was open. He drove forward and parked in the garage. *There can't be anybody here, but the door was closed that morning. The wind? Yes, that's it. The sheriff broke the latching mechanism during the raid, so the wind must have blown it open.* Webster removed a snub-nosed .38 from the glove compartment and exited the car.

Dewey crept to the barn door, revolver in hand, eyes darting every direction. Something was tied to the door handle. He ignored it and inched forward, coming up to the edge of the door and easing his way inside. The dark interior made it difficult to see, and he accidentally kicked a wire cage with an attached note. Webster took the note, recognizing the sloppy handwriting. *Hey bro, this is all I could find this trip. Toby.* The cage contained a little white dog, partially hidden in the folds of a thick blanket. Another damn bait dog. Dewey heaved out a sigh of disgust. *My relatives are so goddamn dumb.* Drunk and stoned. That's how his cousin went through life. No newspapers, no TV, just booze and weed. No wonder he couldn't hold a real job. Webster had tried calling his cousin after the sheriff raided the farm, but he was never home. The dumb-ass didn't even have an answering machine.

Webster dropped the note and went to inspect the thing on the door handle. It was an old dog collar, cracked from exposure to the sun and rain. It must have come from the disposal field, but why was it here? He pitched the collar into a trash barrel and proceeded back inside.

Dewey scratched his head and stared at the blanket inside the cage. It had come from a shelf in a back room, but why would Toby make a bed for a disposable mutt? A dish of water was there as well, not frozen by the cold. They must have just missed each other. Webster pulled something sticky off the bottom of his shoe: duct tape covered with white hair. He leaned over and inspected the dog: tape adhesive around his mouth. Toby had taped the dog to keep from being bit (the usual practice) and then peeled it off? He had to be high on drugs. Here was yet another problem to solve. At least it would be quick and easy.

Webster popped the cylinder on his revolver to inspect the cartridges. Wide-cup hollow points would be overkill, but the sheriff had confiscated his silenced .22. He closed the cylinder and aimed at the dog.

"Looks like you're gonna be number one thousand and one."

Radio music commenced from inside the barn, his favorite country-western station. Webster lowered the gun with a puckered brow. "Toby," Webster called. "What the hell are ya doin?" Dewey walked deeper inside, believing his cousin had parked his van in the workshop. "Yo, skinny dick, ya back there?" He crept toward the music, still holding the gun. His wood-burning stove was open and packed with dry kindling. He continued past the chain-link fence of the darkened arena. "Toby! Stop fuckin' around. We got problems. Those pricks down at City Hall are gonna put the hurt on me."

Bright lights lit the workshop doorway, and Webster went inside. His Kubota tractor was in the service bay with the snowblower already attached. He crept forward, not believing his eyes. The electric coffee maker was plugged in, holding a fresh pot. His toolbox was open with various wrenches laid out in orderly fashion, a half-empty coffee cup beside them. His grease gun rested on the floor beside a dented can of WD-40. *Toby couldn't do this. That idiot can't even change a tire.*

Dewey turned the radio off so he could hear himself think. With air blowing from the overhead heater, he removed his coat, still gripping his revolver. Whoever attached the snowblower didn't finish the job. The PTO safety shield was missing, and the chain guard that should have covered the auger sprocket leaned against the wall. Webster placed his hand on the tractor hood, feeling considerable heat.

A powerful shove from behind knocked Webster down. He aimed his gun just as a man descended upon him. They fought over the weapon, Webster yanking the trigger and firing two shots before the gun was wrenched from his fingers. They continued wrestling until Webster found himself in an unbreakable headlock. The man dragged Webster out of the workshop, hauling him toward the arena. He rammed Webster into the chain-link fence and hoisted him over the top. Dazed and hurting, Dewey dropped to the concrete floor.

Light switches were thrown, and the arena glowed like it was Saturday night. Webster sheltered his eyes from the glaring brightness. More noise—things were being moved around. He rose to his feet, trying to make sense of the pale objects in the surrounding bleachers. More lights came on. Webster wiped his eyes and looked again. Skulls, dog skulls bleached white by the sun peered at him with hollow eye sockets, their skeleton teeth forming hideous grins. He staggered backward.

The arena gate opened, and his attacker stepped inside, latching the gate behind him. He wore workman's coveralls, gloves, and a tight-fitting hat. Webster didn't know him. The running-horse weathervane squeaked in the wind as they stared each other down.

"And just who the fuck are you?" Dewey yelled.

"I want Toby's last name."

"What?"

"The note on the cage, signed 'Toby.' I want his name."

Webster shuffled from side to side. "Smith. Toby Smith."

"And his address?"

"I don't know it offhand."

"What city? What street?"

Webster hesitated. "It's in Cincinnati. On Main Street."

The man eyed him skeptically. "He lives a hundred miles away? In the central business district?"

"I dunno," Dewey hissed. "What difference does it make? Cut the bullshit, and tell me what you want."

"Give me your wristwatch."

Webster tossed him the Rolex. "You want my wallet as well?"

The man hung the expensive timepiece on a fence post and pulled his gloves tight around his fingers. "Defend yourself."

"What the fuck is this? Would ya tell me that?"

"Every dog shall have his day." The man made a sweeping motion to the assemblage of unearthly spectators surrounding them. "This is their day, their moment, so don't disappoint them." He marched forward. "En garde."

Dewey held up his hands. "Now wait, goddammit. We're having a conversa—"

He punched Webster in the stomach, dropping him to his knees.

"I've got cash in the house," Dewey cried. "Lots of money in a safe!"

The man yanked Webster up and shoved him rearward. "Fight me."

Webster swung twice, missing both times. He charged forward and was knocked down again.

"Get up," the man said. "We've only just begun."

Webster stormed headlong at his tormentor, throwing wide-swinging punches that failed to connect. The man struck him several times about the midsection and hurled him into the fence. Webster bounced off the springy barrier and fell on his back.

The intruder promenaded around the arena, gesturing to the canine skulls. "Do you hear them? They are howling. This is a horribly disappointing show."

Dewey rolled over and spat blood, gasping, "We can do a deal. Just tell me what you want."

"I want you on your feet."

Webster remained down, trying to catch his breath. The man unlatched and opened the arena gate. He went to the wall and lifted a long-handled axe and a hatchet from their hangers. He reentered the arena, axe in one hand and hatchet in the other. Webster crawfished back to the fence, shrieking and raising his arms in a defensive posture.

The man dropped the woodcutting tools at Webster's feet. "Listen to me carefully. This is your last chance. We are going to follow the rules, the regulations of this place, canons you created. If you don't fight now and win, you will not leave this building alive."

Dewey grabbed the axe and got up, determined to make a stand. The man waited at the center of the arena, knees slightly bent and fists clenched. Webster raised the axe above his head and made a screaming samurai assault, swinging down with all his might. The man sidestepped the falling blade, striking Webster's jaw as the axe's momentum drew Webster's arms into a vulnerable position. Dewey moved in for another attack, coming from the side with maximum amplitude and speed. The man hit him as he went by, a teasing blow to prolong the battle. Webster stooped over, still gripping the axe, eyes down but watching the man's feet. The man took a step closer, and Dewey whirled the double-bladed cutting tool up from the floor, but only sliced the air. Another punch sent Webster tumbling down.

The man raised his hands like a boxer waving to a cheering crowd. He whirled around. "They want more, much more."

Dewey grabbed the short-handled hatchet and rushed forward, slashing back and forth with controlled swings. His enemy backpedaled, staying just out of reach and hitting with small jabs until Webster dropped to the floor. He got up, panting and bleeding from the face. Dewey hurled the hatchet, striking the man's shoulder, but failing to hit with the sharpened edge. His adversary strode forward and kicked Webster's groin, dropping him flat on his face.

"Get up. Your rules say we fight to the death."

"Over. It's over," Webster wheezed.

"Fight me. I won't tell you again."

Dewey didn't move.

The man grabbed Webster's Rolex and left the arena. He returned with a cylindrical object, something Dewey couldn't clearly see. He finally recognized the grease gun as the man clamped Webster's fingers around the tube and pumping handle. As the man took the lubricating device back to the workshop, Dewey pulled himself into a sitting position. The ruddy floor was sticky, caked with the blood of countless dogfights. The radio began playing again, and the exterior door to the workshop rumbled open. *Is the nightmare coming to an end?*

The Kubota's powerful diesel engine roared to life, and the whir of rotating machinery filled the barn. Webster hobbled his way up and stumbled through the arena gate. The man seized him and dragged him into the workshop. The snowblower blades spun ferociously just a few feet away. He held Webster in a full nelson grip, pushing him toward the terrifying machine.

"Wait," Dewey yowled. "I'll talk. I'll talk. I'll tell you everything."

"What's Toby's last name?" the man yelled.

"Anderson. Toby Anderson, 808 East Peterdale Circle. He drives a black Chevy van. He's the one you want. He made me do it."

With wind from the machine blasting his face and spinning blades just inches away, Dewey shrieked, *"I've told you the truth!"*

The man pushed Webster past the revolving blades and guided him into the gap between the tractor and snowblower. The rapidly rotating PTO shaft came closer and closer, rubbing its grease nipple against Webster's trousers.

The man snatched Webster's hair and yanked his ear close, shouting, *"One thousand and one!"*

Dewey felt a violent jolt.

* * *

The man walked backward, stepping out the open doorway, hardened eyes watching the unfolding event. Webster's warbling banshee wail lasted a few seconds as his body twirled around the rotating shaft. His lifeless arms and legs walloped against the heavy steel bars that held the snowblower. Webster's clothing ripped as he became twisted into a horizontal tornado of unrecognizable pulp. A flopping arm broke free of its frayed ligaments and smacked into a shelf. The other extremities soon followed, spraying droplets of blubbery flesh and blood. Running out of fuel (which had been precisely measured), the Kubota's engine became erratic and sputtered to a stop, chugging out a single smoke ring that floated through the air.

All became still. He scrutinized the scene: radio playing, Webster's wristwatch on the workbench beside a half-filled cup of coffee, snowblower maintenance manual opened to the page on lubrication, grease gun and can of lubricant on the floor, necessary tools (in their correct metric sizes) laid out in all the right places, chain guard against the wall, and everything covered with pristine blood spatter.

He lit the stove and opened the air vent, starting a roaring fire. Burlap sacks were filled with dog skulls and deposited with the pile of canine remains. Webster's revolver was dropped into a barrel of grimy oil, although there were no fingerprint issues to worry about. The hatchet and axe were wiped clean of blood, dipped in diesel fuel, and wiped again before being placed on their respective hangers. A pair of leather gloves found near the stove were used to apply smudged impressions along the wooden handles. He burned the wiping rags, burlap sacks, and the wad of duct tape Webster had found. The man's coveralls, hat, and cloth gloves went into the flames. The bottoms of his rubber boots had been ground flat—proper disposal would come later. He retrieved a cotton duffel bag hidden behind some barrels and withdrew a woodland camouflage coat. The duffel bag was burned as well. He put the coat on along with a fresh pair of cloth gloves. After rummaging through a barrel of trash, he fished out an old rope and tied it around the outside of the coat to form an improvised carrying pouch.

He opened the cage door and gently pulled the little dog out. The pup wandered around, sniffing and urinating here and there. The man picked up the yellow paper and reread Toby's note. He folded the paper and placed it in his pocket. He did a final check for oversights. A bent cigar tube and a button from Webster's shirt were retrieved from the arena and thrown into the stove. He lifted the dog and opened his coat, placing him in the pouch. The center button was left undone, and a tiny nose wiggled its way outside. They made their way across an open field toward some distant trees. He paused a quarter-mile from the barn and looked back. Nothing was visible except the running horse weathervane. He removed a glove and put his hand inside the coat, stroking the dog under his chin. Light snow began falling as they disappeared into the deepest part of the woods.

4 The Assignment

Five a.m. was the best time to travel in Fairfax County. The traffic was light, and no one would bother her at that hour. Valeriya pulled into Rabourn's Restaurant and parked her Grand Cherokee where it would be visible from inside. The temperature was in the mid-forties, just right for what she was wearing. She walked through the scattered raindrops, stopping momentarily in front of the glass doors to admire her reflection. *This is going to be a memorable meal.*

The receptionist approached and whispered, "It will be ready in fifteen minutes."

Val nodded as a hand in her favorite booth shot up and waved. She would have spotted her friend no matter where she was sitting because of that luxurious raven-black hair. Valeriya maneuvered through the tables and chairs, taking her time for maximum visibility.

"Wow. That is one sharp trench coat," Lisa Rogers said.

"You like it?"

"Oh, yeah. And I'm glad to see you're finally breaking out of that ingénue persona." Lisa's eyes wandered over the leather garment, pausing at the bottom. "And Nancy Sinatra would have killed to get those boots. May I?"

With a sidelong gleam of anticipation, Valeriya gave the coat to Lisa and sat down.

Lisa manipulated the black leather. "I've never seen anything like this, so unbelievably soft you could wear it to bed. Must be from Italy."

"Not even close. I picked it up on my trip to that South American cybersecurity conference."

"What kind of leather is this?"

"I have no idea. The shopkeeper said it was a trade secret."

"Lisa examined the stitching and silk lining. "Fabulous workmanship. Bet it's expensive."

"It's like anything else. You get what you pay for."

"The boots are the same?"

Val nodded, discreetly checking her wristwatch.

Lisa peeked below the table. "And I can't believe you're wearing a skirt." She took a better look. "Oh, I see. The boots make that possible."

"I'm wearing knee socks. So I'd be decent even without boots, as long as the wind doesn't kick up."

A waitress brought a pot of coffee and took their orders. Valeriya selected the eggs Benedict with a side order of spicy sausage. Lisa chose the country omelet with hash browns and crispy bacon.

Lisa leaned forward. "Let's go bumming next Saturday night. They're having the grand opening of a fancy nightclub on the north side, and ladies get in for free."

Val's lips curved down. "You're not a party animal, and since when did you start embracing the ways of the wicked white man?"

"I'm stuck on the East Coast. What do you expect me to do, put on ceremonial buckskin and ghost dance around the Washington Monument?"

"If you did, I might see you on television."

"Yeah, for all the wrong reasons. Will you go out with me?"

"Not to a nightclub. And you know why. Let's go for a long hike in Lost River State Park."

Lisa leaned back and sighed. "You need to get out and mix with people. You're wasting your whole life barricaded in that glorified bomb shelter."

"I'm doing what works for me."

"You've got one of those difficult-to-pronounce personality disorders." Lisa contemplated for a moment. "I can't think of the name."

"It's called asshole-phobia."

"I'm trying to be serious, and you're joking around. You need professional counseling. I'll bet you spent Christmas by yourself."

"I spend every Christmas alone. It's no big deal."

Lisa tilted her head. "And New Year's Eve? All alone, right? Just like last year, and the year before, and the year before."

"I was working. New Year's Eve is a flashpoint for terrorism, and they need all hands on deck in case something happens."

"I'm just saying it isn't normal for you to be all alone all the time. You need a flesh and blood companion, someone to get excited with, someone to swap secrets with and talk to on lonely nights."

"This is the bloody scalping knife calling the tomahawk red. I don't see you out looking for Mr. Goodbar. When we were in college, you stayed in the dorm while I at least tried to date someone, even though lots of guys wanted you."

"My point is, Val, I can have a relationship if I want one, but you cannot. Something is wrong."

Valeriya met Lisa's eyes, refusing to become angry with her well-meaning friend. "Some people are cut out for romance, and some are not. I've been down that broken road, and it doesn't go anywhere. Guys will line up to talk with me in a nightclub, ask me to dance and be all over me. But, when the turtleneck comes off, they—are—gone. Just let me live the life I'm supposed to live."

"They wouldn't be gone if they knew you were wallowing in money."

Val rolled her eyes. "Oh, that's a wonderful idea. I'll just go out and buy someone to tuck between my scarred-up legs, listening to him whisper sweet nothings he doesn't mean." She sighed. "I wish I could find a simple solution, however …"

The soft glow of lighted candles turned their heads, providing a much-needed transition.

Creeping carefully to keep everything under control, their waitress wheeled a cart with a birthday cake and two packages. "Your breakfasts will be out shortly."

Valeriya moved the cake to the table. "Happy birthday, Lisa."

"Turning thirty is so depressing. Life never takes you where you think it will." With watery eyes and a somber face, she blew out the candles.

Val gave Lisa the larger package and watched while she tore it open. The rich aroma of expensive leather foretold the gift: a duplicate of Valeriya's trench coat.

Lisa's mouth dropped open. "Oh my God." She stood and tried it on, modelling it for Val. "Fits like a dream, and there's plenty of slack for my shoulder holster."

"Every FBI agent should have a beautiful trench coat."

"Yeah, but this one's so nice I'm afraid to wear it."

Lisa took the second package. "I think I know what this is." She opened it and removed the matching leather boots. She tried them on, still smiling with excitement. "My exact size." She leaned over the table and kissed Val on the cheek. "This wasn't necessary, but thank you."

The waitress served their breakfasts.

Valeriya reached for the salt and pepper. "Was that your handiwork on cable news last night, the guy at First National in Baltimore?"

"Regrettably."

"Does it get any easier?"

"I try not to think about it. I joined the Bureau to get experience so I could go back and help my people, but all I'm doing is squeezing the trigger under a telescopic sight."

Val grabbed Lisa's hand. "You're saving innocent lives, and there's no higher calling. Besides, maybe when you get back from your tour in the Middle East you'll be given other duties."

"I hope so. But I'll be doing the same thing over there, except it will be at a thousand yards, taking out enemy snipers with a 300 Winchester Magnum."

"When are you leaving?"

"Three weeks. I won't be back until next January, but at least my hitch in the Reserves will be finished."

"I'll bet you'll be missed."

Lisa nodded. "Mama for sure. I had to explain that I had to go, that it wasn't an option. The Bureau will do fine without me. They've got Joshua Russell and his trainees."

"Russell? I've heard that name before."

"He's the best rifle shot on the planet. Makes me look like a Girl Scout with a BB gun—shoots groups a third my size."

Valeriya waited with a pensive pause, a knot building in her gut. "Does it ever bother you, working for the government that destroyed your civilization? I think it would bother me."

"The Marine Corps paid for my college education, and whatever happened occurred a long time ago. The Apache have an old saying, 'The branch that bends in the wind stays on the tree.'"

"Maybe that's my problem. I can't bend from what I believe, not for any reason."

Valeriya's cellphone buzzed. She pulled it out, scowling at the flashing red light. "Oh, shit."

"Who is it?"

"Margaret Marshall. I was afraid of this." Val took a large swallow of coffee and pressed the answer button. "This is Valeriya.— Yes, ma'am.—When?—Do I need to bring anything?—I'll be there." Val hung up.

"What's going on?"

"She wants to see me today in the Hoover Building."

"About what?"

"She didn't say, but last Friday we had a messy overseas situation, and I disagreed with Naples on how to resolve it. All our agents were killed."

Lisa scooted forward and whispered, "I didn't see anything in the news."

"You won't. It was a CIA operation."

"Don't look so anxious. Margaret is a fair person, and I know you would never do anything wrong." Lisa tasted her omelet and added

40

Tabasco sauce. "She likes me for some reason, always stops and talks whenever she sees me."

"Good. Maybe you can use your influence to pull my sorry ass out of the fire." Valeriya took a bite of sausage. "Still, the meeting might be about a weird data anomaly."

"What anomaly?"

"You should try this." She passed two of her sausage links over to Lisa. "We've got this pattern that points to a serial killer zapping people who abuse animals, except none of the deaths are homicides, just accidents and missing persons."

"Never heard of anything like that." Lisa tasted the sausage. "This is delicious."

"It is strange. Marshall assigned Mark Blackwell to work with me in figuring it out."

"The Wittgenstein psychiatrist, the guy with all those forensic publications?"

"That's him. He seems like a nice guy."

Lisa wolfed down the sausage and stole another link from Valeriya's plate. "He taught a seminar for the SWAT group on the psychology of hostage situations, giving lots of suggestions to make the perpetrator believe you are cooperating with his demands—until you see an opportunity to take him out. Pretty good advice." Lisa stopped eating and stared at the bottle of Tabasco.

Val pulled the bottle away. "You're not putting yucky hot sauce on that great sausage."

Lisa said nothing, seemingly lost in thought.

"Okay, here." Valeriya pushed the bottle forward. "Hello? Earth to Lisa?"

Lisa looked up and snarled her nose. "Tabasco on sausage? No way." She popped the rest of the spicy meat into her mouth. "What time are you meeting with Margaret?"

"Four o'clock. With the travel to Washington, the whole afternoon will be shot."

Lisa glanced at her wristwatch. "We'd better finish up. I've got lots to do."

"Not before we have our cake."

Valeriya did the honors, slicing an extra-large piece for Lisa. They had their dessert, reminiscing about old times at the University of Michigan and their many travels to Wolverine football games. Val took care of the check and left a generous tip for the mess they made. A favorite *Beatles* song commenced playing over the restaurant speakers. Wearing their leather trench coats and boots, arm-in-arm and walking lockstep, they marched out of the restaurant singing the lyrics from *Yellow Submarine*.

* * *

Mark let out a disgusted groan and pulled the pillow around his ears, livid at the ringing phone. This was the one day of the week where he could sleep in, and now some dingleberry was screwing it up. He peeked through the covers, deciding to let it ring. The answering machine picked up.

"This is Leslie from the director's office. Margaret Marshall wants to know if you would be available for—"

Mark grabbed the phone. "Hello. I was in the bathroom when your call came through.—Noon, today, in conference room B of the DDI?—Tell Director Marshall I will attend." He hung up.

The clock showed 9:38—*get your ass moving!* He stepped into the shower, puzzling over the strange meeting. It couldn't be about his assignment to evaluate Valeriya because that would take several more weeks to complete. And why was Marshall meeting him in the DDI? Mark got dressed, had a quick breakfast, and took his morning insulin injection. He grabbed his topcoat and departed, still trying to solve the mystery.

Margaret Marshall was the first African-American director of the FBI. Blackwell had never met her, although he had seen her speak at various Bureau functions and meetings. Marshall had a reputation for answering questions without mincing words, sometimes turning the tables and embarrassing her questioners. Any encounter with Marshall required his full concentration.

* * *

Two broad-shouldered gentlemen in swanky suits stood at the door of conference room B. Blackwell approached, slowing when he heard Marshall's biting voice through the closed door. One of the guards placed Mark's hand on a portable scanner. A green light flashed, and the other guard opened the door. With flittering angst, Mark straightened his jacket and went inside.

Marshall turned to him. "Professor Blackwell, I'm glad you could join us on such short notice. This is Robert Tyler, Director of the DDI."

Tyler, rigid-faced and perspiring, gave Mark a hasty handshake.

Marshall proceeded to the door. "My schedule is tight. Let's get on with it."

Blackwell and Tyler followed Marshall out of the room. She told her bodyguards to get some lunch in the DDI commissary, and they took off in the other direction. Blackwell and Tyler trailed behind her as she walked uncomfortably fast. Marshall held open the Advanced Queries door, and the trio went inside. Valeriya was leaning over Richard's desk, showing him something on the monitor. Richard cleared his throat, and Val looked up, obviously surprised by the visit.

"Hello, Val," Marshall said. "There's been a change of plans, and I would like to have our meeting here. Will that work for you?"

"Sure. No problem at all."

Valeriya wore a knee-length skirt. Mark moved sideways for a better look: shoeless but with black socks covering her legs.

Val walked around the desk. "There's a conference room in the back."

Marshall pointed to Valeriya's secretive lair. "I want to meet in there." Val nodded, and everyone went inside.

"Take off your coats," Marshall said. "We are going to be here for a while."

Valeriya took each person's topcoat and placed it on a hanger. She slipped into a pair of shoes while Marshall drifted around the room, ostensibly captivated by the artistic creations. The FBI Director paused now and then, eyes contracting when she saw something interesting. Val offered everyone coffee, but there were no takers. Tyler shuffled like something unpleasant was about to occur.

Marshall stood in front of Raphael's masterpiece, admiring the view. She turned to Valeriya. "And this actually belongs to you?"

"Yes. It's my favorite piece."

"Quite remarkable."

"Thank you."

Marshall made eye contact with everyone in turn. "Let's get started."

Marshall and Tyler parked themselves at opposite ends of the sofa while Mark and Val sat facing each other in the leather armchairs.

"We have several issues to discuss," Marshall continued. "Let's deal with the Cairo disaster first. I'm sure you know that six CIA operatives were killed last Friday." Marshall looked at Val. "Anthony Naples has alleged that their deaths are attributable to a delay caused by you in implementing his orders."

Valeriya rested, politely perched, calm and relaxed, her voice lubricated with confidence. "My exchange with Naples is recorded on video."

"I know it's recorded. President Nightingale and I have watched it, but I want to hear your thoughts about what happened."

"The latest decryption of Russian intelligence shows they took our code equipment intact. This means our team never had the opportunity to follow the destruction protocol. The Russians were upon them sooner than we anticipated. One of our operatives shot and killed a Russian agent, and they retaliated with an experimental nerve gas that dissipates after use. The delay Naples refers to is at most five minutes as we discussed alternatives. The delay imposed by Naples' decision to destroy the equipment is at least thirty minutes. Our agents had a better chance of surviving if Naples followed my recommendation for them to leave at once. Naples' choice also ran the risk of allowing the Russians to know that we have broken their encryption algorithms."

Marshall thought for a while, tapping her thumbs together. "As a rule, the Bureau doesn't criticize foreign operations. But we are being dragged into this because of a shared resource, namely you. The President has asked the Senate Intelligence Committee to review what happened and make a recommendation to her. This will take some time because of the technical issues involved, such as the true value of the code equipment and whether it was worth risking lives to save it. In the meantime, your relationship with Naples has deteriorated to a point where the two of you can no longer work together. Naples is the Presidential appointee for the CIA, and he is entitled to make personnel decisions."

Val stiffened like a patient in a dentist's chair, about to feel the drill.

"Therefore, as of this moment," Marshall declared, "you are now working exclusively for the Bureau. We will discuss your new assignment later." Marshall whipped her head around to Tyler. "Henceforth, all CIA queries will go to the CIA Workgroup. Nothing goes to Advanced Queries."

"Margaret, that will create serious problems," Tyler replied. "The CIA Workgroup only does boilerplate queries. If something complex needs to be turned around fast, it goes to Val."

"I'm giving Naples what he wants. Val's employment with the CIA is terminated. Advanced Queries is a Bureau asset coming out of our budget. It is now up to Naples to configure the CIA's use of DDI resources from his budgetary line. I'm sure they have lots of competent people."

"As you wish," Tyler replied.

"You may leave now, Rob. I want to discuss Bureau business."

Tyler, pale-faced and clearly aggravated, took his leave in subdued silence.

Marshall regarded Valeriya. "Now, about this irrational data discrepancy, I've read your report, but I'd like to hear it again."

Valeriya spent the next hour explaining the statistical evidence supporting the notion that a serial killer was slaughtering people charged with animal abuse. Marshall questioned her step-by-step about how she came to this conclusion. Mark remained silent throughout the discussion, focused with quiet attention, favoring Marshall's skeptical attitude but unwilling to oppose Val.

"What about hunters, trappers, and the like?" Marshall asked. "Any evidence they have been targeted?"

"Negative. I've looked at them, plus matadors, rodeo riders, slaughterhouse workers, and people using animals to do medical research. They are not being hunted."

"Val, are you sure this is murder and not just a strange pattern in the data?"

"I know it runs contrary to common sense, but the circumstantial evidence is overwhelming. We have a serial killer."

"Professor Blackwell, my trusted aides tell me you are about the best there is at what you do. What is your opinion?"

Mark swallowed—he must choose between heart or mind. "It's an amazing paradox that runs counter to every previous serial killer case. If it is murder, we are dealing with a meticulous man, an expert in forensic science with a keen eye for the smallest of details. He plans everything out, anticipating things that may go wrong. And, like any project in the real world, when things do go amiss, he adapts and changes the plan to find a way to make it work. It's difficult to believe." He beheld Valeriya thoughtfully, the way he looked at Candy when she gave a brilliant answer in class. "However, Val makes a persuasive case for further investigation. I am with her."

Marshall stared down at the carpet for a considerable time. She raised her eyes. "So far, all you have are accidents and missing persons. And the missing people have been charged with a crime, so they might be on the run. This brings us to your new assignment." She looked at Val. "I want you to verify that a homicide has been committed."

Valeriya glanced at Mark and back to Marshall. "I don't understand."

"You are to investigate these anomalies until we can establish what they are, legitimate accidents or murder."

"But I'm not trained as a field agent."

"No, but you carry a firearm and are trained in its use. And this whole thing is a creation from a database, an archive that you know better than anyone else."

"I don't have the background in forensic science. I wouldn't know what to look for."

"But Professor Blackwell does. Am I right, Mark?"

"Yes. It's required for my academic research."

"Then you have your assignment as well. The two of you will work together to resolve this problem. A data expert and a leader in forensic science, forming an ideal partnership."

Mark's heart galloped at full speed. *Don't smile. Look serious and concerned.*

Val blinked as though she didn't believe what she was hearing. "But neither of us has ever made an arrest."

"I don't want you to arrest anyone or conduct an interrogation. There isn't anyone to arrest or interrogate. Just determine if there has been a crime."

Valeriya drew a sonorous breath. "But we could look for years without finding proof one way or the other."

"It's not a permanent assignment. Just take a good look at some of the more promising cases and render a judgment, myth or maniac. If you get a ruling of homicide from one of the local authorities, I'll turn it over to McMurphy in the Behavioral Analysis Unit, and your work on the case will be finished. If it turns out to be a myth, you'll be assigned to other duties."

"What duties? May I remain here in the DDI?"

"If that's what you really want. We could also use you in the classroom teaching new DDI recruits. I'd appreciate your cooperation."

Val nodded awkwardly.

"Now, on the matter of safety. If either of you even smells a trace of danger, walk away immediately. We don't want a calamity occurring within the Bureau." Marshall regarded them. "All of your previous assignments are hereby rescinded."

Mark shifted in his chair, trying to interpret the ambiguous instruction. *Is the covert mission to evaluate Valeriya canceled as well?* "Everything is rescinded?" He struggled to find the words. "Do you mean …"

"That's correct. Your prior assignment is gone, and you will apply all your knowledge, skill, and powers to the enigma in front of you. Do you understand what I am saying, Dr. Blackwell?"

With meaningful clarity, Mark recognized Marshall's hidden message. "Yes, ma'am," he answered with a straight face.

Marshall extended a card. "This is my private number. Call anytime, day or night." She stood up, indicating the meeting was over. Blackwell and Valeriya escorted her out. She looked back before leaving. "Let me know if you need anything." They both nodded as the door closed.

Val closed her eyes and ran a stressed hand through her pristine hair, turning it into a tangled mess.

"It's not so bad," Mark said. "We shall have ourselves a noteworthy adventure, and at least you are rid of Anthony Naples."

She gave him a half-smile and went to her workstation, pulling off her shoes and those extra-long socks. "I suppose we need to work backward, starting with the freshest cases. We only need to persuade one medical examiner to change his ruling from accident to homicide."

"Sounds easy enough," he agreed, knowing full well how difficult that would be.

"Did you study the Webster death in Ohio?"

"I did." In reality, he had been studying her, more than he should.

"We'll need both reports, the autopsy records as well."

"Two reports for Webster?" Blackwell asked.

"He was arrested for dogfighting, and there is the investigation of his accidental death. I'll send a request for a PDF file of everything, including all the photographic evidence. They can send it over the Internet, and we can review the files before going to Ohio."

"How long will that take?"

"Several days at least. But it will give us time to get organized. I've got a lot to do in transferring my current assignments to the CIA Workgroup, something I should start now."

Mark took the hint. "Call me when you get things straightened out. Or if you just want to talk."

"I will."

He proceeded to the door, not smiling until leaving her office. *Jackpot!*

5 The Yellow Rose

He tore off a piece of duct tape and applied it to the window drapes, tape being the one thing he had in abundance. A sliver of sunlight could still be seen, so Toby Anderson ripped off another piece and pinched it in place. Now he was safe from prying eyes.

The past week had been rough. It started with that phone call from his greasy neighbor, Rick-the-Spic, telling him he was on the six o'clock news. Toby scoffed at the idea. He watched the news at eleven, and sure enough, there he was, hauling a mutt on a restraining pole and slinging it into his van. Even worse, they said the guy stealing the dog was a person of interest in his cousin's dogfighting business. Anderson had tried calling his cousin several times but could never reach him. The TV image looked fuzzy, but it was clear enough for his meddlesome neighbor to finger him. Toby gave the wetback two ounces of Acapulco Gold to forget about it. And this had worked—so far. Still, even the dumb-ass cops would look at his cousin's relatives, and all they needed to see was the photo on Anderson's driver's license. Everything was going down the shithole over a bunch of stupid dogs.

Toby had surveyed the news, and that goddamn TV station showed the video every evening. Then came the bombshell, his cousin dying in a tractor accident. The news broadcast didn't provide any details, just saying the McKinley County coroner was having trouble pinpointing the time of death because the remains had frozen solid.

Dewey just bought that tractor five months ago. *What the hell happened?*

Anderson popped open a can of Coors as he turned on the News at Noon. He watched it through, sipping the beer as he sat in front of the television—finally, a boring broadcast. He brooded about his dead cousin, his only source of cash aside from selling weed. Things were okay last Friday morning because Anderson dropped the last dog off at the farm. It was an unplanned snatch from a rest stop on Interstate 75. The morons went to take a leak and left their car unlocked, so he grabbed their pooch for an easy bait dog. But what happened after he dropped the mutt off at Dewey's farm was a mystery. Toby replayed everything in his head: a pleasant trip down to Louisiana for three weeks to see his sister, then he comes back toting a bait dog—*and bang!* He's the lead story on the fuckin' news. The greedy landlord would pound on the door today, but Anderson hoped to be long gone and on his way to Cajun territory—this time for good.

Toby pitched the empty beer can into a cluttered corner. He kicked more cans out of the way, intending to leave a mess when he left. The Chevy van was almost packed, just four boxes to go. He put on his coat and grabbed the lightest box, carting it down the basement steps and out the rear door. This was a longer trip than going out the side entrance, but no one would see him packing. Anderson opened the sliding van door and placed the box inside, scooting it into place. He looked in the van with the odd feeling that something was missing. He went back inside, locking the deadbolt on the rear door.

Toby decided to load his computer and printer last, placing them on the front seat to cushion the bumpy ride. He wasn't a high-tech guy, but the Internet was useful for selling weed. As he reached for a packing box, the doorbell rang. It couldn't be the landlord because he'd recognize her loud muffler anywhere. Tiptoeing to the front door, he looked through the peephole: a delivery man with a big package. The man knocked on the door.

"What d'ya want?" Anderson called.

"I have a package for Toby Anderson."

Toby peeled back the duct tape on the drapes to get a better look. He couldn't see much, just a guy wearing sunglasses and a heavy coat with a snorkel hood covering most of his face. "What is it?"

"Frangelico."

"I didn't order no Frengeleeno."

"It's already paid for, sir, two cases of hazelnut liqueur."

"Who paid for it?"

The man looked at some papers. "A Mr. Dewey Webster placed the order last December fifteenth, but we were all out due to the Christmas rush, so he backordered it."

"Just leave it on the porch," Toby yelled.

"You gotta sign for this, buddy. It's expensive."

Anderson turned the knob on the deadbolt lock and cracked the door. He scanned up and down the street, seeing no one.

The man shifted on his feet. "Look, I'm freezing my ass off out here. If you don't want it, that's just fine with me." The man grinned like a New Orleans hooker getting a $100 tip.

Toby flew out the door. "Where do I sign?"

The man balanced the load on one arm and laid a packet of papers and a nice-looking pen on top of the box. "Just sign at the bottom."

Anderson scrawled his signature.

He handed over the box, which was much heavier than expected. "You can keep the pen," the man said. "It comes with the booze."

"Stick it in my shirt."

The man groped with his winter gloves, but he got the pen into Anderson's pocket. "Bon appétit," the man said before scurrying down the steps.

Anderson lugged the heavy package inside, kicking the door closed with his foot. He waddled to the dining room table to set the package down. The wrapping was thick, and he went to the kitchen for a knife and a glass. He sliced the box around the edges, opened it, and pulled out a bottle shaped like a monk with a little rope tied around his waist. He counted twenty-four bottles in the top box. Toby twisted the cap off and took a whiff, snickering as he played with the rope.

"Oh man, this shit's fer fags." He poured some into the glass and took a sip: pleasant nutty flavor, something different from beer. His long drive to Louisiana just got a lot better. Anderson filled the glass to the top and drank it down.

A persistent pecking arose from the side door, like fingers knocking on window glass. *That goddamn chili-shitter must be back for more weed. I'll just tell him to come back tomorrow.* Anderson crept down the stairs to the landing, peering through a hole in the window blind: no one there. He separated two panels and looked out again: nothing, not even footprints coming from his neighbor's house. Musta been a bird pecking on the roof. Or was it?

Toby ran back up the steps to secure the front door. He rotated the deadbolt and pulled on the handle to ensure it was locked—the door opened. He took a step back, momentarily stunned. He closed the door, turned the knob, and tried again. Now, the door was locked. *Must be the booze.* After having another helping of the hazelnut delight, Anderson carried two more boxes to the van. He went back for the third when he noticed something on the stairs to the second floor. On the fourth step, prominently displayed like a wedding decoration, was a yellow paper flower. Anderson went up the stairs and picked it up, finding it covered with writing. He unfolded the paper and saw the note he left at his cousin's farm: *Hey bro, this is all I could find this trip. Toby.* What the fuck?

A snakelike thing dropped around his neck, and Anderson was hauled into the air, feet swinging back and forth in the stairwell. He clawed at his throat, struggling to free himself from the pinching chokehold that kept him from breathing. Someone raced down the steps and placed a chair under his feet. Toby stood on the chair, coughing and gasping while his pockets were searched. A man lifted the right leg of Anderson's pants and commenced wrapping something around his lower leg. The tacky clatter and sticky texture were all too familiar: duct tape. Toby craned his neck back and saw he was held by his animal restraining pole, something he had already loaded into the van.

The man strode up the staircase and sat down, facing Anderson at eye level. He was holding a sheet of white paper in each of his gloved hands.

"That's an impressive apparatus," the man said. "Made in the USA and rugged, but I guess it has to be sturdy. Doesn't it?"

Anderson recognized the voice of the deliveryman. He looked different without the hooded coat and sunglasses.

Toby spat phlegm onto the floor. "What do ya want?"

"Your bill is due."

Anderson glanced back at the cases of booze. "You told me that shit was already paid for."

"Not that." He walked down the steps and gave Anderson one of the white sheets of paper.

Toby looked it over: blank on both sides.

"My mistake," the man said. He took the blank sheet from Anderson's hands and gave him the other, also blank, except for Anderson's signature at the bottom. The man snatched the second sheet away.

Toby tugged at the restraining pole. "What do you want?"

The man retrieved the yellow paper Anderson dropped. "I want payment for this, including all prior transgressions."

"Ain't never seen it before."

The man held the white paper with Anderson's signature next to the yellow sheet. "Here is the signature you signed before my eyes just twenty minutes ago. The word 'Toby' is on both sheets in the same handwriting."

"What do you want?" Toby spat more phlegm. "Who the fuck are you?"

"I'm the man who killed your partner, Dewey Webster."

Toby pried his fingers under the rope and yanked as hard as possible, yelling *"Help! Ricky, help! Somebody call the police!"*

The chair disappeared from under Anderson's feet, and the rope tightened, choking off his cries. With sweaty hands that couldn't hold on, Toby grasped the restraining pole, his legs cycling in the air.

The man extended the chair. "Would you like this back?"

Toby gave a quivering nod.

"Then you must be silent." He replaced the chair under Anderson's feet.

Toby balanced himself atop the chair, legs wobbling and fingers fighting the ligature around his neck. The man disappeared and returned with the electric clock from the kitchen. He adjusted the time to ten minutes before twelve o'clock and hung the clock on the wall without plugging it in. After placing the yellow paper in his pocket, he positioned the two white sheets of paper beside Anderson's computer and printer. He removed a paperclip from his pocket and used it to press the start buttons on both machines. The computer began its boot cycle, playing the Windows greeting. The man opened the printer paper drawer and emptied its contents into a trash bag. After mysteriously wiping one side of one of the sheets, he placed it in the printer paper drawer. He added a thick packet of paper from a knapsack, topping it off with the sheet of paper with Anderson's signature. He closed the printer paper drawer and returned.

"Listen carefully. We are going to play a game, an activity you know all too well. Are you listening?"

Toby nodded.

"If you yell again, for any reason, I will remove the chair, and the game will be over. Understand?"

Anderson nodded again.

"I will give you ten minutes to escape from your plaything. If you succeed you will be free, and I will leave you unharmed. Otherwise, I pull the chair away, and you can try your luck picking the lock at the Pearly Gates."

"What kinda' game is that? You ain't givin' me a real chance."

"What chance did you give your innocent victims?"

"Those were animals—*I'm a man!*"

He nodded with a smirk. "There's a box cutter attached to your ankle, held in place with your very own tape. If you can retrieve the cutter, you can use it to slice the rope around your neck. This is part of the game."

Toby touched a bulge beneath the tape. "But what if—"

"Begin." The man plugged the clock into a wall socket and proceeded to Anderson's computer.

Anderson balanced on one leg and raised his foot. He felt all around the tape, trying to find the edge. *Is it wrapped clockwise or counterclockwise?* He lifted his leg again but failed to perceive the edge. He tried clawing with his fingernails, but the tape was too strong. Toby wriggled his fingers between the rope and his neck, standing on his toes and stretching to increase the slack. He tried leaping and pulling himself up, but the other end of the restraining pole was far out of reach. The man typed on the computer keyboard, using the tip of the paperclip to press the keys. The clock showed 11:53.

Toby grabbed the pole, tugging with all his strength. He made another attempt at removing the tape but achieved nothing. *Find the edge. Find the edge.* He tried again and again, wiping lacquered sweat from his face. The clock displayed 11:56. Anderson swung his legs up while grasping the restraining pole. Upside down, legs wrapped around the pole, he tried to reach the knot at the banister post with his feet, but the loop was tied tight with no slack. He continued trying until fatigue caused him to flip over backward, almost missing the chair. The printer activated, and a single sheet of paper popped out. The clock showed 12:01.

The man grabbed Anderson's leg and unwound the tape. He held up the box cutter and extended the blade, slicing a sheet of paper to show the knife was sharp. "The game is over, and you had your chance." He gripped the back of the chair.

"*I'll see you in Hell!*" Toby yelled.

"Pray to your god you aren't that unlucky."

As the man jerked the chair away, the clattering engine of his landlord's car could be heard in the driveway. With sliding hands and kicking feet, Toby mouthed a silent scream.

6 Unreasonable Doubt

He pulled down his lower lip, mouth open wide. His upper teeth were even brighter, so white she would need sunglasses whenever he smiled. *Hm-m, would contact lenses make me even more striking?* Mark took off his eyeglasses and stared in the mirror, head turning side to side. With or without glasses he was a young Brad Pitt. That's what he should have done, departed for Hollywood and a screen test, especially considering his natural gift for acting. The money was well spent: $60 manicure, $150 haircut, $500 for whitened teeth, and a $3,500 custom-tailored suit. Valeriya must see him at his best.

Blackwell inspected his suitcase to make sure he had packed everything: extra shirts, socks, underwear, disposable syringes, and insulin. *Condoms, yes or no?* He hated rubbers, but she might insist. *I'd better take them just to be safe.* The plan was simple enough. After a disappointing meeting with the McKinley County coroner, Valeriya would feel dejected. He would buy her a splendid meal and take her to a nightspot for a few relaxing drinks. He would turn on the charm, dazzling her with brilliance and saying all the things lonely women want to hear. After several generous doses of Jack Daniels liquid panty remover, the rest would be easy. As he closed the suitcase, someone knocked at his front door.

Mark glared through the peephole. *Dammit! Should I pretend not to be home? No, that won't work, not with my car in the driveway.*

He looked again. Sergeant Miller was alone, knocking for the second time.

Blackwell opened the door, wearing his official Wittgenstein smile. "Sergeant Miller? What a pleasant surprise."

Miller returned the grin. "Hello, sir. I was wondering if you could spare me some time?"

"I can, but I must leave in about half an hour—official FBI business." Mark gave a welcoming gesture. "Please come inside. I've been thinking about you and wondering how things were going."

Miller entered the house, still dressed in the same worn-out suit, same workmen's shoes. "I must say, Professor, you're looking exceptionally good this morning."

"Thank you. How can I help?"

"Well, sir, I'm still tying up some loose ends on Miss Rowan's death. Our captain is a stickler for details." Miller stepped closer, as if embarrassed. "Off the record, sir, I'm struggling to explain what happened."

"I'll be happy to help, Sergeant. Sit down and tell me the problem." Blackwell guided Miller to his comfortable easy chair while he sat on the sofa.

Miller opened his notepad and took out a pen. "Have you ever been up to the roof of your building?"

"Several times. One of my colleagues took his telescope up there for some astronomical photography. He showed me some awesome shots of Saturn, Jupiter, and sunspots during the day, although the light pollution from the city streetlights made seeing deep space objects impossible."

Miller nodded. "So you know how to get up there?"

"There's a stairwell in the audiovisual equipment room, up on the sixth floor."

"Did you know that is the only way up there, that there's no other way?"

"I never noticed."

"Well, sir, Miss Rowan fell to her death from that roof, which means she had to go up the stairwell in the equipment room, but the room is locked. Maintenance personnel have the key, as do faculty in the building, but students do not. Accordingly, how did she get to the roof?"

"Maybe the door was unlocked."

"Our forensics staff inspected it, and it's the type of latch that requires a key to open. It's impossible to unlock the door and leave it unlocked. And there is one of those elbow contraptions that pulls the door closed. You can leave the room without a key, but you cannot enter. An internal examination shows the lock was not picked, and the door seems to be working perfectly. We walked all around the building, observing the windows on the top floor, and getting to the roof would be impossible without mountaineering equipment, which she didn't have."

"That is strange." Mark lapsed into thought. *How did Candy get up there?*

"It gets even stranger," Miller continued. "When they dusted the doorknob and door for fingerprints, there were none, none at all—no partials, no smudges, nothing. The technician said someone had wiped all the fingerprints away, like a bank robber wiping down a hot car before he leaves."

"The only explanation I can think of would be the cleaning staff."

"We checked on that, sir. However, that room is cleaned on Mondays, and Miss Rowan died on a Friday."

"Was the scene secured immediately after her death?"

"Regrettably, no. The body fell behind some shrubbery, and it wasn't discovered for about twelve hours. Plenty of students were walking around when she fell, but no one heard her scream."

"All kinds of things can happen when the crime scene isn't secure. Someone may have gone up there to look around, and, realizing he shouldn't be there with a dead body below, wiped his fingerprints away. You get one chance at preserving a crime scene." Blackwell casually crossed his legs, calm as a professor talking to a student. "To me, the relevant question is why Miss Rowan went to the roof. Her not screaming points to suicide."

Miller nodded. "Yes, sir, or to the possibility that she was unconscious when she fell."

Miller turned to the next page in his notebook. "This brings me to the second problem. Once she got up there, Miss Rowan folded her clothes in an orderly fashion. Detectives discovered an opened tube of sexual lubricant in one of her shoes, and traces of the gel were in her vagina."

This was a crippling kick to the crotch, but Mark kept his composure. "That's incredible. What did the autopsy show?"

"There was no autopsy. The coroner did bloodwork and a physical inspection of the body, but in deference to the family's wishes, no medical dissection. He did check for the presence of semen, and none was found."

Miller is hinting at murder. Throw him a speed bump. "By my way of thinking," Mark began, "there are sufficient grounds to have the body exhumed and a proper postmortem performed."

"We can't do that, sir. The body was cremated." Miller shook his head. "You see my problem. It sort of looks like a murder, except we don't have a motive or any suspects. For the life of me, I cannot comprehend why someone would kill such a wonderful girl."

"I still believe it was suicide."

"My captain says no. She's rather firm about it. Miss Rowan went up there to make love, and something terrible happened. I mean, a woman wouldn't be naked and lubricated if she was alone, which means somebody else was there, and it had to be a man because female lovers don't use K-Y jelly." Miller drummed his fingers on the armrest. "Do you see the issue, sir?"

Blackwell nodded. He let the silence sit. *This makes no sense at all. Candy wasn't seeing anyone else, and she wouldn't screw some bloke on top of the roof.* Miller's presence was a problem. Even the appearance of impropriety could be damaging. "Okay, Robert, where do we go from here?"

"We're looking for suspects, trying to find the guy that was with her. Unfortunately, we aren't having much luck. I was hoping a brilliant criminologist such as yourself could help."

Somehow Mark was able to smile. "Well, let's see." He thought for a while. "You could list every person who possesses a key to the equipment room, eliminating female faculty and custodians. There are security cameras at the building entrance, so you can review the footage and determine the precise time when these individuals arrived and departed. Then you eliminate persons not in the building when Miss Rowan died—*such as myself!*"

Miller stared at Blackwell, his jaw dropping open.

"Cameras don't lie," Mark continued. "I would wager you have fewer than twenty men to look at."

"That's so logical. Why didn't I think of that? Now, if you could only help me find the motive."

Blackwell elevated his chin. "Have you looked at Miss Rowan's phone calls, emails, and text messages?"

"Not yet, sir. We would need a court order."

"Then I would proceed in that direction. You have probable cause. Look for phone calls late at night, cryptic emails or text messages indicating stress, or, even more important, show a romantic relationship."

Miller commenced scribbling. "This is fabulous."

"Look at Miss Rowan's credit card transactions, bank transfers, and canceled checks. Look at her social media posts and have a face-to-face discussion with her friends and family." Mark glared at Miller. "Surely the police have her cellphone in their possession?"

Miller's eyes widened. "Oh my. It wasn't with her shoes or clothes."

"You must find that phone! It may well hold a treasure trove of secret photographs and critical information."

Miller kept writing. "You astound me, sir. Whatever they're paying you at Wittgenstein, it isn't enough."

"You got that right." Blackwell checked his watch, dropping a subtle hint. He rose with Miller, each man extending his hand.

Mark grabbed his suitcase and left for the airport. Whatever these bizarre happenings were, he wouldn't allow them to disturb the pleasant prospect of a marvelous day with Val.

7 The Seven Deadly Sins

Mark had never been to Sandy Hook Regional Airport, but it didn't take him long to spot Val's plane. The dual-engine behemoth looked more like a luxury commuter than the type of plane people flew as a hobby. It was dark blue with yellow trim around the windshield, subtly mimicking the football helmet of the Michigan Wolverines. Something this nice had to cost millions, yet it was just a recreational toy, a plaything for a wealthy woman who didn't know how to properly spend money. Someday he would have that kind of wealth—someday. Valeriya hadn't seen him yet, apparently preoccupied with a preflight inspection. He approached along the pathway, lugging his suitcase.

She wore an aquamarine turtleneck sweater and a handsome black trench coat. A mild breeze whipped her hair into a flowing mane of dark, delectable locks, giving her a dreamily exotic appearance. Seeing her in the light of day imparted a ripple of exquisite excitement, revealing just how attractive she was, like witnessing a sudden sunburst on a dreary December day. Any latent thoughts he had about troublesome Sergeant Miller vanished.

"Are we ready?" Blackwell called.

She looked up and nodded. "All gassed up and ready to go."

"You look spectacular in that glitzy leather coat."

"You're looking rather sharp yourself."

She placed his suitcase in the storage compartment and opened the passenger door. The words *Snow Queen* were inscribed below the windshield in elegant yellow script. Mark climbed inside, somewhat overwhelmed by the complexity of the cockpit. Everything was spotless, not a trace of dust or dirt, even on the thick carpet. Valeriya rounded the aircraft and entered from the other side, removing her shoes before buckling up.

Blackwell tried to buckle his safety harness, but the belt would not extend. "This thing isn't working."

"They can be tricky."

Val unbuckled her belt and reached across him, unintentionally caressing his face with feathery hair that smelled like summer strawberries. Her breasts pressed against him as she reached for the seatbelt, sending his pulse skyward. She lingered there, sashaying this way and that, stretching and pulling, elevating his respiration—and more.

She moved back to her seat. "Try it now."

"That did it." Mark pulled the seatbelt across his distended lap and made some cosmetic adjustments.

"Are you all right? You're perspiring."

"Just some preflight anxiety. Sometimes I get motion sickness."

"I'll be careful."

Valeriya helped him with the headset, something she said was necessary to block out engine noise. She flipped cockpit levers and pressed glowing buttons, starting both engines. The plane throttled up and moved to the end of the runway. The control tower gave permission for departure, and the engines roared to full power. With her hands on the flight controls and shoeless feet on the rudder pedals, the *Snow Queen* gracefully rose off the ground, smooth as a yacht sailing a calm sea.

Regaining his physical equanimity, Blackwell wiggled into his seat. "How long before we land?"

"About an hour and forty minutes."

They flew above the Appalachian Mountains, lower than he expected. The rearward sun transformed the wintry landscape into a Thomas Cole painting, showing pristine wilderness and flowing streams, soaring eagles and waterfowl swimming in ponds, primitive wildlife trails that cut through the slopes, resembling the arteries of some enormous creature that couldn't be seen. Val gently banked the plane, pointing to a herd of running deer trotting together as if pulling Santa's sleigh.

Mark leaned toward the window. "This is enchanting."

"I like to fly low, using visual flight rules."

He relaxed as she weaved the plane lazily through the mountains, making steady westward progress yet clutching the progressively unfolding panorama. "And how many people have you treated to this wonderful experience?"

"You're the third. I take Richard up several times each year, and my friend Lisa goes on cross-country trips with me."

"Trips to where?"

"Different places, mostly out west. One year we went to the Superstition Mountains and climbed to the top of Weaver's Needle."

"You, made it to the summit of Weaver's Needle?"

"It wasn't easy, but she got me to the top and back down without me breaking my neck. She's a full-blooded Apache who works for the Bureau's hostage rescue team, so she's trained in rappelling and that sort of thing, aside from being a crack shot with a rifle."

"Hostage rescue. Is that the same as SWAT?" Blackwell asked.

"Not exactly. SWAT is a broader group, but they're pretty close. She and I were roommates in the dormitory at Michigan, taking some of the same classes. She's going overseas until the end of the year, serving with the Marine Reserves."

A voice came over the radio, warning of several ultralight aircraft flying in their vicinity. Valeriya lifted the *Snow Queen* above the clouds, showing him another stunning vision.

They talked about Blackwell's lectures to the FBI SWAT group and about the anomalies each of them found in Dewey Webster's death. Mark suddenly realized he was ensnared in a Catch-22 situation. Val was keen on reclassifying the death as a homicide so she could return to the DDI. But if this occurred, they would send him to work in the boring Behavioral Analysis Unit. Fortunately, the abnormalities they found in Webster's death were inconsequential.

The mountainous terrain flattened when they entered Ohio, still beautiful, but in a different way. Valeriya commenced communications with air traffic control at Dayton International Airport, requesting approach coordinates. She banked the *Snow Queen* for a view of Ohio Stadium.

"Have you ever been to the Horseshoe?" Blackwell asked.

"Lisa and I are there every other November, right on the 50-yard line. We won't make it this year though."

"Perhaps I can be a friendly substitute for Lisa. I love nippy autumn air and the excitement of college football."

The air traffic controller spoke, giving the approach coordinates—she throttled back the engines. As she lowered the landing gear and positioned the flaps, the speed indicator dropped to 175 knots. The control tower granted authorization to land, and she continued the descent, slowing to 100 knots at touchdown.

She guided the *Snow Queen* to a parking location like a mother pushing a baby carriage. "There's a rental car waiting for us. We should be at the coroner's office before noon."

* * *

The McKinley County Courthouse was the tallest structure in town, built the old-fashioned way with hand-chiseled blocks of stone. The uppermost section had a dome shape like the US Capitol building, except there were four enormous clock faces to the north, south, east, and west. After a quick burger and fries, they drove down Main Street, passing a prominent statue of Lady Justice: stern-faced, blindfolded and barefoot, holding a balance in one hand and a sword in the other. Val pulled into the coroner's parking lot, seemingly ready for battle. Mark walked beside her, hoping the meeting would end quickly so they could get onto more important things.

Coroner Harvey Lane was a portly man in his sixties, black hair (dyed too dark for his age), and not much over five feet tall. Lane, speaking with an Eastern-Canadian accent, invited them into his office. Everyone sat down.

"Were the records and photos I sent unsatisfactory?" Lane asked.

"They were excellent," Valeriya replied. "And Sheriff Shank's documentation was also quite helpful."

"I'm rather taken aback that the FBI is interested in dogfighting."

Blackwell folded one leg over the other. "In fact, we're looking at something else."

Lane gave a cartoonish, toothy smile. "How can I help you?"

"You ruled Dewey Webster's death an accident," Valeriya said. "Did you find any irregularities that would point to the contrary, anything at all, even the smallest inconsistencies?"

"Not a single thing. In fact, I will place my professional reputation on the line by saying that Webster died in an accident all too common for novice tractor users. People just don't realize how dangerous farm machinery can be."

Val glanced at Mark, giving him his cue. "One of my friends has a small farm, and I described what seems to have occurred. He said it doesn't make sense."

"Please enlighten me."

"Webster was killed when his clothing became entangled in a spinning tube, something called a PTO shaft."

Lane nodded.

"And the thing that did him in was his removal of the plastic safety shield covering the shaft. In your report, you said you believe he removed the safety shield to make shaft lubrication easier. But my friend tells me any lubrication of the PTO shaft is done when the tractor engine is off. In fact, if the shaft is spinning, lubrication is impossible."

Lane lit a Pall Mall cigarette and took a deep drag, outwardly confident. "An experienced tractor operator can lubricate everything with the safety shields installed, but it's a little more difficult. Tractor rookies, like Webster, sometimes take shortcuts. I spoke with our local tractor dealer, and he theorized that Webster removed the safety shield and lubricated the U-joints and PTO shaft with the tractor engine off. At that point, Webster should have replaced the safety shield. Instead, he removed the chain guard on the snowblower and turned the tractor engine on, deliberately engaging the PTO to spin the snowblower so he could spray the chain with lubricant while it was moving. Evidently while doing this, he fell backward onto the rotating shaft and was killed. We believe he may have stepped on a grease gun while spraying the chain with a can of WD-40."

Blackwell nodded. "I see."

"The forensic support for an accident scenario is overwhelming. We found the grease gun on the floor covered with Webster's finger and palm prints. A film of grease was on his hands, therefore we know he was lubricating the tractor. The room was covered with high-velocity blood spatter, and there were no smudges or tracks in the blood, so no one was there after Webster died. His $10,000 Rolex was left untouched on a workbench, something a thief would certainly take. He also had the snowblower instruction manual open to the page on lubrication. Accordingly, what happened seems perfectly clear. A big snowstorm was coming, and in his haste, Webster cut some safety corners that proved to be fatal. These types of accidents occur all the time on farms across the United States." Lane tilted forward in his chair as if eager to conclude the meeting. "Is there anything else I can help you with?"

"Do you know how astronomers find asteroids?" Valeriya asked.

Lane chortled out an Elmer Fudd giggle. "No ma'am, I don't."

"They take a picture of the sky on a clear night and wait until the next evening, taking another picture of the same area. Then they use a computer program to search for any differences between the two photographs. If the picture has changed, it could be an asteroid or a comet."

Lane nodded his head with a side-to-side motion. "So?"

"I compared the sheriff's photograph of the building where Webster was killed with another photo of the same building taken when he was arrested for dogfighting. I ran a computer scan and found this." Valeriya gave Lane two photo enlargements. "We enhanced the sharpness to provide additional detail, and it appears as though there are bullet holes in the side of the building that were not there before."

Lane grimaced at the photographs. "Are these bullet holes?"

"They are bullet exit holes," Blackwell interjected. "Meaning a gun was fired through the wall from inside the building. You can tell the difference between a bullet entry hole and an exit—"

"Yes, yes, I'm aware of that." Lane crushed out his cigarette. "What's your point?"

"The point concerns why the bullet holes are there," Mark replied. "Did you happen to check for gunshot residue on Webster's hands?"

"No, we didn't. Nor should we have conducted such a test." Lane pulled his chair forward and sat upright. "We know how Mr. Webster died, and it had nothing to do with firearms. He wasn't shot, and no one else was shot. We had no reason to conduct such a test, nor could we now because Webster's remains have been cremated."

Mark continued the verbal assault, championing Valeriya's cause. "Someone fired a gun inside that building, and in a reckless manner. For what reason?"

Lane's complexion reddened. "Look, Mr. Blackwell, these questions are neither answerable nor relevant."

"We are filling out paperwork, the same as you," Mark replied. "There must be an answer for our report."

Lane nodded. "Webster had just been arrested, and he was naturally angry. He might have fired a gun in a wild fit of rage. The circumstances of Webster's death are plain as day, and it couldn't have been a suicide like his cousin because people don't kill themselves in that manner. I know, I know for sure that this is an accident!"

"There was a suicide?" Valeriya asked.

"Webster's cousin hung himself three days ago. We just finished the cut on him this morning. He was involved in Webster's dogfighting operation."

"May we see what you have on that," Valeriya asked, "even if it's just preliminary?"

Lane regarded her as though she had made a foolish request. "The suicide? You want to see the body?"

"Yes, please."

"You're welcome to see it, but it's an airtight case. He killed himself."

Blackwell wasn't eager to prolong this pointless debate, but he had to back her up. "Since the death involved a relative of Webster, we could write a cleaner report if we examine everything."

Lane sighed. "Okay, but you are just wasting your time. The body is in the morgue across the street. I'll meet you there with our pathologist in ninety minutes."

"Thank you," Val replied. "You are being tremendously helpful to our investigation."

Mark nodded in agreement.

* * *

The morgue had a disagreeable odor, reminding Blackwell of medical school classes where he had to dissect cadavers. He and Valeriya entered the examination room, a place filled with stainless steel tables and refrigeration units, save for a single wooden desk in the corner. Harvey Lane talked to a young man wearing a white lab coat and a middle-aged woman dressed in medical attire.

"Ah, our guests are here," Lane said. "This is Mr. Blackwell and Miss Highland from the FBI. And this is our pathologist, Dr. Carla Crosby, and our forensics specialist, José Tori." Everyone shook hands and exchanged salutations.

Crosby stared intently. "Aren't you Professor Mark Blackwell of Wittgenstein University?"

"Indeed I am. I have a faculty sabbatical with the FBI."

Crosby's face brightened. "This is a genuine delight. I've spent countless hours reading your books and journal articles." She went to the desk and returned with a book and pen. "Would you do me the honor?"

Mark recognized his classic: *The Psychological Autopsy*. He opened the book and wrote in his most elegant handwriting: *To Dr. Carla Crosby, Best wishes for solving all your forensic mysteries. Mark Alan Blackwell.*

LESSER EVILS: AN ANIMAL RIGHTS NOVEL

Crosby read the inscription and smiled. "I nearly didn't recognize you without your beard, and those rectangular eyeglasses are different."

Mark bared his best profile, flaunting his handsome face. "I needed a new look for the Bureau."

Lane tapped the toe of his shoe, clearly annoyed with Crosby's idle digression. "Okay, we had better not delay the important work of the FBI." He went to the first examination table and grabbed a white sheet draped over a body, snatching it away like a magician performing a trick. "Mr. Toby Anderson."

Everyone gathered around the nude corpse of a white male with short hair in his twenties. Blackwell scrutinized the neckline while Valeriya read the toe tag.

Lane moved to the front of the examination table. "The FBI has some concerns that Mr. Anderson's death may not have been a suicide."

"Oh, I have seen no indication of that," Crosby replied. "The cause of death was asphyxiation by hanging." Crosby pointed to an inverted-V abrasion on the left side of the neck. "This excoriation and furrow shows he was hanged with a rope. If someone had manually strangled him first, say with a garrote, then you would see a straight mark across the neck, like this." She pantomimed the horizontal pull of a two-handed garrote. "The conjunctivae show petechial hemorrhages around the eyes, therefore he died from slow strangulation. You can also see fingernail scrapings and rope burns on the palms coming from the instinctive attempt to free himself, proving he was alive when hanged." Crosby glanced occasionally at Val as though the explanations were for her benefit. "See how the rope mark has slid past the laryngeal prominence, yet the encirclement is incomplete where the cord met the metal pole that he used to hang himself. There are fractures in the thyroid cartilage consistent with hanging. The body's wounds are in harmony with hanging or the automatic reflex injuries that would occur when he tried to escape from the rope. If he was engaged in a fight, we would expect to see defensive wounds or antemortem bruising, and none are present. The evidence for death by suicide is unequivocal."

Lane rocked back and forth on his heels, displaying a cheeky smirk.

"Who discovered the body?" Blackwell asked.

"The landlord, and if she had been there just a little earlier, this might never have happened. We measured his liver temperature at 97.5, hence he had been dead a short time."

"How short?" Valeriya asked.

Crosby scratched the side of her cheek. "Let's see. Backing up from the time we got there, maybe just a few minutes before she found him."

Val leaned over the dead man's feet. "Did you shave his lower leg? There is hair on one leg but not the other."

Crosby picked up a magnifying glass for a closer look, a slight frown escaping from her lips. "Any thoughts on this, Professor Blackwell?"

"No idea. The hair removal is too high on the leg for a sprained ankle treatment."

"What about this small peninsula of hair in the middle?" Valeriya continued. "It looks like he shaved his leg around it."

"That is odd," Crosby replied. "Nevertheless, the evidence shows he died from hanging."

Val tilted her head thoughtfully. "But was it a suicide? There is still the matter of—"

Lane interrupted her with a smarmy snigger. "If this wasn't a suicide, I'll swim over to Ireland and kiss the Blarney Stone."

Tori stepped forward. "The device he used to hang himself belonged to him. It is the same mechanism he used in capturing dogs for the dogfighting operation. And he left a signed suicide note, stating he felt persecuted by the authorities and he refused to be sentenced to prison."

"Is the note here?" Blackwell asked.

Tori opened a briefcase and removed an evidence bag containing a white sheet of paper. Mark read the note without opening the bag—poor grammar and many misspelled words.

"His signature appears to be genuine," Tori added. "There is a distinctive forward slant with notable top loops and pointed letter bottoms that match the signature on his driver's license. Additionally, his fingerprints are on both sides of the paper and on the computer keyboard where he typed the note. The printed portion of the note uses ink not dissimilar to the ink from the printer cartridge, and the last image from the internal printer roller is the same as the words on the note. The note is from the same paper stock as was found in his printer, and Anderson's fingerprints were on the bottom sheet of paper in the paper feeder tray, proving he loaded the paper into the printer. The ink on the paper where he signed the note is also not dissimilar to the ink in a pen found on the floor, again with his fingerprints. There is no sign of forced entry, and only Anderson and his landlord's fingerprints were found on the doorknobs. All of this proves it was a suicide. QED, I believe."

Lane nodded with confident smugness, as though the issue was closed.

"Are there photographs of the scene?" Valeriya asked.

"That would be helpful," Blackwell added. "And we would like to see the written narrative of the circumstances of discovery."

Tori removed two packets from the briefcase and gave them to Blackwell. Harvey Lane leaned against a refrigeration unit, checking his pocket watch. Mark gave the photographs to Val and opened the packet of narratives.

Crosby touched Mark on the shoulder. "Please sit at my desk. The light is much better."

"You are very kind." Blackwell sat down and commenced reading what looked like a typical crime scene narrative, tedious and technical. He and Val were playing a silly game of *Pin the Tail on the Donkey*, except the donkey wasn't there. He was on the fourth page when Valeriya cried out in a resounding voice:

"Bingo!" She held up two photographs, pinching the corners like they were dead fish. "No way."

Val placed the photos on an empty examination table, and everyone congregated around. The first picture was a close-up of

Anderson's neck while he was hanging by the animal restraining pole. The second photo showed the rope at the opposite end of the pole as it was tied to the banister post. Mark adjusted his eyeglasses, nerves on edge, seeing nothing unusual other than Valeriya watching him with rapturous anticipation.

"Do you see it?" Valeriya whispered. "We just got our 'Get Out Of Jail Free' card."

Mark nodded. "Very interesting."

"And just what is this great revelation?" Lane asked, his smirk disintegrating into a scornful scowl. He looked at Tori and Crosby. José shook his head and shrugged.

Crosby looked at the photos, finger pressed to her chin. Her mouth dropped open. "Oh."

Lane glared at her. "What?"

Tori blurted out something in Spanish.

"English, José," Lane snapped. "This is America."

Crosby drew attention to the neckline. "Look, there's no slack in the rope."

Lane turned the photo towards himself. "Of course not. What would you expect?"

Crosby showed Lane the other photograph. "But there's no slack at the other end of the pole either, just a well-tied knot."

"I overlooked that," Tori murmured.

"Overlooked what?" Lane yelled.

"Anderson had to place the loop around his neck, right?" Crosby asked.

"Obviously!" Lane shot back.

"Then how did he tie the knot at the opposite end of the pole? His arms would have to be seven feet long."

Lane looked back and forth between the photos, turning them sideways and upside down.

Blackwell looked at the pictures over Lane's shoulder, studying the two critical areas: no slack. *Could it be true?*

Lane continued rotating the pictures. "Maybe it's just a funny camera angle, hiding the slack."

"No," Tori replied. "See, we have other photos from different angles showing the same thing. Here, look at this one. It's absolutely clear."

Lane took a breath and blew it out, making a sputtering noise with his lips. "José, see if the sheriff is available. And bring that pole over here so we can study it."

* * *

Sheriff Thomas J Shank was in his forties and walked with a slight limp. He conversed with Harvey Lane at the far end of the room, running a hand through his prematurely graying hair. Carla Crosby and José Tori stood a respectful distance away as Lane and Shank bantered with voices cloaked in heated whispers.

Blackwell rested against a stainless steel table at the back of the room, flipping through the stack of photographs. Valeriya was next to him, reading the crime scene narrative.

"What's the matter?" Val whispered. "You look upset."

"I am angry," Mark whispered back, "fed up with these idiots wasting our valuable time by not seeing the obvious."

Sheriff Shank looked awkwardly at the FBI agents and approached in a roundabout way, as if still contemplating the uncomfortable situation. Valeriya strode forward with Blackwell following.

"May I see your identifications?" Shank asked. Val and Mark held up their FBI credentials. "Looks like you've caught us with our pants down."

"I wouldn't say that," Valeriya replied. "We had information indicating something might be wrong, facts that would have led you to the same conclusion."

Shank took the photos from Blackwell and studied them, frowning a rueful scowl. He grabbed the restraining pole and looped the rope around his neck. "No way for me to pull the rope tight from this end." He held the pole out horizontally. "Yeppers. This don't look good at all. Makes us look like the Keystone Cops."

Crosby and Tori joined Lane as he lit a cigarette, the three of them listening.

"Now before we go down this slippery slope," Shank continued, "there's something that baffles me. The suicide note and fingerprint evidence are overwhelming. I've never seen a stronger case for suicide. How do you explain that?"

"We can't," Blackwell replied, avoiding Valeriya's cool gaze. "And we appreciate your need for caution."

"But these photos refute the suicide hypothesis," Val added, holding the sheriff's eyes.

"There's another explanation," Tori said. "Assisted suicide! Anderson wanted to kill himself, and he had a friend, possibly a neighbor, assist him in the hanging."

Lane looked daggers at Tori, dropping his lit cigarette to the marble floor.

"But that is only speculation," Tori added with a sickly smirk.

"Consequently, we are left with either murder or assisted suicide," Crosby said.

As Sheriff Shank further examined the restraining pole, Lane stood silently in front of a political poster advocating his reelection as McKinley County coroner.

Val nudged Blackwell, whispering, "Help me."

"The psychological profile for suicide is wrong," Mark declared. "Why would he pack his belongings into a van, leaving the van door wide open, and then, in the middle of moving, decide to hang himself? And your report said Anderson had only $182 in cash and no known bank accounts. So where did he get forty-eight bottles of expensive hazelnut liqueur, all but one bottle unopened? The crime scene makes little sense."

"What do you think happened?" Shank asked.

Valeriya tossed Lane's written analysis of Anderson's death onto an examination table. "Anderson was killed by the same man who killed Dewey Webster, someone skilled in manipulating forensic evidence. Anderson and Webster are the latest in a long list of victims."

Lane cackled boisterously.

"If the liqueur was delivered, Anderson may have signed for it," Valeriya continued. "Getting his signature on a piece of paper would be necessary in forging a suicide note."

Shank sat down on a swivel stool, swinging back and forth. "Well, hells-bells. I don't know what to make of this."

"I don't buy assisted suicide," Crosby said. "Somebody killed him. Maybe someone who lost their dog. Those ID chips from the dog carcasses out at that farm should be examined. Maybe we should—"

"I hate to throw cold water on this fanciful discussion," Lane interrupted, "but I'm the person empowered to make this call. We will follow the law, and that means making a judgment based on the preponderance of the evidence at hand. I ruled this death a suicide, and nearly all available evidence supports that conclusion. Therefore, despite these scurrilous speculations, the ruling of suicide is affirmed." Any hint of Lane's civilized veneer was gone. The discussion was over.

Goosebumps heralding probable victory traveled up Mark's arms. *Valeriya will definitely need comforting tonight!*

"Harvey," Crosby whined, her voice kneading him to acknowledge the obvious. "The man did not hang himself."

Questioning eyes fell upon Lane, whereupon he threw his head back, looking down his glowering nostrils. "Carla, have you uncovered any anatomical or medical evidence suggesting something other than suicide?"

"No, but—"

"There are no buts here, Carla. You need to do your job and let me do mine. You are not an elected official. The person who hired you was me. You should remember that."

Shank glared at Lane with a deep frown.

"Now I know there's a fly in the soup," Lane added, "and we'll continue to examine this case for further evidence, quietly, without informing the press or anyone else. And if significant evidence against suicide is obtained, I'll change my decision."

The animated silence was filled with a menacing message for Crosby and Tori.

Shank regarded Blackwell and Valeriya. "We'll continue looking into this, but do you have any specific suggestions?"

Lane raised a twitchy finger. "They need to be aware—"

"Shut up, Harvey!" Shank yelled.

Lane shoved Crosby out of his way and stormed out of the room.

Mark stood upright, feeling the intensity of Val's watchful gaze. "Is Anderson's residence still secure?"

"No," Tori replied. "We turned it over to the landlord this morning. She was positioning a large dumpster in the front yard."

"Many homes have video surveillance or door cams, and a neighbor on the same street might have filmed the perpetrator. You should move fast on this, as those videos are only saved for a short time."

Shank took out a notepad and started writing.

"Those two cases of Frangelico are a clue. Check with the local liquor stores and see if anything comes up. Most of those places have high-definition video cameras."

Shank nodded.

"Doctor Crosby's idea of looking at the ID chips of dead dogs is a possibility, but I don't believe the perpetrator is a local. There was snow on the ground, but I didn't see any photographs of footprints around the house."

"They were all messed up," Tori replied. "The landlord and neighbors were running around before we got there."

"You should identify as many fingerprints as possible. We know the killer wore gloves when messing with the computer and printer, but he might have gotten careless around light switches or doorknobs. Did you gather any trace evidence?"

"We have cigarette butts from the ashtrays, but we didn't search for hair or fiber evidence," Tori replied. "It seemed like such a clear case of suicide."

Mark turned to Crosby. "Are there fingernail scrapings from Anderson?"

"Yes, and I'll have them run a DNA check, but that's not a good bet because he dug into his neck during the hanging."

"Did you comb Anderson's pubic region for foreign hair? A woman may have been involved."

Crosby blinked. "Not yet, but I will."

"That's all I can think of at the moment."

"I hear you have new photographs from the Webster farm," Shank said.

Valeriya gave him the bullet hole photos.

Shank studied the pictures and nodded. "José, take your team out to the farm and see what they can come up with. I know it's late, but do what you can."

Tori nodded.

"And José," Shank added, "report all future findings to me for the Anderson and Webster cases."

Tori smiled. "Yes, sir."

"Is there anything else?" Shank asked.

"Not from me," Blackwell replied. Valeriya shook her head.

The sheriff escorted them out of the building. "I will get back to you on this," Shank said while shaking their hands.

* * *

The bell at the Courthouse tower tolled five times as Mark and Val made their way to the rental car, walking slower than when they arrived.

"Why do you think Lane was so pigheaded?" Blackwell asked, hiding his delight.

"People hate to be proven wrong. There is also the political embarrassment of issuing a correction to the press. It could be an issue in the next election. Everything is money, sex, and power these days, nothing about what's right or wrong." Valeriya started the engine and pulled onto Main Street, heading toward the Dayton airport.

Blackwell loosened his necktie. "What's the plan?"

"We get something to eat and fly home."

"You're going to fly tonight, after such a grueling day? I thought we would return tomorrow when you are better rested."

"I'm not tired, just exasperated. And I hate sleeping in a strange bed."

He nodded. *This is the wrong time to make waves.* "I'm the same way myself, never sleeping well when traveling. Where would you like to eat? I saw a steakhouse close to the airport. My treat to celebrate what we accomplished."

"Which is?"

"You verified your suspicions, and we now know our forensically gifted adversary makes mistakes."

"There were no mistakes. The landlord's arrival interrupted him, so there wasn't time to finish altering the scene. Otherwise, all of those little clues would have vanished, including the lack of slack at the top of the restraining pole. This is the work of a master!"

Valeriya rolled into the parking lot of the Queensland Barbecue. The restaurant wasn't busy, and they were seated immediately. Their waitress arrived, and Mark ordered the 24-ounce prime rib with Australian cheese fries, onion rings, sweet potato pie, and dark chocolate mousse for dessert. Val chose the petite filet mignon and soup du jour, which was French-onion. The weight of the day's unfavorable events showed in her dejected face.

He smiled at her. "You shouldn't let this minor setback get you down. Tomorrow is another day."

"It's not that. I just feel …"

"You just feel what?"

She shook her brown hair. "Nothing."

"What's troubling you? We are partners—you *must* tell me."

"It's this awful case. I hate it."

"Then we should redouble our efforts and get it over with."

Val gave an exasperated sigh. "I don't see the point of investigating these old cases. The crime scene is gone, and we will run into the same headwind we had with Harvey Lane."

"But that's what Marshall wants us to do. If we investigate these previous killings together, I'm sure something will pop up."

"I think we should wait for the next killing and get our best forensic specialists involved while the crime scene is fresh. I'll have a face-to-face with Marshall and try to convince her."

Blackwell nodded, placating her fanciful notion, but not believing the FBI director would agree. The waitress brought their meals, and they made light conversation while eating. They flew back to Virginia, enjoying the nightlights below and the starry heavens above. All things considered, this was an excellent start to a long but worthwhile objective. Mark was pleased.

* * *

Margaret Marshall accepted the waiting strategy, and Valeriya returned to the DDI. Much to his liking, Blackwell received a split assignment, having his mornings free to conduct "psychological research" into the mysterious killings. He slept late and started his day at the civilized hour of 1 p.m., sometimes working with the Behavioral Analysis Unit and sometimes working with Val. She always seemed busy, examining police records and investigating various animal rights groups. A federal judge gave permission to subpoena the employment records of three persons who had been arrested during violent animal rights protests, but they all had a work-related alibi for some of the killings. At Marshall's request, Valeriya spent two days a week training DDI recruits. Mark was able to obtain a small office in the DDI, just five doors down from Val.

Ten weeks after their trip to Ohio, Sheriff Thomas Shank informed them that he closed the investigation. Shank confirmed the bullet holes at the Webster farm, but there was no trace of a firearm. All efforts to further investigate Anderson's death were also negative.

Showing considerable patience, Margaret Marshall maintained the status quo, allowing Mark and Val to await the next murder.

8 For Whom the Bell Tolls

The mahogany and maple checkerboard was his, crafted in thick wood and made in his high school shop class many years ago, the checkers as well. Duke Dyson considered putting them in a cardboard box with his other belongings, but he decided against it because of the memories that would inevitably return. Duke picked up the box (more bulky than heavy) and began the long walk past Engine #14. He paused beside the red door and gazed up at the steering wheel he held many times, some of the best moments of his life. Driving #14 was a joy, something he did with passion and pride, as was watching people's faces as those flashing red lights and screaming siren cleared the road. Everyone in town liked him, would shout out "Double D" and wave, eager to cross a busy street just to shake his hand—until now.

A gruff voice called from behind, "Good luck, Double D."

Dyson looked over his shoulder. "Thanks, Chief. I'm gonna need it." Duke wanted to say more, to ask if he could visit the fire station to play checkers, but he was afraid of the answer. An editorial in the *Nashville Lantern* called for Dyson to be fired immediately. The chief, however, being a decent man, agreed to keep him on the roster until the trial was over, retaining some meager medical and insurance benefits for his family. Duke carried the box outside, feeling the coolness of the evening air, colder than usual for May. Early stars broke through the darkening twilight, adorning a cloudless sky with sparkling globules of crystal-white fire. There was a good chance he would be forced to leave the hills of Tennessee. Hopefully, it wouldn't be for a prison up north.

The firefighter helmet resting on the hood of his pickup truck wasn't there a short time ago. Dyson continued to the passenger side and placed the box on the front seat. The helmet was his, easily recognizable by the crown decals glued to the side, one for each of the years where he won the Tennessee Pool Checkers Championship. The badge on the front, his badge, was turned upside down, and someone had scrawled "Damn Dumb" on the side of the helmet. He didn't look at the two men sitting in front of the Creech Crossing Volunteer Fire Department. One of them surely had done it, but there wasn't much he could do. Duke took a last look at the building that had been a second home for the past fifteen years. The flashing red light atop the siren tower could be seen gleaming at night from his front porch, what used to be a comforting reminder of who and what he was.

As Dyson got inside and fired up the engine, Homer Elliott came running out of the station, possibly to wish him well. Duke lowered the window, smiling at his long-time friend and pool checker opponent. Elliott scooped up a handful of mud and flung it, splattering dark muck all over the windshield.

"Homer!" the chief yelled from the open door. "Get your brainless ass back inside before I let you start what you can't finish."

Duke drove on, sickened by the eagerness of his friends to kick him when he was down. He turned on the windshield wipers, but the fluid reservoir was empty. No matter, it was a short drive home. Dyson pulled into his driveway and stopped to get the mail. Across the road, Granny Foss sat on the front porch of her leaning tar-paper shanty, shotgun cradled in her lap. As Dyson waved, Foss hid the gun under a homespun quilt, within easy reach of her rickety rocking chair. She beckoned him and picked up two canning jars. Duke went to take a look.

Foss hobbled down the steps, wearing her haggard and toothless grin. "Somebody twas up ta see ya, Double D."

"See who it was?"

"Didn't get a good look. Car windows colored dark. Seemed like just one person though."

"Stay long?" Dyson asked.

"A right-smart bit. Where d'ya go off to?"

"Had to drive all the way to Nashville to see a lawyer." Duke looked around warily and scratched the back of his neck. "Ya think this dude was up to no good?"

Granny shrugged. "Never paid him no mind at first, 'cept when he left, he turned right in the creek." She pointed a crooked finger. "Way over yonder."

"He drove inta Hays Branch?" Dyson gazed at the bridge. The fading light on the darkening road made it difficult to see. "What was he drivin'?"

"Can't think what it's called. Onea 'em cars with big wheels and fenders and a flat front, like what Sugar Toes has."

"A Black guy?"

"Couldn't see. No tell'n what he wanted. Might be revenuers huntin' fer shine. Y'all needs ta be a leetle bit careful. Keeps my shotgun ready, just in case."

Duke laughed. "Well, they sniffin' up the wrong tree."

Foss handed over both jars.

He flashed a broad smile. "Lordy, lordy. Pickled corn and pickled beans. I sure am gonna eat good tonight."

"Mind ya don't overcook 'em. Kills the flavor." Granny pulled a shawl around her slumped shoulders. "I don't believe a word a that hog shit they put in the paper. You'd nary do such a terrible thing. I says it twas 'em Tabor boys burnt yer barn, 'cuz ya burnt the hunten shanty they had on yer land. They never got no deer last season."

"I appreciate that, Granny."

"Are 'ya gonna survive this?" She waited while Dyson thought. "I means, whatcha gonna do?"

"I dunno, Granny. Just don't know. Lookin' bad right now. I'll probably be gone for a spell."

"Ya can always count on me."

Duke put a friendly hand on the old woman's shoulder. "How youse doin', livin' alone and all?"

"Gettin' by. My boy Snooky 'ill be out a prison next year. Be easier then."

Foss patted Dyson's arm and hobbled back to her porch. They waved to each other as Duke opened the door to his truck.

Dyson parked outside so he could hose the mud off his windshield the next morning. An orange moon crouched low in the dusky sky, creeping its way up through the blackened ruins on the hill. Once again, that pesky barn owl that had a nest of chicks hidden up in the loft mewled a mournful cry, like it had done every night since the fire. He decided to give it both barrels of his shotgun when the moon was higher and he could see the critter's white feathers. He thought about his wife and daughter visiting her parents down in Birmingham. At least they would have a roof over their head and food to eat while he was away.

Dyson took both canning jars and walked up the front steps to his house, almost not seeing the dark object at the top. He put the jars down and picked it up, jiggling it up and down. It was one of the bells he hung around the neck of his dairy cows, dented and blackened with soot. *How did it get here?* Duke scrutinized the scenery in the last vestige of visible light, observing nothing unusual. The front door was locked, as it should be. He pitched the cowbell on the lawn, hearing its ringing clatter.

The house was frigid beyond belief. *Has the furnace stopped working?* Dyson placed the pickled beans and corn on the kitchen table, noticing three nine-volt batteries stacked next to the salt and pepper. They were his batteries all right, the same brand they sell at Bailey's store, the same expiration date he remembered seeing. As he went to check the furnace, cool air swirled around him—*must be an open window*. He followed the frosty breeze to the living room.

There, against the wall, resting on a table that was previously in the basement, was a strange television. Duke looked it over. Was this something his wife ordered? No, that didn't make sense. She's in Alabama. So how did it get here? A sudden downward rush of chilly air elevated his eyes—the skylight window was cranked open wide. *Somebody's fucking with me, maybe that goofball JoJo from the fire station.* He glimpsed a moving shadow and turned. A man stood in the kitchen doorway, wearing a ski mask and gloves, pistol in hand.

"Goddammit, JoJo," Duke yelled. "I'm gonna beat yer ass til shit comes outta yer nose. Ain't I got enough to deal with without you playin' stupid pranks."

The man pointed at the couch. "Sit over there."

He was JoJo's height, but stocky, and the voice was wrong. Dyson sat down, still believing this was some fireman's practical joke. The man positioned himself in an armchair. He wore ordinary clothes, holding a Colt 1911 automatic. Duke stared disbelievingly. *Blue eyes? Can you believe it? A white man has come to rob me.*

"You gotta be from up north, 'cuz even a fool knows to case the joint before robbing it."

The man looked him over, saying nothing.

Duke considered making a grab for the gun, but the large hole at the end of the pistol persuaded him otherwise. Regrettably, his shotgun was in a bedroom at the other end of the house. "Okay, fine. Just take whatever you want." Dyson spread his arms. "It's all yours."

"We are going to talk."

"Talk? She-it. Just take what ya want and get the fuck out."

"You are going to talk to me. One way or another."

Duke looked at the intimidating pistol again. "If we're gonna chinwag, can I smoke?"

The man nodded.

Having nothing worth stealing, Duke suffered little anxiety. He withdrew a pack of Marlboros and tapped out a cigarette, lighting it with his Creech Crossing fireman's Zippo, *Engine #14* etched into the metal. He took a drag and placed the cigarettes and lighter on a coffee table before him, waiting for the next move.

The man stared at the Zippo, chest rising and falling. He reached for a sheet of newspaper and laid it next to the lighter, print facing Dyson.

Duke recognized the headline: *Fifty-four Dairy Cows Perish in Tragic Barn Fire.*

The man laid down another headline on the other side of the lighter: *Firefighter Burns Dairy Cows Alive*. He leisurely crossed his legs, resting the pistol on his knee. "Tell me about it."

Dammit. It's not a robbery. Dyson sat there, thinking. *Ten feet away—can I overpower him?*

"You are not cooperating," the man said.

"And just why the fuck should I cooperate with you?" Duke stuck out his chin. "You the big man holden that blaster, aren't ya? I ain't afeared a shit."

"You must talk to me. We are both at the precipice."

Duke chuckled. "Pre, preceep. What the fuck are you, some starchy-ass college boy? I'll bet you never once had to wipe yer ass with a corncob."

The man aimed the pistol at Dyson's legs. "Right or left knee?"

"Whoa!" Duke exclaimed with his hands extended. "Everything's cool. Look, the cash wasn't comin' in, man. I got bills to pay, mortgage, truck payments, keepin' the farm going. It's a hard life. Did what I had to do. Ya know being a volunteer fireman don't pay no cash money." Dyson took another drag from his cigarette. "It woulda worked too, 'cept that nosy neighbor kid was hiding in my apple tree. Little shit ratted me out for no reason at all."

The man lowered the pistol and tapped it on his leg. "If you needed money, why didn't you let the dairy cows out of the barn before setting it ablaze? You could have sold them to another dairy farmer."

"The cows was old, man. Not worth havin'. My milk production was way down. But ya see, I had replacement cost insurance on everything. Shoulda got a brand-new barn and a fresh dairy herd. In which case I'd be sittin' pretty.

The man stopped tapping the pistol. "I thought it might be the insurance."

"Ya see, a perfectly logical business decision. Plus it gave me a chance to collect from that crooked insurance company, premiums I paid and never got nutin' back. Cheatin' folks that's cheatin' you ain't cheatin'—it's gettin' even." Dyson flicked ashes into an ashtray. "Course now they won't pay me anything. Thievin' 'sumbitches. Ya know justice and the law is two different things, man."

"We are in complete agreement on that." The intruder heaved a deep sigh and removed his ski mask.

Duke studied the face, having no idea who he was. "Now that we've cleared away the bullshit, would ya kindly tell me what ya want?"

The man rose from the chair. "Did you know your fire department carries a million-dollar life insurance policy on each firefighter?"

Dyson squashed out his cigarette. "Lotta good that'll do me. Completely worthless."

"Not true. The details are described on their website under benefits of membership. And there is a double indemnity clause that pays two million for accidental death."

Duke sat upright. "Ya know, I thought you was just plain-ass stupid, but you're a friggin nutzo."

The man picked up a framed picture of Dyson's wife and baby daughter. "Your family?"

"Yeah, so?"

He shook his head. "Your beneficiaries."

Duke snickered under his breath. "Say what?"

The intruder moved to the strange television, covering Dyson with the gun. He pressed a button on the TV. The kitchen lights dimmed, and sparks shot from the back of the television, creating a crackling and producing dark smoke.

"What the fuck are ya doin'!" Duke yelled.

"Making a perfectly logical business decision." He tossed the pistol to Dyson.

Duke caught the weapon and aimed at his adversary. The man stood in front of the kitchen doorway, blocking the only exit in the windowless room. A pair of flickering flames cavorted across the top of the television, becoming three, then four, then five. Dyson squeezed the trigger—the gun's hammer dropped forward with a click. He racked the slide, finding the chamber empty.

A stream of fire crawled up the wall behind the television, consuming a picture of Dyson and his bride on their wedding day. Duke hurled the empty pistol at the man. The man dodged the gun, still blocking the door, ignoring the growing danger. Dyson charged forward and was thrown back across the couch.

"What's happenin'?" Duke screamed.

"I'm giving you the chance they never had."

Dyson filled his chest with air and vaulted forward, bellowing his most fearsome Parris Island battle cry. He slammed full force into the man, smashing him into the wall. Hanging pictures and knickknacks dropped, breaking on impact. His adversary latched onto him, locking both men together. With eyes assailing eyes and noses touching, Duke squeezed with all his might, shrieking at the top of his lungs. The pillar of fire engulfing the television expanded into a torrent of ever-widening combustion, singeing the hair on Dyson's right arm. The noxious odor of burning plastic filled the room.

Duke bashed the intruder's jaw with an elbow, striking him over and over. The man whacked Dyson's nose with his forehead, blurring his eyesight. Dyson tried to fling him away, but the man's bulldog grip was so strong that both men tumbled to the floor. Duke thrashed and kicked, desperately trying to break loose. The intruder held on tight, flipping Dyson onto his back. Duke shrieked as snakes of flame slithered across the ceiling, licking with a serpent's tongue. The orange moon leered at him through the open skylight, turning blood-red as it oscillated in the billowing smoke. Dyson finally broke free, and the two men leaped to their feet. With a bloodied face and unyielding eyes, the man returned to the kitchen doorway—*you shall not pass!*

Duke sprang ahead and got his immense hands around the man's neck, digging his heels and using his body's weight for leverage. The intruder shoved both of his hands up through Dyson's outstretched arms, breaking his grip by flexing his forearms. Duke swung at him and missed, striking the doorjamb with his fist. He swung again and again. They seized each other, using the other person's body as a battering ram to smash the furniture and walls as fire scorched their arms. Dyson wrenched himself free, falling back to the floor. Intense flames engulfed both sides of the room, turning the pine paneling black and blistering the varnished woodwork. The heat was far worse than anything he had ever felt as a firefighter. The pulsating roar became deafening as the open skylight sucked out heated air. Coughing from smoke inhalation, wiping sweat and charred grime from his burning eyes, Duke gawked at the sentry blocking the doorway, bellowing:

"Who are you!"

Dyson moved to the back of the room and rushed forward, intending to plow through the human barrier. The man met him halfway and caught hold of Dyson's arm, sending him spinning into his wife's china cabinet—glass and bric-à-brac flew everywhere. Gasping for breath and at his wit's end, Duke grabbed a long shard of glass and lunged forward, swinging the improvised weapon back and forth like a hay cutting machine. The man backpedaled and dropped low, allowing Dyson to reach the doorway. He clutched Dyson's leather belt and lifted him into the air. With all his strength, Duke plunged the glass dagger into the man's back, unintentionally slicing open his own hand. The charcoal-faced intruder carried Dyson into the flames, using him as a human shield. Duke screamed and dropped the weapon as he tried to smother his burning hair, arms flailing and legs kicking. The man lugged Dyson to the basement stairway. Duke continued smacking his flaming clothing while the man carried him down the stairs.

"No!" Duke shrieked. "There's no way outta there."

The intruder released him, and Dyson rushed back up the stairs, taking two steps at a time. A vicious tornado of flame rotated beneath the open skylight, turning the room into a roaring furnace. Escape was impossible. Dyson ran back down the steps.

"Ya crazy muthafucka!" Duke yelled. "We're both dead now."

The man removed a handkerchief from his back pocket and casually wiped his face, seemingly oblivious to the fact that they were about to be burned alive.

Dyson grabbed a coal shovel and pounded at the glass block windows. Hefty chunks of glass and mortar fell to the floor as he continued hammering away, eventually clearing the glass and leaving a small opening in the wall. Duke pushed a workbench underneath the aperture and climbed on top, attempting to squeeze through a hole designed to prevent thieves from entering. He took the shovel and beat one of the concrete blocks, trying to enlarge the opening. The shovel handle broke at the base. Dyson jumped down with the wooden handle, drawing back to strike his assassin. The man snatched a chair to defend himself. Charred and bleeding, both defiant, the two combatants stared at each other. Cold air rushed through the broken window and up the staircase, taking the rumbling inferno above them to the next level.

Duke slammed the shovel handle down. "Oh, no. Ya won't get off that easy. I wanna see ya burn. Wanna watch ya scream and cry like a baby when yer hide and hair is burnt away. We'll just see which of us is the tougher man."

The floorboards above them turned charcoal black, and little puffs of smoke pushed through the widening cracks in the tongue-and-groove planks. Dyson followed the man as he walked calmly toward the coal bin. He climbed inside and commenced ascending the coal chute.

"Ha," Duke yelled. "That'll do ya no good. The door is solid steel, locked from the other side."

The man pulled himself up the slippery ramp, gripping the sides to avoid sliding back down. Upon reaching the top, he effortlessly swung the coal chute door open.

"*Goddamn!*" Duke shouted. He leaped into the coal bin and started climbing the metal chute.

The man sat in the small doorway at the top, waiting.

Dyson moved closer. "Outta my way, asshole."

The man sat motionless, peering down at him like a bird of prey.

Dyson reached out. "If I getta hold of that foot."

The man drew his knees up to his chest, and Duke lunged forward. He kicked Dyson in the face, sending him sliding down to the bottom. With scrambling hands and slipping feet, Duke crawled back up the chute, but the man was gone—the steel door closed.

* * *

He jammed an eyebolt through the latch on the coal chute door. The bolt was narrower than the orifice, providing some looseness that allowed the door to jiggle. He retrieved the blackened cowbell from the front yard and attached it to the eyebolt. The steel door sprang out as Dyson battered the other side, the cowbell ringing with each crashing blow. He went to the broken basement window and tossed his gloves inside. Loud pops came from gun ammunition going off in the heat. The bell continued its frantic rhythm, the same horrifying clangs it must have released before.

Thoroughly exhausted and barely able to walk, he staggered up the hill, stopping to remove a shard of glass from his back. He placed it in his pocket, tightening his shirt around the wound. Breathing the crisp air brought him out of the mental maelstrom that made this victory necessary, more valuable than life itself. His eyes drifted up to the shadowy form that had once been a dairy barn—he strode onward.

He stopped at the entrance, scrutinizing the murky shades of black and gray, cattle corpses littering the ground. This was the nightmare that brought him to the mountains of Tennessee, his reason for being alive. An owl glided silently above and landed atop the tallest beam, gazing down upon him. She spread her silvery wings and shrieked a baneful cry. Blackened blood trickled into his hand from an unnoticed wound. He smeared it into the charred wood of what was once the door frame, gripping the crumbling ash. He whirled around and faced the raging fire below.

Long fingers of glistening flame stretched high into the darkness, like some enormous hand reaching up through the ground. The cowbell tolled on, louder and with greater urgency. In the distance, the foreboding howl of the siren atop the fire station tower rose into a high-pitched scream of distress, oscillating up and down, creating echoes upon echoes in the hills and hollows. Clusters of headlights in the valley moved toward the ear-piercing alarm—volunteer firefighters returning to duty. The blazing inferno created a thick column of smoke that arched above him, forming a black rainbow across the moonlit sky.

9 Bigfoot

The *Snow Queen* touched down at Soldier County Regional Airport at 10 a.m., a mere thirty-six hours after the fire. Blackwell and Valeriya waited in the airport lobby for a Bureau technician from Nashville, someone handpicked by Margaret Marshall herself. Their flight to Tennessee was disappointingly quiet, with Mark carrying the conversation. Val chose a different flight path as well, rather ordinary and utilitarian, not making the most of the scenic beauty she had eagerly sought when they made their carefree trip to Ohio. She appeared sullen and preoccupied in her dreary clothes, wedded to a nebulous despondency.

"Is everything all right?" Blackwell asked.

"Why do you ask?"

"You seem depressed, and you look rather pale."

"I haven't been sleeping well."

"Any idea why?"

She waited as if searching for an answer that wasn't easy to see, giving a melancholic sigh. "I've been reading those eighty-three police reports in bed at night. Maybe I shouldn't be doing that."

"Eighty-three reports? There are only forty-one events, forty-two if you count Toby Anderson."

"Except for Anderson, each event has two reports, one for the death or disappearance and another related to animal abuse."

"The animal abuse files? With all those repulsive pictures? They are irrelevant to our case. You are doing too much, Val. You need to relax, learn to enjoy life." He waited for a response that didn't come. "Hey, why don't we spend a day or two down here seeing the sights of Nashville? We could visit the *Country Music Hall Of Fame* and the *Grand Ole Opry*. They even have a—"

"Sorry to keep you waiting," someone said from behind. "Got held up in traffic."

They turned in unison, and Special Agent Ronald Adair extended his hand. After exchanging brief salutations, Adair guided them to his car.

"How much do you know about the fire?" Valeriya asked.

"Just the basics," Adair replied. "They're still doing the forensics."

"Are they being extra careful with the crime scene?"

"We told the fire marshal that foul play was a strong possibility."

"What's the traveling time?" Blackwell asked.

"A little over an hour. It's not far, but there are plenty of winding back roads."

Adair's car was a typical Bureau vehicle, a gray, four-door sedan that wouldn't attract much attention. Val sat in the back, and they spent the trip updating Adair about their case. The Nashville agent was polite but skeptical, and who could blame him? Mark didn't believe it himself.

Adair had short hair and wore a navy blue three-piece suit with a white shirt and silk tie, looking like one of J Edgar's pretty boys from the old days. His stylish garb, however, didn't match his countrified accent—Nashville all the way. Adair listened as Valeriya explained why Toby Anderson's death was not a suicide.

"Photographic evidence can be deceiving," Adair said. "But somebody must think you're on to something. I was told to drop everything and give you my full assistance."

"Are you an arson specialist?" Blackwell asked.

"Yeah, that and explosives. You guys are doing more interesting work. I drifted into it and got snagged because of my strong chemistry background. Spend most of my time analyzing bomb fragment evidence. It's rather boring."

Adair drove by a religious billboard showing God's eyes gazing down from heaven, the underlying caption reading *The End Is Nigh*. He pulled onto a long driveway that meandered across a dry creek bed and around a hill. Gravel crunched under the tires, and dust rose as they traveled past a rusty farm tractor. A deputy sheriff stopped them until Adair flashed his FBI credentials. Police barricade tape was everywhere, keeping approximately twenty spectators away from critical areas. A sheriff's cruiser and a half-dozen other vehicles were parked to the side, including two pickup trucks marked Tennessee State Fire Marshal.

The two burn sites were about 150 yards apart. The house was gone except for a rock chimney and foundation. Further up the hill, the support beams and doorways of the barn were still standing. Everyone exited the car and approached someone studying a clipboard. The man looked up, and Adair introduced Mark and Val. Fire Marshal Andrew Woodford tipped his wide-brim hat to Val and shook their hands. Woodford was a sinewy man with tanned skin, wearing stonewashed overalls and heavy leather boots, not what Blackwell expected from a fire marshal.

"I'm afraid y'all made a long trip for nothing," Woodford said. "It looks like an electrical fire from a defective television, a model notorious for causing problems."

Adair perused the wreckage. "The destruction looks severe. Did you check for accelerants?"

"Preliminaries came back negative for gasoline, kerosene, and fuel oil. We'll have the full results in a few days, but if Trigger didn't find anything, it's not here. His nose is better than any chemical test." Woodford pointed to a corner of the basement. "Doesn't look like the breaker box was tampered with."

"Which TV model was it?" Adair asked.

"A Comet 546. We're checking the serial number stamped into the metal base to be sure."

"Yeah, I remember reading about those. The solder connections were too close, and if they weren't put together just right, time to break out the weenies and marshmallows."

"Where would he get a television like that?" Valeriya asked.

Woodford pulled out a package of Red Man chewing tobacco and stuffed a sizable chaw in his mouth. He offered some to the three FBI agents. They declined. "Oh, it may have been a yard sale or a private transfer. Bartering is a way a life out here."

"That model was recalled several years ago," Adair said. "But you know how that goes, especially in Appalachia."

"What about the deceased?" Blackwell asked.

"Medical examiner has the body," Woodford replied. "Nothing obvious. They're checking for antemortem injuries."

"Are you sure it was Dyson?" Valeriya asked.

"Pretty sure. The local fire chief said he was convinced. Dyson was six-foot-four, and the chief recognized the ring on his hand. We'll know for certain after they get his dental records."

Valeriya eyed the wreckage. "Was there anything unusual about the fire?"

Woodford spat tobacco juice through the air, hitting a stinkbug sitting on a tree stump. "Most fire deaths are from carbon monoxide. Unfortunately for Mr. Dyson, he was trapped in the basement. He broke out a window trying to escape, and that opening fed fresh air up through the stairwell. I'd say there's a fair to middling chance he suffered a gruesome death."

Adair grimaced and nodded.

"It's his own fault," Woodford added. "We found three smoke detectors without batteries. It's pretty clear what happened." Woodford nailed a crawling spider with tobacco juice. "Dyson had the television playing on the first floor. He descended to the basement, and the TV caught fire while he was down there. With no working smoke detectors, he didn't recognize the peril until it was too late. There's no way out except a single staircase and a coal chute door that was pinned shut from the outside. Dyson killed himself through his own negligence. Can you imagine? A fireman leaving his smoke detectors with no batteries?"

Adair shrugged. "A painter's house always needs to be painted."

"So you found nothing strange about what happened?" Valeriya asked.

Woodford wiped a dab of tobacco juice from his lower lip. "There is one thing. We was just here investigating the fire that killed those dairy cows up yonder." Woodford gestured to the burned-out barn. "Now that was arson for sure. A neighbor kid took a video with his smartphone of Dyson setting the fire." Woodford spat at and missed a dragonfly hovering in the air. The winged insect buzzed around him and floated in front of his face before flying off. "So for Dyson to die the same kinda death is mighty strange." Adair cast down his eyes and shifted on his feet. Woodford faced Val. "I see what you're looken at, a revenge thing for the betrayal of his oath as a firefighter. But that faulty television and the lack of batteries in the smoke detectors make a case for accidental death fit like a pair of deerskin gloves, especially considering the clear-cut way he trapped himself in the basement."

A man approached and showed Woodford the results of some chemical tests. Adair stepped closer, and the three men discussed the findings.

"May we look around?" Valeriya asked.

"By all means," Woodford replied. "Y'all watch your step. We're done gathering evidence, but fire scenes can be kinda treacherous."

They approached the remains of the house, stepping through the fallen wreckage.

"Looks like a bomb crater," Mark muttered. "It's going to be difficult to find anything useful." He thought about enticing her down to Memphis, the perfect setting to kindle a bubbling romance. Seeing *Graceland* is every woman's dream—a three-hour romantic drive, the magic of Elvis, and she would be in his arms that night.

Valeriya moved to the edge and looked down, maintaining a pose of enthralled contemplation.

"Do you think he did it?" Blackwell asked.

She neither answered nor turned, seemingly locked in a deep crypt of thought.

"Val? Did he—"

"Yeah. It fits too perfect to be a coincidence. And what a motive—a firefighter burning dairy cows alive. It would be like waving a red cape in front of a bull."

Val inched her way around the foundation, painstakingly scanning every square-foot of rubble. Mark waited patiently for her to realize there was nothing to see, gently tapping the package of condoms in his pocket.

She gazed meditatively up at the blackened structure on the hill, squinting as if seeing some mystical mirage. "We need to go up there."

"For what reason? We know it was Dyson who burned the barn. Any useful evidence regarding our man must be down here."

She continued looking, hand raised to shield her sun-strained eyes. "He must have gone up there. That was the boiler that fired his rage."

Mark chuckled. "You're remarkably good at that, stepping into the shoes of the killer."

They proceeded up the alpine rise, walking side-by-side, naturally at first, then slowing as the foul odor of decomposition grew, a rancid aroma made worse by the lack of wind. A pair of coyotes hustled into the woods, chunks of raw meat in their mouths. The prismatic sunlight made the approaching images of wanton destruction chillingly clear, apocalyptic devastation brought to life. Valeriya took little half-steps as she approached the wooden beams of what had been the barn entrance, her blanched face chiseled in a mask of foreboding horror. She stopped abruptly, as if some invisible sentinel held out his hand.

"He stood right here," she whispered.

Blackwell looked over her shoulder. Dead cows lined each side of the center aisle like church parishioners kneeling to pray. Their rear legs were nothing but splintered bone, shattered from kicking the stalls. The fly-infested bodies were scorched black with ripped open skin, exposing deep fissures of rotting flesh. Every nose pointed up as if gasping for its last breath, a twisted tongue in every mouth. Their intestines had pushed through the abdominal wall, forming what looked like a little calf lying next to its mother. Val's tortured eyes grew wide, darting back and forth, up to the loft and down, as though she was seeing more than there was to see, witnessing their agony, hearing their dreadful cries as they perished in the flames. She pressed a hand to her heart, staggering sideways and grabbing the charred door frame, practically falling upon a carbonized beast. Before Mark could steady her, she whirled around and dashed down the hill, running until she stumbled under an apple tree, falling flat on her face.

Blackwell hurried after her.

"I can't breathe," Valeriya gasped.

She was flushed and dank with sweat, chest heaving in spasmodic jolts. He guided her to a rough-cut wooden bench.

"You're having an anxiety attack." He placed his hands on her shoulders. "Take a single deep breath and hold it." She did as he asked. "One, two, three, now let it out." She forced the air from her lungs, and they repeated the exercise until she ceased trembling.

Val leaned back against the tree, still perspiring like it was one hundred degrees. "I guess you were right. We shouldn't have gone up there."

Mark wiped her face with his handkerchief. "Is there anything I can do?"

She pointed to a fieldstone well, rickety with age and broken edges. "Is there water in there?"

He looked down the grungy pit, a moss-laden hole filled with unsavory black liquid. "There is, but nothing to drink with except an old wooden bucket. I don't think—"

"Bring me some water."

Blackwell filled the pail and carried it to her. She formed a cup with her hands and drank while he poured, gulping like she was dying of thirst. They spent a considerable time quietly resting. She stared into the trees, occasionally closing her dejected eyes and shaking her head. She improved in small increments, as though coming out of deep anesthesia.

"We should call it a day," he suggested. "You're not feeling well, and there's nothing here."

She lifted herself off the bench, brushing dirt from her jacket and pants. "I must speak to Woodford first."

They proceeded down the hill, approaching Woodford and Adair as they talked by the chimney.

"It twas murder!" someone yelled.

All heads turned to a wizened old woman standing near the police barrier tape. Everyone gathered around, including the deputy who was guarding the driveway. She wore a tattered blue dress, patched many times with faded squares of old cloth that didn't match. The ashen shawl was homespun, functional if not pretty, clean if not new, charismatic if not desirable. Her worn-out shoes had the look of hand-cobbled moccasins that had trudged wearily up and down every dusty hill in Tennessee. Her furrowed face was mottled with crusty-brown age spots, probably from spending years toiling under the southern sun.

"Double D twas murdered," the old woman cried. "Kilt by Ziggy and Stevie Tabor."

The group gravitated forward, Valeriya doggedly maneuvering her way to the front.

"Did you see something, Miss Foss?" the deputy asked.

"They burnt down his barn, then they murdered him. Didn't see it, but I knows it."

Several onlookers exchanged amused glances. Blackwell studied the old woman with a courteous smile.

Woodford pushed his way next to Val. "Miss Foss, why don't you come with Deputy Garvey. He'll take you to town where you can tell the sheriff all you know."

"No sirree," Foss snapped. "I ain't goin' ta jail. Done told ya what I has ta say." Foss shook her gnarled fist at Woodford and glared with wrinkled eyes. "'Em that done this evil deed believes in eyes for eye, teeth for tooth, and wounds for wound." She snarled at the grinning spectators with wild maleficence. "The vine watered with blood grows thick but twisted, green but tainted. I knows it's murder, mountain-grown vengeance, and the spirits knows it too. The bell tolled on and on when Double D died."

"I heard that bell," a stout woman called. Several people nodded in agreement.

"What exactly did you hear?" Valeriya asked the heavy woman.

"Well, it was sorta like a cowbell, only different from a cow that's just grazing. It was really loud and just kept going on and on, like the night those cows died. Except there ain't no cows over there now."

Foss pushed forward against the yellow tape, coming within inches of Val and staring vehemently into her widening eyes. "Twas the ghosta of them dead cows ringen that bell, suffern' in undying pain." With rheumatic distress, Foss reached out and snatched Valeriya's hand. "Twas bad, but nothin' like the night of the cows." The old woman held up her other hand. "May the Lord above spare me from ever havin' ta hear a clamor like the dyin' screams of them cows burnin' ta death!"

Valeriya tottered backward, eyes fluttering as she bumped into Blackwell. He stepped back, and she collapsed into his arms. Everyone moved away as he laid her on the grass. With arms flailing, she rolled and writhed on the ground, eventually becoming still as a corpse.

"Should I dial 911?" Deputy Garvey asked.

Mark felt her pulse. "I think she's just fainted. Give me a minute."

Her fingers clutched Blackwell's hand, and she opened her eyes, looking up at the many faces gazing down.

As Mark helped her to her feet, Woodford brought a folding chair from one of the trucks. She sat down, appearing shaken and embarrassed.

"There's an emergency clinic a few miles up the road," Adair said, "if you want to get checked out."

"Thanks, but I just need to—to rest for a while." A spotted hound trotted over, wagging his tail and sniffing her. She reached down to him. "And whose doggy are you?"

"He's mine," Woodford answered. "Been trained to detect accelerants. Come 'ere, Trigger. Leave her be."

Val latched onto the dog, pulling him closer. "He's not bothering me." She applied both hands to rubbing his fur, every finger used to maximum benefit.

Woodford squatted down to eye level. "Can I get you somethin'? We got an ice chest of soda pop and some ham sandwiches."

Valeriya shook her head. "Wait, there is something. Where is Miss Foss? I want to apologize."

"She took off when you fainted," Garvey said, "most likely concerned that we were going to arrest her."

One of the crime scene technicians approached Woodford. "The x-rays and autopsy are done. Dyson has a broken wrist and a cracked cheekbone, but the pathologist said those injuries could have occurred during his efforts to escape the fire." They talked about other negligible autopsy results while Mark and Val listened.

Woodford turned to Valeriya. "How are you feeling, ma'am?"

"Much better, thank you. I think that sight at the barn was a bit overwhelming."

"I should've warned you not to go up there. Is this your first fire?"

Val continued petting Trigger, ignoring the question.

"Do you believe that story about the ringing bell?" Blackwell asked Woodford, trying to change the subject.

"Nah. People's imaginations get carried away. Maybe it was the bell on the firetruck, and folks are just misremembering what happened. You can't have a cowbell ringing without any cows."

Valeriya looked up. "The bell is real. I saw it."

Woodford's eyes narrowed. "Where?"

With Trigger tagging along, Valeriya led Woodford, Adair, and Blackwell to the far side of the foundation. "Here, behind this debris."

Woodford pulled away some charred wreckage, finding a cowbell attached to the coal chute door. "Ah-ha. Seen it from the side but didn't know what it was." He jiggled the bell. "Still, the bell couldn't ring by itself, not unless we were in the middle of an earthquake."

Val stepped over the rubble and grabbed the edge of the door. She pulled it out, and the bell rang. She pushed it in and pulled it out again and again, the bell ringing with each jolt of the door.

"Yeah, that's it. That's what I heard," the stout woman yelled from the police barrier tape.

Everyone exchanged grisly glances.

Woodford called to a man taking photographs, "Chucky, where was Mr. Dyson's body found?"

"Right below where you're standing."

Woodford took off his hat and slapped it against his leg, looking down in a hang-dog way. "Oh, God. I wish I hadn't seen this. I'll be hearing that bell in my sleep for months."

Adair jiggled the coal chute door. "That would explain it all right. And look at the wear on the eyelet and bolt. He must have been pounding hard."

Woodford lingered and looked uneasily at the damaged bolt.

"But do you see the problem?" Valeriya asked.

Silence.

"Why would Dyson hang a cowbell on a coal chute door? Certainly not for security."

"I'm not following you, ma'am," Woodford answered.

"The bell was placed there on the night of the fire, *after* Dyson was trapped in the cellar."

Woodford stared at her with a wrinkled brow. "You're saying ..." He blinked several times. "What are you saying?"

"Miss Foss was right. It's murder."

Woodford leaned back, squinting at her. "That's a pretty damn big leap, isn't it? What about the defective television and no smoke detector batteries?"

Val climbed out of the debris. "It was a setup. The television was placed there just before Dyson came home, and the batteries were removed from the smoke detectors to reinforce the false perception of accidental death."

Woodford looked down and shook his head. "You gotta show me some physical evidence before I can swallow a crazy yarn like that."

She regarded Special Agent Adair. "Suppose someone had that specific television. How difficult would it be to rig it so it would start a fire?"

"Fairly easy. A single drop of solder at the right place would do it. The fire would start when the TV is turned on."

"Now wait a minute," Woodford exclaimed. "We're still going the long way around the barn."

"Did you take pictures in your first investigation, back when the barn burned?" Valeriya asked.

"Took pictures of everything, including the house."

"Where are they?"

"I have a copy on my laptop."

"May we see them?"

Everyone followed Woodford to his pickup truck. He opened the laptop and waited for the machine to boot up. Mark didn't sense that Woodford was defensive or angry. He just didn't believe it. Woodford flipped through the photographs with Val watching.

"There, that one," Valeriya said. "Can you magnify the image?"

Woodford tapped the + key several times.

"That's not a cowbell," she said. "Can you enlarge it?"

He made the image bigger and sharpened the focus.

"Looks like a padlock," Adair said.

Woodford studied the image and nodded.

"A padlock makes perfect sense," Valeriya said. "The latch is on the outside, and the only way to secure the door would be with a padlock. So on the night of the barn fire the coal chute door was padlocked. But when the house burned, the padlock was replaced with a cowbell, something of no security value, but of great importance for the effect it would have on anyone who heard it ringing."

"And just who was supposed to be hearing it?" Woodford asked.

"Duke Dyson!"

Silence.

"Killing is a black art for this murderer," Val continued, "something frightening and invisible. If he comes for you, no one will ever know."

Woodford gawked at the computer screen. "No, ma'am. I still need more. You're telling me Mr. Dyson was killed by a monster, a fiend no one can see. We can't let this turn into a Bigfoot story. Where's the proof?"

Valeriya thought for a second. "May we see the photos?" Woodford stepped back from the computer, and she commenced her examination.

Woodford stood next to her, asking, "Can I hear a complete version of what you think happened?"

"I have a theory, but it's only speculation."

"Let's hear it."

"This isn't an isolated incident, but a campaign that targeted animal abusers for nearly a decade." Woodford folded his arms across his chest as he listened. "Bigfoot, as you call him, read about Dyson in the news media. He staked out the house and waited for Dyson to leave, whereupon he drove up here with the television. He used bolt cutters to snip the padlock on the coal chute door, and that's how he got into the house. He then opened the front door and carried the booby-trapped television inside. He removed the batteries from the smoke detectors, not that it would have mattered to Dyson, but because it was going to matter to you, and it did. Somehow he got Dyson into the basement. Maybe he tricked him, or maybe he forced him at gunpoint. But he used the television to start a fire that blocked the only way out. The cowbell was an exclamation point, sending a message to Dyson about why this was happening."

Woodford leaned back on the fender. "Then I'll ask you the same question you asked me. Where did he get that malfunctioning television? They don't make them anymore."

"He's been doing this for a long time. There would've been stories in the press about problems with that unit. So he bought it years ago and held on to it for just the right occasion, to use as a weapon against someone who burned animals alive."

Val enlarged a photo of the east side of the house. She cropped the picture and expanded a rectangular object on the roof. "This is odd."

"It's a skylight," Woodford replied. "Many homes have them."

"The metal frame is in the cellar, but it's different."

They proceeded back to the foundation, where she pointed to an object under some blackened rubble. Woodford directed one of his helpers to retrieve the item, which seemed rather heavy considering the difficulty he had getting it up the ladder. They went to examine it.

"It's the skylight," Woodford said while lifting it up, "made of steel. That's why it survived the fire. I don't see the problem."

"It's open," Adair said. "It's been cranked wide open."

Silence.

"Was the weather warm two days ago?" Valeriya asked.

"No," Adair replied. "It's been unseasonably cool. The furnace at my house has been running."

"Then why was the skylight cranked open as far as it would go?"

Woodford continued studying the metal object.

"It answers one question," Adair added. "It explains why the destruction was complete. With an air supply from the basement and an open skylight, the place would go up like a tinderbox."

"Maybe he burnt somethin' on the stove and wanted to air the place out." Woodford eyed Valeriya. "You're still not showing me proof."

"Unless an eyewitness comes forward, we'll not get the kind of proof you're looking for. Show Dyson's widow a picture of the Comet 546 and ask her if she's ever seen that television."

"I'll do that. I'll do it personally," Woodford replied. "But even if she says no, it proves nothing. He may have just acquired it."

Blackwell nodded. "I understand your logic, although I agree with my partner. Mr. Dyson was definitely murdered."

"You know I'm only the fire marshal. I determine the cause of the fire, and it's up to the medical examiner to rule on whether it's an accident, suicide, or a homicide."

Val shrugged half-heartedly. "But if you rule the fire as accidental, then the medical examiner's ruling is almost predetermined."

"Yes, ma'am. I expect that would weigh heavily in his decision."

Silence.

"Is there anything else?" Woodford asked.

Valeriya extended her card. "Would you please send us a copy of your final report? The photos as well, if that's feasible."

"I'll be happy to do that, ma'am."

"You've been very helpful." She sank down and looked into Trigger's dutiful eyes, massaging the animal about his neck. "Does he have a proper home? I mean, you don't keep him locked in a cage with your equipment, do you?"

"Lordy, no. He piles into bed every night with my kids—part of the family. Much obliged to you for your concern."

Val smiled, and the three FBI agents shook hands with Woodford before departing.

* * *

They entered the car like before, Mark up front and Val in the back. Adair drove around some moseying mountain folk, spectators returning to the hollows of their homes. He stopped at the end of the gravel drive, waiting for a large truck to go by.

"Wait," Valeriya called. She unbuckled her seatbelt and moved forward. "Is that Miss Foss across the road?"

Blackwell looked around. "Where?"

She pointed. "Up higher."

Mark focused on a figure struggling with a water-carrying yoke. "I think so. At least that's what she was wearing."

The threesome watched Foss lug two pails of water up the steps to a tiny shack, a crude dwelling without telephone wires or electricity.

Val pulled out a pen and pad. "Drive slow when you go by so I can get the mailbox number."

Adair did as she asked. "Am I taking you to the airport?"

"Just to pick up our luggage," Valeriya replied. "We'll spend the night in Tennessee and fly back tomorrow morning."

Mark suppressed a smirk. *That was easy.*

Adair followed the truck for a while before finding an opportunity to pass. "I'm going to be honest with you. I have some serious reservations about the viability of your 'Bigfoot' killer. I just don't see how someone could pull this off. The detailed planning required, and then the execution of that plan would be prone to error. It seems impossible."

Mark chuckled. "At least Fire Marshal Woodford has given us a name for him."

"Bigfoot doesn't have an overly detailed plan," Valeriya said, "at least not initially. He's like a chef who walks into a strange kitchen. He knows he wants to prepare something but waits to see what resources are available before 'cooking up' the killing. This event was an exception because he brought the television with him."

Adair nodded, although still showing his skepticism. "Suppose he couldn't get Dyson into the basement?"

"Then Mr. Dyson would have vanished, and everyone would consider him a fugitive from justice."

Adair made eye contact with Val in the rearview mirror. "When the two of you were up on the hill, Woodford said he received an information request from an insurance investigator. Apparently, Dyson's widow and daughter will receive a large life insurance settlement. A million dollars minimum, and two million if the death is ruled as an accident."

"Lucky break for her," Blackwell replied. "Woodford might think about that in making his decision. How old is Dyson's daughter?"

"She's still an infant. They've only been married a couple of years."

Mark looked back at Val. "Are you going to send Miss Foss a thank you card?"

"That, plus something else."

"Like what? This isn't the city. Most mountain people won't accept charity, at least that's what I hear."

Adair nodded. "I'll bet she doesn't even have a bank account."

"Then I guess it will have to be cash," Valeriya replied, her firm lips sealing the decision. "I'll have my attorney take care of it."

Blackwell arched his brows and turned forward. *Once Valeriya makes up her mind, that's it. It's time to change the subject.* "I heard a rumor that Margaret Marshall might run for president, Nightingale being in her second term."

"I'd be sorry to see her leave the Bureau," Adair replied. "Douglas McCracken will probably be her successor, and I hear troublesome things about him."

"McCracken is a political opportunist," Val added. "Doesn't care about anyone but himself."

Adair slowed the car for a tight curve. "There's word that CIA Chief Tony Naples may be in the doghouse. I don't have the specifics, but a southern senator told me that Naples threw a tantrum in front of the Senate Intelligence Committee, tossing papers and dropping the F-bomb before walking out on them. The senator says Naples has screwed up so many times that this last debacle could put him down, professionally anyway. The guy's temper is his own worst enemy, and Big Alice's patience is wearing thin."

Mark nodded. "Will Nightingale fire him?"

"Who knows?"

Adair and Blackwell spent the rest of the trip discussing the psychological traits of serial bomber Ted Kaczynski. Valeriya remained silent, spending most of her time gazing out the window. Upon arriving at the airport, Mark and Val thanked Adair for his assistance and watched him drive away. They proceeded to the *Snow Queen*, where she removed their overnight bags. Valeriya also took out a large briefcase.

"Is that a computer?" Blackwell asked.

"It's just a laptop with the data set for our case, nothing classified. I'll play with it before going to bed."

With long shadows approaching from the forested mountain slopes, they checked into a nearby motel, each having separate rooms next to each other.

Mark walked her to the door. "Are you turning in early? I thought maybe seeing a movie or going to a show would help you relax."

"Thank you, but it's been a devilishly difficult day."

"You should at least have a proper meal. You'll sleep better on a full stomach."

"I couldn't eat if I tried. I just want a long, relaxing bath and bed."

"Call me if you need anything, anything at all. I can bring you a nightcap if you have trouble sleeping."

"I'll see you in the morning."

Disappointed but not discouraged, Blackwell dined alone at a Waffle House across the street. Project Valeriya would require patience and persistence, and he had plenty of both. He returned to the motel, retiring for a boring evening of television and microwave popcorn. He watched Gregory Peck's *Moby Dick* until falling asleep.

* * *

A harsh ring from the motel phone awakened him. Blackwell groped, dropping the receiver before pressing it to his ear.

"Hello," he said in his best wide-awake voice. The motel clock showed 7:14.

"Did I wake you?"

"No, no. I was just about to get into the shower."

"I found something important. Come over when you're ready."

"Right. Be there in a jiffy."

Mark grumbled his way into the shower spray, soaping up and rinsing off. Shave or not? Yeah, you'd better. God knows what she found, probably some irrelevant nonsense about her white whale. After making himself presentable with jacket on and necktie straight, he went next door.

Val was barefoot but fully dressed, laptop open, coffee and protein bars spread across a table. She poured him a badly needed cup of coffee, and they sat down.

"I've made an oversight. How do you think Bigfoot is locating his targets?"

Blackwell took a large gulp. "The same way anyone finds anything these days. He's using the Internet."

"That's what I thought. Every newspaper has its own website, and I assumed he was using a search engine to hunt for press reports about abused animals and related arrests. I've spent weeks pouring over metadata from Google and the other search engines to unearth people trolling for such headlines, finding nothing of consequence. But a timeline exploration shows five cases where the victim was killed before any reports of animal abuse appeared in the press."

"What does that mean?"

"Bigfoot is using a restricted database to find his targets, possibly one of the online criminal justice databases."

Mark commenced eating a protein bar. "Run that by me again."

"There's a significant gap between the time the police obtain evidence of criminality and when those results are released to the press, usually when a defendant is arrested and charged with a crime. However, those unreleased police reports and evidence summaries are digitized and made available to the law enforcement community via restricted databases."

"Are you saying Bigfoot is a police officer?"

"I doubt that. The police are tied down to specific locations, and their accountability for where they are is easy to establish. But we can check to see if anyone is searching the restricted databases with queries related to animal mistreatment."

He took another protein bar. "Who has access to those databases?"

"It's still a large number of people, tens of thousands. But it narrows the search from what we had before, which was everyone with an internet connection."

"Okay, what's next?"

"We fly home, and I'll run queries to see who is making these types of searches. We'll have a list of names by nightfall."

"When do we leave?"

"Now. Pack your things."

10 Lions, Tigers, and Bears

Upon returning to Virginia, Blackwell suggested an early lunch, telling her the protein bars he had for breakfast left him feeling hollow. Val politely declined, saying she wanted to return to the DDI ASAP to check her interesting theory. They got in their separate cars and departed with the plan of Mark joining her later. He stopped at a fast food restaurant, contemplating his slow and demoralizing progress with Val. She spent most of her time squirreled away in her secretive sanctuary. And when she wasn't there, she was teaching DDI recruits, allowing little time for him. He needed a legitimate excuse to see her on a regular basis. With that in mind, a marvelous idea popped into his head—and he had exactly what he needed in his suitcase.

* * *

Blackwell entered Advanced Queries and told Richard Val was expecting him. The unopened insulin bottle and packet of disposable syringes in his coat pocket had been inspected and cleared by DDI security, as he was a registered diabetic. Richard announced him, and the thick door to Valeriya's unassailable bunker rolled open.

Mark went inside. "How goes the hunt?"

She had changed into comfortable clothes and sat at her workstation, scowling at the largest monitor. "I'm having problems. This doesn't make sense."

She typed some indecipherable computer code and pressed enter, her face aglow with confounded curiosity, whereupon the machine flashed *No results found.*

"Would you mind if I stored some insulin and syringes in here? I don't have a refrigerator in my office."

She pushed herself back from the workstation. "No problem. I have plenty of room."

Blackwell followed her to the kitchenette, and she opened the refrigerator. "Here's two empty shelves. Help yourself."

He placed the insulin and syringes on the top shelf and closed the door. "Only the insulin needs to be refrigerated, but I'll keep them together. What's wrong with the search? You sounded confident this morning."

She commenced making a fresh pot of coffee. "This is a genuine mystery. There have been no unusual searches for information about animal abusers in any restricted databases. And I've looked at every possible query phrase. Animal cruelty, animal abuse, animal deaths, animals killed, even replacing the word 'animal' with dog, cat, cow, horse, goat—even lions, tigers, and bears."

"Oh my!"

The corners of her mouth turned up. "I ran an integrity check on the restricted databases to see if anything was wrong, and they appear to be working perfectly. Which means I'm back to square one, having nothing."

"It simply means your theory of him using a government database is wrong."

"Can't be. There's no other explanation because he's using information that never appeared on the Internet."

"Can he search the databases without leaving a record?"

"No. The search would be recorded in the activity log, and it's impossible to erase information from that file."

"Then how do you explain the contradiction?"

She let out an exasperated sigh. "We are missing something, a critical piece of the puzzle. I'll try expanding the timeline beyond the known killings."

They took their coffees back to her workstation. With exquisite pleasure, Mark pulled up a chair and plonked himself down, silently watching as she ran query after query. He enjoyed being close to her, smelling her scent and observing subtle changes in those predacious eyes. His primordial hunger swelled, as did unbearable desires. *Tell me my delectable darling, what do you taste like? Tart cherries or peaches and cream? Do you like it slow as a peaceful pond, or fast like running rapids? Oh, the exquisite imagery, the rising rhythm, the precipitous palpitations in that compact cavern—Plato's Cave blissfully dripping with dazzling dew. I'll wager I can make you scream.* After some additional mental meanderings and fastidious fantasies of what might be, Mark went to the kitchenette and returned bearing two fresh cups of coffee, sliding her cup across the workstation with his middle finger. *Sigmund Freud is smiling.*

Val studied the monitor, chin in hand. "This is interesting. Bigfoot has killed sporadically over the past nine years, generally in the eastern half of the United States. But twenty years ago there were two disappearances, two accidental deaths, and two animal deaths. And everything happened at the same place over a single summer." She turned and faced him. "The son of one of the men who disappeared has unrestricted access to every database in the DDI."

"Are you saying he works here?"

"No. The file says he's a civilian consultant for the United States Navy."

"What's his name?"

"Roy Lawton."

"Can you examine his database activities?"

Valeriya typed the request, and in a split second, a bright yellow banner flashed *Classified—USCC.*

He regarded her. "I thought you had access to everything?"

"Everything except the military. United States Cyber Command is blocking the search, but Marshall can get me the password. I'll send her a request." Val composed and sent a high-priority email.

"How long before she replies?"

"It depends on what she's doing. I can still get the stuff that isn't classified." She continued punching the keys, and Lawton's driver's license appeared. "He's thirty-two years old, stands five foot eleven, weighs 195 pounds, has brown hair and blue eyes. He's practically a match for you."

Mark leaned forward to inspect the photo. "Yeah, but I'm much better looking."

She typed more commands. "He owns a house east of Columbus, Ohio, but his primary residence is in Bedford County, Kentucky, the same place where the deaths occurred." She typed again. "He pays taxes on a lot of Kentucky land, but he's not listed as a farmer."

"Does he have a criminal record?"

"Arrested in Youngstown, Ohio when he was thirteen for assault and battery on two students, but the charges were dropped. He reported a break-in to his car when he was nineteen. The thieves got away with a laptop computer and a notebook with a black cover and red corners."

"What about the deaths twenty years ago?"

"There's not much here, just condensed summaries. People were drinking, and there was a quarrel between neighbors. Things went from bad to worse. The detailed records are in Kentucky." The computer emitted a shrill double chirp. "Shit. It's a video call. I was hoping Marshall would just send the password."

Blackwell moved out of view of the camera while Valeriya adjusted her turtleneck sweater. She pressed the red button.

Marshall's tone was snappy. "Admiral Christian wants to know why I'm playing in his sandbox."

"Excuse me?"

"Your request for a top-secret password," Marshall huffed. "He wants to know the reason, and so do I."

Val recounted her motivations for investigating Roy Lawton, citing the limited information she had. Mark moved to a position to watch the exchange without being seen.

"Go on," Marshall said.

"That's what we have so far."

"We can't breach top-secret protocol based on a wild story about a hillbilly feud that occurred twenty years ago. Can you place Mr. Lawton at the scene of the recent killings?"

"No."

"Has he been doing anything suspicious?"

"We can't tell because everything about him is classified. That's why we need the password."

"It's not enough. The Bureau is almost at war with that nincompoop running the CIA, and I can't afford to pick a fight with the Navy's ICBM commander."

"Lawton is the only blip on our radar screen."

"Where's Professor Blackwell?"

He stepped in front of the camera, trying to look prim and proper. "Right here."

"Do you concur with Val's assessment?"

"Yes, ma'am. I fully believe we are tracking a serial killer, and Val has found something significant."

"I take it both of you know what 'probable cause' means?"

"Yes, ma'am," they said together.

"Well, that's what it will take. Get out there and do some investigating!" The screen went dark.

Val slumped back in her chair. "Investigate how? This happened two decades ago. There's no crime scene and probably damn few witnesses."

Mark put on a stern face. "Orders are orders. When are we leaving for Kentucky?"

"I need to make some phone calls to see what evidence is available and try to locate any living witnesses. It could be several days."

"We should travel by car this time. That way I can drive if you have another anxiety attack."

She nodded without enthusiasm, obviously preferring to fly her plane. "Maybe you should check your phone messages and emails."

This was a polite way of kicking him out. "I was thinking the same thing myself."

"I'll call you when I know the details."

He took a last gulp of coffee before leaving. *Perhaps the third time will be the charm.*

11 Kentucky Backwoods

They planned the trip to Kentucky for the following Thursday. Mark rose early that morning, and Val picked him up in her Grand Cherokee at 6 a.m. Aside from some brief emails, they hadn't talked to each other since he was in her office. She spent the first part of the trip explaining her research results. They had a lucky break because Bedford County Sheriff Harold Trimble was the deputy who investigated the deaths and disappearances near the Lawton farm. Trimble was also there when Lawton's home burned down, a seemingly significant event. Valeriya also found Clarita Fernandez, a guidance counselor at Riverside High School in Youngstown. Fernandez was Roy Lawton's advisor, and she had first-hand knowledge of the assault charges against him. The tentative plan was to meet with Sheriff Trimble, spend the night in Kentucky, and then drive up to Youngstown to meet with Fernandez.

"What do your instincts tell you?" Blackwell asked. "Is Roy Lawton Bigfoot?"

"I don't understand how someone working for the Navy is going to have time to be a serial killer. Still, he could gather information from DDI databases and pass it on to someone else. He's worth looking at."

"Are you losing weight? Your cheekbones seem more pronounced."

"I never weigh myself. Don't even have a bathroom scale."

They continued west through the Blue Ridge Mountains. Mark hoped she would be in a better mood, like when they made their trip to

Ohio. Regrettably, this wasn't the case. He broached the difficult subject.

"Are you happy?"

"Happier than some, less than others."

"It seems like you haven't recovered from our trip to Tennessee. If anything, your melancholy is worse. I'm worried about you."

"You needn't be. I'm fine."

"That anxiety attack at Dyson's barn could be a symptom of a serious psychological issue. It might be related to your social isolation, your lack of friends and family. Working alone all the time is extremely unhealthy."

Val lowered her oversized sunglasses and made brief eye contact. "It's not my lifestyle. It's this damnable case—it's hurting me. Let's just change the subject."

They spent the next hour discussing whether Margaret Marshall would be a good successor to President Nightingale. Blackwell opined that Marshall couldn't win the Democratic nomination because she was a moderate. Valeriya countered that the Democratic Party was becoming less liberal and that Marshall's chances were equal to those of the current candidates.

With 200 mountainous miles behind them, Valeriya pulled into a rest stop. Mark took his time in the restroom, exercising his arms and washing his face to clear the mental cobwebs caused by rising early. He left the building and waited on the sidewalk, wondering why she was taking so long. Then he spotted her standing beside a wooden fence, petting a brown horse with white feet—a Clydesdale. He approached them, voyaging between bouquets of blooming lilacs and crossing a field of thick clover.

"A gorgeous animal, isn't he?" Blackwell called.

"He's magnificent. I've had a special thing for horses ever since reading *The Black Stallion* in elementary school." Val fawned over him, rhythmically stroking the massive animal about the neck while talking to him in a soft, little-girl voice. The horse turned his head and moved closer, succumbing to the temptation of her lavish affection. She combed his mane with her fingers and scratched him behind the ears.

"Did you ever ride one?"

"No. But they were in my childhood fantasies of owning a country farm, a mystical place with mountainous meadows and babbling brooks. I wouldn't ride them. I'd just let them run free through the fields and spoil them rotten with carrots, apples, and other treats." She fondled the plume of silky hair between his ears, gazing into his dark eyes, as if they were speaking to each other in some silent but eloquent language. "You're being very patient with me."

Mark smiled. "Take your time. He's obviously enjoying it."

"I could do this all day, but alas … We'd better get going."

Like two children they strolled briskly across the grass, Blackwell matching her vivacious walk and carefree grin. The wild daisies growing around their feet harmonized her mood—the melancholy was gone. Mark almost took her hand.

They continued on Interstate 64, snacking on her peanut butter and jelly sandwiches. Kentucky and West Virginia seemed much the same, nothing but a magnificent spread of green hills and valleys, the same primitives populating the cabins on knolls and shacks nestled back in the smoky hollows. If civilization collapsed, these were the people who knew how to survive, denizens of living in hard times, ready to shoot to defend what was theirs. Valeriya selected the appropriate exit and drove along a road that followed a stream. The dashboard map gave directions as they approached the sheriff's office.

* * *

Sheriff Harold Trimble asked to see their credentials and led them back to his office. With his no-frills uniform and laid-back demeanor, Trimble looked more like a small-town constable than a county sheriff. The missing finger on his left hand seemed in harmony with the military decorations displayed on the wall. Blackwell recognized the Purple Heart, but he hadn't a clue about the other medals. The man was pleasant enough, although he seemed apprehensive. The sheriff offered them a seat and sat behind his desk, face rigid, rubbing his thumbs back and forth against his index fingers.

"What's this about?" Trimble asked. "Something to do with the Lawtons?"

As planned, Val took the lead, taking a different approach than before. "The Bureau is gathering some routine demographic data on clusters of unusual events, and Bedford County popped up because of what happened here twenty years ago."

"It's not an actual investigation," Blackwell added.

Trimble crossed one leg over the other while calling out, "Tiny, please bring some coffee and goodies for our guests." He gave the FBI agents a chilly smile. "What would you like to know?"

"Just your recollections of what occurred," Valeriya replied.

"At the Lawton farm?"

"And the deaths that ensued nearby."

Swinging in his swivel chair, Trimble gave the matter some thought, as if a simple retelling wasn't enough. "The whole situation got started in early June when Kevin and Larry Slade were racing on horseback across the Lawton acreage. There wasn't any reason for it, just two liquored-up fools making asses of themselves. Kevin's horse stumbled and threw him. So he's all pissed-off." Trimble looked apologetically at Val. "Please excuse my foul language, ma'am."

"Don't apologize. I say worse things every day."

Trimble smiled and nodded. "Kevin tied his horse to a fence post and began beating it with a bullwhip. Jim Lawton was there, cutting down a tree with his son, Roy, and he told Kevin that he will not beat a horse on his land. Kevin grins, tells him all right, then he pulls out a revolver and shoots the horse between the eyes. A scuffle ensued, with Kevin and Larry fighting Jim. Now the Slade brothers were mighty fearsome, but they were drunk, and Jim won the battle, breaking Larry's jaw in the process." Trimble stopped talking and eyed Valeriya. "Is something wrong?"

She swallowed and shook her head.

"Was his son involved in the fight?" Blackwell asked.

"No. Now had his father been in any trouble, I don't have any doubts that Roy would have jumped in—*pronto!*"

Tiny brought three coffees and a box of Dunkin Donuts. Tiny was not tiny, as she looked big enough to give the average man all he wanted in a wrestling contest. Mark picked through the nice assortment, selecting a jelly doughnut.

Trimble reached for a chocolate cream stick and took a bite. "Two weeks go by, and Denny Boyd, Jim's cousin, calls and wants Jim to stop by his house and look at some old family photos he found under the floorboards at their old home place. Jim leaves for Boyd's residence and is never seen again."

"How do you know about the phone call?" Valeriya asked.

"We interviewed Roy after his father disappeared, and he told us what happened."

"Were there any suspects in the disappearance?" Blackwell asked.

"I'm coming to that," Trimble replied. "Kevin and Larry Slade were both meaner than drippy owl shit on a hot summer night, and folks was afraid of them. Larry in particular, cause anyone talking with him could see right off he wasn't right in the head. Larry toted a black stone about the size of a softball in his pickup truck, and any time he argued with somebody he'd say he was going to show them his 'pet rock.' People complained to me, fearing Larry was going to conk them in the head and bury them someplace up in the hills. Therefore Larry was a definite suspect. To make things even more complicated, the Slade brothers knew Denny Boyd very well. They sold him moonshine, and he was one of their best customers. Boyd had been trying to get Jim Lawton to sell the timber rights to his land for years, but Jim would never sell. So there was some family friction there."

Tiny appeared in the doorway. "Boyd wanted Jim to give him the timber rights on credit, and he'd pay him back when the logging company took the trees. Wasn't a decent price neither." Tiny explained that she was a neighbor of the Lawtons when it happened.

Mark nodded and took a vanilla cream stick. "So Boyd would have been a logical suspect as well as the Slade brothers."

"Definitely. Although Larry Slade was higher on my list. We investigated and talked to the Slade brothers about Lawton's disappearance but couldn't find a thing. Denny Boyd claimed Jim Lawton never showed up at his place. We asked to see the family photos in question, but Boyd said they were accidentally burned when he got rid of some trash. Something didn't smell right about that. Anyway, we didn't have a body, and there weren't any witnesses. Our hands were tied."

"I believe the three of them were in it together," Tiny said. "The Slade brothers killed Jim for breaking Larry's jaw, and Denny Boyd wanted Jim out of the way 'cos he thought he'd have a better chance of getting the timber. Taxes on all them acres were so high that a young kid couldn't pay 'em. Boyd figured Roy would be forced to sell the timber to keep the farm."

Trimble took a glazed doughnut from the box. "Well, Jim was gone, but now we had another problem—a twelve-year-old boy living alone with his dog. I talked to Roy, trying to get him to go and live with his aunt over in Elliott County, but he refused to leave. This goes on for weeks until Child Welfare issues a decree that he's to be moved by force, only there's a serious glitch—we couldn't catch him. It was that damn dog. Roy knew we were after him, and anytime we snuck up on the house that mutt would sound the alarm. The whole situation was an ugly mess."

Tiny moved further into the room. "Roy told me his father was alive, and he was going to come home. I offered Roy a chair at our dinner table many times, but he would never accept. I think he was afraid it was a trap, and the sheriff would ship him off to Elliott County. He lived off their garden, I guess."

Trimble nodded. "We knew a deputy from Carter County who was a marathon runner, and we brought him over to catch Roy. I'm sure he would have if they were running down the road (Tiny shook her head), but back in those woods among them hills, the guy said he never had a chance. He came out all scratched up from briars and limping with a sprained ankle. He said trying to catch Roy was like a house cat climbing a tree to catch a squirrel. Just ain't gonna happen. One day we cornered Roy when he ran into the abandoned limestone mine on their property. We stationed two deputies there to wait him out. I stopped by to see how things were going, and Roy was standing on the far hill with his dog, waving at me. We were dealing with someone who knew everything about that area, including the mine shafts and natural limestone caverns, some of which ran under the farm. Then came that horrible fire." Tiny left the room.

Valeriya sat with hands clutching her stomach.

"Do you need to use the restroom?" Mark whispered.

She cleared her throat. "I'm staying."

The former uneasiness in Trimble's eyes returned. "I'm out on patrol with my partner, Donald Lohr, and we get a call about a fire at the Lawton farm. We arrived at the scene, and the backside of the house is burning. Roy's dog is running around the cruiser, barking at us, but there's no sign of Roy. We're back on the driveway, still a fer piece from the house, and the damn dog is blocking our way. Roy comes running out of the woods and sees his home burning. He hears the dog barking but doesn't see him. He runs into the house through the front door, yelling 'Shiloh' over and over. The dog hears him and runs into the house. Roy climbs out a side window to escape the flames, only now the front of the house is on fire. We're both running towards the house, and Roy has come to the front, still searching for Shiloh. He realizes his dog is trapped inside the house, and he's going in to bring him out."

Blackwell took the last cream stick.

Trimble procured an extra-large swallow of coffee. "The house was a wall of flame, so we had to stop him. Don tackled Roy, and World War III began. I went to help Don, who needed all the assistance he could get. Roy managed to rip the pepper spray off my utility belt, and he zapped us good in the face. Don and I were sightless but still holding on. The dog was whimpering and crying inside the house, and Roy is going wild. It's hard to say what happened next, other than it was a horrifying melee." Trimble pointed to the left side of his head. "I still have a scar where the doctor stitched the top part of my ear back on, and I lost both of my front teeth from a head-butt." Trimble tapped his incisors. "These are implants." He drank more coffee. "Roy got free by kicking at our elbows, and Don cried out his arm was broken. A fireman collared Roy, at least until he weaseled his way through the firemen's legs. Barely able to see, I got to my feet and wrestled him to the ground. The ornery little shit grabbed me by the balls, realigning my priorities in a hurry." Trimble winced. "This time Roy makes it all the way to the front steps before another fireman knocked him down. Two more firemen come to restrain him, so he's not going anywhere. Me and Don are sitting on our asses in the dirt, blind and bleeding, me toothless and Don with patches of missing hair and a busted arm. The dog is yelping now, most likely being burned alive, and with three firemen holding him, all Roy can do is scream—*God awful shrieks folks heard a mile away!*" Trimble jiggled his cheeks. "Makes my flesh crawl just thinking about that day."

Pale as death, Val's hands were clenched into white-knuckled fists.

Mark took a napkin and wiped chocolate frosting from his lips. "No offense, but how do you account for a kid besting two trained police officers?"

"It was the circumstances of the situation. He was just trying to save his dog, and we didn't want to hurt him. That gave him an enormous advantage. We hesitated, he didn't. We didn't use our full strength, and he fought like a mother grizzly protecting her cubs. Roy did considerable logging work with his father on their farm, moving heavy trees and such. He was a lot sturdier than your average twelve-year-old, practically a man. And, we were overconfident, not sensing any danger until we got sprayed with pepper mace." Trimble leaned back in his chair, eyeballing Blackwell. "Ya know, if I had it to do over again, I would've let him rescue the dog."

Mark shifted uncomfortably and nodded.

"Other deputies arrived," Trimble continued, "and Roy, despite his significant injuries, was handcuffed and carried to the back seat of a cruiser. The fire was contained, but the house was a total loss. Several deputies helped Don and me to another cruiser, along with a fireman with a bloody nose and broken finger. We followed the first cruiser down the driveway, both of us heading for the emergency room at Clearview. As we get to the road, there were the two Slade brothers and

Denny Boyd, standing off to the side, laughing and joking with riotous delight."

Silence.

Mark glanced briefly at Val—she seemed calm. "Well, that's certainly an amazing story. How did the fire start?"

"It was arson. There was gasoline residue all over the place."

Tiny walked in carrying a framed photograph. "I'm sure it was Denny Boyd. He was there the week before, still trying to cook up a deal with Roy for those timber rights. Roy pelted him with rocks, cracking the windshield on Boyd's car."

Tiny handed Blackwell the picture. "Here's Roy with my boy Timmy, taken the Christmas before the fire."

Valeriya leaned over for a better look. "Is this the dog that died in the fire?"

"Yes, that's Shiloh."

"May I take a photograph?" Tiny nodded, and Val took several images of the picture with her cellphone.

"Where is Timmy now?" Blackwell asked.

"He's a Chief Petty Officer on the *USS Ronald Reagan*," Tiny said proudly.

"Did Roy blame you for what happened?" Blackwell asked.

Trimble gave a dismissive wave. "Nah. I went to see him the following week at the Juvenile Justice Center. He apologized and said he knew we were just doing our job. I still see him in town now and then— treats me like an old friend. His wife, Carolyn, plays first board at the Morehead Chess Club. Beats me like a child every time we play."

"Roy came back to the farm three weeks after the fire," Tiny said. "He dug through the rubble and found Shiloh's bones. Took them up behind the barn to be buried with his mother. He would've buried Jim up there if they had ever found the body."

Trimble gazed up at his secretary. "You never told me Roy came back. The Elliott County sheriff was lookin' all over for him."

Tiny folded her arms. "You never asked."

"And if I did, would you have told me?"

"Oh, of course not!"

Trimble's hue became florid. "And why not?"

"Maybe 'cos you did such a wonderful job catching him the first time."

"How did he get back from Elliott County?"

"Walked sixty miles along the railroad tracks. He spent the next two months living in the barn—wasn't the same person though. Then he stayed with his aunt Bessie until moving to Youngstown in the fall. Bessie's younger sister was up there." Tiny left to answer the phone.

"What about the other deaths," Blackwell asked, "the ones that occurred later?"

"Larry Slade disappeared a month after the fire. We weren't too concerned at first because mountain folks takes off all the time—especially drunks." Trimble puckered his lips. "But Larry's pet rock turned up in Kevin's mailbox, and that sent a pretty clear message."

"Which was?"

"Larry used his pet rock threat once too often, and he ran into the wrong guy. We investigated, but nothing came of it. It was just like the disappearance of Jim Lawton. He just vanished. Kevin was complaining to everyone, including the Kentucky State Police, but without a body or any witnesses, there wasn't anything to work with. We found Larry's pickup truck near his moonshine still, but no trace of foul play. May have been a liquor deal gone bad. Then, in one for the record books, Kevin dies two weeks later from copperhead bites. Five of them to be exact."

"What happened there?"

"We're not entirely sure. But it looks like he was in his barn, and he tilted over a wooden barrel up on a shelf to get a riding bridle for his horse, and several copperheads poured out on top of him."

"Sounds ghastly," Mark replied.

"I'm sure it was. One copperhead bite won't kill a man. Even one snake biting several times won't kill. But the autopsy results showed several full-charge venom injections, which means at least three copperheads had to be in the barrel. They found him on the ground, all twisted and tangled up in leather riding straps, but no trace of the snakes, which would have crawled away."

"Remarkable."

Trimble nodded. "That was a first for the State of Kentucky. Then, a week later, Denny Boyd was driving down a muddy logging road not far from the Slade farm, and he sets himself on fire with moonshine. A passerby saw Boyd running from his car, completely engulfed in flames, trying to make it to the creek at the bottom of the hill. He collapsed a few feet from the water."

"Are you certain about the circumstances?"

"The Slade brothers sold their moonshine in one-quart Mason canning jars. We found an open jar in Boyd's car. Boyd was a chain smoker, and that just doesn't go with 180-proof white lightning, particularly when bouncing over a bumpy logging road."

Mark plowed through the Dunkin' Donuts, finding the last pastry with cream filling. "How would you summarize this event for our records?"

"It's pretty simple. I believe the Slade brothers and Boyd killed Jim Lawton. Larry Slade was murdered by someone who hated him, which narrows it down to half the folks in Bedford County. Kevin was killed in an accident, and Denny Boyd died by his own negligence."

Blackwell finished off the delectable treat, licking his lips. "Is there a pattern there, or is it just my overactive imagination?"

Trimble stared at the two FBI agents, eyes shifting between them. "You can see meaningless patterns everywhere if you look long enough. They're still arguing about who killed John Kennedy. But I believe things happened just the way I said." He glared at Blackwell. *"Exactly that way!"*

Silence.

"The Lawton farm is only a thirty-minute drive," Trimble continued, interlocking his fingers around his knee. "Roy is up in Ohio during the first part of the week, but he's likely home now. I could give him a call, and we can drop by for a friendly visit. The home is new, but the same barn and graveyard are there. You could see everything first-hand." He passed them a mischievous smile. "That is, if you want to get the story straight from the horse's mouth."

"We appreciate the offer," Blackwell replied, "but that won't be necessary."

Trimble stretched out his legs. "You know, the wheel of justice isn't round. It's got flat spots that make for a bumpy ride. But people must answer for what they do, either in this life or the next. Whatever happened up in them hills was seen by God. And He took care of it."

Tiny reappeared at the door. "The mayor is on the phone. He says the County prosecutor has agreed to plea-bargain that 1740 on the mayor's nephew down to a 1730, providing you will agree."

Trimble scowled at Tiny. "I can't remember all those damn penal code numbers."

"Seventeen-forty is video voyeurism, a felony. And 1730 is voyeurism, a misdemeanor."

"He wants to replace the felony with a misdemeanor?"

Tiny nodded.

"That pervert took movies of those schoolgirls naked in the shower and showed them at his stag party. Tell him I said absolutely not."

"The mayor also said to remind you that you owed him a 'special favor,' and he's calling in your marker." Tiny elevated her flaring nose. "Whatever that means."

Trimble looked sheepishly away. "Tell him I'll call him back." He composed himself and regarded the FBI agents, "Is there anything else I can help you with?"

Blackwell passed a copy of the police report filed by Roy Lawton thirteen years ago. "Were either of these items ever recovered?"

The sheriff studied the paper. "I don't remember this. Ah, I was toting a rifle in Afghanistan at the time." He continued reading. "Let's see, a stolen laptop computer and a black notebook with red corners? You can check with Property Recovery, but after all this time it's unlikely. They're in the gray building two blocks down on the other side of the street. Is it important?"

"Probably not," Blackwell replied. "We just want to tie up all the loose ends."

They thanked Sheriff Trimble and Tiny for their assistance before departing. Upon entering the open air, Val quickened her pace, moving with a clear purpose in mind.

"The ladies' room is inside," Mark called.

She kept going, around a corner and into a patch of tangled woods.

With clumsy haste, Blackwell jogged after her, maneuvering his way around a multitude of thorny bushes. "What's wrong?"

Valeriya pushed her way through thick mats of foxtail grass, breaking into a run. The swish of running water grew louder.

"Val, what's the matter?"

"My skin is burning."

Mark stumbled in the tall weeds, losing sight of her in the thick debouchment. He followed the rustle and aroma of flowing water, finding her at the edge of a stream, barefoot and shucking off her jacket. "You're not going in there?"

"Yep." She pulled off her turtleneck and removed her pants.

"Listen to me. Your skin is not burning. You're just having a psychosomatic reaction."

She removed her bra and pitched it.

As Mark reached for her, Val flung her panties in his face and jumped in the water. She popped up a short distance away, moving to some sloping rocks, water covering everything up to her chin. Blackwell paced back and forth. He couldn't reach her without going in.

"Can you swim?" he called.

"Never learned, but the water's not deep."

"For God's sake, Val."

"Just chill out. This feels good, and I need to recuperate."

Blackwell looked around dismally and rested against a sloping willow. She perched on the rocks, legs folded up against her chest, eyes closed, breathing deeply and thinking God knows what. A multitude of curious minnows circled her, nibbling and inspecting the strange new creature. Mark skipped a flat stone across the water, almost making it to the other side.

Valeriya finally opened her eyes, lifting her brows with a mournful sigh. "Did you see it?"

"See what?"

"The missing piece. When we were in Trimble's office."

He stood upright, securing his foot on a jagged rock. "I sure did. Lawton killed them all—the Slade brothers and Denny Boyd. It's amazing the sheriff couldn't figure it out."

A Mona Lisa smile appeared on Val's lips. She looked away, saying nothing.

"Homicidal children aren't uncommon," Mark continued. "Val, I never believed in this case—not until now. Lawton committed three murders twenty years ago, and he has never stopped killing. He's right up there with Ted Bundy and Richard Ramirez, only worse because nobody knows what's happening." He regarded her distant gaze. "Are you listening to me?"

Silence.

"Please tell me what you're thinking?"

"It's hardly expressible in words."

"Try me."

She stared across the rippling water. "Do people who are slowly going insane realize they are losing their mind?"

"Serial killers aren't crazy. They are evil—Lawton in particular."

"I'm talking about me."

He said nothing, stunned by her statement.

She glanced his way. "Well, you're the expert. Do they?"

"Sometimes. But having an anxiety attack does not mean you're becoming irrational."

"I'm leaving the case."

Mark swallowed. "You're … You're what?"

"I can't do this anymore. Marshall can put me in a fucking classroom."

"Val, you're overreacting. You can't just walk away."

Silence.

"Look at me," Mark called. She scooted around, legs crossed Indian-style in the water. "There has never been a serial killer like Roy

Lawton. We are breaking the mold of forensic history. The names Blackwell and Highland could become household words, better known than Holmes and Watson. This is the opportunity of a lifetime."

"I'm very happy for you."

"Us, Valeriya. Be happy for us. You must come with me."

She shook her head. "I'm having physical reactions—serious pain. You have no idea what I feel, the chaos, the anguish, the *horror!* "

"Valeriya, that's all in your head. It isn't real."

"Are you wearing your pistol?"

He gazed up at the sky. "No. I forgot to bring it."

"Then take mine and shoot yourself in the foot."

"Why would I do such a crazy thing?"

"So I can tell you the pain is all in your head, that it isn't real."

"Are you telling me you are suffering actual physical pain from being on this case?"

"*Yes!* It is killing me."

Val submerged herself before coming out. She showed no modesty, as if wanting him to see the scars. At a loss for words, Mark passed her her clothes. *Don't argue. Just wait until things calm down.*

They strolled back to the car, steadily uphill, with Valeriya barefoot and carrying her shoes. He let her choose the motel and didn't contest the skipping of dinner. Later on, he would visit the diner across the street. Somehow, someway, he had to prevent her from leaving the case.

12 From Worm to Man

Blackwell slept poorly, worrying this would be his last outing with Val. They went for breakfast at 7 a.m. In all the time he had known her, she never once changed her mind. Nevertheless, he had to try. She seemed normal enough, wearing a snow-white turtleneck sweater, matching white slacks, and a different jacket from yesterday. He pretended nothing had happened, waiting for the right moment to attempt the impossible. An interesting idea came as Valeriya held open the restaurant door for an elderly couple. *Don't try to change her mind— just delay the decision.*

The waitress at Margie's Dinner Bell seated them near an old-fashioned jukebox, the kind you saw in movies from the '50s and '60s. This was a genuine farmhouse eatery with wood-fired cookstoves, exposed beam ceilings, rough-cut floors, and knotty pine furnishings. The seductive aroma of fresh-baked bread and delectable pies seemed irresistible, even for the morning meal. There were no shortcuts in preparing this food—everything was made from scratch. Valeriya queried the waitress about the menu, seeking options that weren't listed. Mark ordered bacon and eggs, hash browns, hickory-smoked sausage, and blueberry cobbler for dessert. Val chose cheesy grits and collard greens with buttermilk biscuits and honey. Disliking the quiet interior that could carry their voices, he passed several quarters to the waitress and asked her to play something on the jukebox. The young woman went to the machine, made a selection, and Claude King's *Wolverton Mountain* began playing.

Blackwell gazed out the restaurant window. "It's a beautiful day for traveling. Should make our trip to Youngstown very pleasant."

"It's a nice day."

"I hope you will stay with me during the transition, at least until Marshall can assign your replacement."

No answer. *Silence is good—it means she's thinking.*

He put on a puzzled expression. "What will you tell Margaret? You can't tell her the truth without losing your top-secret security clearance."

Val glowered with unblinking eyes, still saying nothing.

Mark poured coffee. "We need to get our stories straight, so there will be no discrepancies. Just tell me what you want me to say, and that will become the truth." To someone who worshiped Aristotle, his last statement was sacrilege. Her color flushed like a traffic light turning red. *So far, so good.* "Let me make a suggestion. Why don't we continue as before, and you can exit the case later, when your leaving will be less conspicuous? If you don't see or hear about acts of violence, no discomfort will occur."

She met his eyes—*here it comes.* "All right, I'll postpone my exit. However, acts of violence aren't the problem. It's something else, a creeping feeling I don't understand."

They had a delightful breakfast, making small talk about how many household items in impoverished Appalachian homes would be considered valuable antiques in the East. His dream was still alive.

* * *

The doors at Property Recovery had just opened for business when they arrived, and a smiling female desk clerk greeted them.

Blackwell gave her the police report about the theft of Lawton's laptop and notebook. "I know this occurred a long time ago, but we wondered if either of these items were ever recovered."

The clerk adjusted her bifocals and scrolled through a list on a computer screen. "The laptop, no. We hardly ever recover computers, and this Dell model isn't listed. Now the other, let's see …" She continued looking and disappeared into a back room, returning a short time later with something in her hand. "A black notebook with red corners." She gave the book to Blackwell. "I remember now. It came from a drug dealer's storage locker that the sheriff opened two years ago. There's no name, but someone put a lot of work into writing it. I've been reluctant to throw it away."

The book was a hardbound journal about three inches thick with sewn-in pages full of writing. Each chapter began with a small ornamental design, hand-sketched with epigraphic assuredness, as though the author knew exactly what he wanted. Mark flipped through the tome, impressed by the artistic exactness, the perfect penmanship, the lack of corrections, but flummoxed by the weird mathematical symbols and indecipherable hieroglyphics. "There must be a name somewhere, or at least a nom de plume." He passed it to Val. "What kind of math is that?"

"It's predicate calculus, a form of symbolic logic."

"It doesn't look like what we're looking for. Not that I know what we're looking for."

Valeriya opened her cellphone. "I have his driver's license image." She blew up the signature and compared it to the handwriting in the book. Mark looked over her shoulder. "Look at the similar slant and cross of the t's, and look at the y's and the w's."

"Very close," Blackwell agreed.

"May we have this?" Valeriya asked the clerk.

"Yes, you may. I'm glad somebody wants it."

They checked out of the motel and went to her Grand Cherokee. Val asked if he wanted to drive, and Mark accepted. She helped him adjust the driver's seat and foot pedal positions, bringing back pleasant but less titillating recollections of their first ride in the *Snow Queen*. They got two large coffees before getting onto Interstate 64, heading east to Charleston. The morning sun was irritating, floating back and forth with each turn on the highway, and Blackwell had to keep moving the sun visor. Valeriya removed her shoes and socks, loosened her seatbelt, and wiggled into a comfortable position. She opened the strange book and began reading, borrowing a pen from Blackwell to take notes. He spoke to her once, but she shushed him, saying she needed absolute concentration.

Mark relaxed and began a silent debate about whether he would be interested in her if she was poor. After some serious haggling with his practical side, he reaffirmed an unwavering yes. She was a pillar of propriety, a statuesque intellectual (nearly his equal), trustworthy to a fault, chaste, and unspoiled by other men. And even though she was an incurable idealist, almost infecting him with a yearning for virtue, he still adored the lucid timbre of her ethereal mind, thoroughbred reason and concision conjoined. Those trivial burn scars on her body meant nothing. Every little gesture or change in posture and every glance from those saucy feline eyes suggested exotic lovemaking—miming erotomania to the nth degree. Even the slightest incidental contact between them ignited a bewitching arousal that would not go away, a tottering torment to his senses, further aggravated by her earthly indifference toward him.

She lolled languorously in the car seat, his borrowed pen pressed between her voluptuous lips, seductively rocking one foot like a beckoning brownie, all while granting him provocative peeps of her suggestively posed legs in the reflecting window glass, those body-hugging white pants revealing every anatomical curve. Mark continued his mental voyage, eventually mollifying himself by firmly believing he would solve the mystery, finding a way to enter and taste the intoxicant nectar of that prettily painted Pandora's box. Val looked up when they entered Charleston, taking several swallows of coffee.

"Have you figured it out?" Blackwell asked. "Possibly a set of boring lecture notes for a college course?"

"It's too precise for lecture notes. This is mathematics without numbers, an abstract treatise on the philosophy of Friedrich Nietzsche."

"Nietzsche? Good Lord. That was Adolf Hitler's hero. It's just some philosophy professor's scribblings, notwithstanding the handwriting similarities."

"Nope. This belongs to Roy Lawton."

"How can you be sure?"

"There's a list of passwords on the last page, and every one of them is some variation of the word 'Shiloh' and the mailbox number at his Bedford County home."

Mark shook his head. "It figures. Lawton couldn't have picked a bigger crackpot to analyze. Nietzsche said it all. 'God is Dead, I Am the Antichrist, Will to Power,' and volumes of other vile nonsense. The Nazi party adored him. Either Lawton is a skinhead Hitler lover, or it's a bunch of old lecture notes from a course he took in college. When was it written?"

"I haven't seen any dates, but he reported it stolen seven years after the fire, thus he was nineteen when the theft occurred. He's writing what he thinks, praising Nietzsche sometimes and criticizing him in other passages, backed up by symbolic logic proofs. There's even a poem. Would you like to hear it?"

"Lay it on me."

"With an utterly inadequate and fallible brain,
we picture and ponder the cause of our pain.
Yet the answer is simple and perfectly plain,
we seek the quota, the leisure, and frivolous gain."

Mark chuckled. "These are hardly weighty words of wisdom, and Lord Byron has nothing to fear."

The traffic in Charleston grew heavy, and he became preoccupied with selecting the proper lane. Valeriya turned the pages unhurriedly, like she was reading every word. Finding Interstate 77 was easier than he anticipated, and the sun was finally at their back as they headed north. Neither of them spoke as she continued studying, slumped down in the car seat and grasping the book by its top edges.

Road construction signs diverted all traffic to two lanes. The car shook from the bumpy ride, rousing Val from her deep concentration.

"So, what have you learned about our Nazi sympathizer and tutor of despicable doggerel?" Blackwell asked.

"Nothing about a master race. It's an indictment of the master species, meaning homo sapiens."

"How so?"

"Lawton says that Nietzsche's colorful metaphors for mankind are marvelously accurate. Nietzsche writes, *'We have made our way from worm to man, yet much of us is still worm. Once we were apes, and now man is more ape than any ape.'"*

135

Mark chuckled. "Frivolous poppycock. What's Lawton trying to say?"

"He says ruthless dinosaurs still walk the earth, only now they are giants of unenlightened intellect. They prey on one another and lord over the other animals without compassion or mercy. He says man's lust for power has created abominable suffering for himself and the other beings of the planet."

"It sounds like another Unabomber Manifesto. Perhaps the book is valuable after all. It was his own megalomaniacal writings that hung Theodore Kaczynski. How far have you gotten into the book?"

"Not far. I'm skipping the proofs and just reading his words. It would take months to absorb this."

"What's the purpose of the logic proofs?" Blackwell asked.

"He's reducing Nietzsche's writings to a set of premises and extrapolating all valid conclusions. Some of his inferences run contrary to the beliefs of Nietzsche."

"Like what?"

"He says Nietzsche held the belief that life should be embraced as it is, the bad with the good, such that we would be willing to relive the exact same life over and over, even if that life was filled with nothing but misery. Lawton spurns that view, claiming there's a better way." The road construction ended, and she picked up the book.

They continued north, crossing the Ohio River and driving into country that still looked like West Virginia. Valeriya read for over an hour, silently purring like a contented cat that had found something fascinating to watch. She sat upright, beaming with delight.

"Here's Lawton's explanation for human evil, something only visible in what he calls the mind's blind spot." She read aloud. *"A dark whirlpool spins in the mind of man, a spiraling vortex that is always unseen and largely unknown, even though it alters every thought and changes every hope, frequently laying waste to mental order and rational action. At the core of this maelstrom is the recognition that we are mortal and will one day be swept away, as well as everyone we know and care about. This is the subconscious origin of greed and envy because the window of opportunity is progressively closing, gradually depriving us of our ambitions and desires. It creates veiled thoughts of emptiness that leave man endlessly searching for meaning in a cruel and difficult world, misdirecting our limited resources and mental energies away from what is relevant and real."*

"The man is a sordid enigma, spouting nothing but vapid gibberish."

"He says we should face death with Buddhistic tranquility and strive to make a difference while we are here, making personal sacrifices to benefit future generations—the opposite of what we do now. His core idea is Preemption, which means striking at the cause of our difficulties rather than just addressing the symptoms. He advocates population control and establishing a world government where each country would operate as a separate state but without large armies or nuclear weapons. He argues for fiscal restraint and taking responsibility for solving your own problems. He maintains that Preemption is the correct way to defeat nihilism since it provides a clear and constructive purpose to life. You become your own endeavor, working to make the world a better place, fighting against the evils of society when necessary, regardless of the personal consequences. He argues that a society practicing Preemption will achieve the best possible world."

Mark laughed disparagingly.

Valeriya opened the book. "I want to keep working." She read in silence all the way to Youngstown.

* * *

Youngstown was different from most cities. There were vast stretches of open land where massive steel mills had once towered back when the Rust Belt was an industrial superpower. Valeriya gave him directions without looking at the dashboard map, explaining that her middle school in Massillon made an annual visit to Mill Creek Park to view the beautiful scenery and take boat rides on the lakes. They ate a late lunch at a Mexican restaurant, Mark having two burritos and Val choosing a salad with tortilla chips and guacamole. A sudden thunderstorm blew in from the east, flooding the parking lot and delaying their departure. More clouds loomed on the horizon, making for a rainy afternoon.

Riverside High School was aptly named since it was on a knoll overlooking the Mahoning River. The redbrick edifice seemed old-fashioned with boxlike construction that differed from the current style of building schools with irregular angles and winding connections. School was out for the day, although there were still a few students roaming around. Parking, however, was a problem. The school lot was protected with gates requiring a keycard for entry. Blackwell pulled into an open spot marked "Handicapped" but yielded to Valeriya's vehement objections, and he was forced to park on the street several blocks away.

They approached the school, quickening their pace as intermittent raindrops fell from a threatening sky. Midway into the school grounds, Val stopped abruptly, bending down to examine a low spot in the water-covered sidewalk. She pulled out a handkerchief.

"What are you doing?" Blackwell asked.

"These little critters breathe air. They will drown if I leave them here." She plucked earthworms from underneath the water and transferred them to her handkerchief.

The falling drops grew thicker, becoming mixed with scattered sleet. Mark shielded his eyeglasses. "Come on, Val. We're going to get soaked."

"Wait for me at the building entrance." She continued the task, undaunted by the increased precipitation.

"You can get them after our meeting. Look at that nasty black cloud."

She didn't look up. "There's no drainage here. They'll be dead by then."

"May I assist you?" a male voice asked.

Blackwell turned to a beefy security guard.

"Almost half-finished," Valeriya called.

Mark smiled with embarrassment. "She's rescuing the earthworms."

The guard bent down and looked. "Worms? Fishing worms?" He turned to Blackwell. "This is a restricted school zone. Unless you're a parent, you cannot—"

Mark showed his ID. "FBI. We have an appointment with Clarita Fernandez."

"Oh, well, a ... Mrs. Fernandez is in the second to the last office in the administrative section of the building. Just follow the signs."

Both men flinched when a Biblical clap of thunder shook the ground. The tall trees across the river bowed like blowing wheat, and dark clouds swooped menacingly down, blasting everyone with bullets of hail and a thick torrent of whirling rain. Blackwell and the security guard dashed to the building, guarding their faces from stinging ice. They got inside just before the rain thickened into Niagara Falls. The overhead lights went dark, and the nearby church steeple vanished into a sea of wispy gray. Mark removed his glasses and dried the lenses, turning to find Valeriya—*she wasn't there!* With dismal dismay, Blackwell scrutinized her from the doorway, now on her knees, shielding the pool of water with her body, ignoring the ping-pong sized hail and wind that roared like a demoniacal beast. Val continued the rescue, working methodically to save the worms, accepting all the wrath. Watching in stunned silence, his mouth hanging open, the security guard stood beside Blackwell.

"She's a Ph.D.," Mark said. "They do things like that."

Valeriya rose and hid the handkerchief under her jacket, transporting the living cargo to higher ground. Back on her knees, she deposited the worms underneath some dense shrubbery on the side opposite the storm, covering them with leaves and mulch. Valeriya strolled across the hail-covered lawn, white pants ruined and shoes muddy, hair straight and running like a wet mop, yet smiling through the rivulets flowing over her rosy cheeks.

Mark reached for the glass door and held it open. "Did you have a good time?"

"Yep. I got them all."

The emergency lighting provided enough illumination to find the restrooms. Blackwell's feet were wet, and he was uncomfortably damp, yet still presentable. He waited outside for Val, at a complete loss to figure out what happened. *She's too young for dementia, and this isn't schizophrenia. Maybe she's bipolar.*

Val came out with her hair tied in a bristly ponytail, no longer dripping but still visibly wet, saying she hand-washed her pants. They followed the signs and progressed down the hall, her shoes squelching with each step. Mark tapped on Fernandez's door, and she invited them in, opening the blinds to illuminate her darkened office.

"Oh, my. You were caught out in that awful storm?"

Val nodded with occasional droplets still running down her cheeks. "It came up rather sudden."

Hot coffee was offered, and they both accepted. Fernandez looked to be in her mid-forties, speaking with a mild Puerto Rican accent.

"Is Roy in some kind of trouble?"

"Not at all," Blackwell replied. "This is a routine security review for a government job. We'd like you to give us your recollections of him as a student, as best you can, given he was here twenty years ago."

Fernandez nodded. "Some students stick in your mind, and Roy is one of them." She opened a folder and laid it flat on her desk. "He was a transfer student from Kentucky with good grades and high placement test scores, although most teachers believed he was somewhat autistic."

"Did he have difficulty speaking?"

"No. Nothing like that. It was his impaired social interaction, although he could converse wonderfully under the right circumstances. His math and science teachers saw nothing wrong, and he was gifted in those areas, especially math."

"Like an idiot savant?" Mark asked.

"Idiot isn't the right word. We never had the impression that he couldn't do something. He just chose not to, being headstrong with those he didn't like. He wouldn't speak unless spoken to, never smiled, and pretty much kept to himself. It was a tragedy because there was so much potential. He could've been somebody."

Mark looked at the folder. "We noticed the assault charge."

"Oh, I wouldn't let that become an obstacle to being hired."

"May we hear about it, just for completeness?"

Fernandez spent a few moments collecting her thoughts. "He'd been here about a month, and two of the roughhouse boys backed him into a corner in the outdoor handball court, intending to shake him down for his lunch money. I guess Roy looked like an easy target, a southern kid with an accent and no friends. He told them he didn't have any money, and one kid popped open a switchblade, waving it under Roy's nose and telling him to cough it up or bleed. Roy punched the kid in the throat, and he collapsed to the ground. The other boy grabbed Roy, and they began wrestling. Roy pulled the boy's arm behind his back, literally lifting the kid into the air and breaking his arm. There was total pandemonium, and the police showed up and arrested Roy."

"What about the other two boys?" Valeriya asked.

"Ambulances took them away."

"But were they charged with anything?"

Fernandez shook her head. "There was too much confusion, and the boy with the broken arm claimed they were the ones who were attacked, the switchblade belonging to Roy. They also looked like victims. The boy who got punched nearly died, and he spent a month on a ventilator. He talked in a raspy voice after that. Fortunately for Roy, the event was witnessed by two teachers looking out of a third-story window, and the prosecutor had to drop the charges. Nevertheless, it shook up everyone. The two witnesses said everything happened incredibly fast, not like the typical brawls boys have. The mother of one of the injured boys claimed the eyewitnesses misunderstood what had happened. She was also on the Board of Education, so you can imagine the issues in play. Our school superintendent, Mr. Clay, was feeling the heat, and he wanted Roy expelled, arguing he was a danger to the other kids because of the autism issue."

"What was Roy's demeanor during all this?" Blackwell asked.

"After the fight they hauled Roy into the boy's locker room to wait for the police to arrive. Both of the injured kids played for the varsity, and one of the football coaches bellowed at Roy, calling him names and asking if he wanted to fight him. He struck Roy about the face several times, bloodying his mouth. I wasn't there, but I was told Roy took the beating without batting an eye. He was as calm and cool as if waiting for a school bus. He had no fear of anyone or anything. Nothing really mattered, which proves something was wrong with him. Two days later, Mr. Clay sent Roy to be evaluated by the school psychologist."

"Who was the psychologist?"

"Dr. Philip Fleming. He had a contract to work with troubled students in Mahoning and Trumbull Counties, providing up to a month of free counseling."

Mark didn't recognize the name.

"Fleming conducted his examination and said Roy wasn't autistic and there was nothing wrong with him. This upset Mr. Clay immensely, especially since his employment contract for superintendent was up for renewal. Clay demanded that Roy continue seeing Fleming for therapy as a condition for remaining a student at Riverside. I think this was Clay's way of driving Roy out since he could never afford the cost of therapy. But when Fleming heard of this condition, he became so incensed that he agreed to treat Roy free of charge, and he remained under Fleming's care until he graduated two years later."

"You mean he went through four years of high school in two years?" Mark asked.

"Most kids from the wrong side of the tracks don't do well academically, but Roy was the exception. His high test scores enabled him to skip ninth grade, and he did so well on the competency examinations that he skipped the eleventh grade as well. Clay was eager to get rid of him."

"Did Dr. Fleming ever provide any insights or comments about Roy?" Blackwell asked, knowing the answer in advance.

"Not to me. Fleming would sometimes have discussions with the parents of troubled kids, but he said nothing to teachers or administrators." Fernandez looked away for a moment. "I do remember one comment. In the first year of therapy, Fleming and I were sitting behind a partition, secretly listening to Roy having a discussion with his math teacher. The topic was differential equations, whatever that is. When it was over and we were back in my office, I asked Fleming how

Roy could be so advanced in academics yet be socially impoverished. Fleming let down his guard for a moment, and he said there were great peaks and deep valleys with this kid. He lived in his own world, an enigmatic place we wouldn't understand. Fleming also said once Roy got something in his head, dynamite wouldn't get it out. But once something starts to happen with him, *look out!* It's like the solid rocket boosters on the old space shuttle. Once they're lit, there's no way to turn them off."

"Does Fleming still work for the Youngstown school system?"

"Unfortunately, no. The failure of the tax levies hit everyone hard, and the administration elected to spend the money elsewhere."

"Is Fleming still in the area?"

"I saw him once at the Eastwood Mall several years ago. He said he was providing counseling services for the prison systems. Don't know where he lives."

Mark nodded. "What else can you tell us about Roy?"

"He had little money, and it showed in his worn-out clothes. He never ate in the cafeteria, and when he did eat, it was inexpensive food. You know, peanut butter sandwiches, beans, cornbread, and the like. I got him a voucher for a government-sponsored lunch program so he could eat in the cafeteria for free. He turned it down. I think it was part of his psychological difficulties. He definitely was autistic, regardless of what Fleming said." Fernandez pursed her lips as if regretting her previous comment. "He was a worker though, bagging groceries at Simpson's Market, and he mowed people's grass with a push mower during the summer."

"He avoided everyone all the time? No friends at all?"

Fernandez nodded. "He did work out regularly in the weightlifting room, but he did it at odd hours when no one was there. Not that he needed to lift weights."

"What do you mean?"

"After demolishing two of the toughest bullies at Riverside, the word was out. This kid plays marbles for keeps. Everyone steered clear of him, which was what he wanted. The football coaches tried unsuccessfully to get him interested in joining the team. Only one kid was stronger, but he was three years older than Roy and outweighed him by sixty pounds."

"And when did you last see Roy?"

She drummed her fingers on the desk, staring out the window. "I know he skipped the graduation ceremony, to the surprise of no one. It would've been when we talked about colleges—roughly eighteen years ago." Fernandez chuckled. "That was another blooper. The kid had perfect grades and fabulous test scores. He could've had a free ride at any Ivy League school, yet he chooses Ohio State because it's closer to Kentucky."

Mark smiled. "You couldn't talk him out of it?"

"Believe me, I tried. But like Dr. Fleming said, once he made up his mind. Not that it turned out bad. He entered the fall term just after turning fifteen, and he graduated in six years, completing a Bachelor's summa cum laude, a Master's in computer science, and a Ph.D. in artificial intelligence, which was a good choice for him. The nerdy computer types tend to be loners anyway."

Valeriya didn't return Blackwell's roguish grin. He regarded Fernandez. "What's your overall opinion of Roy Lawton?"

Fernandez pondered the question as if wanting to choose her words with caution. "If he's applying for a job where he has to work with the public, it's not a good match. But if the situation is something analytical, where he can work alone, he is going to blow you away!"

They thanked Mrs. Fernandez for her time and visited the restroom before leaving. Val's wet shoes squeaked merrily along the sidewalk, reminding him of needful desires. He had already seen her naked, a monumental step forward in their tacit relationship. Perhaps they could dispense with formalities.

"What's the difference between Lawton's Ph.D. and yours," Blackwell asked, "aside from you attending a much better university?"

"My specialty is searching through databases, looking for faint patterns in the data, finding the proverbial needle in a haystack. Artificial Intelligence deals with teaching computers to think and make decisions on their own, like playing chess or diagnosing disease based on the medical symptoms."

"We need to get you out of those damp clothes. There's a Holiday Inn down the road. We can get a room now and go to dinner."

"We can't spend the night. I got a text message from Marshall asking me to attend a meeting tomorrow morning."

"On a Saturday?"

"The Bureau never sleeps." Valeriya pulled out her cellphone and showed him the message.

Shit. It's always something. "I'm surprised that your phone is still working."

"It's waterproof. The back windows of the car are tinted. We can change clothes there. We'll grab some fast food, and I'll have you home before midnight."

They paused at a crosswalk, waiting for the light to change. "It doesn't seem like we've met the legal threshold for 'probable cause' with Lawton, does it?" Blackwell asked.

"Not even close. All we have are stories of what might have happened twenty years ago."

Mark accepted the disappointment. *Patience and persistence will eventually win the day.*

13 Skeleton Key

True to her word, Valeriya had Blackwell home before midnight. Bone tired and sulky, he went to bed but couldn't sleep, thinking about his lack of success with Val. If she was mentally ill, it would explain a lot: her compulsive desire for seclusion, the bizarre behavior in Tennessee, skinny dipping in Kentucky, braving that fearsome storm to rescue earthworms, and her apparent rejection of him. Taken together, this was persuasive evidence of a deranged mind, manifestations of her incipient psychosis arising from repressed sexual frustration. The human mind desires sex, needs sex to be functionally normal. Take it away, and mercurial neuroses will come. Mark kept telling himself she wasn't worth it, and he should just move on. Regrettably, it didn't work. Like some decrepit drug addict needing his fix, he constantly craved her, wanted her, and was pathologically drawn to her presence, savoring the imagined bliss of countless fleshly fantasies. *Not having her is smothering wrath!* Eventually, he drifted off while strategizing about those academic publications he was supposed to be writing for Dean Shoemaker. That would put anyone to sleep.

Blackwell arose later than usual the following day. Clad in his velvety slippers and burgundy smoking jacket, he had breakfast at noon and settled down to check phone messages and emails. There was nothing important aside from emails from Margaret Marshall and Dean Shoemaker, both requesting an update on his sabbatical. Mark replied to Shoemaker, telling the old fart things were going well and his work with the FBI would lead to groundbreaking discoveries and the identification of a new type of serial killer. This was no stretch of the truth. Once Lawton is arrested, it will be Blackwell at the podium, briefing a news-hungry public on the psychological intricacies of this diabolical fiend. Scholarly journal editors would call him up, begging for manuscript submissions about the killer no one could see. Valeriya had coined him right: "If he comes for you, no one will ever know." This would be his golden parachute, just in case things didn't work out with Val. Needing to give the matter some careful thought, he postponed his reply to the more inquisitive and intellectually sharper Margaret Marshall.

The hurried hum of an automobile engine sent Mark to the window, standing back where he couldn't be seen. *Oh crap. It's Sergeant Miller.* Blackwell waited until the detective rapped the knocker and waited a bit longer to simulate the response of a busy man. He swallowed his annoyance and opened the door.

"Robert? Working on a Saturday? "

"Yes, sir. Am I disturbing you?"

"No, no. Please come in."

Miller entered and regarded Blackwell's casual attire. "Are you feeling all right?"

"Never better." Mark slid a thumb inside his smoking jacket. "I dress for comfort when writing. Been up since six o'clock working on an important manuscript, something I'm sure you will read about when it's published. Would you care for some coffee or tea?"

"No, thank you. I can't stay long, but I'm afraid I still need your help. This is a real mystery."

"Have a seat."

Both men sat in the same locations as the previous visit, Blackwell on the sofa and Miller in Mark's favorite leather chair. Miller's gray eyes were always roaming, looking here and there, seemingly searching for some minute oversight that might topple Mark's house of cards.

"Well, sir, as you suggested, we tried to locate Miss Rowan's cellphone, but without any luck. Her family was cooperative, looking throughout their Allentown home, Miss Rowan's car and her apartment in Boston, and searching the secluded cottage they have up in Pike County. That's near the Delaware State Forest, a beautiful place. Have you ever been there?"

"No," Mark lied. "I'm a city boy, liking bright lights and an active nightlife."

Miller chuckled. "My daughter is the same way. We checked with her cellular provider, and unbeknownst to her family and friends, Miss Rowan had two phones registered in her name, each having different phone numbers. The first phone, her primary phone, made many calls and sent text messages to many people. However, the second phone, the one nobody knew about, was seldom used, and it only made calls to the first phone. We know Miss Rowan wasn't calling herself, so what was going on?"

"Hm-m."

"You see the difficulty, sir?"

Blackwell nodded, silently thinking. The second phone was his idea, enabling them to talk without leaving a digital trail that would lead back to him. After her suicide he smashed the phone and pitched the parts into the Charles River. He regarded the detective. "The only thing I can suggest is you talk to her friends, especially the other cheerleaders. Someone must know something."

Miller nodded and scribbled in his notebook, apparently satisfied with the response. "What do you know about triangulation?"

"It's a means of determining the location of a cellphone based on measuring the time delay for a signal to return to the cellular towers. It's accurate and useful in police work." Mark raised a eureka finger. "Let me guess. You used triangulation to determine the transmission locations of Miss Rowan's phones."

"You're right again, sir. There was nothing unusual about her primary phone. She received and placed calls from her Boston apartment, her parent's home in Allentown, their hideaway cottage in Pike County, the Wittgenstein campus, and a goodly number of calls while driving down the highway—which is illegal because of the distracted driving issue. Transmissions from her second phone also

148

show calls from various places, but never near people. We were hoping to spot the mystery caller with either highway cameras or surveillance footage from gas stations or stores, that coverage being widespread. But in every instance, the caller made the call from a place where he couldn't be photographed. Professor Wolf in the Wittgenstein Statistics Department did some computer simulations, and she said the likelihood of that occurring by chance is over a million to one. It seems as if the caller knew all about triangulation and how police use security camera footage."

"Triangulation is common knowledge," Blackwell replied. "It appears all the time on television crime shows." Not liking where this was going, Mark opted to change the focus. "What about the security camera footage for Bradley Hall? You were going to check to see who was in the building when Miss Rowan died."

"We've encountered a problem."

"Don't tell me the cameras weren't working?"

"They were functioning normally. However, they don't cover every doorway in the building."

"The north side fire escape?" Mark asked.

"Yes, sir. It runs from the sixth floor all the way to the bottom. Someone could exit the building without being photographed."

"This is of no consequence for three reasons. First, you can't get to that stairwell without opening a fire door and tripping the alarm. Second, the relevant question is not whether they could get out, but whether they could get in. And third, the outside door on the ground floor only allows people to leave."

"Would you explain that again? Why entry into the building is the relevant question?"

"We want to establish who was in the building when Miss Rowan died. Accordingly, if the security cameras show someone leaving the building, myself for example, and not reentering, then that person could not have killed Miss Rowan. Follow?"

"Yes, sir."

"As I said before, the exterior door to the fire escape stairwell cannot be opened from the outside. It has a smooth surface with no door handle, no external lock, nothing but a solid sheet of steel. None of the windows open without dismantling the window frame, a laborious process requiring specialized tools. Accordingly, you can determine with absolute certainty who was not inside the building. Even if someone somehow left via the fire escape door without setting off the alarm, the security cameras would show an entry for that person but no exit. It's simple arithmetic. One in and one out equals zero, and that person is not a suspect."

Miller nodded. "Okay. Now I understand." He smiled. "I sure wish I had your smarts for figuring things out."

"I'm delighted to be of service. Are we finished?"

"There is one more thing. May we have your key to the sixth-floor equipment room? The lock has been changed, but the boys in the lab want to inspect all the old keys for differences in wear patterns along the teeth."

"That's no problem," Mark replied. He proceeded to his desk, opening and closing drawers until he found his ring of keys. He circled through the keys and spun them again, eliminating them one by one. *What's this? It isn't here?* He went through the keys again with the same result. *This is impossible!* He turned to Miller, who had followed him and was watching. "I can't seem to find it. Would you recognize it?"

"Yes, sir. I've collected everyone's but yours." Miller slid one key at a time through the ring. "It's not here. Are you sure this is where you kept it?"

Mark nodded, feeling a tinge of panic at this mishap of memory. "On second thought, I believe it might be in my desk at Wittgenstein. You can get inside the faculty offices, can't you?"

Miller nodded. "If the faculty member gives their consent."

"Well, you have my full permission to search for that key." Blackwell imposed a reassuring smile. "And take it with you when you find it."

"Thank you, sir. I'll do that."

The police officer shook Mark's hand and departed.

Blackwell slumped down in his favorite chair. Keys don't disappear from a keyring unless they are deliberately removed. How did

Candy get to the roof? That, now, was abundantly clear. She had taken his key. But what happened to the key? Why wasn't it with her? And why would she do such a senseless thing? There was no shortage of tall buildings where one could leap to eternity. Mark drank a double brandy to settle his nerves, mentally replaying what had happened for the rest of the day. *This is a mystery.*

14 The Three Fates

Blackwell arrived at the DDI on Monday morning, eager to hear about Valeriya's Saturday meeting with Margaret Marshall. Richard said Val left for Washington and would be gone all day. Mark quizzed Richard, trying to extract more information about what she was doing. Either Richard knew nothing, or he was protecting his boss. Mark hid his annoyance and went to his office, settling into the slumped weariness of working on his literature review.

Journal articles on homicidal juveniles weren't that common, and Blackwell downloaded what was available from Wittgenstein's digital library. The DDI archives had more, but he hadn't quite learned the intricacies of navigating that vast but complex informational warehouse. He formed a theory that explained everything. Roy Lawton was a child in a man's body, someone with the higher brain functions of an adult, yet emotionally undeveloped and lacking a fundamental sense of right and wrong. Sigmund Freud's expatiations could be used, and Blackwell could work in a discussion of the rebellious son (Lawton) slaying the primal father (society). This would lay the rudimentary foundation for the first research paper, an ingenious work of art entitled *The Maestro of Murders*.

After returning from his 3 p.m. lunch, the office telephone rang, showing the caller ID, *V R Highland*.

Mark grabbed the phone. "How are things going?"

"Margaret and I are being interrogated by the Senate Intelligence Committee."

"About the Cairo deaths?"

"Yeah. It's a chaotic mess. Lots of contradictory statements from CIA officers about what I did or failed to do. Naples is here as well, but I don't know what he's telling them. I've also been appointed as the Bureau's Official Liaison for the US Cyber Command."

Blackwell chuckled. "That's a mouthful. What does it mean?"

"It won't change my job much, but I'll have access to all the classified stuff on Lawton."

"Was that your idea?"

"Margaret came up with it. Looks like I'll be stuck in Washington all week, so you'll have to manage the investigation alone."

"I have everything under control."

"Gotta go. The next session is starting."

* * *

Valeriya returned to the DDI late Friday afternoon. Mark proceeded to her office, practically starving for her presence. She was smiling and upbeat, barefoot but still wearing the formal clothes appropriate for Washington.

"You're looking mighty fine," Mark said.

"I'm feeling good. Margaret and I spent a lot of time together. We're becoming good friends."

"Now that you have this new security clearance, what's the scoop on Roy Lawton?"

"He designs computer viruses for the US government."

"You mean like the malware that sometimes infects people's computers?"

She nodded. "But his software alters the programming of high-tech machines."

"Like the virus that destroyed the uranium centrifuges in Iran back in 2011." He scratched his head. "What was it called?"

"Stuxnet. Today's military viruses are more sophisticated. Stuxnet was a single piece of code that was easy to detect. The new cyber worms are nearly invisible. They send false signals to alter machine behavior and fool automated protective logic monitors, causing the devices to malfunction."

"And what target is Lawton working on?" Blackwell asked.

"It's classified as 'Need to Know,' but it must be something for the Navy."

"If Lawton is developing superbugs, how could he find the time to commit intricate murders?"

"He's the architect, not the builder. The detailed drudgery of writing complicated computer code is done by others."

Mark nodded. "What else have you discovered?"

"Lawton works out of the Burns Cybernetic Institute, east of Columbus, Ohio. He's only there on Mondays, working from his Kentucky home the rest of the time, which is interesting."

"Why is that?"

"There are fourteen cases where we can identify when the critical event took place, and there were no killings or disappearances on a Sunday, Monday, or Tuesday."

"That might be enough for a conviction if we can place him at the scene of the crime. What about his database searches? Has he been trolling for animal abusers?"

"He only did eleven searches, and none are related to animal mistreatment."

Mark stared at her. "You said he was definitely using the restricted databases to identify targets."

"I'm still thinking about that."

"What about his wife, Carolyn?"

"Her maiden name is Morgan. They took several computer classes together at Ohio State. She was on the women's swim team and still holds several college records for freestyle swimming. She has a Master's degree in computer science, so she might be involved, doing some of the computer virus design while he's 'on the road.'"

Valeriya said she was hungry, and Blackwell happily accompanied her to the DDI commissary. She chose the eggplant parmesan, and he had a large burger with fries. They sat at Val's favorite table, a nook hidden back in the corner. They commenced eating.

Mark pondered his dilemma with Candy. No one had seen her suicide letter but him. He regarded Val. "Suppose you saw a tombstone with nothing on it except the number three, three being a number and not written. What would you think?"

"Have you seen such a thing?"

"A long time ago. But I've never been able to get it out of my head."

Valeriya arched her brows. "No dates or years, just the number three?"

"That's all."

"An old gravestone?"

"I couldn't tell."

"What about the surrounding markers? Were they new or old?"

He thought for a moment, trying to spin the fictitious tale in the most productive way. "Fairly new. If you had to hazard a guess, what did it mean?"

She swallowed her food and took a drink of water. "It means three things are buried there. If they were human, there would be names. Maybe they are somebody's pets."

Mark nodded. "Yeah, dogs or cats. I guess that makes sense." *But Candy didn't have any pets*. He pushed the disturbing thought out of his head. "You will never guess who I saw dining together at the King's Table Restaurant. Go on, take a guess."

Val gave a half-shrug. "I have no idea."

"Douglas McCracken and Anthony Naples." She didn't seem surprised. "Marshall and Naples are fighting like Bobby Kennedy and Jimmy Hoffa, and the number two guy in the FBI sits down and breaks bread with Naples. They were even laughing and joking together."

"Their mothers are first cousins, and they played together when they were children, same baseball and football teams."

Blackwell's grin faded. "Ah, I see. But how does Marshall deal with that? It must make her uncomfortable."

"Margaret and Doug are professionals. They get along well."

* * *

The Stealth Killer case slowed to a crawl over the summer months, mostly because no new suspected murders were discovered. Val's teaching activities expanded to three days per week, and Mark was given another leave to conduct in-depth research into the mindset of serial killers. He had occasional lunches and dinners with Valeriya, but they were few and far between.

FBI specialists secretly installed a GPS tracker on Lawton's pickup truck while it was parked at the Burns Institute. Lawton had two other vehicles, but both remained inaccessible for the installation. The Bureau also rented a house across from Lawton's Columbus residence, and surveillance cameras were installed at that location. However, neither the GPS tracker nor the security cameras provided any evidence of improper conduct. Mark contacted Dr. Philip Fleming by phone, and as expected, Fleming declined to discuss Roy Lawton, citing the confidentiality rules between therapist and patient. Fleming also said he discontinued his private practice.

* * *

On the day after Labor Day, Blackwell received a telephone call from Sheriff Tom Shank about some newly discovered evidence in the Webster and Anderson deaths. A forensic specialist found a DNA match between a pair of drinking glasses, one from the house of Dewey Webster and the other from Toby Anderson's kitchen. The specimen was not in the national DNA databank, but it proves that some individual visited both Webster and Anderson. Shank said he put little stock in the match since Webster and Anderson were related, and it could be just a family member or a mutual friend. Nevertheless, Shank thought Blackwell should know. Mark thanked the sheriff and proceeded to Val's office to report the good news.

Valeriya listened with interest as Blackwell explained the new evidence. She typed a search command and watched the screen.

"What do you think?" Mark asked. "At least it's something to work with."

"As I feared, Roy Lawton is not in the DNA databank."

"How can that be? He's a government employee."

"He's not in the military, and civilian consultants don't submit a DNA specimen."

"There must be a record of it somewhere."

Val conducted several more searches. "Nope. Nothing here." Her eyes brightened. "However …" She entered a long password and waited while the screen flickered through a series of coded transmissions. The Bald Eagle emblem of the United States Cyber Command appeared, followed by a text document. "There's a cyber worm training session at the Burns Institute in October, and Roy Lawton is the morning presenter. It's an all-day event with breakfast, lunch, and dinner served to the participants, and with my new Cyber Command security clearance, I can attend."

"How will that help?"

"All I need to do is snatch a spoon or fork from his plate after he has finished eating. We may be able to obtain a DNA sample from the saliva. He's a presenter, so lots of people will be talking to him, providing ample distraction. It's a longshot, but worth a try."

Mark disliked the idea. "We should get someone else."

"How? It's a top-secret government facility. US Cyber Command certification is necessary to be there. Plus, I have enough technical background to understand what Lawton says during the presentation. Even if I don't get the sample, we're still going to learn about what he does, which could benefit the investigation."

"There has to be some other way."

"You can't knock on his door and ask him to pee in a jar. You're the one who said secrecy was necessary to catch him."

"Can I come with you?"

"Not a chance. Cyber Command would never allow it."

Blackwell hesitated, not wanting to send Val alone, yet needing something to break the impasse. "How many people will be there? Is he going to notice you?"

"About sixty from Fort Meade, and others fly in from California, well over 100 participants. Hiding in that crowd will be easy."

"All right, but stay away from Lawton. Don't talk to him. Don't go near him. Don't even look at him unless he's giving a presentation. Get the DNA sample and *get out!* Do you understand?"

"You're being silly, Mark. It's a government-protected facility, and I'll be surrounded by people. You know how careful I am. What could possibly go wrong?"

15 V for Valeriya

The distant streetlights of Columbus glowed orange-yellow when Val broke through the dark clouds. The approach controller at John Glenn Airport provided alignment coordinates, and Valeriya piloted the *Snow Queen* to the proper flight corridor. He passed her off to the airport tower, and after receiving clearance to land, she glided in for a rougher than normal touchdown. A ripping crosswind was the culprit, shoving the plane to and fro. The external thermometer provided a telling clue: twenty degrees cooler than predicted. Usually airport weather forecasts were on the mark, but not today.

Traveling in semidarkness and hindered by construction, Valeriya taxied the plane to the designated parking region. The airplane door pushed hard against her, and a chilling breeze bit through her turtleneck sweater, lashing her nicely combed hair into a tangled heap of hay. Val hurried to the luggage compartment and put on her black leather trench coat, raising the collar and fastening every button. With purse in hand, still fighting the blustery onslaught, she pushed her way to the terminal and hailed a cab. She opened the door and got inside, telling the driver, "Burns Cybernetic Institute."

The dark-skinned cabbie wore an indigo turban and spoke slow but precise English, quoting the fare for the thirty-mile journey. She nodded and buckled her seatbelt. He wasn't chatty, which suited her troubled mood. The dwellings grew further apart as they continued away from the airport, barely discernible in dawn's early light. Yielding to creeping curiosity, Valeriya asked the cabbie to slow down as they approached Lawton's Columbus residence. It was a plain-looking green A-frame, similar to the surrounding homes, a sharp contrast from his sprawling Kentucky cabin. She scrutinized the house that the Bureau was renting for surveillance. The observation camera was under the eaves (pointing at Lawton's property), although it could pass for a home security system. There was also a large picture window, perfect for watching with binoculars, although Lawton's infrequent use of the house didn't warrant a full-time human surveillance team.

Now they were in full-fledged farmland, unbounded meadows of flatness and gradations of gorgeous green. That nasty wind whipped up again, jostling the car as it weaved to stay on the road. To her left, a small herd of cattle huddled together behind a barbed-wire fence. There was neither barn nor outbuilding nor any place to drink. *Surely someone must look after them—surely.* She turned to the rear window, craning her neck until they were out of sight.

* * *

At first glance, the Burns Institute appeared unassuming. Other than stone walls, dual gates, and extra security guards, it was just another office building. The tall windows had a faint copper tint, a technique used to make electronic espionage difficult. An array of antennas circumscribed the building, providing a radiofrequency firewall. The DDI didn't require such countermeasures since it was located deep underground. Valeriya paid the cabbie and gave him her usual 200% tip. He seemed flustered at first, repeatedly telling her the price. She smiled and pushed the cash into his hands. A flashing sign at the bank across the street showed a temperature of forty-seven, but the steady wind made it feel colder. Val pulled the leather trench coat around her and scurried to the first security gate, showing her FBI identification and NSA pass. The guard signaled the second gate, lowering the massive barrier used to thwart car or truck bombs, and Valeriya went inside.

She surrendered her firearm, purse, and cellphone. The security rules were the same as the DDI: clothes and shoes only. No pens, wristwatches, jewelry, or anything else. She removed her shoes and trench coat and stepped into the high-resolution body scanner. The shoes and coat were scanned with a powerful x-ray machine. Valeriya entered a processing area where a blondish woman approached.

"Hello. I'm Monica."

Val returned the friendly smile. "Nice to meet you. I'm Valeriya Highland"

"You're early."

"I was told to come early because it's my first time."

Monica studied a clipboard. "You've already been cleared, so this will be easy. Just follow me."

Monica led her through a suite of offices and into a room filled with what looked like optometrist equipment. She had Valeriya sit upright in a chair and place her chin on a rest to steady her head, explaining that she was taking a picture of her irises and retinas. Val's stomach growled, anticipating the breakfast that would soon be served. Monica used bobby pins to pull back Val's hair and expose her ears, and she told Valeriya to sit still while a camera rotated around her head.

Voices emanated from down the hall—a woman and man conversing. "How about this?" the man asked. "No. They may see the general designs but no specifics," the woman replied.

Monica's final procedure was scanning finger and palm prints. She punched several buttons on a machine, saying, "Your electronic ID will be ready in a few minutes."

The room seemed overly warm, and Valeriya removed her trench coat.

"I love your coat," Monica squealed. "It's a real looker." Her eyes refused to leave the leather garment. "May I?"

Val smiled and passed it over.

Monica squeezed the leather like she was testing bread for freshness. "This is amazing. Can I try it on?"

"Be my guest."

Monica went to a mirror attached to her office door, rotating to get the best view. It fit her well. She had the wistful gaze of a penniless kid looking through the window of a candy store. "If my sisters could see me now. Martha would die of envy." She twirled around, pressing the coat against her body. "Back in college I worked in leather goods at Bloomingdale's, but I've never felt anything like this." Monica removed the coat and scrutinized the leather. "This isn't cowhide. I'm pretty sure it's horse, but the leather is so unbelievably soft." The ID machine activated, sending Valeriya's United States Cyber Command identification badge sliding into a tray. Monica held out the ID. "Here you are."

Val sat perfectly still.

Monica waited, arm extended. "Ms. Highland?" Monica inspected the badge and offered it again. "Ma'am?"

Valeriya slowly took the badge, a black rectangle with a holographic picture of her marked with serial number K954. As with other high-security identification badges, her name was not shown. She pinned it to her sweater. "Would you like to have it?"

Monica blinked. "Have what?"

"The trench coat."

Monica smirked like she was being teased. "Yeah, right. And I want a Rolls-Royce as well."

"I'm serious."

Monica tossed her head back and laughed raucously, revealing a mouthful of sparkling white teeth. "No you're not."

"I'm very sincere."

Monica hesitated, presumably thinking it over. She passed the coat back to Val. "I can't accept this." She laughed again. "We're complete strangers."

Someone called from outside, "Monica, the Fort Meade troop is coming."

"It's not a problem," Monica replied. "They already have their IDs. I just need to check them in." Both women moved to the door with Monica still smiling at Valeriya. "You're so funny."

Val navigated through the empty building, trench coat draped over her arm, trying not to think about what she was carrying. Her temples throbbed with migraine intensity, but her ibuprofen was locked away at the screening station. *Maybe some food will help.* She followed the wall signs, moving steadily toward the Murphy Conservatory, the place where the training session was located.

She pushed through a set of double doors, striking something on the other side. A large bucket sloshed dark liquid, covering Valeriya with grungy filth. She jumped back and wiped the irritating fluid from her face. A janitor holding a mop apologized for leaving the pail near the door, saying he didn't think anyone was around. Val hurried into the ladies' room and washed her face, flushing both eyes with water. Her clothes reeked of ammonia, and stains covered her sweater. She continued rinsing until the burning sensation was gone. The unlighted mirror showed some redness around the eyes, and her vision was slightly blurred. She applied damp paper towels to the spots on her sweater, achieving little to nothing. *I cannot believe this!* Val marched out of the restroom, intending to smite the negligent janitor with a piece of her mind, but the man was gone. At least she had found the conference location.

A metallic coat rack stood in front of some cathedral arch windows, and Valeriya hung her trench coat on the last hanger. She entered the Murphy Conservatory and found a typical conference facility with tables and chairs surrounding a carved wooden podium and projection screen. The décor was lovely, although not ostentatious: knotty pine paneling on the walls, bookshelves loaded with tomes of military history. A long row of portraits circumscribed the room, heroes from World Wars I and II, Korea, and Vietnam. A twenty-four-hour military clock showed 6:45. Breakfast was supposed to start at 7:15, and the training session would begin at eight. She toyed with the idea of going back to her plane to get clean clothes, but there wasn't enough time. Then, to her astonishment, she spied the janitor through the open doorway. He was at the coat rack, examining her coat.

Valeriya rushed toward him, heels clacking across the hardwood floor. *"Get your grimy paws off my coat, you careless creep!"*

He froze in place. She was well into the hall when she glimpsed another man with a mop, cleaning up the spilled liquid. Val blinked several times, trying to clear her blurred eyesight—it was the janitor.

She turned back to the man at the coat rack, a dark silhouette back-lit by the sun-filled windows.

"That's a very costly coat," the man said. "And you probably paid a lot of money for it as well."

The shadowy figure crept toward her. Valeriya swallowed hard. She recognized the voice—the man she heard in Monica's office.

He smiled and extended his hand. "I'm Roy Lawton."

Val forced her arm forward and gave him a perfunctory handshake.

"And you are?" Lawton asked while scrutinizing her badge.

"I'm … I'm Ms. Jones. Lisa Jones."

"I'm delighted to meet you, Ms. Jones. Are you new to the Ares Project?"

Ares was the Greek god of war, but she had no idea what he meant. "Yes I am, and I hope to learn a lot today."

"I'm sorry about handling your trench coat. I have a reason, if you would care to hear it."

Valeriya took a step back. "Yes, but some other time. I need to make an important phone call from the security office."

Lawton bowed slightly. "Another time."

Val exited through the double doors and hurried down the corridor. The full import of what had happened hit like a rolling avalanche. What was simple and easy had become complicated and difficult. She had been noticed in the worst possible way. Valeriya descended a staircase and made several random turns into deserted hallways, fighting the urge to scream. She entered a vacant storage room and quietly closed the door. Her reflection in the door glass stared back at her. *You stupid idiot!*

Taking an arduous intake of breath, Val descended into thought. Not returning until the conference started seemed wise. That would eliminate any further conversations with Lawton, although it meant skipping breakfast. She pulled down her pants and inspected the plastic evidence bag taped to her inner thigh—still sealed tight. If everything fell apart, Margaret Marshall would come to her rescue. She waited until eight o'clock.

Hearing the amplified voices of a formal presentation, Valeriya went through the double doors. Coffee was still available in the hall. She poured a cup and peeked through the doorway window. The conservatory was filled with men and women dressed in military fatigues, all wearing the same type of security badge. She guessed they were mid-ranking officers—lieutenants, captains, and majors—although no armed forces insignias were displayed. A few senior officers wore military uniforms, possibly supervisors.

Val eased the door open and slipped inside. Most seats were taken, and she was forced to sit in the front row. An admiral spoke at the podium, discussing the secrecy rules. Valeriya recognized the admiral's voice—the woman talking to Lawton earlier that morning. Spouses and loved ones were to be told they were working on a boring assignment involving logistics software. Details of the fake assignment would be distributed to make the misrepresentation convincing. A color portrait of Audie Murphy loomed above the admiral, his chest loaded with medals and military decorations. The admiral said the morning agenda would cover strategy and theory. They would break for lunch, and the afternoon session would explain the new computer code writing machines. She introduced Roy Lawton without mentioning his name, referring to him as our "Deep Dive Specialist." Lawton stepped to the podium and inserted a flash drive, activating the overhead display. He glanced at Val and pulled the microphone to his mouth.

Lawton described the Ares Project as a program to incapacitate Russian intercontinental ballistic missiles. He said the Ares 1 worm had already infected a third of the ICBMs on Borei-class submarines, and the number of compromised missiles was increasing at the rate of approximately one-half percent per month as the Russians conducted routine maintenance procedures with software updates. The Ares 2 worm would target land-based ICBMs located inside Russia, and the coding of Ares 2 would be the mission of the personnel in the room. The project would last three months and take place at several undisclosed locations.

Lawton explained that conventional computer viruses were ineffective because the Russians regularly checked their equipment, including the launching of test missiles. Thus, to be successful, Ares worms needed to be smart enough to allow test missile firings to go as planned while blocking genuine attacks on the United States. When activated, the Ares worm sent false signals to the missile's navigation system, and it prevented warhead detonation by fooling the positional sensors into believing the missile was still in transit high above the earth.

Lawton played a computer simulation of the Ares worm in action. Upon entering the missile software, the worm erased specific computer coding and rewrote the program to perform the originally intended function while adding a small module. The rewriting of binary data was more compact, so file size remained unchanged, and only a microscopic line-by-line examination would reveal that the software had been altered. Lawton further illustrated a serious flaw in the Russian system due to its reliance on digitized testing to verify software accuracy. Ares would not activate during a computer simulation and was therefore invisible to Russian missile technicians. After Ares installed its payload of eleven modules in different locations, the worm would self-destruct, removing all traces of itself.

Upon seeing the aura, clarity, and elegant unexpectedness of Lawton's architectonic designs, Valeriya had the impression of seeing Mozart at the piano or Michelangelo sculpting the face of David. The euphonic finesses were a little higher, the fine points a little richer, the words a little sharper. No one doubted him or asked why he was enthroned as their guru of malicious malware ideas.

One participant asked Lawton how Ares 2 would be introduced into the Russian system. Lawton smiled, saying, "It won't be the Internet." Someone asked if an Ares-infected missile could strike China with a nuclear warhead. However, the admiral interrupted, saying there would be no more questions. Lawton exhibited numerous slides on the technical aspects of Ares, and the conference members made notes in the handbooks and pens that were distributed to them. Each person would be assigned the job of writing part of the code for one of the Ares modules, and each piece of code would be cross-checked with the work of others who were given the same assignment, although no one would know which person or group had the same coding task. The code writers were not allowed to show or discuss their work with anyone except their assigned supervisors. Specialized code writing machines would be used so the actual blueprint of the Ares worm remained concealed.

A ninety minute lunch break was announced, and everyone filed out in military style, eyes straight, foregoing the chitchat one would expect at a civilian conference. Valeriya blended in as best she could and went to find a distant restroom. She now understood Lawton's role in the project. The Ares worms made complicated decisions regarding which parts of the Russian code should be erased and where to put the secret modules. Lawton's doctoral dissertation on autonomous neural networks was tailor-made for what was happening.

Upon returning to the double doors (now propped open to accommodate heavy traffic), Valeriya observed kitchen staff wheeling carts of luscious-smelling food into the conservatory. She was finally going to have something to eat. Many people chatted outside, waiting for the tables to be set. Val took advantage of the social exchange by watching Lawton from a safe distance. His open-collar shirt and casual slacks set him apart from the rest. No wonder she mistook him for a janitor. Lawton appeared fit and trim with broad shoulders and moderately long hair. His shoes were interesting, different from the spit-shined footwear of the military participants, more like those of long-distance runners.

Valeriya ambled closer, approaching Lawton from behind. He conversed with a Naval Captain in fluent Spanish, apparently having a friendly dispute. Val couldn't follow the conversation, but it had something to do with General George S. Patton. Lawton had one commonality with his military friends—the nylon belt around his waist. *What does this mean? This guy is more precise than a Swiss watch. There must be a reason.* She moved near enough to touch him. *Aha. The leatherless belt goes with the leatherless shoes. That's why he went after her leather coat.* As Lawton turned to speak with another officer, almost enough to see her, Val slipped into the crowd, shuffling with them to the conservatory.

Various food entrées and nonalcoholic drinks were positioned on the conference tables, now covered with snowy-white linen. Valeriya gazed around the room, trying to choose the most inconspicuous location. She sat at the furthest table in the back row, last seat in the corner, under a handsome portrait of Alvin York. This gave her a good view of the room, and it would minimize the chance of idle conversation, talk that might be embarrassing due to her lack of knowledge about the secret project. Lawton stood at the front of the room, amiably chatting and being friendly.

Valeriya grabbed a plate and scooped out a generous helping of cheese lasagna from one of the heated trays. She added toasted garlic bread, sweetcorn, green beans, and selected a glass of unsweetened iced tea. With a watering mouth and growling tummy, she dug in, relishing the tasty food. There was real butter for the garlic bread, and the corn and beans were superb.

Lawton was still cornered by eager questioners, mostly guys and gals with thick nerdy glasses, semi-encircled and leaning towards him like adoring towers of Pisa. This was not the autistic boy described by Clarita Fernandez, nor a polished parody of a backwoods redneck. This was someone you wanted in command during a crisis, a man who had all the answers, and the monster who knew even more. Touching their shoulders in a fatherly gesture, he pulled free and approached the admiral, whispering something in her ear. The naval officer peered directly at Valeriya and then typed on a computer console. She and Lawton studied the monitor, heads down, whispering to each other, the admiral shaking her head.

Val gritted her teeth with the troubling thought that she might be discovered. She mentally kicked herself for not having a bailout strategy. She was legally there with the blessing of Margaret Marshall, but how would she respond to the coming barrage of questions? *Oh, shit. He's coming this way!*

Lawton meandered through the maze of tables, crisscrossing to avoid congested areas.

Valeriya crouched low in her chair, eyes down, hiding behind her hair, yet watching those foreboding shoes coming closer and closer.

I'm screwed. This is the way he wants to play it—direct confrontation. She gave herself an internal pep-talk. *Protect the mission—tell him nothing.*

Lawton stopped in front of her, rock steady, polished brass belt buckle shining in her face. "May I join you and Sergeant York, Ms. Jones?"

Val looked up, parting her disheveled hair with casual calm. "Of course." She somehow managed to smile. "Please be our guest."

Lawton loaded his plate, skipping the meat entrées and choosing the same food as her with spaghetti instead of lasagna. He sat down and unfolded a napkin, smiling with a sidelong flicker of pleasure.

Valeriya regarded him calmly, ready to play the game. "That was a fascinating presentation. You must be very good at what you do."

"Thank you. However, I have some serious misgivings. The cyber worm is becoming a cyber serpent, and I'm afraid it will turn and bite us. The underlying technology is now in the hands of hostile countries."

They conversed about the threat of computer terrorism and how it was spreading via the Internet. Lawton was sociable and pleasant company, a far cry from her expectations. Val relaxed, pretending to pick his debonair brain about the intricacies of cyber warfare, yet all the while maintaining her awareness of his fork and spoon. They were well into the meal when he surprised her.

"I will soon leave government service to work on my final project."

Her mind flooded with questions—dare she poke a sleeping Grizzly? "And what might that be?"

He forked some spaghetti into his mouth, thinking before answering and wiping away a diminutive yet indefinable smile. "I believe you already know."

She looked at him narrowly. "I assure you I don't."

"I'm an advocate for animal rights, and I will devote my remaining time to that cause."

"And why did you choose animal rights?"

"There have been at least three holocausts in North America, the first two being perpetrated against African-Americans and American

Indians. Our society is turning a blind eye to the third, the systematic torture and destruction of animals. Something needs to be done."

"Human catastrophes abound everywhere. Why not apply your efforts there?"

"That's a good point. There's far too much human misery in the world, but my chosen cause is clear—helping those who have no chance to help themselves. Our society treats animals as property, something to be exploited for profit or idle pleasure, irrespective of the pain and suffering inflicted upon them."

"Aristotle claimed the exploitation of animals by humans is only right because they lack reasoning ability."

Lawton inclined his head. "Aristotle also argued that women were inferior to men because they lack reasoning ability, but we both know that isn't true."

"Touché." Val regretted the gaffe, being outmaneuvered on her Greek idol. "But surely, you're not claiming that animal rights are comparable to the discrimination issues women and minorities have faced?"

"Why are they different?"

She lapsed into silent deliberation, seeing the need to answer with absolute precision.

"I'm not disagreeing with you," Lawton added. "Just tell me your reasons."

"Human suffering is different. It's deeper because people have elevated emotional levels. Our advanced intellect causes us to suffer in unique ways, beyond what animals are capable of."

Lawton took a spoonful of sweetcorn and nodded. "I agree. But you will concede that many animals experience joy and sadness, fear and anxiety, love for their young, and grief upon their separation or death. They have many of our emotions, and they certainly are capable of feeling physical pain."

"I suppose that's true."

"Then you must agree that needless suffering among sentient animals should be prevented whenever it is reasonably possible."

"Not at the cost of human lives."

"I said reasonably possible."

Valeriya nodded fractionally. "You did. You seem like such a reasonable man." She spread butter across her garlic bread. "Are you reasonable?"

"Not about some things."

She bit into the bread, relishing the savory blend of garlic and butter. "What things make you unreasonable?"

"That, for one, on your lower lip."

Val wiped a dangling dab of butter with her finger. "This?" She placed it on her tongue.

"It's part of the animal Holocaust."

"*Oh, please!* Are you claiming the American dairy industry is abusing cows? There would be rioting in the streets."

"That is exactly what I am saying."

Valeriya scoffed at him. Only yesterday she watched a dairy commercial with a girl hugging a lovable Jersey. "How are they being mistreated? Precisely how?"

"Today's dairy cows are pumped full of antibiotics and hormones to produce more milk. This places a heavy metabolic burden on the animals and increases stress and disease. The calves are taken away from their mothers when they are just one day old, and they are fed milk replacements that include cattle blood so the real milk can be sold to humans. The overwhelming majority of cows spend their entire lives tethered in little cubicles, unable to exercise." Lawton lowered his brow—veins bulged on his neck. "They spend their nights lying on concrete floors, slippery with urine and feces. Proper bedding material is sparse or nonexistent. Over eighty percent never know what real grass tastes like. Cows have a natural lifespan of twenty years, but dairy cows succumb to lameness or disease when they are four or five years old. Many of these 'farmers' have implemented the paradoxical procedure of restricting food to further increase milk production. Starving them also means higher corporate profits."

Val tried to look away, but Lawton's hypnotic gaze held her tight as the throttling tirade continued.

"Multiple ovulation embryo transfer is done to increase the calving rate, a painful procedure. They cut off over half of the tail without anesthesia, and the cows suffer from fly bites to the open wound. Semen to impregnate cows is gathered by inserting a device into the bull's rectum and delivering an excruciating electric shock. Dairy cows are milked like machines, irrespective of their inflamed mammary glands. And if mastitis curtails milk production, they are sent straight to the slaughterhouse to become hamburger meat. Female calves are kept alive to endure this long-term torment, but male calves are placed in solitary crates too small to permit them to turn around or sleep in a natural position. They are butchered after eighteen weeks and sold as veal. Can you imagine the horror that mother and child withstand in this continuous cycle of misery, both enduring never-ending pain and wretchedness?"

Valeriya sat in stunned silence, unsure of whether to believe him.

"Nothing to say, *Ms. Jones?*"

"There will always be a few rotten apples, but I can't imagine …" Words failed her. The idea was unthinkable.

"Rotten apples? Brutal treatment isn't the exception. It has become the industry norm." Lawton gestured to the heated meat trays. "As bad as dairy cows have it, life is worse for factory farm chickens and hogs."

An emergent thought came to her aid. Every state has animal welfare laws, and there are federal regulations to protect farm animals. He had to be lying.

"*Now, wait a minute. This is a bunch of vile crap!*" Her voice dripped with scathing acid. She leaned forward, scarcely able to withhold a hard slap to his face. "*You think you can finger-fuck me with these ungodly fabrications!*" People at the next table glanced her way. Valeriya grabbed a clean plate and proceeded to the heated trays. She scooped up a generous portion of pork roast and added a large chicken breast for good measure. She plunked back down and took a fresh napkin, snapping it open and placing it on her lap. She glared at Lawton, ashamed of her childish gullibility.

Lawton tapped his fingers together. "I seem to have fumbled the ball. My apologies."

She applied salt and pepper to the meat. "You should be sorry. Telling such macabre lies."

"My method of persuasion has failed, but I haven't lied to you."

Val devoured the pork, rolling her eyes. "You have more fairytales? Let me hear them."

"Maybe this isn't the right time."

"Nonsense. You say it gets worse? Tell me about the pigs and chickens."

He regarded her silently.

"I'm waiting." She ate more pork, licking her lips and pretending to enjoy the blood-rare flesh. There was method to her madness. He might become disgusted and walk away, leaving his eating utensils behind. She took another bite. "Come on, Charlie Brown. I'll hold the football, and you come running and kick it."

With rouged cheeks, Lawton settled into his chair, affability gone. "Factory farms have become legalized chambers of horror where over 100 million mammals and several billion birds are gruesomely mistreated and killed every year. Far more in other countries."

"That must be a gross exaggeration. There are laws. Federal inspectors oversee those places."

"The *Humane Slaughter Act* says nothing about the living conditions of factory farm animals. All it requires is for animals other than poultry to be rendered unconscious before being cut into pieces. The federal inspectors are at the other end of the slaughterhouse, checking the meat for any obvious signs of contamination. They don't witness the killing, or the all too frequently lack thereof, nor the dismemberment. And they don't inspect the living conditions of the animals, which are in many cases indescribably appalling. Factory farms are businesses designed to maximize company profits, saving a few dollars by creating meat as cheaply as possible. Traditional farmers would be appalled if they witnessed the gross abuse currently taking place."

Valeriya squirmed in her chair, still not believing. She forced herself to think of the mission and placed another slice of pork in her mouth, more determined than ever to drive him away. "There are trade-offs with everything. Making food less expensive for the economically disadvantaged is important."

"That's a laughable argument. The cost of meat protein is ten times higher than the equivalent nourishment from grains and vegetables, so you could feed ten times as many people, not to mention the trillions of dollars saved in healthcare costs for treating heart disease, diabetes, and obesity. Four percent of all greenhouse gases are attributable to the meatpacking industry, so there is much to be gained from its elimination."

Val switched to the chicken breast, hoping it would go down easier. Tiny beads of sweat appeared on her brow. "Every state has animal cruelty laws. I see people prosecuted all the time."

"Factory farms are exempt from animal cruelty laws in most states, and the enforcement of what laws exist is practically nil. There was even a case where a factory farm operator repeatedly killed sows by stringing them up alive, claiming this was the safest and most economical way to kill them. Animal welfare officers tried to intervene, showing video evidence of the hangings, but the local prosecutor refused to file charges."

Valeriya's fork slipped from her fingers, dropping to the floor and mercifully ending the self-immolation. "That can't possibly be true."

His icy-blue eyes bored into her. "You want proof? Do an internet search for the video, if you can stand the sight of it. Everything I've told you is available on websites like the Humane Society, ASPCA, or dozens of other charitable organizations—thousands of photos and video evidence of terrible suffering." With a disdainful sneer, Lawton glanced around the room. "But no one is looking. They're keeping their bellies full and heads buried in the mud. Commercial dairy farms are luxury hotels compared to what factory farm animals endure. The chicken you are eating lived her entire life in a wire cage so small that she couldn't even stretch her wings. Sometimes she wasn't given food or water for days because it extends the 'life' of egg-laying hens. The cages are stacked on top of one another, so she was covered with excrement and swarming flies."

Unable to think, Valeriya raised a trembling hand, but the onslaught continued, his razor tongue cutting her with every word.

"They chopped off the end of her beak without anesthesia so she couldn't peck the birds in cages beside her. She was hung upside down, alive and kicking on a motorized conveyor like some inanimate machine part in a fucking factory. She wasn't rendered unconscious when sliced open and disemboweled since the law doesn't require it. The male chicks, having no commercial value, were ground up alive or tossed into barrels to slowly suffocate. Factory farm hogs suffer similar mistreatment. The same confined spaces, lack of sanitation and proper bedding for sleeping, living shoulder to shoulder in what must be considered an absolute hell. Hogs have remarkable intelligence, at least as high as dogs, and yet they are being systematically tortured with the full blessing of the US government." His contemptuous eyes dropped to her plate. "While you're sitting there enjoying that 'delicacy,' there are tens of millions of animals trapped in small cages, suffering the tortures of the damned with no hope for anything but the mercy of death."

Scarcely able to breathe, Val instinctively reached across the table, lips parting in a silent sob.

Lawton dipped his finger in the red pork juice and glided it voluptuously across the back of her hand, painting the letter V. Hot pins slithered up her arm, across her shoulder and down her breasts, ensnaring her belly in a maelstrom of convulsive agony. Mustering all her self-control, Valeriya rose and maneuvered through the tables, pork blood dripping from her hand, urine trickling down her legs. No one noticed her misery aside from the hanging portraits, their eyes watching her every move. With orderly footfalls she continued toward the door, in ripe silence, not hurrying, maintaining her dignity. She nuzzled the door open, and when finally alone, dashed headlong into the restroom, banging the toilet door open and plunging to her knees. Everything came up, all she had eaten, and more. Groveling low with one arm clinging to the porcelain bowl, Val gasped for breath—not thinking, not feeling, just surviving.

The excruciating minutes seemed like hours, but Valeriya pulled herself off the soiled floor. *What a disaster! Beaten and trampled with fast-footed lies—emotionally raped by the devil himself.* Never in her life had she stumbled so badly. If Margaret Marshall could see her now … Val was physically frail, but the intense pain was gone. She gazed into the mirror. *There's only one way to redeem yourself. You must complete the mission!* Valeriya rinsed her underpants in the sink and wrung out the excess water. The evidence bag was still sealed tight, a necessity for going on. She got dressed and took an abysmal breath. With moral strength and supreme conviction, she marched back to the conservatory.

Lawton was sitting where he was, talking with an Air Force Colonel. Nearly everyone had finished eating, and military busboys were clearing the dishes. Valeriya picked up a tall glass of ice water and sat across from him, taking small sips and waiting. Lawton told the Colonel he would be at the Burns Institute through tomorrow evening. The officer nodded and departed. Lawton's wily blue eyes swung to her with a scintilla of glee. She expected a glow of competitive victory, yet he regarded her warmly.

He picked up a chocolate brownie. "Most people eat dairy or meat because they like the taste and switching to a vegetarian regime requires some modest effort, but there are wonderful alternatives. Fortified plant-derived milks taste just as good and provide all necessary nutrients without cholesterol. Supermarkets sell eggs from free-ranging chickens for just a little more money, and plant-based 'meat' is difficult to distinguish from the real thing. It's provides a healthier diet."

The busboys were three rows away, gradually working their way closer. Val sipped her ice water.

Lawton bit into the brownie. "If one is going to consume flesh, eating 'cultured meat' is a better choice because it's created in a laboratory and does not involve slaughtering innocent animals. A less desirable but still better alternative would be eating fish from the ocean since they lead normal lives before being killed. Eating meat from free-ranging cattle would be next, although many of them are terribly abused during slaughter."

He seemed so sincere, so believable, but so was Ted Bundy. Valeriya coughed and took a large drink. "If dairy cows and factory farm animals are being abused like you say, why is nothing being done to stop it?"

"Because people are just like you. They don't realize what's happening. There's more to this story, tales of what happens to rodeo animals, racehorses, and what they do to create 'cultured' pearls. But no one is paying attention." He placed the rest of the pastry in his mouth. "Someone needs to send them a wake-up call."

The admiral announced that the next session would begin shortly. Lawton stood up. "Please excuse me, but I'm needed up front. It's been delightful meeting you, Dr. Highland." He gave her a brazen wink and walked away.

Val snatched Lawton's fork and hid it in her lap, careful to touch only the handle. She acquired a clean paper napkin (middle of the pile) and rubbed the prongs to transfer any saliva remnants. The napkin slid easily into the evidence bag, flat and inconspicuous. She ambled toward the conservatory doorway, taking a lingering last look at Audie Murphy. She left the room, pausing to think, and then went to the coat rack. Val draped the leather trench coat over her arm and pushed through the double doors, knowing she could never wear it again.

Monica was busy at the front desk, talking to someone about a scheduling conflict. With shoes in one hand and her trench coat in the other, Valeriya crept into Monica's office. She draped the coat across a chair and snuck out the door. The body scanner was the next problem. The paper napkin might be flagged because the entry and exit images wouldn't match.

Still in an interior hallway, Val slid the evidence bag inside her underwear, folding the edges to match her pubic region. She rested there, still feeling lightheaded, still quarreling with her queasy stomach. *You must do this. Deep breaths—one—two—three—go!* Valeriya walked casually out and deposited her shoes in the x-ray machine. The attendant motioned her forward, and Val stepped into the body scanner, smiling at the woman who was about to see her naked. The attendant took a long look at the images, wrinkling her brow and pursing her lips, but she waved Valeriya through without any questions. Another staff member returned her firearm, purse, and cellphone. *Almost there—keep going.*

Val called for a cab and waited in the atrium, watching the falling rain. The temperature display at the bank had dropped to thirty-five degrees, cold enough to snow. The cab arrived, and she dashed through the drizzle and hopped inside. It was the same cabbie as before. She closed the door, telling him, "John Glenn Airport."

The ride back seemed longer, as though time itself had slowed. The automatic windshield wipers accelerated as the rain intensified, each distended droplet smacking the glass with hateful anger. The sky grew dark with black thunder clouds swirling low—the cabbie slowed the vehicle. Through the rain-peppered window glass the same herd of cattle could be seen scurrying into the trees, seeking what little protection there was. A rise in the road afforded a better view, confirming her earlier suspicions about the lack of shelter and available water. Several animals staggered sideways as though they were sick, and others were lying flat on the ground. *This is disgusting.*

Valeriya called the Humane Society, describing what she had seen and where. The officer told her someone would be out as soon as possible.

She hung up, pressing a hand to her gut. "Do you have something for an upset stomach?"

"No, madam. But I have cold ginger ale. It works for me."

"I'll give it a try."

The cabbie opened a cooler and passed her a bottle of Canada Dry. She twisted the cap and took several medicinal swallows, trying to think positively about what had happened. After all, she called the authorities. What more could she do? Yet, her discomfort grew with each passing mile, intensified by flashbacks to McKinley County and Tennessee, Kentucky and Youngstown, hearing the wavering words of Sheriffs Shank and Trimble, Tiny and Fernandez, Blackwell and Marshall, all talking at the same time. And then there was Lawton, his vivid images of animal torture parading across her mind. She gulped more ginger ale, asking for another bottle to squelch the growing fire. At her wit's end, Val picked up her cellphone. *I must know if it's true.*

Valeriya found the Internet awash with articles and photographs documenting the severe mistreatment of dairy cows and factory farm animals, countless examples of forlorn eyes trapped behind iron bars and in minuscule cages. The small screen on her phone yielded some protection from the ghastly images, partially hiding open sores and bleeding wounds. She found "Ag-Gag" legislation that made it illegal to report or document farm animal abuse. There were "Right to Farm" laws that limited the ability to regulate conditions on farms, including cruel confinement and the mistreatment of animals. The sources seemed like legitimate organizations. Val located the video of the hog farmer hanging sows. She watched it through to the end, biting her lip raw as the animals died a slow and gruesome death. Everything Lawton told her was true.

"You need to pull over."

The cabbie looked over his shoulder. "Madam?"

"I'm going to be sick."

The cab stopped, and Valeriya leaped out, stumbling across a trench and falling to her knees. She vomited a torrent of brown gunge, gasping for air between each purge. The cabbie came to her assistance, holding an umbrella over her until she was finished. She pressed her burning face into the muddy earth, releasing a gut-wrenching sob.

He lifted her by the arms and held her till she was stable. "I will take you to hospital."

"No. Just … Just get me back to the airport."

"You are ill. You must seek medical help."

Val slid her hand underneath her pants and pulled out the evidence bag. "This is all I need." The cabbie stared open-mouthed as she tore the bag open and ripped the paper napkin into confetti, tossing it high in the swirling wind. "I'll be all right now."

16 Postmortal Passion

His Bureau cellphone announced an incoming call, no doubt Valeriya reporting on the success of her secretive undertaking. Blackwell pulled into a gas station and turned off the engine, staring contemptuously at the caller ID: *RF Miller-Wittgenstein Police Department.* The phone continued ringing, and Mark continued thinking—answer or not? *That pernicious detective is calling my FBI number, guaranteeing a permanent recording of the conversation. Sit tight and wait—let him be transferred to voicemail.*

Blackwell continued to the DDI, intending to be there by noon. He arrived at the parking deck and pulled into a spot with the engine running. *Oh, hell. I'd better listen to the message.* He opened his phone and went through the complicated rigmarole of accessing his Bureau voicemail.

"Professor Blackwell, this is Sergeant Miller calling. There have been some troubling developments in the Candace Rowan murder investigation, and I need to speak with you at your earliest convenience."

Son of a bitch! This guy is a runaway train. Now there's a Bureau recording that makes me sound like a common criminal. Scratching his bushy sideburn, Mark mused over the situation. Not responding was a terrible choice and might bring in his FBI superiors.

After checking his other messages and emails to ensure there was nothing from Val, Blackwell called Sergeant Miller, purporting to be his helpful self. Following standard police procedures, Miller wouldn't say anything other than a face-to-face meeting was necessary. Mark suggested his Virginia residence (the most discreet place), and Miller agreed to meet him at 4 p.m. As much as he wanted to be in the DDI when Valeriya called, this recurring hindrance with Miller had to be eliminated once and for all. He placed his car in reverse and proceeded straight home.

* * *

Miller arrived a few minutes late, driving the same car but this time bringing a briefcase. He was alone, which was comforting news. If an arrest was going to be made, other officers would be there. Blackwell feigned gestures of welcome and attempted to lead Miller to the same easy chair, but the detective said he would rather sit at the dining room table. They sat opposite each other, Miller less affable than before, grim and aloof. Mark remained relaxed and confident. The detective couldn't have anything because there was nothing to be had.

Miller opened his briefcase. "I believe we're getting close, sir, close to solving the case."

"I am delighted. Please tell me how I can help. Did you find my missing key to the equipment room?"

"I did not. However, you gave us some good advice about checking Miss Rowan's credit card transactions." Miller gave Blackwell a cryptic cash register receipt. "Look at the third item, the one for $19.95. Do you know what that is?"

"How could I? It's just a bunch of numbers and a price."

"It's for a book, sir. This book." Miller held up a colorful paperback showing a title for expectant mothers.

Mark nodded. "Okay. She bought a book. Is that the actual copy?"

"No. We used her credit card statement to locate the store, getting a copy of the receipt and watching security footage of her buying the book. Do you see where this is going?"

"Not really. Are you suggesting the possibility that Miss Rowan was pregnant?"

"Yes, sir. It's more than a possibility."

"I don't wish to appear contrary, but there's a mistake in your reasoning. The book may well have been purchased as a gift for a friend."

"But we also have this, sir." Miller produced another receipt, this time from a drugstore. "Miss Rowan purchased a pregnancy test kit a week before buying the book. The same as this one." Miller pulled out a pink box from the briefcase. "You don't buy a pregnancy test kit for a friend. She purchased it for herself, which means she had reason to believe she might be pregnant."

"It's a plausible theory, but just a theory. As you told me before, there was no autopsy, and Miss Rowan's body has been cremated."

"You're right, sir. It's just a theory. But I believe most people would look at the timing of these separate events and conclude that Miss Rowan was probably pregnant."

Blackwell shrugged. "What of it? She was on a college campus, where lots of girls get 'probably pregnant.'"

"Captain Sheldon believes that was the motive for the murder. She calls this case 'Chappaquiddick without the stupid blunders.'"

"But that's absurd. You don't kill someone over an unwanted pregnancy. And what happened at the Dyke Bridge was an accident, nothing more."

Miller lowered his eyes and nodded. "An accident. Yes, sir. That was the conclusion of the Edgartown inquest." He regarded Blackwell again. "But Miss Rowan's case is different and quite unusual. You see, we believe she was having a secret affair. She was hush-hush with her friends and family about dating, but we know she was spending weekends with someone at the cottage in Pike County, Pennsylvania."

"How do you know? You said their cabin was secluded back in the hills."

"A neighbor woman was in the habit of walking her dog at night. She observed Miss Rowan arriving at the cottage on several occasions, with a companion, a man she could not describe because of the distance and poor lighting. We cross-checked the approximate dates, and Miss Rowan's family believed she was at her apartment in Boston and that the cottage was empty."

Mark shook his head. "You're forging a chain made with links of pretzel dough. Good police work must be based on provable facts that will hold up in court. Look at the holes in this case. No autopsy—body cremated—crime scene never secured, and now this hypothetical pregnancy. Any responsible judge would throw it out of court."

"We all gathered around the station one evening, asking ourselves why the need for secrecy? Miss Rowan wasn't married, wasn't engaged, didn't have a jealous boyfriend—or any boyfriend for that matter. She was perfectly entitled to date whomever she wanted—almost. We believe her Wittgenstein lover held a prestigious position, an endowed chair with a high salary and reduced teaching load. As you know, faculty are prohibited from dating current students, an offense punishable by termination whether tenured or not. Based on the available facts—"

"Not facts, speculative theories," Blackwell corrected.

Miller nodded grudgingly. "Based on what we believe may have happened, this professor got Miss Rowan pregnant. And, sharing the religious beliefs of her family, Miss Rowan refused to have an abortion. She wanted to get married, to start a family with the handsome man who swept her off her feet. She wanted him to keep his promises and fulfill his moral obligation. Had she not been his student—your student—for two consecutive semesters, you could have married her and retained your esteemed appointment. But her pregnancy was too far advanced for any razzle-dazzle—everyone would know what had happened. The moral turpitude scandal would break you, leaving you jobless and permanently unemployable at any reputable university. When you couldn't change her mind about terminating the pregnancy, you had to make a choice. You could have this beautiful and talented woman, the loving mother of your future child, or you could maintain your easy lifestyle, but not both. *Not both!*" Miller leaned back in his chair. "You chose wrong. A man with your intellect could have started over and found a different career."

Mark let out a gregarious laugh, not revealing the slightest tinge of annoyance.

"This isn't funny. A woman has been murdered."

"I wasn't laughing at her death. I was cackling at this ridiculous accusation. Have you told Captain Sheldon I wasn't in the building when Miss Rowan died, that the security camera footage would prove I wasn't there?"

"There's a serious problem with your alibi. The security video does confirm you left the building and did not return through the regular doorways. But you could have reentered through the fire escape stairwell."

"We discussed that before. And it wasn't possible because the fire escape doors will let people out, but not in. There is also the matter of the fire alarm that would be triggered when someone entered the stairwell."

"The fire alarm is activated when someone opens the door by pushing the handle. But you can open the door without setting off the buzzer by sliding a thin object, such as a letter opener, into the lock and depressing the plunger. All you had to do was tape the plunger back, and you could enter or exit the stairwell. You then taped the plunger at the bottom of the stairwell so the door could be opened from the outside. With the top and bottom doors rigged, you could leave the building in front of the security cameras to create your phony alibi and come back after dark, using a magnet to pull open the door to the stairwell. Our forensics technician found traces of tape adhesive on the doors, proving the locks were jimmied. I found a roll of tape hidden behind some books when I was in your office looking for the missing key. The magnet you used to open the fire escape door was attached to the underside of one of your filing cabinet drawers."

Blackwell bolted upright. "Tape? A magnet? In my office?"

Miller nodded. "The adhesive residue from the tape is identical to what we found on the fire escape doors. And the magnet base had microscopic scrapings of paint that matched the paint of the exterior door."

His perfect alibi was gone. Mark could almost hear the click of Miller's handcuffs clamping around his wrists. "This is preposterous! The tape and magnet had to be planted to incriminate me with false evidence."

"The fingerprints on the magnet were too smudged to be read." Miller raised a jovial finger. "However, your fingerprints are on the roll of tape, plain as day."

Blackwell's mind raced with unpleasant possibilities. He had helped Candy package some books two days before she killed herself, sealing the boxes with tape. And Candy was in his office the following day, briefly alone while he went to pick up some exams.

"As you already know," Miller continued, "that was supposed to be a night of celebration, Miss Rowan believing you agreed to marry her. The family cottage was unavailable since her parents were entertaining friends. Miss Rowan willingly accompanied you to the roof of Bradley Hall for the romantic spectacle of making love under the stars. You struck her with something, rendering her unconscious, and then you threw her off the building. You couldn't wear gloves because Miss Rowan might become suspicious. So you wiped away the fingerprints on the door leading to the roof. Then you made your getaway down the fire escape, pulling off the tape as you left. If you had disposed of the tape and magnet, you might have committed the perfect murder."

Mark calmly regarded Miller. "Am I under arrest?"

"Not yet, *sir!*"

"I'm sure you know the basic criminological principles of means, motive, and opportunity. You cannot get a conviction without them. Now, which of those three essential items is missing?"

"They are all there."

There was no alternative. Blackwell would have to ask the question he swore he would never ask, knowing his freedom rested on the answer. "Do you have any evidence that Miss Rowan and I were having an affair?"

Miller's facial features hardened.

"And what does that tell you?" Mark asked.

Silence.

"You didn't find any evidence because it does not exist. Miss Rowan and I were never romantically involved."

"There's an old saying, professor. 'The night has a thousand eyes.' I'm going to keep looking, as long as it takes. Someplace, somewhere, someone saw something." Miller derisively closed his briefcase and rose. "You'll be seeing me again."

Mark followed him to the door. He tried to shake Miller's hand, but the officer walked by. "One day you will come back and apologize, Bob, when you find out what actually happened."

Blackwell locked the door. He waited until Miller's car turned the corner and poured himself a stiff brandy—liquid courage to face a cold reality. *Candy tried to frame me!* She had taken his earlier course on forensic science and was using that information against him. This explains the meaning of the number three on her sketch of the tombstone—Candy, her fetus, and him. The clever girl knew he would destroy her suicide note, making him an accomplice to his own destruction. She had, however, made a miscalculation, believing his missing key, the roll of masking tape, and the magnet would be sufficient. They weren't. Mark knew that, and so did Miller. The police would need to find evidence that he and Candy were having an affair, and that, thanks to his careful precautions, simply did not exist. The brandy kicked in. *I am safe.*

17 Disco Inferno

Blackwell arrived at the DDI by noon the following day. Richard stood near the open doorway to Valeriya's office, hands on hips, watching with interest.

Mark approached, peering over Richard's shoulder. "What's going on?"

"They're installing some new equipment. Looks like there's still a lot to do."

"Where's Val? She wouldn't allow strangers to be poking around her office without being there."

"She knows these guys. In fact, she had them start yesterday because she knew she would be out of town."

"But where is she?"

Richard gave a puzzled shrug. "I thought she would be back today."

Blackwell went to his office and called Sandy Hook Regional Airport, identifying himself as FBI and asking whether Valeriya Highland's plane had returned from Columbus. The tower supervisor said she arrived yesterday evening around 7 p.m. Mark thanked him for the information and punched in Val's home number. The phone rang and rang, suggesting her answering machine was turned off. He was about to hang up when a bedraggled voice groaned out, "Hello?"

"Val?"

"Yeah," she replied with a long yawn. "What time is it?"

"Almost one. Are you sick?"

"No. Just catching up on some sleep."

After considerable hemming and hawing from her, pleading and begging from him, he enticed her into a late lunch. She agreed to meet him at Rabourn's Restaurant in two hours.

* * *

Mark arrived on time and was seated with a complimentary pot of coffee. The minutes ticked by: ten, twenty, thirty. He finally glimpsed the distinctive walk of the woman he wanted, the one that really mattered. Valeriya approached, appearing less than her usual sunny self. Blackwell adjusted his eyeglasses, trying not to stare. She bent forward to slide into the booth, wearing a V-neck blouse that practically advertised the burn scars on her neck and chest.

Stunned into carefulness, he gave her a priestly smile. "No turtleneck today?" The question didn't seem to register. She appeared remote and raggedy, terribly wan with dark circles under her eyes, lower lip swollen like she had been in a fight. He poured coffee for two. "Are you sure you're feeling okay? You look ..." He couldn't say it without offending her.

"Everyone should see me as I am."

"Which is brilliant and charming, beguiling and exceedingly good company."

She ignored his compliment, seemingly lost in a cloud of abject gloom.

"What happened to your mouth?"

Val rolled her wistful eyes. "I ran into a brick wall."

"Be serious. Did Lawton do that? Did he hit you?"

"No. I just had a horrible day."

"Tell me about it."

"I'm not sure I can. I don't ..." She shook her head.

Blackwell took a sip of coffee, hiding his frustration. "Val, tell me what happened."

"I failed horribly, bombing in the worst imaginable way."

"I take it you didn't bring back the DNA sample?"

"Obviously!"

"Was Lawton there? Did you make an attempt?"

"I saw him. And I tried, but I couldn't do it."

Mark reassuringly patted her hand. "Police work is always a crapshoot. However, I'm quite sure you gave it your all, and that is a moral victory."

"Moral." She gazed down at the table. "I don't know the meaning of that word, not anymore."

"What about Lawton? I know you didn't get close to him, but what was he like?"

"Different. Not what I imagined." Her swollen lip quivered like jiggling Jell-O. "We should change the subject."

A smilingly plump waitress approached with pen and notepad in hand. Blackwell ordered barbecued spareribs with a baked potato and a wedge of apple pie for dessert. Valeriya ordered without looking at the menu: a double-helping of oatmeal with fresh blueberries.

Mark picked up one of the free chocolate-chip cookies, extra-large and freshly baked. "I noticed men working in your office today." He offered her a cookie—she declined. "They were installing something against the wall."

"It's a new interface to the DDI mainframe, provides faster searches when looking for specific images in video files."

They talked about the new technology until the waitress brought their food. The generous plate of spareribs appeared dark and delectable with the aroma of hot-off-the-grill freshness. As soon as the waitress placed the oatmeal in front of Valeriya, she began wolfing it down.

Blackwell unfolded his napkin, marveling that she preferred gooey wallpaper paste to genuine food. "Must be damn-good oatmeal."

"I didn't eat yesterday."

"Not at all?"

"Nothing that stayed down."

"Well, that explains everything. You can't work with an upset stomach."

For some inexplicable reason, Val ate her entire meal while gazing out the window. She talked at him rather than to him, maintaining her fixation on the boring parking lot. Her color and mood improved with the food, and Val started behaving like her old self. She picked up the check, leaving a huge tip. They departed together, agreeing to meet again at the DDI.

* * *

Richard greeted them when they arrived, not saying anything about Valeriya's unusual appearance. She stepped inside her office, conversing about having to relocate her glass display case. There was still work to do, and Val suggested they wait in Mark's office until the final hookups were done. He agreed, of course, eager to be alone with Val.

Valeriya approached his modest workstation. "Let me use your computer. I want to check the latest news."

Blackwell typed in his PIN, whereupon the computer flashed *Password Incorrect*. He lifted his desk calendar to read the pain-in-the-ass frustration, typing it again and still getting it wrong.

Val pulled him out of the chair. "If you miscue again, NSA will terminate the connection, and you will have to go through tons of red tape to get it back." She seated herself, gave the password a skimming glance, and with fluttering fingers entered the long combination of numerals, upper and lowercase letters, and mathematical symbols.

He pulled up a chair and sat beside her, grumbling, "I don't see why they make those so difficult."

She adjusted the height of the chair and slipped out of her shoes, a clear sign of recovery. Usually she wore socks, but not today. The monitor flashed a series of cryptic matrices and documents.

"Has anything happened?" Mark asked, hoping the answer was "no" so she would pay attention to him.

"Doesn't look like it. No new deaths of animal abusers." She scooted closer, fidgeting with the ill-fitting chair, tucking one bare foot under her leg. "This is strange."

Blackwell perked up, reading a headline about a recent communal beheading in Iran. "That's normal over there. Public executions are part of their culture."

"But I know this guy. He was a visiting professor of computer science when I was getting my doctorate at Michigan. He presented a research paper at our colloquium, and several Ph.D. students, myself included, went to dinner with him afterward." A somber expression fluttered across her face as she continued reading. "It doesn't say why he was killed."

Richard announced over the intercom that Valeriya's office was ready. She thanked him and continued searching for information about the dead professor.

The computer emitted a shrill double chirp, and a red banner flashed across the screen: *Encrypted Video Call.*

Val pushed herself back. "Who the hell is this?"

Mark let out a groan of revulsion. "It has to be Margaret Marshall. She sent me an email wanting an update on my research activities, and I forgot to respond."

Valeriya moved away from the monitor camera. "Don't tell her I'm here. I don't want her to see me like this."

After swiftly fabricating a believable response, Blackwell sat down at the terminal and pressed the red button. To his surprise, the bulldog face of CIA Director Anthony Naples appeared.

"Blackwell," Naples snarled. "Where are you?"

Silence.

Naples tapped his microphone. "I can see you. Can you hear me?"

"I hear you, sir. I'm in my office."

"Well, where is it? I've been waiting seven goddamn months."

"Where is what?"

"Your psychiatric evaluation of Valeriya Highland."

Still keeping out of Naples' view, Val crept closer, arms folded across her chest.

Mark cleared his throat. "Er … That assignment was canceled, sir."

Naples' bushy caterpillar brows climbed his bald noggin. "Canceled? No way! On whose authority?"

"FBI Director Margaret Marshall rescinded it last March."

"Vaffanculo!" Naples slammed the top of his desk, his jowls quivering. "That fuzzy-hair has no control over the CIA. I signed that order myself. It's goddamn important, critical to the security of our Nation. Do you realize what's at stake here?"

"Sir, I'm just—"

"That communist cunt has gained the highest security clearance possible, access to everything but the nuclear launch codes." Naples leaned forward, his cheeks and voice quaking. "Highland is a Russian mole, a Mata Hari spreading her legs for our defense secrets."

Silence.

"You have been working with her as instructed, right? Undercover? The way we arranged?"

Mark answered before thinking. "Yes, sir, but—"

"No buts. I want her out. Understand? O-U-T! Now write your report and get it to me this week, without fail. And I hope you're smart enough to read between the lines on what I'm telling you." Naples smacked his keyboard, ending the call.

Valeriya bolted out of the room like a slapped child.

"Val, wait."

Blackwell hurried after her, racing down the hall while calling her name, seeing nothing but wind-borne hair and bouncing bare feet. Fortunately, Richard was on break. Valeriya slapped her palm to the scanner, and the heavy door rolled back. She darted inside, but he caught the edge of the closing door before the lockers activated. He shoved it back and entered.

"Val, just hear me out."

She whirled on her heel and faced him, cheeks aflame, hair awry. "Anthony Naples? All this time you've been working for that bastard!"

"Will you calm down and let me explain?"

She stood there, dripping with mule-tempered anger. Then she rounded her workstation, heading for the comfortable chairs, watching him with a cynical eye.

Mark approached her, hands extended.

She pulled away, shouting, "Don't touch me!"

They sat across from each other like they had done many times before. He peeked dolefully into the kitchenette. "I could use some coffee."

"Not a chance. If you have something to confess, say it and leave."

"Can Richard or anyone else hear us? Is this a private conversation?"

"You know better. Eavesdropping devices are prohibited in the DDI, and this room is soundproof."

Blackwell collected his jittery thoughts. "It's true. My initial assignment came from Anthony Naples. He directed me to perform a psychological evaluation of you—*for security purposes only!* But Margaret Marshall canceled that task. You were there when it happened. It was at the meeting last March when she revoked all our prior assignments."

"Then why the fuck didn't you tell me before now? Why keep it a secret?"

"I considered telling you several times, but I thought it would damage our relationship."

"Relationship—shit! You can't have a relationship without trust." She gestured toward Blackwell's office. "Then why is Naples still demanding your phony Freudian fuckery?"

Mark raised his hand like he was taking a solemn oath. "I swear to you, I have no idea. I have always been loyal to you, always looking out for your best interest. I would do anything for you, anything at all. I know I handled this wrong, and I apologize. I should've told you, and I didn't."

She looked down, twitching her nose. "Apology accepted. You may leave."

Her eyes were still injured. He needed to say more. "Let's get out of this awful place. We'll go back to my office and get your shoes, and we can go somewhere where I can mentally unwind and tell you everything that happened."

"I have another pair of shoes under the bed, and I've had all I can stand in one day. Just go."

Their heads turned in unison to a pleasant ping. The large monitor on the wall sprang to life, showing a new email. Blackwell rose from his chair, pushing his eyeglasses up his nose—the sender was Roy Lawton. He regarded Valeriya. "Am I seeing this right? Roy Lawton—sending you an email?"

She stood up, creeping forward with slumped shoulders. "I guess so."

"The subject line says, *Per our Previous Conversation*. You spoke to him, to Lawton himself?"

Silence.

"Val, did you talk to Lawton or not?"

Blackwell followed her to the workstation. She opened the email, which said *See attached file*. The attachment was named *Video for Valeriya*. She typed a query, asking the machine to analyze the file. The monitor answered:

High Definition Video. Threat-Level 0.

Mark looked at her. "What the hell is it?"

She thought for a bit, rolling a wisp of hair between her thumb and forefinger. "It's a film showing a hog farmer stringing up live sows."

"What?" He shook his head. "Someone hanging pigs? Why would Lawton send you such a ridiculous thing?"

"We talked about it over lunch." Val turned to him. "Would you like to see it? I'll put it up on the big screen. Might give you something to think about the next time you're cramming your maw with pork."

Blackwell hesitated, glancing between the large monitor and her witch's grin. "Yeah, sure. Play it."

Valeriya positioned herself in the chair as though something significant was about to happen, eyes firm, face grim. She pressed a key, and vivacious music filled the room, the kind that brought tired feet back to life. Blackwell recognized the old '70s song—*Disco Inferno, Burn Baby Burn*. A gorgeous Latino model, red rose in hair, strutted across a stage, frolicking and dancing a fabulous rumba.

Mark snorted out a chuckle. "This is a joke. He's making fun of you. Either that, or he sent you the wrong file."

Valeriya rose from her chair and rounded the workstation, staring at the big screen. The bikini-clad model flashed her ravishing body as she opened and closed a leather garment—high-stepping, breasts bouncing, and hips swaying. The big monitor made her larger-than-life, realer than if she was dancing in the room. She allowed the full-length coat to hang like a matador's cape and fought an imaginary bull, bobbing and weaving, twirling and swinging in perfect time with the music. She came closer, flaunting and manipulating the luxurious leather as though it was silk spun on the looms of the gods.

Blackwell scrutinized the distinctive lapels. He gazed back at Val. "Isn't that your trench coat?"

With shuddered breath and widening eyes, Valeriya crept backward. Mark whirled around, not seeing the cause of her alarm. The beautiful model was dancing her best routine.

The twirling girl faded away, and the video transitioned to a strange setting, a place difficult to define. Blackwell discerned a pregnant horse under heavy restraint and confined to a miniscule stall. A man with an enormous syringe injected something into the animal, calling to someone in Spanish. A male narrator, someone not in the video and speaking American English, described what was happening as a forced miscarriage to abort the unborn pony. The mother horse moaned, and a moving fetus—still in the fetal sac—dropped to the floor. With head and legs thrashing, they hoisted the baby pony upside down. Another man approached with a long knife. He placed the serrated blade against the pony's throat.

"Oh, Jesus!" Valeriya shrieked. She dashed back to the workstation and smacked the keyboard, stopping the offensive film. She tried to sit down but missed the chair, landing flat on her rump.

Mark pulled her up and held her steady. "Val, it isn't real. It's only a movie." Her face was panicked, eyes bulging and unable to blink. "Was that Lawton doing the narration?"

She gave a barely perceptible nod and grabbed her stomach. Valeriya coughed once, and a volcanic torrent of bluish vomit erupted from her mouth and nose. She staggered to the bathroom, extending her blouse to catch another upsurge. She slipped and fell on the tile floor, crawling on her hands and knees. Blackwell lifted her to the commode, where she continued heaving large amounts of partially digested oatmeal. She gasped for breath between puking sessions, coughing and spluttering globules of bile until there was nothing but dry heaves. Panting and covered with sticky vomit, she rested on the floor.

Mark stooped over her. "Should I call for help?"

"No," she wheezed. "Just get me into the shower."

He steadied her while she shed her dirty clothes and guided her through the shower door. He grabbed several towels and cleaned the bathroom, mopping up vomit and crud. He went back and cleaned places where she soiled the carpet. The shower door squeaked open.

He scurried back and delivered a clean towel. "I did the best I could. But the place will need a proper cleaning."

"Thank you. The carpet needs shampooing anyway."

Val put on a terrycloth robe and limped out of the bathroom, making her way to one of the reclining chairs. She adjusted her robe so it would cover the leather surface.

"How do you feel?" Blackwell asked.

She passed a hand through her wet hair without saying anything.

"The film is a fake. You are being conned."

"He wouldn't do that, not about this."

"You must tell me what happened between you and Lawton."

She reclined the chair and closed her eyes. "I'm too disgusted to talk."

Mark instinctively knelt and took her foot, massaging the arch and heel. She made no objection, and he settled into a rhythm, rotating the ball and flexing the metatarsals, gently pulling and popping each toe. Her breathing slowed to a child-like rhythm, as though she might fall asleep. He progressed to the other foot, applying the same technique. She became calm, eyes still closed, melting into the chair. He alternated between feet, applying deeper pressure, firm but not hard, top and bottom, thoroughly probing her flesh.

"What are you thinking?" he asked.

Her eyes stayed closed. "I see my mother running down concrete stairs in her bare feet."

"Going shoeless seems to run in your family." Each of his fingers found a metatarsal groove, steadily moving back and forth.

"She abandoned her high heels to keep up with my father, who was carrying me down as fast as he could."

"How old were you?"

"Five."

"Where was he going in such a hurry?"

Her voice slowed to a dream-like crawl. "I didn't know, but I was frightened. The elevators didn't work, so we descended the emergency staircase, going down and down for a long time. We were close to the bottom when the building began shaking. My father tucked me under the concrete stairs, way back in a corner. Everything started collapsing, and I curled up into a ball. When the shaking stopped, I was pinned in a small place. The dust was terrible, and breathing was difficult. I couldn't get out or even turn around. I called for Mom and Dad, but all I heard was the wail of emergency sirens. Scalding liquid came trickling over me, not fast, but steady. I screamed until I lost consciousness."

"I'm sorry. Why did you think of that now?"

Valeriya opened her eyes and pulled her feet from his hands. "That was a pivot point in my life, just like today."

"You were wearing shoes. I guess that's why your feet are unscarred."

She nodded. "It's time for you to go."

"With you in this condition? Let me at least take you home and get you settled."

With calm resolve, Val planted her feet on the floor and rose. "I need some time to relax, and that means being alone." She laid her hands upon him, tugboating him toward the door. "I'll call you when I'm feeling better."

Mark kissed her on the cheek and left.

* * *

After a brief hesitation, Valeriya returned to her workstation. She rewound the video and clicked the play icon. She allowed her robe to fall away and returned to the leather chair, lying supine with arms and legs parted. With tear-filled eyes she watched, listening to fetal gasps and gurgling squeals. Cherry-red blood geysered aloft, spurting higher as the knife cut deeper into the arteries. The mother bellowed and kicked the side of the stall. Other men approached, skinners with smaller blades. They began peeling the hide from the still moving pony. In the dignified tone of a British butler, Lawton explained that fetal horsehide made the trench coat exceptionally soft, creating a truly unique product for well-bred ladies who demand the most exquisite attire from their couturières. Only select portions of the hide are used, and three pony fetuses are required to make one full-length coat. The travesty went on, showing close-ups of the skinning process and describing the patience and surgical skill needed to remove the delicate hide without damaging the valuable outer surface. Without a trace of sarcasm, Lawton commended the efficiency of the operation, saying they would breed the mother again as soon as possible. His choice of words and calm delivery were exceedingly effective, sending curls of horror and mind-ripping hysteria throughout Val's naked flesh. He knew how to pull her down, how to make her bleed, how to slowly apply his vocal branding iron. The film ended, and Valeriya closed her eyes. *I am destroyed.*

* * *

Val had an ugly cry. She ambled nude around the room, ignoring the artifacts she once held so dear. Unending nightmares would be lurking, waiting and watching, watching and waiting—*unless?* She glanced up at the clock: 7 p.m. Her pulse quickened. *He might still be there!*

She washed her face and put on a turtleneck sweater. She grabbed Lawton's journal and went to her workstation. The book had a unique logic proof, one that Lawton had finished in the margins with arrows and distinctive markings. She dimmed the overhead lights to hide her compromised appearance and typed her US Cyber Command password, entering the Dark Channel. By Presidential order, the clandestine activities of Cyber Command did not exist. The DC provided a means for communication between operatives that could not be intercepted, and no recordings were made. Valeriya typed Lawton's security badge number and pressed enter.

Roy Lawton's face appeared on the monitor, left eyebrow arching high. "Valeriya? How delightful. I thought you might be angry with me." Lawton's smirk broadened into a playful grin. "And you're using the DC as well. Are we at war with Russia, or just each other?"

"I plead guilty, six times over."

"Six times?"

"I bought two coats, and you said each one takes three ponies."

"What a pity. But I admire your honesty."

"I want to see you."

Lawton swiveled in his chair, raising his palms. "Here I am."

"No. I need to meet you face-to-face, someplace private where we can talk."

"This is as private as it gets. No one can see or hear us, providing you are alone."

"I have something that belongs to you." She opened his journal to the page with the fancy logic proof and held it steady in front of the camera.

His eyes narrowed with interest. "My, my. Where did you find that?"

"At the sheriff's property recovery facility, a few miles from your Kentucky home."

"You've been a busy girl." He regarded her with confusion. "Your voice sounds different. Why are you sitting in the dark?"

"Do you want the journal? Because even if you don't, I still need to see you. It's important."

Lawton consulted a notebook. "I'll be in Washington in two weeks. We could—"

Val slammed the book closed. *"It can't wait!"*

His face became serious. "All right, when?"

"Tomorrow would be ideal, if you can make it."

"Where?"

"Are you familiar with Mill Creek Park in Youngstown?" She had several alternatives, but this was the best.

He nodded assent. "I once lived in Youngstown, as you no doubt already know."

"Can you be at the suspension bridge at 2 p.m.?"

He pondered her question.

"There is a reason," Valeriya added. "You'll understand when I see you."

"I will be there. Is there anything else? I have a meeting to attend."

"Tell no one, and don't drive your truck to Youngstown."

Lawton's smirk returned. "I'll see you tomorrow." He disconnected.

Val finished dressing and left the DDI, intending to make preparations for tomorrow's journey.

18 Deliverance

Valeriya pulled into the Lily Pond parking lot, the same place her school bus had parked many years ago. Handsome painted turtles with heads raised high sunned themselves on leaning logs while youngsters tossed bread and biscuits to Mallard ducks and Canada geese. Several people took photographs or movies with their cellphones. There were closer places to the suspension bridge, but she wanted to retrace the historic journey. With sunglasses on and hefty hair covering most of her face, she snatched Lawton's journal and zigzagged down to the creek, avoiding cameras, following the same path her eighth-grade class had taken, many of them wearing the football logo of the Massillon Tigers. She took her time, strolling along and watching chipmunks play amid the fallen hardwood leaves. She paused at the tallest pine tree, remembering a secret wish that had sadly vanished with the passing years. The air was crisp, a poignant reminder of the time her mother took her trick-or-treating on a blustery Halloween night.

Valeriya stopped at the waterfall, listening and watching, clearing her mind of every unpleasant thought. She had the sudden urge to stay within the boundaries of nature, to forget about her job and troubles. But alas, this wasn't possible. She continued along what was now called the Artists' Trail, eventually emerging at the Pioneer Pavilion. This was a place where picnics and family reunions were held, and a small gathering was taking place. She veered left to the lake, following the West Cohasset Trail. The calm water formed a mirror that reflected the colorful foliage, a riot of russet and red, creating a voluptuous vista that simply begged to be painted in oils. She came upon a pair of young lovers, hand in hand, ambling leisurely ahead of her. The boy unexpectedly grabbed the girl and wrestled her to the ground. Laughing and squealing, she offered fake resistance, clearly loving the amorous moment as they tussled like puppies in a basket of clothes. A steady stream of scarlet maple leaves fluttered down from above. They ceased "hostilities," melting into each other's arms, eyes closed, kissing deeply and savoring what had to be the most romantic moment imaginable. Valeriya crept silently by.

She arrived at the suspension bridge at 1:58 p.m. and wandered onto the walkway. A group of teenage boys played football in a nearby field, and a woman walked her German Shepherd among the colorful trees, but there was no sign of Lawton. She turned little by little, perusing the scenery, sun, and shadows, eventually spotting someone perched atop a gray boulder on the west side. He wasn't there before. The figure wore blue jeans and a dark sweatshirt with an attached hood covering his head. *Is that him?* He hopped off the rock and gave a small wave, pulling back his hood. The winsome farm boy grin was unmistakable. Valeriya smoothed back her hair and went to meet him, heartbeat quickening with each approaching step.

"I didn't recognize you with those sunglasses," Lawton called. His self-assured smile faded as she drew near. "What happened to your lip?"

"I bumped into something. I'm kind of a klutz."

With his lips curving skyward, Lawton focused on her new shoes. He placed his foot beside hers—identical except for shoe size. He eyed the nylon belt around her waist—same as his. "I have the impression you're trying to tell me something. Or is this just a black widow's web?"

Val thrust the journal into his hands. "It's in mint condition."

Lawton passed through the pages. "This brings back a lot of memories. It was the beginning, Volume One."

"There's more?"

"I wrote a follow-up analysis using the philosophy of Martin Heidegger, but the first volume contains the fundamental ideas." He looked up from the book. "What did you think of it?"

"It's hard for me to warm up to Friedrich Nietzsche, but your ideas on Preemption were on the mark."

"Ah, but you only see the shell of what Nietzsche would have been if his health hadn't failed. Nietzsche and Heidegger are the two most misunderstood men in history, geniuses of their time. Did you understand what I was saying?"

"Part of it," Valeriya replied. "It's a lot to grasp. Can you give me a summary in simple words, something the average person could understand?"

He pondered her request, apparently trying to collate and condense 400 pages of Nietzschean intricacy. "You're an aviator. What do you think of Amelia Earhart?"

"She was an early feminist, a champion of women's rights. I like her a lot."

"But what was she all about?"

Val pondered the puzzling question. "Social equality of the sexes, I guess. Righting the wrongs of her time."

Lawton's cheeks plumped up. "Excellent. 'Righting the wrongs of her time.' And what was her method?"

"She showed what women could do, refusing to accept the role men had forced upon them."

"True, but what was her core, the essence of her being?"

After some intense but unsuccessful cerebration, Valeriya shook her head.

"Amelia was a doer of great and difficult things. She went beyond the acceptable, always thinking the unimaginable, like falling snow in the Amazon or what it would be like to visit the dark side of the moon. She took risks that created a far-reaching imbalance in our social order, a role model for those who dare."

Val nodded. "But she was quite lucky to have had the opportunity to make a difference."

"You create opportunities, sometimes molding irrational ideas to make something from nothing. What you do determines who you are."

"There has to be a door. You can't walk through a brick wall."

"Heidegger said we are hurled into this world, unable to choose neither our parents, our natural gifts, nor the time of our existence. He talked about being authentic, discovering and following your own unique possibilities based on where you are in history. Amelia was dripping with authenticity. She shunned the routine and conventional, not hiding from her true potential, as many couch potatoes do today. Amelia would go around a wall, over a wall, or under a wall. And if that didn't work, she would smash her Lockheed Electra into the wall—which she did. Winning isn't defined by 'success.' Victory is achieved by giving your best effort to achieve your own authenticity, whatever that might be. Amelia followed her highest and most noble destiny, achieving her full potential. She lived a life worth living."

"That is interesting, something worthy of deep reflection." Valeriya stood upright, inhaling to face the coming task. *This will not be easy, descending from doubting Thomas to Judas.* "There's something I want to tell you. It's complicated, and I need to get into it gradually. Will you walk with me?"

Lawton elevated an appraising brow and looked around suspiciously. He must have suspected a trap.

Val raised her arms and rotated, revealing her skin-tight sweater and jeans. "I mean you no harm. You can frisk me for weapons or recording devices." She unbuckled her nylon belt. "I'll strip behind that boulder if you want."

His color reddened as though she had embarrassed him. "That won't be necessary. Lead the way."

Valeriya ambled back the way she came, staying off the road but keeping it in sight. Lawton's attentive gaze constantly searched the trees. He glided easily beside her, like a light-footed Indian wearing soft-soled moccasins. Val could hear her own footfalls, but not his. He stepped around twigs and debris as if making a sound was considered a mortal sin.

"Where did you park?" she asked. "You didn't drive your Ram pickup, did you?"

"Close to Lanterman's Mill. I drove something else."

"So no one knows you're here?"

"No one except you."

"Your animal rights project. Tell me about it. Do you want everyone to become vegetarians and wear synthetic shoes and belts like us?"

A disdainful frown tugged at his lips. "Us? You put on a pair of leatherless shoes and a nylon belt, and I'm supposed to trust you?"

She smiled up at him. "No. I don't expect you to trust me." They continued onward.

"Converting everyone into vegans isn't a practical goal, at least not at this time. It runs contrary to our history and social conditioning, what people were taught and how they were raised. If your father took you to bullfights or into the fields to blow birds apart with a shotgun, you'll believe such activities are normal, even enjoyable. That's what's holding us back. We believe what we were taught in our youth, and we adopt the culture of our family, even when that culture is flawed. Nietzsche pointed out that mental conditioning in our youth becomes a barrier, a psychological roadblock that restrains us from seeing better possibilities." He stopped to admire the view of the lake. "My wife would love these woods. She adores the hues of fall, which are richer in Ohio."

"You should take her around the Cohasset Trail. It's the best way to see the colors." They continued on. "How did all this start? I mean, how did you come to believe what you believe?"

"I'd have to give credit to Nietzsche and Heidegger. They got me thinking on a different level. And there are other thoughts and things."

"What thoughts and things?" Valeriya asked, wondering how far he would go.

"Superior race and superior gender and superior species are all branches from the same unforgiving tree. We have made some inroads in addressing race and gender, but we are still grunting Neanderthals when recognizing the rights of other species. What I find most offensive is when civil rights activists mistreat women or when devout feminists become outraged when speciesism is compared to sexism. These hypocrites are the essence of what they profess to be fighting."

"That is *not* what you find *most* offensive!"

Lawton smiled down at her. "Touché." He grabbed her arm and pointed. "Hornet nest." They steered their way around the hanging globe of insects.

"Getting back to animal rights, tell me what you want. No philosophical bullshit, just plain talk." They sat side-by-side on a fallen tree.

"At a minimum, we need legislation to reform factory farms in America. These animals need to be raised under humane conditions, with quality food and the freedom to move about and enjoy what life they have. We need surprise inspections of their living conditions and treatment during slaughter, along with stiff fines and serious jail time for offenders."

"We are running huge deficits now. Who would pay for the new inspections?"

"We tax gasoline so we can pave roads and fix bridges. We should tax meat consumption the same way. People will complain that we are raising the price of food for the poor, but as we discussed earlier, protein from meat is far more expensive than nourishment from healthy grains and vegetables." Lawton lifted a praying mantis clinging to her hair and moved it to a tree. "We must modify our culture so animals are not harmed unless it is necessary."

"There must be exceptions. Deer hunting is essential in some places to prevent overpopulation, and some Native American tribes hunt to put needed food on the table."

Lawton nodded. "We live in a difficult world, and killing animals to reduce suffering is appropriate behavior. But harming them for mere sport or spectator amusement is wrong. Modern-day hunters killing deer with archery equipment should rethink their methods."

"Because of the misplaced shots and wounding?"

"Deer that are hit often die a lingering death." He helped her over a fallen log, lifting her as though she weighed nothing at all.

"Anyway, the corporate mentality of factory farming is for greater efficiency, which equates to animal suffering. Society needs to bend away from animal exploitation. Automobile manufacturers force customers to buy leather seats and interiors to get the most advanced electronic safety equipment. And there's a flawed perception that equates leather with status in furniture and clothing. Learning to treat other animals with compassion is a necessary condition for evolving out of the cycle of human aggression against our own species."

"That's a lot to ask. Is it sensible to believe you can change people's minds?"

"You can't change someone's mind about anything. The right approach is to present the pertinent facts in a way that isn't threatening to their pride or self-image. Vanity rules the world. This gets them thinking with an open mind, and change will follow. Most people are fundamentally decent. They just lack the light to show them the way. But first, you must get their attention, and that isn't easy."

She turned to Lawton. "This animal rights project, it's important to you?"

"Paramount."

"Then you must do what is necessary. *Whatever is necessary!*"

"No argument there."

"I don't know how to say this, so I'm just going to say it." She moistened her lips. "You have to stop."

Valeriya waited for the question that didn't come, his sphinxlike expression giving little away.

"You can't accomplish anything if you're dead or locked away in a prison cell. I know you think this is a trap, and I'm trying to trick you into a confession. But I'm not." She blocked his path. "They are watching you now. But there isn't any evidence, nothing that would justify your arrest. If you quit now, you'll be free, free to fight for the cause."

He still said nothing.

"Try something else, peaceful protests or civil disobedience."

His silence continued.

"At least nod or give me a sign that you understand what I am saying."

He clasped both hands around his journal as though it was a defensive shield. "You are being perfectly clear."

"Good. At least you know. That's as much as I can do." She looked down, pawing the ground with the toe of her shoe. "I did it for them."

"Really?" He eyed her distrustfully.

The clank of a slamming car door turned their heads, and a vehicle drove away, leaving something behind—it moved. They jogged toward the road, slowing and staring.

"Is that what I think it is?" Val groaned.

"Yep. He dropped her off and left."

"Bloody bastard."

They approached a multicolored kitten with patches of creamy brown, satin white, and charcoal gray. The animal ran upon seeing them, scurrying through the trees and hiding between some rocks.

"She won't survive out here by herself," Lawton said.

Valeriya crept closer, cooing, "Here, kitty kitty kitty." Val reached for her, but the cat was too quick. Lawton tried to block her path, but she ran between his legs. The pursuit continued through a steeper part of the hill, ending when the animal disappeared inside a burrow.

"Dammit!" Val yelled. She laid her sunglasses on a rock and bent down, inspecting the dark hole. "Here, kitty kitty kitty. Come on, come on," she said in her sweetest voice. "I don't suppose you have a flashlight?"

Lawton stooped down beside her. "Wish I did." He looked into the black opening. "It's probably a fox or groundhog den."

Valeriya continued her calls without success. She reached inside, scooting closer until her head and shoulder touched the entrance.

"You shouldn't do that," Lawton called. "You don't know what's in there."

She kept trying, shoveling earth with her hands, prying and probing.

"Valeriya, there could be snakes, and if an animal bites you you'll have to get rabies shots."

She swirled out a large rock and went deeper inside, head first, scooping with her hands.

"Did you hear what I said?" Lawton yelled.

She kept going, leaving her rump and legs sticking out. Lawton grabbed her feet and began pulling. She kicked him back, squealing, "Let me go. I felt some fur." He released her, and she pulled herself further into the tunnel, arms stretched out, grabbing tree roots to pull forward. Now she was fully inside, in the dark, still groping and reaching.

Lawton bellowed into the tunnel, "It's going to look pretty damn bad if I have to call the fire department to dig you out. It'll be in the newspapers, and there will be a police report with tons of questions for both of us."

She pushed on, eyes closed to shut out the falling dirt, feeling her way forward. A tuff of soft hair grazed her wrist, and Valeriya gently pulled the kitten into her hands. "Okay. I got her. Now get us out." Something touched the tip of her shoe. She heard digging and Lawton cursing under his breath. "Come on!" Val called. "What are you waiting for? I did the hard part."

"I can't reach you," he yelled. "I'm going to try slipping my belt around your feet. Push them together."

The earth collapsed, pinning her in an immobile position. Valeriya held onto the kitten, taking shallow breaths of the available air. Something dangled around her ankles—she felt a powerful pull but didn't move.

"You seem to be stuck," Lawton called. "Should I pull harder?"

"With all your might!" Val screamed. *"We're suffocating!"*

Her ankles tightened together, and she began sliding rearward. A sharp tree root snagged her turtleneck sweater, digging into her side. She gritted her teeth, ignoring the pain, passing the kitten from hand to hand as her turtleneck sweater ripped away. With a sudden jolt, she was free, naked from the waist up and filthy, but still holding the cat. Lawton took the squirming animal and helped her up.

She wiped dirt from her eyes and beheld the kitten, smiling like a gold medalist at the Olympic Games. "How's that for authenticity?"

"I think I've created a monster." He examined her rib cage. "You're bleeding. Is anything broken? Can you walk?"

Valeriya tested her legs and surveyed the damage. "It's just a scrape. I can get cleaned up at the pavilion." She took the kitten and held her up. "She's a calico cutie. I'll call you Shingles."

Lawton gave her his hooded sweatshirt. "You're going to keep her?"

"After all that? Absolutely."

They continued down the road with Val cuddling her prize.

* * *

The restroom at the Pioneer Pavilion was open, and Valeriya took a G.I. bath at the sink, scrubbing her flesh wounds with soap and water. The bruising was apparent now, and she was feeling the damage. She filled a paper cup with water and carried it outside. Lawton sat at a picnic table under a tree, feeding Shingles some meat.

"Where did you get that?" Val asked.

He pointed to a trash bin. "Someone was here earlier. They left half a chicken." He regarded her. "How are you feeling?"

"Not bad. Scraped up and a little sore." Val took over the job of feeding the kitten. She offered her water, but the animal was more interested in food. She looked back at the woods. "I left my sunglasses at that hole."

"I'll get them on my way back." He grew strangely quiet, watching her feed the cat. "You surprised me back there. I thought you were working, playing the role of a devious detective."

Valeriya flashed her pearly whites. She dipped her finger into the chicken juice and painted a capital R on the back of his hand.

He returned her smile. "What would you do if I satisfied your curiosity?"

"About what?"

"About what you want to know?"

She rolled her eyes. "I've already changed sides, becoming a fucking traitor. Maybe I shouldn't know."

He nodded and watched the kitten. "Is this your first cat? If it is, you may want to get her a playmate to pass the time while you're working."

She nodded back, mentally chiding herself and feeling the sting of a missed opportunity. The pressure mounted. "Oh, hell! Just tell me. I won't get a night's sleep if you don't."

"You might not get a night's sleep if I do. We're going way past Nietzsche and Heidegger."

Val took a deep breath. "Tell me. I will remain silent."

He leaned forward. "About every 200 years something momentous happens in our moral evolution. Not slowly, but a sudden eruption that radically changes our perceptions of right and wrong. It last occurred when Abraham Lincoln plunged the Nation into a war that killed over 600,000 American soldiers. There was suffering and carnage the likes of which was never seen. Entire families were destroyed, and hundreds of thousands starved to death. Lincoln knew the likely consequences of his actions, yet he did it anyway. Our social structure changed, and the world became a better place."

"I'm not sure I understand what you're saying."

"Lincoln perceived a difficult problem and solved it by choosing a lesser evil. That's what the important decisions in life are all about, choosing lesser evils. We are ready for the next big move, only this time we cannot free the remaining slaves, but we can lessen their suffering."

"How?"

"It will begin in a year or two. The trial of the twenty-first century."

Valeriya stared in disbelief. "But that won't work. You can't leap from killing animal abusers to helping animals suffering on factory farms. It might even have the opposite effect."

"Nietzsche said truth is whatever promotes our advancement. You need to get orthogonal, go beyond conventional reasoning."

"Truth is truth. But you're telling me two plus two equals five."

"You're locked in the prison of conformity. Success in this difficult situation will not be easy, and it requires relentless innovation, looking at the changing situation and adapting to overcome obstacles. You must look for the wrong answer that's right from a different perspective."

"Okay. I'm listening."

"As we speak, a legal team is working on a 'hypothetical' research project. It's all about introducing the right evidence in court as part of the defense. The news media will be there in force, and countless millions will be watching. I want them to see the pictures and watch the videos of animal abuse. I will have just one job." His blue eyes flashed with precipitous passion. "*Make—them—squirm!*"

"It doesn't matter how good your attorneys are. You'll be executed. They'll strap you down on a gurney and pump poison into your veins."

Lawton smiled whimsically. "A slight pinch in the arm and then peacefully drifting away, knowing I did what I thought was right. Therein lies *my* authenticity."

"But what's your strategy? The insanity defense?"

"That would be self-defeating."

"Diminished capacity?"

"Same answer."

Val shook her head. "That's all there is unless you're going to enter a guilty plea, in which case there is no trial."

"Again, that's linear thinking. When flying a plane, the shortest distance between two points isn't a straight line but rather a great-circle plot to your destination. I cannot be any clearer without implicating others."

"The prosecution will object to your evidence as being irrelevant. There's a good chance the judge will agree."

"You're not telling me anything I haven't considered. There's a backup plan."

"It's a dangerous dualism between right and wrong. You cannot sublimate murder."

Lawton stroked the kitten, keeping his eyes fixed on Val. "One must consider the moral trade-off, the good that new evil helps to create."

"What of the people lying in their graves to make this transformation happen? What about justice for them?"

"How many thousands of innocent women and children were blown apart in Civil War mortar shelling or were burned alive in Atlanta while hiding in basements and attics? There will always be civilian casualties in war, but I am not combating noncombatants."

"How can you be so sure? You are playing judge, jury, and executioner."

"There were no mistakes. I took care of that personally. This is a battle against barbaric cruelty, and the strategic application of violence is required, like setting a backfire to smother the burning woods. If there was another way, I would do it."

"Committing violence against humans violates the essence of what it means to be human."

"If humans were more human, you and I would have different occupations. Violence is always permissible in defending the innocent. No virtue is greater than helping the helpless."

Shingles climbed off the picnic table and into Valeriya's arms, snuggling into the folds of her sweatshirt. "Why make them look like accidents? It would have been simpler to just kill them."

"That would've set off alarm bells too soon. There's a big difference between six and sixty. The press has a twisted taste for blood, and I had an ample supply of worthy targets. However, the killings are over with one exception, a big one to light the fuse and get everyone's attention."

Val elevated her brows. "Seems like you already have enough. Is there any way to stop it?"

"It's already happened. They will be aware of it soon." He looked at his wristwatch. "I need to get going. Are you well enough to drive?"

"Yeah. My car's close by. There were a lot of people taking pictures at the Lily Pond. I guess we shouldn't be seen together." She stood up. "Is there anything I can do to help, short of helping you whack someone?"

He smiled. "Not for now, but I'll keep you in mind."

"I'll have to owe you for the sweatshirt."

"Don't concern yourself. Got it at Trade Day in Olive Hill for fifteen bucks."

Lawton gazed at the cat and then into her eyes, giving a silent goodbye. They went in opposite directions. Valeriya hesitated at the edge of the woods and glanced over her shoulder: no one was there.

19 Rude Awakening

Blackwell approached the DDI parking deck on Friday morning, sipping his coffee and thinking of Val. He hadn't seen her since Tuesday, and he hoped she'd be back at work. Extra guards stood at the entrance, carrying AR-15's and making everyone show their ID. Mark pulled out his wallet and lowered the window, asking, "What's going on?"

"Terrorist attack about an hour ago," the guard replied. "They got the FBI director."

"Margaret Marshall?"

The guard nodded.

"Has she been killed?"

"I don't know. The story is still breaking."

Mark parked his car and hurried to the main entrance. Normally the body scans took twenty seconds, but today it was over a minute. He placed his belongings in the security box as usual and went to the elevator door. The regular foot traffic inside the DDI had diminished greatly, possibly because everyone was watching television.

Upon entering Advanced Queries, he found Richard viewing a news broadcast. He told Mark that Marshall was hit with a flying bomb, and they transported her to Walter Reed. Blackwell asked if Val was in, and Richard nodded. Mark almost asked if she was available, but he went to his office instead, hoping to find a phone message or email. His voicemail was empty, so he booted up his computer and waited, entering the long password and clicking the email icon: nothing but junk. Valeriya booted him out of her office on Tuesday, telling him she would call when she was feeling better. *Should I call her or not? She might be busy with the Marshall bombing.* Then he remembered the insulin stored in her refrigerator, the perfect excuse for seeing her. He picked up the phone and punched Val's number.

"This is Val."

"It's me. I hate to trouble you in a time of crisis, but I forgot to take my insulin. Can I get some from your refrigerator?"

"Sure. Come on over."

Her office door was open when he arrived. Unlike Tuesday, she was dressed as usual: turtleneck sweater, dress slacks, watching the same news broadcast as Richard.

"Is she alive?" Mark asked.

"They're not saying. Looks like they attacked her with a drone."

"I thought the military watched for those things."

"It was a small drone, the kind available to the public for taking aerial pictures. Her bodyguards spotted it coming but believed it was the press seeking some high-angle footage. A sign on the side read *CBS News*."

Mark nodded. "Sneaky." He proceeded to the kitchenette, hoping Valeriya wouldn't follow—but she did, coffee cup in hand. The pot was empty, and she took a fresh container of Native Grounds from a cupboard. Her face was bruised and scratched.

He gestured to her cheek. "What happened?"

"I slipped and fell while rescuing a cat."

He smirked at her. "You and your thing about animals. What did you do with it?"

"She's at my apartment along with another kitty. I can check on them with a camera monitor."

Blackwell opened the refrigerator and acquired an unopened vial of insulin. He rolled it gently between his fingers and opened a ten-pack of disposable syringes. Two shots in two hours would be too much. He cut back the dosage, loading a quarter of the normal amount.

Val observed him while the coffee brewed, saying, "That isn't much."

"I don't take a lot. Underdosing with insulin is no biggie. It's overdosing that's dangerous, especially on an empty stomach." He removed his jacket and lifted his shirt, injecting the medication into his stomach.

She poured two cups of coffee—his invitation to stay. They went to her workstation, and Mark pulled up his favorite chair. They watched the live coverage, although not much was said. A security camera attached to a building caught a distant view of the attack. The drone was so small it could barely be seen. News commentators said the perpetrator might have been miles away because these devices broadcast signals back to the controller. Valeriya did a few searches but came up with nothing, saying data on publicly available drones was practically nonexistent. The Bureau hadn't issued a statement other than sending an internal notification announcing that Douglas McCracken had assumed temporary command of the FBI as acting director.

Mark constantly thought about Val. What could he say or do to make things better between them? Flowers and cherry chocolates might work with other women, but not this rare bird. He'd have better luck catching a will-o'-the-wisp.

Valeriya remained fully absorbed and watched the screen without paying any attention to him. A news conference informed the public that Margaret Marshall had undergone surgery for shrapnel injuries and was in intensive care. The bustling banter of eager reporters ended as President Alice Nightingale went to the podium. Val turned up the volume, hinting Mark should remain quiet. The President vowed to bring the bombers to justice, saying the FBI would have a blank check for investigative resources and no stone would be left unturned. Douglas McCracken stood tall behind her, nodding in agreement. Nightingale surrendered the podium to McCracken, and the acting FBI director summarized what was known about the bombing, which seemed little.

The workstation monitor chimed the arrival of a new request. Valeriya clicked on the file.

Blackwell leaned forward when he noticed there were photographs. They showed a young girl in her late teens or early twenties, posing with family or friends. "What's this about?" he asked.

"She went missing last week, disappearing without a trace. They want me to go through video footage at all the airports to make sure she didn't board a plane."

Mark squinted at the screen, reading the request himself. "How can you do that?"

"With a facial recognition scan. We've got photos of her from several angles, so there's a reasonable chance I can find her, providing she went to a major airport." Val scooted forward and typed.

"You're saying you will scan ordinary airport observation footage to find the face of a single person?"

"Yep."

He gave her a bull-eyed glare, throwing up his chin. "That's impossible, at least not with our current technology."

"I do it two or three times a week." She loaded the photographs into a file and activated a program. The machine began working. "This may take a while." She stood up and proceeded toward the bathroom.

Mark followed her, pushing open the bathroom door. They had to be misunderstanding each other.

"Do you mind? I have to pee."

"I've seen it all before." He entered the bathroom. "The images from airport security cameras are too fuzzy for facial recognition scans."

Val pulled down her underwear and urinated.

"You can match her to driver's license or passport photos," Mark continued, "but not to wide shots of many people moving about in a crowd."

"I do it all the time."

"How?"

She dabbed herself with toilet paper and flushed. "It's a process of elimination, discarding images that aren't even close. Then the computer takes the reasonable candidates and looks at the same person from different camera angles, combining the pixels into a matrix that would be meaningless to human eyes but yields sharpened vision for machines." She washed her hands. "It's analogous to the way radio telescopes that are spread far apart combine their images to form one picture of a celestial object." Her computer chimed its unique eureka ping. "We have a hit. Usually it takes much longer."

Blackwell tailed her back to the workstation, still not believing her claim.

Valeriya sat down and manipulated an image, expanding and sharpening the picture. "What do you think?"

He said nothing, stunned into silence.

She zoomed in on an ear and showed a blowup of the missing girl's ear for comparison. "There's no doubt about it. She boarded a flight from Dallas Love Field and flew to Toronto."

Mark studied the images, stomach tightening into a knot. "Why has nothing been written about this in the forensics literature?"

"Because the technique is classified, and the United States government doesn't share its best intelligence-gathering techniques."

He thought of Sergeant Miller. "Do local and state police departments have access to this?"

"No. We do individual searches on a special request basis, but we don't tell them how we found the person."

"And you can do this search with any video footage?"

Val nodded. "Pretty much. It works best at modern airports since they have many high definition cameras, which means the pixels pile up to form sharper images." She grimaced up at him. "Is something wrong? You're white as a ghost."

He tried to appear relaxed. "It's just stress. I'm worried about Margaret."

Shaken but still confident, Mark returned to his office. Candy Rowan was never a missing person, wasn't a criminal, and was never suspected of terrorist activities. And if the Wittgenstein police were going to use this technique, they would have certainly done so by now.

* * *

Over the next several weeks Blackwell kept a low profile, still concerned that concrete evidence might prove his romantic relationship with Candy. Useful information about the Marshall bombing was nil.

Bomb fragment analysis showed the drone was available to anyone with the cash to buy it, and the explosive and shrapnel were homemade and untraceable. There were no suspects, and no terrorist organizations claimed responsibility. Margaret Marshall's condition improved, but she was seriously injured and would not be returning to work anytime soon—if ever.

Much to Mark's annoyance, Valeriya spent considerably less time working, taking vacation and cutting her days to eight-hour shifts. Their occasional conversations left him with an empty feeling, having no more intimacy than passing the time of day with a boring colleague. All in all, things were not going well.

20 Hoisting the Jolly Roger

Blackwell spent his time diligently working on the three research papers, reading everything available on serial killers. Roy Lawton would soon be apprehended, and that gave Mark energy to toil until the red-winged Blackbirds sang their early morning songs. He dreamt about Lawton, ate with him, bathed with him, and mentally pictured the mind of this murdering machine. He wrote with insight and precision, gliding into a different dimension, taking the *Death Instinct* theories of Sigmund Freud to an unprecedented level—beyond mere criminology or psychology, further than philosophy itself, touching the inner essence of a psychotic mind. *This scholarly work will be universally acknowledged as a stroke of genius, my own private Picture of Dorian Gray.*

* * *

On a sunny day in the third week of October, just after breakfast, his home telephone rang. Mark rushed to pick it up, hoping it might be Val.

"Hello," he said with enthusiasm.

"May I speak with Mark Blackwell?" a woman replied.

Disappointment—it wasn't Valeriya. "Speaking."

"This is Mrs. Hamilton calling on behalf of Douglas McCracken."

"Yes, ma'am."

"There is an important meeting today at 1 p.m. at the J. Edgar Hoover Building in the William Webster Conference Room. Mr.

McCracken would like you to attend and bring all the files and records for the Stealth Killer investigation."

Mark's heart fluttered with primitive palpitations. "Has there been an arrest?"

"I'm not privy to any details, Mr. Blackwell. I'm simply conveying the wishes of Douglas McCracken. He was adamant that you bring absolutely everything you have to that meeting."

"All the files are with my partner, Valeriya Highland."

"I have already spoken to Miss Highland, told her about the meeting and the need for all available files. She will be attending. Will you be there?"

This was not a request. "I will. One p.m. in the Webster conference room."

"Thank you, and have a good day."

Blackwell turned on his cellphone, ready to punch in Val's number. There was a text message from her:

Have the files and am leaving shortly. Will meet you there.

He tried calling her but got no answer. Recognizing a golden opportunity, Mark selected an elegant French-cuff dress shirt in glowing white, the one that looked best with his gold cufflinks. He chose a tasteful sharkskin suit and a pair of Italian leather shoes, the ones he saved for special occasions. A Prometheus Society pin was the final touch for his imported silk tie. He checked his immaculate appearance in the mirror: perfection for meeting his new boss. Douglas McCracken was a highbrow bureaucrat, but practical and utilitarian. He might give a speech and take an undeserved bow for capturing Roy Lawton, but the press would want more, dirty details about this new and unheard-of serial killer. Blackwell should be that spokesman. He had the facts and investigation details, the necessary psychological background, and the panache to give hungry reporters everything they wanted. Who else could McCracken choose? After all, Valeriya was so demure and reclusive. This meant all his articles would be published in the most prestigious journals. There would be book deals and forensic textbook opportunities galore. Maybe then Val would see him in a different light, and he could rekindle her interest.

* * *

Mark filled the drive to Washington with rehearsals, working out what he would say. He deduced that Lawton had been arrested while caught in the act. Otherwise, there would be no need for an emergency meeting. Douglas McCracken would want to know the background of the case before calling a press conference: the who, the where, and the when of the Lawton murders. Having outlined three Lawton research papers, including a spectacular literature review of serial killers, Mark would become the eliminator of chaos, bearing stone tablets of indisputable truths. He would be generous to Valeriya, lauding her helpful efforts and computerized acrobatics. Yet, all free-thinking academics would see, bathed in the light of his Freudian analysis, that Mark Blackwell had discovered something exceptionally new, and his name would be written into the annals of forensic psychology.

With shoulders back and chin held high, Mark bounded into the J. Edgar Hoover Building, taking expansive steps of zeal, making ready for the apotheosis of his career. Valeriya had a special appreciation of art and beauty, and she would no doubt study his papers, being impressed by their intellectual depth and profundity. He rounded a corner, and seeing the elevator doors closing, clasped the edges and gave a prodigious heave. The big doors rolled back like the parting of the Red Sea, and mighty Moses stepped inside. Blackwell blinked, looked, and blinked again. There stood Valeriya, a deep frown creasing her face, dressed in absolutely dreadful clothes: frayed blue jeans, jogging shoes, and a dumpster-diving sweatshirt that looked like it was abandoned by a homeless tramp.

"I can't believe you came here dressed like that."

She pressed the button for the top floor. "My clothes are clean. I brought the files on a flash drive."

"Val, you can't meet Douglas McCracken looking like a street beggar." The elevator hummed ominously upward. She held his gaze with unmoving eyes, obviously pissed about something. "Okay. What's wrong?"

"You don't know?"

"Know what?"

"As soon as I downloaded the files, my security clearance was canceled. They have shut me out of the DDI databases, with the sole exception of doing routine searches for police investigations. Your security clearance is canceled as well."

Mark scowled at her. "It has to be a mistake or a glitch in the system."

"Richard examined the order. It came from Douglas McCracken himself, written with the specific intention of shutting us out."

"All right, just calm down. I'll talk to McCracken."

Her eyes bored into him. "Your words won't help. I need a sledgehammer."

"Just give me a chance. It would be easier if you got rid of that ghetto hoodie."

"I can't."

"You can't, or you won't?"

"Can't."

Mark grabbed the sweatshirt zipper and pulled it down: nothing underneath. "Oh my God. Are you losing your mind?" The elevator slowed. "Give me the flash drive, and I'll meet with McCracken. You need to sneak out of here. Just go home and rest."

Valeriya zipped up as the elevator door opened. She darted out with Blackwell in pursuit.

He caught up with her. "Val," he whispered, "you're having a mental breakdown. Now listen to me. This is a crucial meeting. Roy Lawton has been arrested, and—"

"He hasn't been arrested. I checked before downloading the files, and nothing has happened."

He struggled to keep up with her. "Then why are we having this meeting?"

"I have no idea."

Further down the hall, Douglas McCracken and Senator Jackson appeared to be having a heated exchange, Jackson poking McCracken's chest with his index finger. Val ducked into a drinking fountain egress, one eye peering around the edge. Blackwell did the same, but McCracken and Jackson were too far away to be overheard. A firm but

LESSER EVILS: AN ANIMAL RIGHTS NOVEL

friendly hand landed on Mark's shoulder. He turned around, and Assistant Director Patrick Greene grabbed his hand.

"Long time no see, Mark." Still smiling, Greene studied Valeriya's unconventional wardrobe. He shook her hand. "I'm delighted to see you in person. Margaret constantly sings your praises, saying you can squeeze blood from a stone."

"How is she doing?" Valeriya asked.

"We're hoping for the best, but there's some spinal cord damage."

"I know she isn't seeing visitors, but is she taking calls?"

"I think so. If it's important."

Val tilted her head toward Douglas McCracken, who was now nodding in agreement with Senator Jackson. "Why did he call this meeting?"

"Your Stealth Killer may have struck Senator Jackson's family, and Alex McCracken is taking over the case."

Val rolled her eyes. "When it rains, it fucking pours."

Greene chuckled. "Everyone's gonna be wear'n raincoats with those two in charge."

"Alex McCracken?" Blackwell asked.

"Alex is Doug's nephew," Greene whispered, "the newest and youngest-ever assistant director in Bureau history. Doug promoted him to help with the new transition, bypassing better-qualified candidates. But no one dared challenge the word from on high. They don't believe Margaret is coming back, although she is technically still in charge—I think." Greene eyed his boss. "Bureau scuttlebutt says Doug was furious when Nightingale chose Margaret over him to lead the FBI. He complains about subsisting under her shadow, although never to her face."

The threesome watched Douglas McCracken shake Senator Jackson's hand before departing. Whatever the disagreement was, it was apparently resolved.

"Yeah, smart Alex," Greene continued, "the Bureau's go-getter and wunderkind. He worked for me for a while, always saying one day he'd be my boss. That's probably true, unfortunately. He's a tough cookie. Plays to win every game, regardless of the rules. You'd better steer clear of him if you can." Greene glanced up at a clock. "Gotta go." He hurried off.

"Have you ever met Alex McCracken?" Mark whispered.

The corners of Val's mouth twisted down. "Never had the 'pleasure.' But I've heard plenty, all bad."

They traveled to the other side of the building, the corner closest to the Washington Monument. Several unknown persons chatted at the conference room entrance, one of them gesturing with calming nods. Valeriya attempted to enter when a man wearing wire-rim glasses and a fashionable three-piece double-breasted suit extended his arm, blocking her path.

"This is a secured area," the man said. He snapped his perfectly manicured fingers and beckoned a security guard. The thin-framed fellow was the same height as Val, wearing a Wyatt Earp black bowtie with a matching carnation boutonniere. Give him a wide-brimmed fedora, and he would've been a perfect addition to the old Western streets of Tombstone.

Val opened her FBI credentials.

Tensing his brow, the man studied the photograph and badge. "You're Valeriya Highland?"

"I am."

The approaching security guard looked menacingly at her, hand resting on a taser. "Is there a problem, Mr. McCracken?"

Alex McCracken looked her over with stiffening distaste, like the revulsion of a Marine drill sergeant inspecting a sloppy recruit. "No problem," McCracken replied. The guard went back to his post, maintaining a watchful gaze. McCracken took a step forward, getting right in her face. "This is the Federal Bureau of Investigation, and I expect you to dress professionally, not like the mop lady of a skid row soup kitchen."

Without blinking an eye, Valeriya plowed forward, literally battering the newly appointed assistant director out of her way. McCracken backpedaled and bounced off the propped-open door, disjointedly rolling his modest shoulders. He removed a handkerchief and wiped smudges from his eyeglasses, nodding slowly to himself.

Totally flabbergasted, Blackwell swallowed and entered the conference room. Val was seated in the last row, resting as casually as if she was in a cinema.

Mark sat next to her, whispering, "That was exciting. What will you do next, set the building on fire?"

Silence.

"Val, what happens now will change things for the rest of our lives. Our careers are at stake. I want you to be quiet and let me do all the talking. Where is the flash drive?"

"I have it."

"Give it to me."

"I'll give it to McCracken when he asks for it."

With perspiring hands, Blackwell slumped back in the seat. *Mark, preserve thyself!* Valeriya sat beside him, calmly kneading the sweatshirt like she was petting a dog.

"Why are you wearing that ugly thing, that and nothing underneath?" he whispered.

"It feels good."

More people streamed inside and took seats. Mark recognized several individuals connected to the Bureau's surveillance operations. Alex McCracken led a distinguished gentleman to the front, someone of importance based on the way McCracken was treating him. The security guard closed the door.

McCracken went to the lectern and glanced around the auditorium, pausing when he spotted Valeriya. "All of you undoubtedly recognized Senator Jackson in the hall this afternoon. There has been a dark turn in the story regarding his son, Scott Jackson, and that is why we are meeting today."

McCracken recounted a prior FBI investigation where Scott Jackson was scrutinized as a suspect in the Forest Glades case. Forest Glades was a premium pet food company that went bankrupt several years ago when harmful chemicals were discovered in its products. Scott Jackson was married to Rosanna Glades (owner of the company), and the prevailing theory held that Jackson and two accomplices poisoned the pet food with a rare substance not tested for by the authorities. Thousands of dogs and cats developed cancerous tumors and had to be euthanized. The perceived motive was revenge because of the bitter and very public divorce proceedings between Scott Jackson and Rosanna Glades. The FBI confirmed that Scott Jackson purchased a large quantity of the rare poison, but the case could not go forward because a judge rendered the evidence inadmissible due to a questionable search of Scott Jackson's automobile. McCracken further reported that Senator Jackson claimed Rosanna Glades planted the incriminating evidence to discredit the Jackson name in the next election, and there was no reason to doubt the Senator's word.

"Do you remember that brawl between Scott Jackson and Rosanna Glades?" Blackwell whispered.

Val nodded. "It made the biggest Hollywood divorces look like pillow fights."

McCracken brushed back a bothersome strand of hanging hair, a remnant of his physical skirmish with Val. "Both of the men who allegedly assisted Scott Jackson in the poisoning are dead from cancer, and Scott Jackson has entered a hospice center with terminal cancer spread throughout his body." Muffled conversations gathered and built momentum. McCracken spoke louder to quiet them. "We believe these three men were targeted by a serial killer who has been murdering people charged with animal cruelty, and catching this individual will be the mission of this important task force."

A woman in the front row raised her hand. "Were the men poisoned with the same chemical?"

"No," McCracken replied. "That substance is detectable, and none of it was found in their bodies. Our toxicology laboratory has conducted every known test, and we can find no trace of any poison in the men or their families or homes. Their relatives and work colleagues remain cancer-free. We believe we are dealing with a weaponized carcinogen that kills without leaving a trace." Chatter rose from the audience again. "Allow me to introduce Sir David Carlington from British Intelligence. He will elaborate on what we think is happening."

Sir David, a tall and handsome man with a touch of gray at his temples, hair brushed straight back, approached the lectern. His marked British intonation and noble bearing seemed reminiscent of the House of Windsor. "Back in 2004, MI6 intercepted and decoded an exchange between two foreign governments that complained about the untidiness of Yasser Arafat's demise. Both leaderships agreed upon the need for a clandestine way of dealing with persistent political difficulties. They subsequently began developing weaponized carcinogens. These substances cause the targeted individual to develop terminal cancer. Unlike conventional poisons that need to be ingested or injected, these compounds are absorbed through the skin via dimethyl sulfoxide. A fatal dose could be administered by placing two or three drops of liquid on the clothing. The application would be painless and unnoticeable. The carcinogens are water-soluble and quickly eliminated from the body, but they damage the cell structures so cancer will develop at a later time. The victim would be unaware that he is a 'walking dead man' because he would feel no discomfort until cancer emerged. The poisonings could occur with casual contact in an elevator or on a crowded street. They are, as far as we know, the perfect assassination weapon because there is no known way to prove they were used."

"Which countries have this weapon?" someone asked.

"His Majesty's Government would never think of using such an undiplomatic contrivance. However, MI6 is aware of five regimes that have the armament. The Russians have it as well as a similar compound that produces debilitating dementia in about six months. And we believe the Chinese may have used it to address political unrest, targeting key individuals." Sir David elevated an illustrious brow at Alex McCracken. "I cannot speak for the United States."

McCracken smiled brazenly, his Wyatt Earp machismo shining through. "America is too civilized to be on the cutting edge of efficiency." Several people in the audience laughed.

"Could a lone-wolf manufacture this?" someone asked.

"Not the average person," Sir David answered. "Even an experienced chemist would have difficulty arriving at the formula because published research focuses on curing rather than causing cancer." Sir David somberly scanned the listeners. "However, a fortnight ago, MI6 discovered that the formula can be deduced from the current medical literature, but the terrorist would need to be a skilled logician and a competent organic chemist—a rare combination of skills."

Alex McCracken stepped forward. "Thank you, Sir David." The English knight returned to his chair and seated himself in a prim and proper way. McCracken paused dramatically, mimicking the stance of his taller and more famous uncle. "The Bureau believes that an active serial killer is now in possession of a weapon of mass destruction, an invisible bludgeon that could eliminate everyone in this room in a single day." Audible gasps arose.

Sir David raised his hand. "If you'll permit me?"

McCracken nodded.

"Carcinogenic weapons are more appropriate for targeting specific individuals than mass killings. If a terrorist bent on wanton destruction has the intellectual wherewithal to develop this sophisticated poison, he could create nerve gas or anthrax that would kill a thousand times as many people."

"Could this person apply a carcinogenic weapon to five random individuals?" McCracken asked.

Sir David nodded. "Even more."

"Could he do this day after day, week after week, month after month, without being noticed?"

"I see your point."

McCracken gazed into the assembled listeners like a pretentious politician running for office. "This individual could poison thousands of people, and we wouldn't even know it happened until they developed cancer months later." McCracken waited for the audience to be silent. "We have a person of interest, a government employee who has the means, motive, and opportunity to perpetrate this crime." McCracken activated a projector, and the image of Roy Lawton appeared.

McCracken spent the next hour summarizing the circumstantial evidence against Lawton, using the weekly summaries that Valeriya had filed, reports that chronicled their travels throughout Ohio, Tennessee, and Kentucky. McCracken reviewed the accidental deaths and disappearances of numerous animal abusers, and he discussed Lawton's unrestricted access to law enforcement databases. Some of McCracken's "evidence" was misleading, such as the fact that unalterable computer logs failed to show that Lawton had accessed the databases to search for animal abusers.

McCracken clasped his hands together. "The time has come for decisive action." The audience nodded in unison. "Our task is to bring Mr. Lawton to justice. Some preliminary work has already been done by one of our interns in the Behavioral Analysis Unit. He and his underling will turn over their work and be transferred to other cases." McCracken checked his wristwatch. "Let's take a fifteen-minute break, and we will reconvene to discuss strategy."

Blackwell rose but sat back down when Val didn't move. She waited until the aisle was clear and got up. He followed her, becoming alarmed when she made the wrong turn, heading toward McCracken. Sir David shook McCracken's hand and excused himself, explaining that he had to catch a plane. McCracken spotted her and waited with a clever smirk.

She halted in front of him. "I'm not leaving this investigation."

He chuckled and looked down. "This. Is not. A democracy. You are free to have your preferences, and even your opinions, but mine is the opinion that counts." He glanced up at Blackwell. "Both of you are off the case."

"Are you sure this is wise?" Mark asked. "We have direct knowledge of the investigation that could be extremely beneficial."

The FBI chieftain's smile disappeared. "Neither of you is a Special Agent. You never went through the FBI Academy, and you don't know shit about running a proper investigation. Two judges have already turned down my request for a search warrant on Lawton's property because of a lack of evidence—based on your incompetence." McCracken's gentlemanly voice rose until it reached grating proportions. "The 'work' you've done over the past eight months is a masterful guide of precisely what not to do. You are both out."

Valeriya planted the toe of her jogging shoe behind her heel and did a military about-face. She walked swiftly up the aisle.

"Where are you going?" McCracken called. "I want those files." She kept walking, not breaking her stride. "Did you hear me?"

"You'll get them," Val called over her shoulder. "I need to use the restroom."

McCracken cast Blackwell an icy stare, and Mark returned to his seat. He tried to think but couldn't, flummoxed by the lack of alternatives. If he was alone, there might be some chance to salvage the situation, but with Valeriya there it seemed hopeless. Time passed, and meeting participants shuffled back to their seats, Val being the last to return. She sat next to him, not showing the slightest bit of distress.

McCracken called to someone in the first row. "Tommy, I want you to put together a surveillance team for Lawton. I want to know where he is and what he does all the time. Spend whatever you need." McCracken looked at another man. "JP, you have the behavioral background, so let's put together a trap. Time is of the essence, so think of something that will work with one try."

JP and McCracken conversed for another ten minutes, reviewing possible scenarios when McCracken's cellphone rang. He took a quick glance and then an extended look. A small red light in the corner of the phone flashed repeatedly. He regarded the group. "I need to take this. Be back in a sec." He hurried out of the room.

Valeriya watched with a satisfied smirk.

"Please tell me you didn't," Mark whispered.

"I did."

"Margaret is injured too badly to return, and Douglas McCracken will be the new director. What will you do then?"

"Whatever it takes."

Bustling conversations ceased when the back door opened, and Alex McCracken proceeded onto the stage. He stood rigid, pulling his jacket straight. "I will brief each of you individually on your specific assignments. Our meeting is adjourned for today, and you may continue working on your other cases." His eyes drifted to the back of the room. "Miss Highland, please remain here."

Everyone filed out, murmuring while stealing subdued glimpses of Val. Mark remained beside her. They got up when everyone left and went to the center aisle.

McCracken folded his arms. "Kindly leave us, Mr. Blackwell. I want to have a private conversation with Miss Highland."

"I'd like to stay, sir. We are partners."

McCracken belched a repulsive chuckle. "Partners?"

"Yes, sir. To the end."

"Very well." McCracken approached them, smiling while composing what seemed like wavering thoughts. "You know, the name McCracken is already big in the Bureau, and it's going to get a lot bigger. You should think about your future."

Silence.

"I propose a compromise," McCracken said with delectable charm. "Allow me a free hand to conduct this investigation—in your absence—and, when the time comes to make an arrest, you can be there to clap the bracelets on Roy Lawton. We'll even have you pose for the press when we take him in for booking. Now, how does that sound?" His seductive smile grew wider. "You'll be famous, a recruiting example for the Bureau, clearly needing a promotion and a substantial salary increase."

Mark held his breath. *This is our last chance!*

"No." Her single syllable had the jolting finality of a closing bank vault door.

McCracken's nostrils narrowed like he was being assailed by some detestable stench. "Just another bossy bitch who wants to jump up and down on my balls."

Blackwell cleared his throat. "Sir, maybe if you give us time to—
"

"We clear this up now!" McCracken yelled. "I've got a job to do."

"I must be involved," Valeriya replied. "It's your show, and you can do as you please, but I want to be there until he's taken into custody."

The hue in McCracken's face deepened. "That's the problem with government service today, too many women in positions where they don't belong." He sneered at her. "They look over your shoulder, micromanaging every move, making the job take twice as long and turn out half as good."

"I won't interfere, providing you follow accepted Bureau procedures."

"But why do you insist on being here?"

"I have my reasons." Val removed the flash drive from her pocket. "Here are the files you requested—*Sir.*"

McCracken snatched the device. "I have a long memory." He stormed around them and departed, slamming the door.

Mark released an exasperated sigh. "What the hell are you doing? You can't gather honey by kicking over the beehive."

"I'm going to do nothing, but do it well."

"Nothing? You're already doing something. Who or what are you fighting?"

"Murphy's Law."

They proceeded together out of the building and toward the parking deck, Blackwell silently fuming. All the bridges were burned, and there was no place to go.

Valeriya slowed and stopped. "I have to go back."

"Why?"

"I need to look at some documents, things that haven't been digitized for remote viewing."

"You told me your security clearance was canceled."

"I'm not seeking classified information."

"I should go with you. I'm good at researching paper records."

"I'm not sure what I'm looking for, and it might take a long time. I'll let you know what I find."

With unspoken consent, Mark went to his car. *She's the one playing with fire, but I'm getting burned.*

21 Turtles and Toads, Frogs and Dogs

Blackwell spent the next several days pondering the possibilities. The silver lining in this dismal cloud of continuous calamities was the imminent arrest of Roy Lawton. The Bureau was finally going to bring him down. Mark didn't need anyone's permission to write research papers about Lawton, and he would have a running start, writing with firsthand insights and experiences no one else possessed.

He arrived at the DDI on Monday morning, impatient to discover what Val had found. She was back in her usual office attire, busily typing at the computer.

"Did you find what you wanted at the Hoover Building?" Mark asked.

"I'm not sure. I sent a request for more documentation, but it's coming by snail-mail. It will be a week or two."

"What are you doing?"

She heaved a sigh. "Just puttering around, trying to see what's available on drones."

"You're wasting your time. The bomb squad collected all the drone parts, and nothing could be traced. They drilled the serial numbers out."

"They know the manufacturer. It was an expensive model with a nine-mile range, large enough to carry an explosive charge." She turned to him. "Drones like that are supposed to be registered with the Federal

Aviation Administration. If you purchased a drone with the intent of killing someone, would you register it?"

"Of course not."

"And would you use a credit or debit card to buy it?"

"Never. I would pay cash."

She turned to her machine. "Then I know what I'm looking for. A Mirage 3, purchased from a specialty store, paid for with cash, and never registered with the FAA." The screen flashed several cryptic displays. She gave an offended snort. "The information isn't here. We'll have to get it the old fashioned way."

Valeriya picked up the phone and called Patrick Greene. Mark listened as she told Greene what she wanted: video surveillance footage from all retail outlets that sold the Mirage 3, including cash register records.

She hung up. "He's going to try." Her computer flashed an incoming email. She opened the message. "Look at this."

Blackwell moved closer.

From: FBI Director Margaret Marshall

To: Assistant Director Alexander McCracken

CC: Acting Director Douglas McCracken, Valeriya Highland, and Mark Blackwell

The security clearances for Valeriya Highland and Mark Blackwell are hereby reinstated. In the future, if you wish to revoke a security clearance, you must follow established procedures. You will make Dr. Highland and Professor Blackwell fully aware of all Bureau activities involving FBI Investigation B3690 (serial killer of animal abusers). Each of them shall have the right to be present for any Bureau meetings, substantive discussions, or active operations involving the case.

Mark shook his head. "The fat's in the fire now. Bet they're pissed."

"That's an understatement."

Her monitor flashed an activation notice for camera LCX 62— she opened a video image.

Blackwell viewed the film, not recognizing the setting. "What is this?"

"Footage of Lawton's Columbus residence, taken from the camera we have in the vacant home down the road."

"Is it live?"

"It's a thirty-second delay." Val pressed a button, and the video clip replayed from the beginning. The film showed Lawton's Ram pickup pulling into his driveway. Lawton exited to get the mail, and a little white dog ran across the road to greet him. Lawton kneeled and played with the spirited animal.

"Is that Lawton's dog?" Mark asked.

"Belongs to a neighbor."

"It sure seems to like him." A young girl ran up to Lawton. "Who's that?"

She moved the computer mouse over a street map on another monitor until it rested on a house with a large pond in the back—an information box popped up. "My best guess is Cecilia Logan, age eleven. She and her mother are Lawton's neighbors."

Lawton placed the dog into the girl's outstretched arms. He pointed at the road and said something. The girl nodded obediently and hugged the dog, cuddling and kissing it like he was her baby.

"Do you have audio?" Mark asked.

"It's too far away. But he's reprimanding her for allowing the dog to be on the road without being on a leash."

Blackwell pondered the friendly gestures. "Do you think he poisoned those three men with a carcinogen?"

"Yeah," Valeriya whispered. "Deliberately poisoning pet food— killing all those dogs and cats—he'd dig all the way to China to get them." The little girl wrapped her arms around Lawton and gave him a hug.

"Funny, isn't it? How terrible monsters can appear normal."

"There are monsters everywhere we look, often where you least expect them." Val's face grew weary, dragging into downward lines of melancholy. "You should go. I have things to do."

* * *

The bright October colors faded to early-November browns and mid-November grays with no word from Alex McCracken. Val remained isolated, either locked in her office or traveling to Washington or going who knows where. There was no news about Lawton or the Marshall bombing, although numerous agents collected the information Valeriya wanted. The one frightening event (which might occur) would be for Lawton to do nothing. Then he couldn't be arrested, and all of Mark's research papers would be meaningless.

An unexpected call from Alex McCracken's personal assistant came on the morning before Thanksgiving. She told him the Stealth Killer Task Force was meeting that afternoon at the same time and location. Once again, Alex McCracken had given him short notice, and being there on time would be a challenge. Blackwell tried to call Valeriya and got a busy signal. He hung up, believing she was attempting to call him. His phone rang, and Val said she would pick him up in thirty minutes.

Mark showered and shaved and dressed in a drab gray suit. He waited on his front porch, relishing the unseasonably warm weather. Women on the street were still wearing summer clothes, mostly shorts and sandals, showing as much leg as if it were July. Time drifted by. He was about to call Val when a white Honda pulled up to the curb and tooted its horn. Valeriya waved, and Blackwell jogged to the car. He got inside, finding her wearing the same decrepit hoodie, running shoes, and tattered jeans that Alex McCracken found so offensive.

All right. Stay calm and don't lose your temper. He buckled his seatbelt. "Did you buy a new car?"

"It's a rental. I saw dark liquid dripping underneath my Grand Cherokee. Looked like brake fluid."

She got onto the highway and accelerated faster than usual, not reckless, but assuredly aggressive. Just as they reached cruising speed, she slowed, cursing under her breath. She activated the right turn signal, driving onto an exit ramp.

"What's the matter?" Mark asked.

"There's a turtle along the edge of the road. I'm going back to get him."

"You can't be serious." He whipped his head around. "We're already going to be late." Valeriya made a left turn and then another. She got back on the highway going in the opposite direction. "First it was 'save the earthworms,' and now it's 'save the turtles.'" He glared at her. "What's going to be next, 'save the toads and frogs?'"

"If I see one that needs to be rescued." She exited and did another double-left, reentering the highway.

"You're being revoltingly absurd. We should just turn around and go home. McCracken would be happy, and I would be delighted. Why don't you admit it? You're only going there to piss him off."

Val activated the emergency flashers and parked in the grass. She picked up the turtle and looked it over, breaking into a broad smile.

Blackwell left the car as she disappeared from view. "Val!" he yelled. "Where are you going?" He followed her down to the highway fence, where she proceeded to claw the ground. She placed the turtle in the depression and climbed the fence, retrieving it on the other side. Valeriya took the turtle to a wooded pond and watched it swim away.

He met her at the car. "I've had enough of your frivolous freewheeling. I'm going to drive."

She pushed him aside and got into the driver's seat.

Mark entered the passenger side, slamming the door before she raced away.

"You've gone crazy, Val. I mean absolutely wacko!" He thumped the armrest. *"You've got to pull yourself together!"*

"He was a beauty, long yellow stripes covering his feet and legs, crimson-red underbelly. A really magnificent guy."

After several minutes of uncomfortable silence, Blackwell turned on the radio, using the scan feature to find a news report. Nothing interesting was happening aside from more executions in Iran. Val turned up the volume and listened.

"They're killing some of their best people," she said, "government scientists and technological leaders. It's very strange."

* * *

They arrived forty-five minutes late for the meeting, entering quietly and moving to the back row. The group appeared to be the same, although there were a few new faces, the most prominent being Senator Jackson. Alex McCracken wore a different suit but maintained his Wyatt Earp bowtie and black carnation boutonniere. The man McCracken had called "JP" stood on the stage, explaining a map. He projected photos of a two-story house, showing it from different angles and perspectives. The rolling hills around the residence suggested Appalachia, but this was not Roy Lawton's home. JP returned to the map and highlighted key locations, access points, and areas of interest. Valeriya took her cellphone and scrolled along a Kentucky map, eventually finding the place JP was talking about. Mark studied the screen: Bedford County, about twenty-five miles from Lawton's home. JP passed the meeting off to Alex McCracken.

McCracken whispered something to Senator Jackson and went to the lectern. He scanned the auditorium, pausing for a split second upon seeing Val. A prison mugshot of a handsome man appeared on the overhead screen, an inmate with blue eyes and sandy-blonde hair. McCracken identified him as Franco Larue, a member of a ruthless Colombian drug cartel and the chief importer of synthetic fentanyl into the United States—fentanyl being the leading cause of overdose deaths for Americans. McCracken explained that Larue's method of operation was to force dogs to swallow sealed packets of the drug and bring them across the border as pets. Cartel-paid veterinarians issued the necessary paper documentation, including proof of rabies vaccination and fit-to-fly health certificates. Other forged documents included vaccinations for Bordetella, distemper, hepatitis, and parvovirus. It was a well-run operation. After transporting the dogs to a secret location, they would be butchered to retrieve the valuable contents from their bellies.

McCracken said Larue was in federal custody and awaiting trial. US Attorneys, however, had worked with the Bureau to arrange for a sentence of deportation to Columbia on the condition that he never return to the United States, and that he cooperate with the Bureau in setting up a sting operation. A sneaky smirk crossed Valeriya's lips when McCracken said Lawton would find Larue a tempting target because of the widespread media coverage of his drug mule operations with dogs.

The Bureau would feed the news media a false report stating Larue was freed on a legal technicality, drawing Lawton into the trap.

McCracken further explained that the Bureau had chosen the identified residence because it was located on the road traveled by Lawton when making his weekly journey to Columbus. The house and utilities would be placed in Larue's name, backdated by three months. The county tax map would show Larue as the owner, making his address available to everyone with an internet connection. Larue would live at the house and be protected by Bureau bodyguards. The trap was grounded on the premise that any unusual interest by Lawton in the house or Franco Larue would breach the legal threshold of establishing probable cause for a full search of Lawton's residences in Kentucky and Ohio. Hopefully, the Bureau would find the sophisticated apparatus Lawton used in making the weaponized carcinogen that poisoned Scott Jackson and his two accomplices. And if Lawton attempted to break into the home, that in itself would be grounds for his arrest.

"Stupid," Val muttered.

A man in the second row feebly raised his hand. "May I ask a dumb question?"

McCracken nodded. "I get those all the time."

"If Roy Lawton is the killer you've described, isn't the Bureau putting Larue's life at risk, not to mention our own personnel?"

"Not at all," McCracken replied. "The entrances to the house have high-security doors with pick-proof locks that use uncopiable keycards, and all windows are thick polycarbonate that can withstand rifle fire. Security cameras cover the perimeter, showing every door and window. The house is large enough to accommodate Larue and a substantial protective force. We've anticipated every possibility, and Larue will not be in danger."

A woman spoke out. "What makes you think Lawton will go after Larue rather than another animal abuser?"

"That's a good question, and we have the answer. An expert has assessed the viability of JP's plan, someone who knows Lawton extremely well, the psychologist who treated him for aggressive behavior in high school." He beckoned a man in the front row. "This is our counselor, Dr. Philip Fleming."

Valeriya shoved her hands into her sweatshirt pockets as if they were cold.

Fleming was significantly older than McCracken, perhaps mid-fifties. He repositioned the microphone for his taller frame. "Assistant Director McCracken has sought my opinion on the feasibility of this deception. I can say with reasonable certainty that based on my prior psychological evaluation of Roy Lawton, he would find the freeing of Franco Larue infuriating, and action may be taken."

"What kind of action?" someone asked.

"When he was my patient, Lawton was a precipitous individual, someone prone to engagement. People like that rarely change."

"And if Bureau personnel get in his way," someone else asked, "are they at risk?"

"Even if Lawton becomes aware that law enforcement is involved, he may view you as benefactors of Franco Larue. Which you are, from a certain point of view. Considerable caution is needed."

Fleming had a hypnotically soothing voice, imparting a beatitude of calm correctness—just what McCracken would want to settle disquieting questions.

Val scrutinized the psychologist with intense concentration. "Watch Fleming's left hand," she whispered.

A barely noticeable tremor was evident.

"Maybe early Parkinson's, or just nervousness," Mark whispered back.

"He's not nervous. He's enjoying this."

McCracken answered several more questions before dismissing the meeting. People started filing out with Senator Jackson leading the way.

Valeriya and Blackwell moved toward the door. Without warning, Val made a sudden left and proceeded down the aisle.

Mark tried to grab her arm, whispering, "We're in enough trouble."

She pulled free. "I just want to talk."

He followed her, bracing for another battle with Alex McCracken. However, she approached the psychologist instead. Philip Fleming froze in place. He studied her, owlish eyes moving up and down, and then he broke into a face-splitting grin.

Valeriya's cheeks blazed scarlet red. "Isn't there some ethical canon that protects communications between patient and therapist?"

Fleming's smile vanished, and he addressed her with solemn eyes. "There's a moral imperative here, my dear. I must do all I can to stop the killing."

Alex McCracken approached, and Fleming turned to speak with JP.

McCracken elevated his nose. "My instructions say the two of you are permitted to be present at any Bureau operations. We have an upstairs bedroom available for you, but Mr. Blackwell will have to share a room with one of Franco Larue's bodyguards."

Mark mentally cringed.

"Thank you," Val replied. "But that won't be necessary. You may proceed without us for the time being."

McCracken nodded and walked away.

"I'm relieved we won't be sharing a roof with a Colombian drug lord," Mark whispered.

"It's an obvious trap, having Larue coincidentally living close to Lawton. A sixth-grader could come up with a better plan."

They continued back to her rental car. Blackwell said he was famished, and they dined in Washington before returning home. He hid his beliefs, not agreeing with Valeriya's assessment of JP's trap. All the Bureau needed was a search warrant, and any infraction—even a sidelong glance caught on film—could be enough to convince a judge. Then the Bureau would have an army of agents searching, x-raying, and chemical-sniffing every square inch of the Lawton properties. And if Lawton was foolish enough to attempt the elimination of Franco Larue, so much the better.

* * *

The auto mechanic who serviced Val's car said the brake lines had been damaged, probably when she ran over something. She began parking her Grand Cherokee only in places that provided good security camera coverage, and her airplane was placed in a locked hanger with nighttime security guards. Mark believed she was overly cautious, and what the mechanic told her was true—just an accident.

Alex McCracken set his trap on the twenty-seventh of November, and the full-time surveillance of Lawton intensified. Roving teams of FBI agents followed Lawton in an assortment of mundane cars, trucks, and even from above in a single-engine Cessna. Each group passed off the surveillance to another crew after fifteen minutes to avoid being "made." Aside from these facts, McCracken kept Blackwell and Valeriya in the dark, revealing no information about what was happening.

The first half of December was the warmest on record, and long-range forecasters pointed to the possibility of a snowless winter. Following Valeriya's criteria and working with orders from Patrick Greene, Bureau agents gathered a disorganized hodgepodge of video footage from stores that sold drones. Sales of the Mirage 3 were rare because of the price, but it had distinctive packaging, and Val was able to use video scanning software to identify relevant transactions. Only one person purchased the drone for cash, a bearded fellow dressed for cold weather despite it being summer. Even though the drone was purchased six months ago, it was never registered as required by law. Her facial recognition scan turned up nothing, undoubtedly because the guy wore a disguise. However, the store also had video parking lot coverage, and she was able to get the license plate number when he carried the drone to his car. It was a phony registration showing a plate from California that expired nine years ago. Using a much deeper search that took several days, she pinpointed the location and time of the car's travels by scanning highway camera footage, machine-reading the license plate. The vehicle entered the parking lot of an abandoned business outside Austin, Texas, stayed a few minutes and left, followed by another car. The license plate of the other vehicle was registered to Ryan Hancock, an employee of the Central Intelligence Agency. Valeriya sent the information to Patrick Greene.

* * *

Christmas came and went with no news from Alex McCracken. Scott Jackson died of cancer on New Year's Eve and was entombed at the Jackson family mausoleum. Blackwell finished all three research papers by the middle of January. They were gigantic rocket ships sitting on the launchpad, all fueled up and ready to go. All he needed was the arrest of Roy Lawton. Waiting was the hard part, and it seemed strange that his fate rested solely on the actions of a serial killer.

Eight weeks and three days after McCracken set his trap, the big phone call came. It was Saturday night, and Mark had just finished a languorous glass of wine. Valeriya told him Patrick Greene would be stopping by to convey an "important development." Blackwell dressed quickly and left for the DDI. It was only natural that Greene would break the news. Alex McCracken would rather drink nitric acid than talk to him or Val. *Had Lawton tried to kill Franco Larue? He must have done something.* Blackwell made good time through the evening traffic, thinking about when and where to send his research articles. Douglas McCracken's press conference seemed like the right time, maybe early next week.

When Mark entered Valeriya's office, Greene was already there, giddy with excitement.

He grabbed Blackwell's hand. "I think we did it. Val's tip about Ryan Hancock is a crusher. We picked him up at Langley, and he immediately invoked his Fifth Amendment privilege. A federal judge viewed the clip of the Austin footage and issued a search warrant. We discovered an abundance of electronic parts in Hancock's basement workshop, some of which matched the bomb fragments found at the scene. We believe he used the picture-taking feature of the drone to detonate the bomb. He has no alibi for the time he met with the mystery man, and no alibi for the Marshall bombing. He's burnt toast!"

Dripping with bitter disappointment, Mark tried to appear delighted. "That's marvelous. It establishes a link between the Marshall bombing and the CIA."

Val folded her arms. "Yeah, but Hancock is only a pawn on the chessboard. Who's moving the pieces?"

Greene regarded her thoughtfully. "That's a touchy question that no one seems to be asking. Doug McCracken is lying low."

"What about Anthony Naples?" Blackwell asked. "Surely he has something to say."

Greene shrugged. "I haven't heard a thing."

"Motive is the key," Val continued. "Who gains from having Margaret eliminated? It isn't just one person."

Greene rubbed his forehead. "That's a deep and dangerous thought." He glanced at Valeriya's clock. "I guess I better get going."

Mark raised a frustrated finger. "By the way, what's going on with the Stealth Killer investigation? We know Alex McCracken has set a trap, but has anything actually happened?"

Greene belched a frothy chuckle. "This is hilarious. Alex is spending tons of money and getting nowhere. Senator Jackson is livid about the lack of progress, so he visits Doug and tells him he expects immediate results. Otherwise, Jackson will vote against him in the upcoming FBI confirmation hearings. Jackson is a heavyweight, and he carries a lot of influence with other senators. Take a guess at how Alex responds to this new pressure on his worried uncle."

Valeriya beamed with a satisfied sparkle, showing every tooth she had. "More surveillance? Another trap?"

Greene laughed again. "Alex assigned twenty-five agents the task of looking for a dog."

Her smile vanished. "A dog?"

"And not just any dog. It had to be an exact match for a dog in a photograph, an odd-looking mongrel that wouldn't be easy to find. They combed animal shelters across the country. Finally found one up in Oregon, and they flew him to Kentucky two days ago. What do you make of that?"

Her breathing quickened. "Did you see the photograph?"

Greene nodded.

Val turned to her workstation and entered a lengthy password. She searched through a list of items and clicked on an icon. "Is this the dog?" The monitor displayed the twenty-year-old snapshot of Roy Lawton with Shiloh.

"That's him," Greene replied. "It's the craziest thing I've ever seen, but with Uncle Doug in command, Alex knows he's King Shit and can do as he pleases."

Veronica's voice came over the intercom. "Mr. Greene, Robert Tyler is trying to find you."

Greene headed for the door. "I'll be in touch with any developments. Congratulations and thanks again."

As soon as Greene left, Valeriya snatched the phone, fingers hovering over the keypad. She slammed the receiver into its cradle. *"I'm a fucking idiot!"* She shut down her computer and rushed to the bedroom.

Mark followed her. "What's the matter?"

She grabbed her overnight bag and began packing, not saying a thing.

"Are you going somewhere?" Mark asked.

"Bedford County."

"Kentucky?" Blackwell rounded the bed to face her. "To that madhouse—with Franco Larue?"

"Yep."

"For God's sake, why?"

"McCracken is going to use the dog as a weapon."

"You're being silly. How can a homeless dog be a weapon?"

She commenced peeling off her clothes. "I don't know. That's why I'm going."

"We're not leaving tonight."

"It's already Sunday, and whatever McCracken has planned will happen Monday morning when Lawton travels to Columbus. You're not coming with me."

"The hell I'm not!" Mark pursued her into the bathroom. "You read Marshall's order—*you and I together for all meetings and operations involving the case.*"

She turned on the shower and got inside, yelling, "I'll pick you up in front of your house in sixty minutes. If you're not there, *I—am—gone!*"

"An hour? I'll need more time." He took a deep breath. "Look, Val, it's only a six-hour drive. We should both get a good night's sleep and leave tomorrow morning. We'll be there Sunday afternoon, which is plenty of time."

"Fifty-nine minutes!"

Mark hurried out of her office, rushing through the DDI. He broke into a full run upon reaching the parking deck.

22 The Throwdown

The halogen headlights of her Grand Cherokee flashed in the driveway, and Blackwell ran out the door. Valeriya raised the hatchback for his overnight bag. He loaded the luggage and got inside, pleased she had brought him hot coffee. Her fractured face glowed goblin green from the dashboard lights, enough for him to see she was still terribly upset. And of course, he would've been shocked if she hadn't been wearing the same homeless tramp outfit—sweatshirt, jeans, and jogging shoes.

"Would you have left without me?" Mark asked.

She backed out without answering, driving into the murky night.

He peeled back the plastic tab on the coffee cup and took a sip. "You know I'm supposed to be with you."

"You're with me, but not *with* me."

The record-breaking warm January had a downside for nighttime drivers, and that deficiency was particularly evident: dense fog blanketing everything. Valeriya drove below the speed limit, sometimes creeping through the soft mist at thirty mph. Ordinary roadside objects took on an eerie aura, floating by and swirling like ghostly phantoms. Val was in no mood for conversation, and he couldn't understand her capricious change in temperament. They entered the Appalachians, and Blackwell reclined the seat, closing his eyes, listening to the whirring tires and the occasional swipe of her windshield wipers. Numerous fixations rattled inside his head: Alex McCracken and Roy

Lawton, the three completed yet unpublished research papers, and, most importantly, Val. He fell asleep.

Dawn broke when they were close to Kentucky, if one could call it dawn. The soupy haze continued, making the hills and countryside impossible to see. Sunday morning traffic was practically nonexistent, and they breakfasted on Val's old standby: peanut butter and jelly sandwiches. He ate them without complaining.

* * *

They arrived after 10 a.m. Valeriya slowed and made an unexpected turn onto an unmarked gravel path, a trail more for horses or farm tractors than cars. Visibility had improved, but there was still enough fog to hide distant trees.

Mark studied the dashboard map. "I thought the house was on Wendover Road?"

"It is, but everyone is parking here to preserve the impression that Larue is alone. It's about a half-mile hike." With the press of a button, Valeriya elevated the riding height of the car. She swung a broad right, driving through matted-down weeds and parking in front of a weathered Mail Pouch tobacco barn. Three cars were there: a typical FBI undercover sedan in drab gray, a black Wrangler with oversized tires, and a white Chevrolet with a sticker showing it was from a car rental company. She pulled out her cellphone. "I'd better let them know we're coming."

She punched in a number and waited, making a brief announcement of their arrival while Blackwell retrieved the overnight bags. She unzipped her sweatshirt (still shirtless with no bra) and withdrew a Glock pistol from a nylon shoulder holster, racking the slide to chamber a cartridge.

"Did you bring your gun?" she asked.

He exhaled forcefully. "I forgot. Didn't bring my insulin either."

She glared at him with a look that could peel boiler paint.

"I was in a rush, Val. There isn't going to be any shooting, and I only take a small amount. I'll just watch what I eat." He looked down the winding trail. "Who did you talk to?"

"Some guy. He didn't give his name."

They picked up their bags and ambled into the woods, stepping lightly to keep their shoes dry. Snowbirds twittered amongst the bushes, and hanging droplets of morning dew created hundreds of jeweled spider webs in the intricate leafless foliage—unbelievable for the middle of winter. A ramshackle shed contained the remnants of what may have once been a moonshine operation. The air had a pleasant hickory aroma, possibly from someone's smokehouse. Mark craved his regular bacon and egg breakfast.

The back of the century home was recognizable from JP's photographs: empty chicken house off to the side, open woodshed piled with kindling, rain barrels beneath the spouting, and an old millstone walkway leading up to a covered porch. Cars could be heard going by, but none could be seen. The Bureau's stealthy security cameras were barely noticeable, hidden in the eaves and angled to cover the door and windows. They walked up the wooden steps, and Valeriya knocked on the door. A dog barked three times, and a single blue eye peeked through a slit in the curtains.

Two deadbolt locks popped, and a dark-haired woman leaped out of the door, yelling, *"Surprise!"* The door pulled itself shut behind her.

Valeriya bounded back as if struck by a poisonous snake. "Lisa?"

"In the flesh." She embraced Val and kissed her on the cheek. "You have no idea how much I've missed you."

Valeriya pressed a hand to her chest.

Lisa laughed and clasped her hands together. "That look is priceless."

"What on earth are you doing here?"

"Working, of course, but I never expected to see you."

"Working? But you're a shooter."

"Yeah. They wanted Joshua Russell, but he's sick, so they sent me instead. Kinda' flattering if you think about it, me being a replacement for the greatest rifle marksman in FBI history."

Blackwell considered the intriguing tomboy. She wore Marine Corps fatigues and combat boots, had an hourglass figure with squeezingly plump breasts, Beretta 9 mm strapped to her side. Her pert nose, raven-black hair, and desert-sand complexion didn't quite go with those Scandinavian-blue eyes—no wedding ring.

"Just got back to the States last Thursday, and they called me out Friday morning. Told me to grab my gear and get on a plane to Lexington." She looked Valeriya over with a wry wrench in her mouth. "What's with the frumpish clothes?"

Val took a spasmodic breath. "Do you know why you're here?"

"They didn't tell me a thing. All I've been doing is puppy sitting." She ogled Mark, as if expecting to be introduced.

Valeriya did not oblige—he extended his hand. "I'm Mark Blackwell."

"Lisa Rogers." She pumped Mark's hand with a he-man grip. "This is so cool. Val sent me several emails about you, and I was hoping we could get together."

"Is Alex McCracken here?" Valeriya whispered.

"No, but he's on his way—could arrive any time."

"Not so loud. Who's inside the house?"

"Two FBI and two other guys. One of them is a prisoner, I think. What's going on?"

"Do the men know we know each other?"

"I don't think so. What difference does it make?"

Val grabbed Rogers' shoulders. "This is important. We don't know each other. We have never met before now."

Rogers blinked several times. "Okay. We don't know each other."

Valeriya regarded Blackwell. "Lisa and I have never met. Understand?"

He nodded.

"*Say it!*" Valeriya hissed.

"My hearing is not impaired. You and Lisa do not know each other."

She turned back to Rogers. "We've gotta talk, someplace private."

"That's easy enough. I need to walk the dog."

"Do it now." Val turned to Mark. "Take the bags inside and see what's happening. If anyone asks, Lisa and I are getting acquainted."

"Shouldn't I come with you?"

Valeriya's eyes flamed. "Not now. Just do what I say."

Rogers slid a white keycard underneath the door handle assembly, and the deadbolt locks flipped open. She opened the door and called, "Silver Bells." A sizable pooch leaped outside, tail wagging and bouncing with enthusiasm. "I'm walking the dog," Rogers yelled into the house. The four-legged critter sniffed Blackwell and Valeriya as Rogers hooked a leash to his collar. He was a dead ringer for the dog in the photograph. Rogers slid the key card again, and with considerable reluctance, Mark carried their bags inside.

Two men in casual dress approached, firm frowns fixed on their faces. Blackwell showed his FBI credentials, and they gave him a terse greeting, identifying themselves as Special Agents Greg Johnson and Jason Kenton. Kenton unceremoniously turned his back and left the room, apparently aware that Mark was persona non grata. Johnson, speaking with a southern accent, lingered and made an effort to be civil. He explained this was easy but boring duty. Their prisoner was confined to an upstairs bedroom where he had cable TV and a refrigerator full of beer. The food was poor, just frozen TV dinners, canned goods, and military MREs. There was a full bathroom upstairs and a crude but functional toilet in the basement. Johnson told Blackwell to make himself at home, and he disappeared into the room Kenton had entered. Mark peered out the kitchen window: no sign of the women or dog. He went upstairs to find the bathroom.

The cast-iron bathtub had the old-fashioned ball and claw legs and the original plumbing. Closing the door, he discovered the lock had been removed, conceivably because they were housing a federal prisoner. After relieving himself, he explored the house.

The original knotty pine woodwork was there, dark with age, and it appeared the Bureau had made no modifications aside from installing heavy security doors and bulletproof windows. The ceilings were high, the way they built homes back before energy efficiency was the dominant theme. He traveled down a hallway, pausing upon seeing someone's shoe. Blackwell stepped inside an old-fashioned parlor, decorated with an assortment of well-worn chairs, brass reading lamps, and a battered Chesterfield sofa strewn with cushions and patchwork throws. The bluish walls had the eerie imprint of a crucifix that had once hung near a sunlit window. Philip Fleming sat on the sofa reading a book. Mark cleared his throat, and Fleming rose to greet him.

"My apologies for not recognizing you when we met before," Fleming said. "I've read several of your journal articles and two of your books. *The Psychological Autopsy* was a thought-provoking read."

Blackwell shook Fleming's hand. "You're too kind. I'm rather surprised to see you here. When did you arrive?"

"Yesterday afternoon. Mr. McCracken called and said something important was happening, but he didn't want to discuss it over the phone. After comparing our schedules and various alternatives, we decided I would join him here, which is a shorter drive than traveling to the East Coast."

"I take it McCracken is paying you?"

Fleming nodded. "An obscene amount I couldn't refuse."

"Any idea why the dog is here?"

Fleming drummed his fingers on the book he was holding. "No, but that's an interesting question."

Mark reached for the book. "May I?" Fleming handed it over. The slight trembling in Fleming's left hand seemed more pronounced than before. The book was hefty for its modest size. Blackwell opened the cover and read aloud from the first page: "'*It was the best of times, it was the worst of times, it was the age of wisdom, it was the age of foolishness, it was the epoch of belief, it was the epoch of incredulity …*'" He looked up. "Truly, this was Charles Dickens' most celebrated novel. The characters are fascinating. I especially like Madame Therese Defarge for her steely determination and will to win." He gave the book back to Fleming.

"I love reading Dickens, although Madame Defarge is not my favorite character."

Mark accepted Fleming's offer of a chair, and the two men spent an hour talking about the struggles of being a practicing therapist.

Mental health treatment no longer provided the financial rewards of the past, primarily because of socialized medicine and the fee limitations imposed by insurance companies. Blackwell asked Fleming how he dealt with uncooperative patients, particularly women who refuse any treatment. Fleming espoused the virtue of perseverance and that a therapist needed to wait for an opportunity to break through their phobic defense mechanisms. They discussed the accelerating executions in Iran until the deadbolt locks on the back door popped. Mark excused himself.

He found Val and Lisa in the kitchen, whispering to one another. They stopped when he approached. Rogers' previously cheerful demeanor was gone. She had wandering eyes and looked every bit as grim as Val. But the dog was happy, bouncing and pulling playfully at Rogers' camouflage jacket.

"Is everything all right?" Mark whispered.

Valeriya nodded. "What's the situation in here?"

"Don't know much, other than Philip Fleming is down the hall."

Val grimaced. "That doesn't surprise me."

Rogers opened a cellophane packet of dog food. She refilled the dog's water dish and commenced hand-feeding him.

Blackwell bent down and scratched the spirited mutt. "Looks like the two of you have hit it off."

"He's adorable," Rogers replied. "There's no way he's going back to a dog pound."

The dog's ears perked up—Val shifted to the kitchen window. "Alex McCracken is here."

Both women proceeded in opposite directions, Rogers leading the dog into a side room while Valeriya went down the hall. Blackwell followed Val past the parlor and to the front of the house. They entered a room with a large picture window and fireplace.

Mark whispered, "What did you and Lisa talk about?"

"I gave her the short version. Not everything, but enough. Milk Fleming for all the info you can get. He's here for a reason."

"Will do."

Blackwell peeked down the hallway as a pounding knock came from the back door. Special Agent Johnson slid a keycard through the lock, and Alex McCracken entered with JP and two other men, each loaded with baggage and equipment. They were dressed in casual clothes. Johnson conversed quietly with McCracken.

"What!" McCracken exclaimed. "When?" Muffled dialogue ensued until McCracken roared in a voice brimming with malice, "And just who the hell are you?"

Sharp barks and belligerent growls sent Valeriya bounding toward the commotion. Mark hurried after her.

Rogers knelt on the floor and restrained the dog. "No, no. It's okay," she cooed with a soothing intonation. The dog ceased hostilities but scrutinized McCracken with a steady, distrusting gaze. Rogers stroked him. "Good boy."

The assistant director glared down at her. "Who are you?"

She stood up. "Special Agent Lisa Rogers from Hostage Rescue, reporting as ordered, sir."

"SWAT?"

"Yes, sir."

The muscles in McCracken's jaw bulged. "I requested Joshua Russell."

"He's sick, sir. A ruptured appendix. He'll be out of commission for at least six weeks."

"When did it happen?"

"He was on his way here when they rerouted to a hospital. I got called out shortly after."

McCracken and JP exchanged anxious glances. JP suggested trying again in March.

With a practiced gaze, McCracken regarded Rogers, looking her over meticulously. "What are you?"

"Sir?"

"You're not black, and you're not Caucasian or Hispanic."

"I'm a Native American from the Fort Apache Reservation."

He quirked an eyebrow. "An American Indian—with blue eyes?"

Silence.

McCracken bared the faint twitch of a condescending smile. "What's your real name, the one your Apache parents gave you?"

"Naiche."

"And what does that mean in English?"

"Mischief maker."

McCracken humphed once, tilting his head. "Did you bring your rifle?"

"Yes, sir, but I don't have a spotter. I don't like shooting without one."

"Your spotter is here." McCracken made imposing eye contact with everyone. "We're going to have a rotation of personnel. Johnson, Kenton, you are dismissed. Report back to the Louisville field office. Blackwell and Highland will report to the Hoover Building. I'll have an assignment waiting for you."

"We're staying," Valeriya replied in a calm voice.

Everyone froze as though someone had yelled a cuss word in church. JP whispered something in McCracken's ear.

"Where's Larue?" McCracken asked.

"In his bedroom," Johnson replied, "drinking Coors and watching the tube."

"Take his beer away. I want him cold-sober for tomorrow morning."

McCracken introduced the new arrivals, all young men in their late twenties. JP's last name was Madison, and the two new Special Agents were Lee Hopkins and Steve Livingston. Hopkins and Livingston looked like common mill workers, guys who drank Mad Dog 20/20 and shaved every two or three days. Hopkins was shorter than everyone else, maybe five-foot two or three. He had a young and innocent face, the kind you see in church choirs. If there was ever an agent perfect for undercover work, it was him. Livingston had an eagle-beak nose and a troubling aura, like he didn't want to be there. JP was calmer than the others, confident like Clark Kent before changing into Superman.

JP directed Hopkins and Livingston to move their equipment into a large room on the first floor (a place he called the den). Blackwell and Valeriya drifted to a far corner and listened to McCracken pummel

Rogers with questions. How long had she been a member of SWAT? How many shooting assignments? How many men had she killed? McCracken's surly tone improved when Rogers acknowledged killing eleven men and two women. McCracken wanted dirty details, curtly interrupting her: how far away, how many head shots, how many had survived, and whether she understood the rules for using lethal force to protect citizens. He seemed satisfied with her answers.

Rogers requested permission to walk the dog—undoubtedly an excuse to end the unpleasant discourse. McCracken consented, and she made a quick trip upstairs before taking the dog outside. Mark and Val escaped to the parlor. Fleming was gone, and they made themselves comfortable. She pointed out that there were no security cameras inside the house, a sharp contrast to the exterior and a break from normal protocol when monitoring federal prisoners.

"What do you think," Mark asked, "having no cameras inside?"

"The Watergate tapes hung Richard Nixon. McCracken doesn't want to make the same mistake."

A toilet flushed on the second floor, and Philip Fleming appeared soon thereafter. Wanting to return Fleming's gracious hospitality, Blackwell invited him in. Val walked out with her nose high in the air. Fleming sat down, seemingly oblivious to Valeriya's snub. He complained about the steep staircase being hard on his arthritic knees. They continued discussing Blackwell's latest book on the psychological elements of suicide. Fleming disagreed with the premise that suicidal people are presumed to need psychiatric treatment—blasphemous words coming from a mental health professional. He cited the examples of Navy SEAL Michael Monsoor, who threw himself on a grenade to save his comrades, and Buddhist monk Thích Quảng Đức, who set himself ablaze to protest what was happening during the Vietnam War.

Rogers returned with the dog, and McCracken went to meet her. He summoned Blackwell and Valeriya as well, gathering everyone in the kitchen.

McCracken regarded the two women. "Sleeping arrangements are tight. It would be helpful if you could share a room."

"Yes, sir," Rogers replied.

Val grimaced as though it would be an inconvenience, but eventually nodded.

"Mr. Blackwell, you'll have to share a room with Mr. Larue."

"I'll be perfectly happy on the sofa," Mark replied. "It'll be just like home."

"I also require the surrender of your service pistol." McCracken looked at Valeriya. "Yours as well."

"Why?" Valeriya asked.

"Bureau regulations grant the field commander absolute authority in matters of security. A federal prisoner is here, and neither of you is a trained peace officer." McCracken raised a noble chin. "I am responsible for everyone's safety."

Blackwell watched with apprehension as Valeriya opened her zipper and slid a hand into the sweatshirt, but she retrieved the firearm without revealing she was naked underneath. She gave the pistol to McCracken, butt first. Blackwell said he was unarmed. McCracken pointed, and JP patted him down to be sure. McCracken and JP entered the den and closed the door.

Valeriya and Rogers climbed the stairs with the dog close behind. Relieved yet annoyed at being separated from Val, Blackwell returned to the parlor and sat next to Fleming. The psychologist offered to share his room, but Mark declined, thanking him just the same. Things were quiet upstairs except for muffled audio from a television.

McCracken sent Hopkins and Livingston on a food run, telling them to bring enough for everyone. They returned an hour later, and the delicious aroma of chargrill drifted into the parlor. Blackwell continued talking to Fleming, although his mind was on food. JP and Hopkins carried several fully loaded plates into the den, which had become McCracken's bunker of operations. Soon afterward, Livingston appeared at the parlor door and told them to come and eat. Mark eagerly rose and took several steps, pausing and looking back at the still-seated psychologist.

"Aren't you coming?" Blackwell asked.

Fleming smiled and picked up his book. "I had a large breakfast. Perhaps later."

259

The kitchen countertop was laden with delicious-looking containers of roast beef, barbecued ribs, and fried chicken. There were side dishes of potato salad, coleslaw, and corn. Mark went for the ribs, loading his plate to the max. Franco Larue appeared next to him, dinner plate in hand, obviously impressed by the wonderful spread. Blackwell introduced himself as Larue took several chicken thighs and drumsticks. Out of curiosity, Mark sat at a woodworm table and asked Larue to join him. The offer was accepted, although the prisoner seemed more interested in eating than having a dinner conversation. Blackwell kept a keen watch for the girls, but they never came down the stairs. Valeriya probably had food packed away in her luggage.

Larue was the perfect candidate for a Colombian drug smuggler: tall, blonde, and muscular, the opposite of what one would expect. Give him a surfboard, and he would fit right in with the sunny beaches of California. And most important, Larue spoke perfect American English. He did have one notable flaw on those powerful arms: needle marks— not fresh, but definitely there. Larue had once been a hard-core drug user. They both went back for seconds, and Mark continued raiding the ribs while Larue sampled the roast beef.

The pace of activities increased at sundown. JP unlocked the back door so Rogers could walk the dog, and McCracken summoned Philip Fleming to the den. Hopkins and Livingston put together a large tripod and fitted a pair of military binoculars to the mount. JP reminded them the assembly would have to be done in the dark. There was some discussion about why they weren't using the Bureau's electronic binoculars with image stabilization. JP said Alex preferred the primitive tripod setup because nothing could go wrong.

Blackwell recalled Valeriya's comment regarding the lack of security cameras inside the house. Electronic binoculars automatically record the images seen. Here again, McCracken was avoiding everything except an eyewitness account of what was about to happen. Yet the pieces didn't fit together: a dog, giant binoculars, Fleming, a rifle marksman, and Franco Larue. *What is McCracken planning?*

After spending ninety minutes alone with McCracken, Fleming reentered the parlor. Rogers was next, and JP led her into the den. JP joined Hopkins and Livingston in the kitchen for another round of food. If they wanted any of those delicious ribs, they were out of luck. Fleming rejoined Blackwell, uttering a tiresome sigh.

"Did you find out what's going on?" Mark whispered.

"I know less than when I went in."

"What did he want with you?"

"He asked about Lawton's flashpoint, about how quickly he became angry. There were many suppositional questions—suppose Lawton saw this, suppose Lawton saw that, lots of 'what ifs.' But the hypotheticals made no sense, at least to me."

"And what did you tell him?"

"I said it was difficult to say without knowing the specific scenario, yet he refused to divulge any details. From my perspective, this is nothing but an exercise in meaningless dissipation."

Blackwell and Fleming talked for another twenty minutes, speculating about what might be transpiring. Rogers left the den and ascended the staircase, stepping almost as silently as Val. Both women moved like cats creeping across a bed. If you didn't see them, you would never know they were there.

Nature called, and Mark traveled up the stairs. Rogers was nowhere in sight, although the rush of running water came through the closed bathroom door. The opening that had once contained the door lock revealed appealing pink flesh, and the thought of seeing the Indian beauty in all her natural glory was too much to resist. Peeking through the hole seemed risky with vigilant Val nearby. Blackwell waited until the water stopped and pushed the door open. His sphincter tightened upon seeing a stark-naked Franco Larue and his gargantuan male member. Mark apologized and went to find the basement privy, grateful he wasn't Larue's cellmate in prison.

After trying several doors on the first floor, he found the lower staircase. It was a typical rural basement: stone walls, rough-cut wooden steps, musty odor, and dim lighting with no doorway or windows to the outside. The toilet was crude, just a curtain wrapped around a ceramic basin next to a coal cellar. Blackwell relieved himself without touching anything. He had just zipped up his trousers when he overheard McCracken talking—the den was straight above. Mark gently pried open a heating vent, and McCracken's conversation with JP became crystal clear.

"Did you scout the side road?" McCracken asked.

"Thoroughly," JP replied. "It runs parallel to our location, and there are no houses or farms until it rejoins the highway. The county uses it to reach its road salt bins and snow removal equipment, but the warm weather makes that irrelevant. We'll put up a detour sign when Lawton approaches and take it down when he turns onto the road."

"What about the surveillance team?"

The tinkle of wrinkling paper came through the heating vent. "They stop at this bridge. They'll go no farther."

"Do you think they suspect anything?" McCracken asked.

"They believe we plan to arrest Lawton if he shows aggressive intent toward Larue. Nobody knows what's happening except us."

"Do you have the throwdown?"

"An untraceable six-shot revolver," JP replied. "We'll only need it if Lawton is unarmed."

"I don't want to take any chances, so have it ready. And do the fingerprints right. We don't have to worry about powder residue because it doesn't matter if he fired the gun. He only has to have it on his person."

"It's going to take some time," JP said. "I've got to get his prints on the gun and the cartridges—specifically the thumb, index, and middle finger of his left hand around the shell casings. You've got to keep Rogers away."

"I'll send her back to the house as soon as she kills him. Lots of drivers have dashboard cameras that record their journey. If Lawton has one, you've got to get rid of it."

"Understood, but we're taking a big chance. We need Joshua Russell."

"I know," McCracken answered. "Shouldn't be using a pair of tits for serious work, but we're running out of time. The confirmation hearings are one week away, and it will be iffy. Doug needs Jackson's support to prevail, and Lawton's death will satisfy the Senator's lust for revenge."

"What if Rogers doesn't shoot?"

"She will. I'll be her spotter. She won't have a choice."

"But what if she doesn't?"

"In that unlikely event, I'll make the fucking shot myself."

Silence.

"Do you want me to do it?" JP asked. "We could leave Rogers here."

"It's 265 yards, maybe longer, depending on where Lawton stops. You'll need a head shot if he's in his truck, and he'll be a moving target if he gets out. You must kill him. Can you do it?"

"Fifty-fifty chance," JP replied.

"That's not good enough, Jonathan. Even I can do better than even money. Is there any way to get closer?"

"Unfortunately, no. The county has security cameras posted at several locations to prevent people from stealing their road service equipment. This is the only stretch of unmonitored road, and there's nothing up close to hide behind. A long-distance rifle shot is the only way. Of course, I assumed we'd have Russell behind the trigger."

Silence.

"Let's proceed as planned," McCracken said. "I called the SWAT commander, and he said that Indian squaw is lethal as cyanide. Besides, we can use her as insurance. If she only wounds him, I have the option of claiming she fired before I gave the order to shoot. She'll take the fall. It'll be my word against hers—no contest."

"Good thinking."

A thin shaft of yellow light illuminated the basement stairway. Blackwell closed the vent and proceeded casually forward. Valeriya's jogging shoes came stealthily down the steps, toe first, testing each board for creaks, and then moving to another spot upon hearing the faintest sound. The eeriness of her silent progress was unnerving, reminding him of the old nursery rhyme about the infamous Borden murders: "—so close your door and lock and latch it, cause here comes

Lizzie with her hatchet." Mark met her at the bottom, buttoning his jacket as though he had just finished.

"You can't use that," he whispered while pointing to the commode. "It's plugged up."

"I couldn't find you. Did Fleming tell you anything?"

"Nothing useful. He doesn't even know why he's here." Fearful that Valeriya might hear McCracken talking, Blackwell tried to ascend the stairs.

She held him back. "Have you discovered anything else? We can't figure this out."

"It's a mystery to me."

Valeriya followed him up the stairs. The hallway was empty, and she continued to the second floor. Fleming's book and papers were gone, so he had also retired. Mark carried his suitcase to the parlor and closed the door. He stripped to his underwear and rearranged the sofa into an improvised bed, using the patchwork throws as sheet and blanket. There he rested, staring at the featureless ceiling and contemplating McCracken's scheme.

The dog will be used as a diversion, and Lawton will be killed under the pretext that he drew a gun on federal agents. Throwdowns were an old police trick used when an officer had shot an unarmed man, a means of justifying deadly force when circumstances were questionable. This wasn't the first time law enforcement used executive action to solve a problem, nor would it be the last.

Actually, this imaginative exploit might be quite beneficial. Lawton attacking federal officers would be grounds for the search warrant, and having him die in no way diminished the validity of Blackwell's academic papers. On the contrary, Lawton would not be alive to be examined or contest what Blackwell wrote. Lee Harvey Oswald's untimely demise only increased his infamy. A shrewd smile cracked across Mark's face. *Alex McCracken is helping me, and he doesn't even know it.*

23 Boomerang

JP's harsh voice jarred Mark awake:

"It will be daylight soon. Get your asses moving with that setup."

Blackwell put on clean underwear and dressed, wearing the same suit as yesterday. Stepping into the hall, he observed Hopkins and Livingston carrying the tripod and binoculars out of the house. He freshened up in the bathroom and continued down the steep stairs. Philip Fleming's voice came from the kitchen:

"Can you open this? My arthritis is bad this morning."

Blackwell entered, and Franco Larue twisted the top off a canning jar of what looked like green beans. Larue placed the jar in front of Fleming and continued eating.

"Where is everyone?" Mark asked.

"We're the last ones up," Fleming replied. "Looks like a busy day."

Blackwell peeked out the kitchen window. "Where are the girls?"

"They walked the dog about forty-five minutes ago. They're upstairs now." Fleming tilted his head, listening. "Sounds like one of them is in the bathroom. Mr. McCracken and Mr. Madison are in the den."

Blackwell heard nothing but went to investigate, eager to see what was happening. The bathroom was empty, so he approached their bedroom. The dog barked before he arrived, and Valeriya cracked a narrow slit in the door.

"Are you all right?" Mark whispered.

She nodded. "Have you uncovered anything new?"

"No, other than Livingston and Hopkins are out of the house, setting up a tripod with binoculars. Can I come in?"

"Not now. We're busy. We'll talk later." She closed the door.

When Blackwell returned to the kitchen, Fleming and Larue were gone. He raided the refrigerator, breakfasting on cold chicken, biscuits, and various leftovers from yesterday. However, he couldn't find the jar of green beans. While eating, Mark spied JP ascending the stairs. He brought Rogers down and guided her to the den. She wore woodland camouflage and was carrying her rifle. The door was open, and Mark moved closer to listen.

"Caliber?" McCracken asked.

"7.62 NATO."

"Ammunition?"

"Match bullets—150-grain mushrooming soft point."

"I want deep hollow points, the type that explode on impact. Do you have them?"

"Yes, sir."

"This isn't a Remington 700."

"It's a custom rifle from Shilen. Match barrel and chamber with a nine-ounce trigger. The scope is a Steiner 5–25 variable with a mil-dot reticle."

"Let me have it." Jangle of rifle bolt being opened and closed. "For precision shooting?"

"Yes, sir."

"How precise?"

"Shooting from rest with match ammunition and no wind, dime-sized groups at 100 yards."

"And at 270 yards?"

"I can hit a silver dollar all day long."

"Good. We'll be leaving soon. Get ready. I'll be your spotter."

Rogers carried her rifle upstairs. Hopkins and Livingston returned to the house and told McCracken everything was prepared. McCracken took Franco Larue into the den and closed the door. Mark could not hear what they were saying, but Larue's raised voice suggested aggravation.

With Valeriya in tow, Rogers descended the staircase with her rifle. Blackwell and Fleming joined them. McCracken and Larue exited the den, and everyone moved to the large room with the picture window and fireplace. JP checked the drapes to make certain no one could see inside. He made some adjustments to the body armor Franco Larue was wearing.

Larue rubbed his hand across the bulletproof vest. "My attorney didn't say anything about this. This is some weird shit, man."

McCracken put his hand on Larue's shoulder. "Just do what I told you, and you'll be on a plane to Bogotá this Friday."

Larue nodded with a jittery smile.

McCracken regarded JP. "Bring the mutt."

JP brought the tail-wagging pooch and replaced his collar with a choke chain. He gave the leash to Larue, but the dog's bristling brown eyes dawdled over to the girl with the rifle, never leaving her.

McCracken approached Rogers. "I'll take your service pistol. You won't be needing it." She gave him the firearm, and McCracken handed it over to Hopkins. "Take this to the den." He turned to Rogers. "Empty your pants pockets."

Rogers showed him a folding pocketknife and a handkerchief. He scrutinized her utility vest. There were two rows of ammunition clips—three on top and three on the bottom. McCracken pulled out the middle clip from the top row, probably making sure the bullets were hollow points. He tucked the magazine back into her vest and pointed at a device on her utility belt. "What is this?"

"A laser rangefinder, sir. It's needed for accurate bullet placement."

"I checked it yesterday," JP said. "It's okay."

Rogers stood upright, face firm and eyes straight ahead as McCracken knelt and frisked her below the waist, thoroughly prodding and probing her legs, groin, and buttocks. Hopkins smiled, raising a curly brow. Val unobtrusively left the room.

Appearing satisfied, McCracken rose and pressed a transceiver button on his lapel. "Radio check." A screeching arose from the transceivers Hopkins and JP were wearing. McCracken handed Livingston a keycard and told him no one was to get in or out of the house until he returned.

Livingston nodded in a servile manner and slid the card to open the front door. Hopkins went into the early morning light, followed by Larue and the dog, then JP, then Rogers with her rifle, and finally Alex McCracken. Livingston trekked into the den and locked the door. Valeriya drew back the drapes and watched Lisa until they were out of sight. Blackwell gazed over her shoulder. Unlike yesterday's foggy morning, visibility was good, a lucky break for McCracken. Hopkins and JP took Larue and the dog to the west, while McCracken and Rogers went east. The stairs creaked, and Mark glimpsed Fleming ascending to the second floor.

Val pressed closer to the cobwebbed windowpane, her breath clouding the bulletproof glass. "They're using short-range radios with a scrambler, too short for any NSA eavesdropping."

"But what's going on?" Mark asked, feigning his ignorance.

"Isn't it obvious?"

A radio squelch emanated from the den as JP talked about detour signs. Blackwell was just about to say something when Philip Fleming spoke:

"Excuse me, Dr. Highland. My cellphone doesn't seem to be working. May I use yours?"

"None of the cells are working," Val replied, maintaining her gaze out the window. "McCracken is using a radiofrequency jammer."

"I see." Fleming cleared his throat. "I believe this belongs to you."

They turned to see Fleming holding Valeriya's sunglasses.

She gaped at the darkened spectacles, chest rising and falling. "Thank you. They must have dropped out of my overnight bag."

More radio chatter from the den—this time McCracken talking. Blackwell moved to another window and looked through the leafless locust trees. "Can't see a damn thing." He unfolded a handkerchief and cleaned his eyeglasses. "Why would they split up like that, going in different directions?"

Silence.

Mark turned around to an empty room.

* * *

Lisa followed McCracken through the damp woods, rifle cradled in her arms. They went by several No Trespassing signs and stepped through a barbed-wire fence. McCracken paused at a fork in the trail and consulted a hand-drawn map, seemingly confused. Lisa silently removed the bottom-right ammunition magazine from her vest, turned it around, and swapped it for the middle magazine in the top row.

McCracken called JP on the transceiver and asked whether he should veer left or right. JP said left, and they continued on.

Lisa adjusted the straps on her vest to ensure they wouldn't block the tiny camera and microphone. She was ready.

"I need to be briefed, sir."

McCracken kept walking. "You are here to protect Franco Larue."

"I've been trained to apply lethal force in hostage situations. I don't see—"

"This is the same thing."

"How is it the same, sir?"

He ignored her question.

"Sir, how is this a hostage scenario?"

"This is an assignment, just like any other. You will utilize your marksmanship skills to the situation at hand."

"I—rescue—people!"

"And today you're going to rescue Mr. Larue."

They came to a clearing with a camouflaged shooting bench and horizontal rifle rest. The binoculars and tripod pointed toward the road.

McCracken tapped the rear sandbag with his hand. "You'll be shooting from here."

"Sir, Bureau regulations require that I understand what is happening."

McCracken held up his hand. "Mouth closed, ears open."

Lisa lowered her rifle and faced McCracken, standing as steady as possible.

"Do you understand that lethal force is warranted when citizens face a violent attack?"

"Yes, sir."

"And you understand that even a gesture toward what could be a hidden gun is just cause for shooting?"

"Yes, sir."

"You're taking part in a sting operation. A man is approaching in a pickup truck. He's a serial killer who has murdered dozens of innocent people. We believe he may try to attack Mr. Larue, and Special Agents Madison and Hopkins will arrest him if he does. Your sole concern is to protect Mr. Larue from any lethal weapons that may be used against him. If the suspect attempts to shoot Larue, or even if he goes for his gun, you will shoot him in the head. I will make that call."

"Sir?"

"I'll be looking through the binoculars. When I ..." McCracken paused. "If I tell you to take him out, you will fire your weapon and kill him."

"But that's not FBI—"

He lunged forward, practically touching her nose. "*I am the FBI!* This is a special situation, and you will follow my orders to the letter. I have the high-powered binoculars and the legal authority to make the call on using lethal force. Now am I being perfectly clear, Special Agent Rogers?"

Lisa snapped to attention. "Yes, sir. The situation is clear."

"Good. Now make yourself ready. ETA is twenty-five minutes. Show me you are a worthy replacement for the great Joshua Russell, and a promotion and pay increase are guaranteed."

Lisa placed the rifle on the gun rest. She focused the laser rangefinder on a speed limit sign beside the road: 283 yards. She noted the mil-dot conversion in the rangefinder for that distance. McCracken busily worked the binoculars on the tripod, focusing and refocusing the lenses to accommodate his eyeglasses. Lisa turned the elevation knob on the rifle scope counterclockwise. She continued turning the knob until the point of bullet impact would occur at the fifth dot above the crosshairs—impact would be six feet above the point of aim. Lisa made a mental note of the number of complete turns and clicks. She scrutinized the other side of the road for any homes or buildings that could be damaged by a high-flying projectile—nothing but trees. She settled in and waited.

JP spoke from the transceiver: "I hear a diesel engine."

McCracken pressed his transceiver button. "Lee, get Larue started." He looked down at Lisa. "Get ready."

Lisa racked the bolt of her rifle, chambering a cartridge. She positioned herself at the shooting bench, keeping both eyes open—one eye at the scope and one eye to see the overall situation. Franco Larue came into view, walking the dog down the middle of the road. A silver pickup truck rounded the corner and slowed. Larue blocked the path of the truck, forcing it to stop. He yanked at the chain leash, choking the dog—the dog struggled. The driver lowered his window, and Larue moved closer, still holding a strangling grip.

"Get your finger on the trigger," McCracken whispered. "This could happen fast."

Lisa did as he asked. She noted the vertical dot above the crosshairs that marked the actual point of aim. Larue started shouting and lifting the chain, practically hanging the dog. The driver's words couldn't be heard, but Larue was yelling, *"Pussy—Motherfucker—Mind yer own goddamn business. It's my fuckin' dog!"*

"Come on. *Come on!*" McCracken jeered.

Lisa flinched when Larue kicked the dog in the ribs. Her heart raced as he kicked him again and again. The dog yelped and cried out in pain.

"He's going for his gun," McCracken called. "Take him out."

"His hands are on the steering wheel, sir."

"He moved a revolver to his lap. I saw him do it. Shoot him now."

"His hands have never left the steering wheel, sir."

"Fire your weapon. That's a goddamn order!"

Lisa didn't move.

McCracken whirled around. "Get the fuck up."

Lisa engaged the safety lever and rose from the bench, calmly facing McCracken.

He hurriedly embraced the rifle and moved the safety lever into its firing position. He aimed, and the gun discharged with a loud boom.

"Got 'em!" McCracken bellowed while shaking his fist. Larue and the dog bolted in opposite directions. With smoking tires and the squeal of burning rubber, the truck sprang forward. "What the fuck?" McCracken racked the bolt and fired again, but the accelerating vehicle disappeared from view. He yelled into the transceiver, "Finish it, Jonathan! Use your pistol. You must stop him. Don't let him get away." McCracken dashed toward the road.

Lisa picked up the rifle and rotated the scope elevation knob clockwise. She returned the bullet impact to the crosshairs and jogged after McCracken. JP and Hopkins came running with pistols drawn, wide-eyed and breathing heavy. The three men converged on Franco Larue. Lisa arrived to find the dog's neck bleeding from the chain collar. He ran to her, ears folded back and trembling. She removed the offending restraint and tossed it into some nearby weeds.

"Was he hit?" McCracken called breathlessly. "I couldn't see."

"Didn't look like it," JP answered. "No broken glass or bullet holes in the truck."

McCracken looked down the empty road. "Goddamn it."

"The clock is ticking, Chief," JP said. "We gotta do something. The surveillance team is too far away to give chase. Do you want me to call the Kentucky State Police and have him pulled over?"

McCracken searched the road for signs of broken glass. "Shit. There's nothing here, nothing at all." He looked at JP. "Was there a dash cam?"

"Couldn't tell. He was moving fast, and the sun was on the windshield. Kentucky Police, yes or no?"

McCracken wiped sweat from his wrinkled brow. "No police. There'll be a shit-load of questions, and we need time to think this through. Just let him go." McCracken reeled around as if swinging a battle axe. *"Son of a bitch!"*

Larue wandered over. "Look, man, I did my part, just like you told me. A deal's a deal. I'm free, right?"

McCracken nodded. "Yeah. I'll sign the papers myself and put you on a plane. The sooner the better."

Hopkins threw up his hands and yelled at Lisa, "You missed an easy shot like that? *You missed twice!* You were shooting from a bench, and you couldn't even hit the fuckin' truck?"

Lisa said nothing.

McCracken regarded her suspiciously. He looked around and pointed to a distant tree with a cluster of hanging gourds—Purple Martin houses during the summer. "Shoot that birdhouse, the one on the far left."

Lisa racked the bolt and raised her rifle—the empty birdhouse blew apart.

McCracken stared in disbelief. "Again. The far right." She destroyed the second birdhouse. "Jonathan, you try. Shoot the one at the top."

Lisa removed a loaded ammunition clip from the bottom row of her vest and inserted it into the rifle. She gave the weapon to JP.

JP chambered a cartridge and rested the gun atop an old fence post—the birdhouse shattered into pieces. He obliterated two more birdhouses. "The weapon is dead-on." He gave the rifle back to Lisa. "You musta had a bad case of buck fever."

McCracken kicked the empty shell casings off the road. He turned to the group. "Now listen up. The sting was unsuccessful. Lawton just drove by, and nothing happened. The shooting was just some unscheduled target practice and nothing else. Got it?" Hopkins and JP nodded. McCracken approached Lisa. "Did you hear what I said?"

She stood stone-faced and silent.

He glared into her eyes. "I've got three eyewitnesses who'll say it never happened." He waited. "Don't fuck with me, or you won't be able to get a job guarding moldy buffalo skins outside your daddy's tepee."

Silence.

McCracken turned to JP. "Call Steve and have him get rid of Fleming, and see if he can also dispose of our unwanted guests." He regarded Hopkins. "Tell the surveillance team to break off for the day. Let's get the hell out of here."

"What about the tripod and shooting bench?" Hopkins asked.

McCracken looked back at the distant woods. "Nobody can see them. We'll get them later. And put that mongrel back on his leash."

Lisa formed a double loop in the rope and slipped it over the dog's head.

"Franco, take the dog," McCracken called.

"I've got him," Lisa answered.

"Franco, take the dog now."

Larue pulled the rope out of Lisa's hand, and the dog clamped his large jaws around Larue's leg. The Colombian spun around, yelling and screaming. Lisa jumped into the fray and pulled them apart. Larue rolled on the ground, holding his bleeding ankle.

"Shoot the fucking mutt!" McCracken yelled.

Lisa's mind raced. If she ran into the woods, the dog would follow. She was just about to take off when JP spoke.

"Not now, Chief. Someone's watching us."

McCracken looked around. "Where?"

"Ten o'clock, at the top of the hill." JP raised a pair of binoculars. "Looks like a security guard for the county. Their equipment barn is in the valley behind him. He must have heard the shooting and came to investigate. This land is posted, and somebody owns those birdhouses. We gotta get outta here now. I have a silencer back at the house. We'll do the dog there."

McCracken ordered Hopkins to take the dog—Lisa remained close by. JP tied a handkerchief around Larue's bleeding leg and helped him to his feet. Larue could walk, and everyone traveled into the woods. They paused long enough to contact Livingston and the surveillance team.

* * *

Blackwell strode up to the window, eyes forward, teeth clenched. *What went wrong? Lawton has more damn lives than an alley cat!*

He turned to Val. "We should have left with Fleming. You heard what Livingston said. Lawton never showed up."

"Then why was there shooting?"

"It's nothing but hunters."

"Deer season is over."

"Could be someone target shooting. These inbred rednecks are in love with their firearms."

Valeriya ignored him.

"Look, Val—"

She raised her hand, cutting him off. "I'm not leaving until I know Lisa is safe."

"How could she not be safe? Nothing happened."

McCracken's brassy voice came over Livingston's transceiver. They followed Livingston to the back of the house, where he slid his keycard through the lock. Franco Larue limped through the door. McCracken and JP came in next, followed by Rogers toting her rifle.

"What happened?" Livingston asked. "Where's Lee?"

"He's tying the mutt out back," McCracken replied. "The dog turned vicious."

Livingston looked out a small window in the door. "Vicious? I played with him last night. He's an overgrown puppy."

Larue raised the leg of his pants and exhibited a blood-soaked handkerchief. "Motherfucker bit me." He grabbed his stomach and groaned. "I'm feeling really sick."

McCracken gestured to Livingston. "Help him up the stairs and into his room—and give him his beer."

Larue hobbled up the steps with Livingston lending support.

Blackwell glanced out the kitchen window. The dog was tethered to a tree at the edge of the woods, about eighty yards away. McCracken slid his keycard, and Hopkins entered, appearing just as rattled as the others.

Livingston returned and regarded Hopkins. "You okay, Lee?"

He heaved a long sigh. "Yeah, I'm fuckin' fine."

The dog barked, and Livingston gazed out the door window again, fidgeting with a button on his shirt. "What do we do with him?"

"I've got a silenced pistol in the back," JP replied. "Lee will take care of it."

Livingston shook his head. "I think we should take him to an animal shelter—or something."

McCracken gave Livingston a hostile shove. "I'm not running a debate, Steve. The dog is dangerous, and there are liability issues for the Bureau." He regarded the woman holding the rifle. "Special Agent Rogers, your duties here are finished. Pack your things and report to your supervisor." He glared at the unwanted. "Mr. Blackwell and Miss Highland, this operation is terminated, and you are hereby dismissed."

Rogers ascended to the second floor with Valeriya close behind. Mark proceeded toward the parlor, ostensibly to gather his things. He passed out of sight and stopped to listen.

"She missed the shot," Hopkins whispered. "She missed the whole truck. Lawton just drove away."

"How could that happen?" Livingston asked. "She killed eleven men."

"That has to be more of Marshall's equal opportunity bullshit," JP replied. "They fudge the results to make women appear equal to men. Female agents can sometimes punch pretty holes in paper targets, but they will choke when it counts. They can't function under pressure, not like men. Joshua Russell would have put one in Lawton's ear."

"The Bureau keeps sinking lower and lower," Hopkins added.

"There will be some serious changes when Doug takes over," McCracken said. "We are going to assign jobs and promote people based on talent and performance."

Creaking floorboards under Mark's feet hushed the private conversation. He ducked into the parlor and reemerged with his suitcase. Rogers joined him with her gun case and duffel bag.

"Where's Val?" Mark whispered.

"She's coming."

Rogers entered the kitchen, and with no sign of Valeriya, Blackwell followed. JP slid a card through the lock and opened the door. Rogers passed the snooty faces and went down the porch steps. McCracken closed the door and watched her through the small window.

"Are you going to tell us what happened out there!" Her derisive voice was grating as chalk squeaking across an old schoolroom blackboard. Every head turned to see Val standing in the kitchen doorway. Elongated seconds ticked by. "Cat got your tongue, Mr. McCracken?"

McCracken moved toward her, puffing out like a toad. "You've lost your shield, sugar britches. The Queen Bee's retirement became official this morning." He flashed a wicked smile. "You are nothing but a scrawny little bug in my chicken coop, and it's dinner time for the birds." His eyes darted between her and Mark. "Both of you are fired. I want your offices cleaned out by tomorrow night, or I'll have all your shit thrown into the trash." He proceeded back toward the door window, smiling as if the problem was resolved.

"Shall we talk about transcripts, Alex? College transcripts?"

McCracken halted in his tracks. He swiveled around, head first, body reluctantly following. They glared at each other without blinking, without breaking the uneasy silence.

Valeriya stepped contentiously into the room, hands on hips, elbows turned out. "Every FBI applicant must submit a college transcript, a document printed on official transcript paper with the raised seal of the Registrar. The transcript in your personnel file is marked 'Official,' but it's only a photostatic copy—a fairly convincing forgery created with a scanner and high-tech printer, but without the raised seal."

JP blurted out a crazy-eyed laugh. "Oh, what a crock a shit." He looked at his boss, eager to watch the ensuing rebuttal. But McCracken's hollow expression said it all.

Val regarded McCracken's sweaty face. "I used the consent form you signed in your application to get another copy of your academic record from Cornell. And there it was. Alexander Maximilian

McCracken, expelled two semesters for cheating on a math exam. That alone would have prevented you from joining the FBI."

Mark's temples throbbed. *Where is this going? Why hadn't she told me before?*

McCracken's thunderous eyes fell upon her, twitching like livid bumblebees. "This is slander." He glanced at his subordinates as if about to give a command, opening his cavernous maw, but words failed him.

"The phony transcript exists right now in your official personnel file," Valeriya continued, "unqualified proof of my allegation." She beamed like someone about to taste a delicious dessert. "Just think of the implications."

"There are worse things than losing a job," McCracken roared. "Both of you could just disappear. We could cut you up into little meatballs and feed you to the fucking dog, and it would all be blamed on Lawton."

Livingston and Hopkins exchanged uneasy glances.

"Relax, Max," Val cooed with cool composure. "I'm not after you." She folded her arms. "You see, it's not possible to submit a fake transcript to the FBI. All transcripts are acquired directly from the respective university, therefore no one can prove you did anything wrong." She inched closer. "I want the inside man, the sordid mastermind within the FBI who could make the substitution, the con artist who hand-picked his kiss-ass cronies for the Application Committee, the heavy presence who had the clout to make everyone a little less observant about the fine details of applicant documentation, the unethical bastard who wanted to bring his tarnished nephew into the Bureau." Valeriya licked her lips . "Douglas McCracken will never be appointed as director of the FBI. *I'll see to that!*"

McCracken lunged toward her, drawing back his fist. Val whipped out a pistol—the 9 mm Beretta McCracken had taken from Rogers. Mark nearly shit his pants.

The FBI chieftain's eyes grew wide, but then he broke into a far-reaching smile. "Thank you. You have just doused your professional career with gasoline and lit a match. Drawing a gun on federal officers is a felony."

"You threatened me with physical violence. I had no choice."

"It will be your word against ours," McCracken replied while gesturing to his underlings. "Who do you think will win?"

"Open the door. Come on, Mark, we're going."

Blackwell froze in place, unsure of what to do. "What about our things?"

"Leave them. We're going now."

"Make your choice Dr. Blackwell," McCracken said while folding his arms. "Stay with us, and your job and professional reputation will be secure. I give you my word."

Mark joined her, and McCracken's smile vanished.

She pointed the pistol at McCracken, cocking the hammer. *"I said open the fucking door!"*

McCracken slid his keycard and held the door open. He raised a calming hand to his subordinates. "Let them go. They'll be behind bars tomorrow morning."

Valeriya sent Blackwell out first and walked backwards out the door. The rope tethering the dog to the tree was still there, but the animal was gone. They jogged into the woods.

Mark paused halfway to the car to catch his breath. "You have really done it now. Our goose is cooked."

"Keep going. I want to get out of here."

He hurried after her. The cars came into view: Val's Grand Cherokee and McCracken's Mercedes limousine. She unlocked the doors to her vehicle, and they got inside. Two minutes later, they were on the main road driving away.

"Was it worth it?" Blackwell asked. "Sacrificing your career so Lisa could save the dog?"

She said nothing.

"Was that truth or bullshit about McCracken's transcript?"

"I can't talk about it."

"Can't or won't?

"Both."

Mark was mostly quiet during the return journey, sensing the gathering storm. Valeriya made one stop for gasoline and food before they arrived home.

24 The Sting

Blackwell stayed home the following day. Valeriya said she was taking some time off, so there wasn't any point in going to the DDI. What was going to happen regarding Val's gun drawing escapade? Imprudence and ingenuity are two sides of the same coin, and she may have overreached with crafty Alex. Who would win the battle of he says, she says? Mark would be a witness for Val, but McCracken had his own witnesses. Push a slithering snake underwater, and he will pop up someplace else.

The Kentucky debacle was as much a blow to Mark as to Alex McCracken. Lawton was still free, and the Bureau's one chance to nail him was gone. There they were, three finished research papers, all dressed up with no place to go. His sabbatical was two-thirds over, and hard-nosed Dean Shoemaker expected more than work-in-progress. Wittgenstein University invented *publish or perish!*

Bored and aggravated, Blackwell turned on the television. All five networks showed live coverage of the plunging stock market and a massive cyberattack on the US banking system. The assault originated somewhere in the Middle East, and several CIA commentators said Iran was behind the plot. Computer experts said this new virus was radically different from anything seen before. The worm altered the financial records of millions of bank customers and wrote fictitious information into computer backup files. Small account balances were exchanged for large, creating a bookkeeping nightmare. Some bank customers had already withdrawn large amounts of money that wasn't theirs, and the three largest banks announced they would be closed for a week to reconstruct their financial records. Mark tried to log on to his Chase checking account without success.

Later that evening, the television news reported from anonymous sources that a major break in the Marshall bombing case was imminent, and a shocking arrest would soon be made. The news anchor also discussed reports of electric power plants mysteriously blowing up in Iran, plunging large parts of the country into darkness. A power plant expert said the computers controlling the steam boilers malfunctioned, keeping visible pressure gauges normal while leaving the gas jets wide open. One cable news commentator speculated that the United States had launched a retaliatory cyberattack. He said we were seeing the first cyberwar between nations. Other TV pundits opined that Russia had given the virus to Iran, and they were "laughing their asses off" while Iran and the United States pounded each other with devastating economic damage.

* * *

Two days later, Blackwell received an early morning phone call from Amanda Harrison, an investigator from the Office of Professional Responsibility. OPR was analogous to Internal Affairs for a police department, and they investigated FBI misconduct. Harrison requested Mark's immediate presence in Washington. Blackwell knew this was coming, and it would be a serious meeting. Lying to OPR investigators was a criminal offense, and prison time could follow.

Upon arriving at OPR Headquarters, Blackwell was ushered into a room where he was given a quick physical exam: temperature, blood pressure, questions about how he was feeling and had he been sick. Mark said he had no complaints. He asked the physician why he was being examined, but the doctor seemed evasive, saying it was just a routine checkup.

They took Blackwell to an interrogation room: hard wooden chairs, bright lights, and a video camera. Harrison introduced herself and OPR agent Martin Callaway. Mark gave each of them a firm handshake to shroud his anxiety. Troubling questions popped into

Mark's head. *Are they after me or Val? Do I need a lawyer?* He sat down at an oblong table, wiping his sweaty palms across his pants.

Harrison began the interview by requesting a meticulous accounting of his actions at the house on Wendover Road. She wanted a sequential description of everything he did, who he met, where and when, and how long he was with them. Blackwell lied as little as possible, giving an accurate account of Valeriya's gun-drawing confrontation with Alex McCracken. He couldn't admit to knowing about McCracken's plot to kill Roy Lawton—he would be complicit in a conspiracy to commit murder. Harrison worked methodically, slowing him down and requesting finer details about everything. She had no qualms about making him rehash his story out of sequence, obviously looking for inconsistencies. Strangely, there were no questions about Valeriya or why she pulled a gun on her boss.

Blackwell requested a bathroom break, and Callaway accompanied him to the men's room. Mark stood at the urinal and overheard several men discussing the late-breaking news: CIA Director Anthony Naples was now a fugitive. *Even Hell has its rainbows.*

Bottled soda and two large pizza boxes were in the room when Blackwell returned. He raised a lid and helped himself to the biggest slice while Harrison talked on her phone.

"Yes, sir," Harrison said. "We are doing it now. I'll submit my report as soon as possible." Harrison conversed for another five minutes. She regarded Blackwell. "Was anyone sick during your stay in Kentucky?"

"Not to my knowledge," Mark replied. "As I said previously, Franco Larue suffered a dog bite and was feeling poorly."

"You're quite sure?" Callaway asked. "No one was sick at all?"

Mark nodded. "Not as far as I know." He looked back and forth between Harrison and Callaway. "What's this about?"

"Mr. Larue died yesterday morning."

Mark gawked at her. "I didn't think the dog bite was that serious."

"It wasn't," Harrison replied. "He complained of stomach pains and had difficulty breathing, at which point he was taken to a hospital. The doctors tried to save him but were unsuccessful."

"They must have some idea as to what killed him."

"The symptoms are consistent with food poisoning, specifically clostridium botulinum, also known as botulism. However, the autopsy is still underway. Unfortunately, the leftover food at the house has been thrown away, making an accurate diagnosis difficult."

Blackwell readjusted his position on the uncomfortable chair. "I'm skeptical of that diagnosis. Everyone was eating everything, and botulism is a serious toxin. If the food was tainted, others would have become ill."

Harrison nodded. "We'll know more after the toxicology report."

Mark thought for an instant. "I'm rather surprised you didn't want more information about the fight between Alex McCracken and Dr. Highland."

Harrison and Callaway exchanged furtive glances. She regarded Mark. "Two months ago, Dr. Highland contacted our office about the possibility of fraudulent FBI employment documentation. The situation was awkward because it seemed to show a conspiracy within the Bureau involving upper administration. The questionable document contained Dr. Highland's fingerprints along with the prints of the Bureau's Acceptance Committee, but no other prints, such as administrative assistants or mailroom workers. The other employment documents in the file were covered with many fingerprints, but not the document in question—very suspicious. However, we had to consider the possibility that the document was planted to falsely incriminate a senior FBI official. With this in mind, we made a copy of the phony document and placed it in the file. We also installed a hidden surveillance camera in the document examination room. Dr. Highland was instructed to, at the proper time and place, drop hints about discovering the fake document. Someone openly objecting would imply innocence—someone attempting a cover-up would suggest guilt. Last Monday afternoon, we received a report that Alex McCracken's personal assistant had accessed the file. The video shows him removing the copy in question and smuggling it out of the personnel office."

Callaway perked up from his relaxed position. "We were watching the video of McCracken's secretary when our office received a call from Special Agent Lisa Rogers. She alleged that Alex McCracken had attempted an illegal killing and OPR intervention was needed. She said she had body camera footage to back up the allegation, and she would be available for questioning."

Blackwell acknowledged Harrison's inquisitive eye. "I'll help in any way I can."

"We interviewed Lisa Rogers on Tuesday and viewed her body camera film. The camera was hidden in a rifle ammunition magazine, and Mr. McCracken didn't know he was being recorded. I can't discuss specific details, but the film is alarming. It shows serious violations of FBI procedures and breaches of federal law. Regrettably, McCracken and Rogers were looking through telescopic devices, and the body camera could not record what they were seeing. The video does, however, invalidate Mr. McCracken's sworn statement of what happened that morning."

Mark said nothing.

"Dr. Highland also had a body camera during her clash with Alex McCracken. The camera was turned on but hidden in her pocket, so we have a recording of what was said but no video. Here again, the soundtrack supports Dr. Highland's version of events."

Mark nodded. "I guess she couldn't wear the body camera because it would be seen." He felt hurt that Valeriya had not confided in him. After all they had been through together, she still didn't trust him.

Harrison closed her notebook. "You may go now, Professor Blackwell. We will be in touch about your role in the upcoming trials. Please don't discuss the facts of this case with anyone except the appropriate governmental representatives."

Blackwell shook hands with Harrison and Callaway before leaving.

* * *

The toxicology report for Franco Larue said he died from foodborne botulism. The most plausible theory suggested that Larue ate food that was left unrefrigerated for too long. Such instances are rare, but they occur. Based on the evidence and autopsy, Franco Larue's death was ruled an accident.

President Alice Nightingale accepted the resignation of Douglas McCracken and named Patrick Greene as the new director of the FBI. Alex McCracken, Jonathan Madison, Stephen Livingston, and Lee Hopkins were charged with multiple felonies, including conspiracy, falsifying official documents, and lying to FBI investigators.

The Stealth Killer case was placed on hold as everyone adjusted to the change at the top and Patrick Greene's consensus-building managerial style. February passed into March, and record cold gripped North America, negating the balmy winter everyone previously enjoyed. Relations between Val and Mark also cooled, and she kept a professional distance between them. There were no more lunches or dinners, just strict business conversation, and only when necessary. Mark was devastated, and his remedial efforts to restore their close friendship were unsuccessful.

With Bureau operations approaching normal, Patrick Greene convinced a federal judge to grant search warrants for Lawton's properties in Columbus and Kentucky. The judge restricted the search to chemicals and laboratory devices that could create the carcinogenic poison suspected (but never proven) in the death of Scott Jackson and his alleged conspirators. In an extensive meeting between Blackwell, Valeriya, and a host of Bureau specialists, the group decided that the search of the Kentucky property was more important because the acreage was riddled with limestone mines and natural caverns, suitable places for hiding a chemical laboratory. The committee further agreed Lawton should be taken into custody in Ohio to prevent the possible destruction of evidence that may occur once he realized federal agents were upon him. The lightly traveled road in front of Lawton's Ohio home was considered the best place to make the stop. FBI professionals would take Lawton into custody. Another team of agents would simultaneously execute the warrant in Kentucky and scour the Lawton farm for evidence of a chemical laboratory.

Bureau surveillance of email communications revealed that Lawton would travel to Columbus on March seventeenth, and Patrick Greene chose that time to perform the search. Val insisted on being there when Lawton was detained, saying this was her case. Patrick Greene acquiesced, saying she and Blackwell could make the journey to Columbus together. In a private conversation with Blackwell, Greene promised that Mark would be the Bureau's press agent and spokesperson for the Stealth Killer case—providing Lawton was charged with murder. At least that was something of value.

25 No Colder Place

They traveled to Ohio the day before the planned arrest. Val drove, as usual, and Mark was content to allow her to navigate the snow-covered roads. She still had her shields up, being cordial in a business-like way, but only listening with half an ear, not talking to him like a friend. He had to do something, make an offer or give a grand gesture, otherwise he would never see her again. When they crossed the Ohio River, Blackwell made his play.

"Patrick Greene told me I would be the spokesperson when Lawton is charged with murder."

"Congratulations. You finally got what you wanted."

"I'd like you to be there with me. We could manage the press together."

She gave a contemptuous snort. "I'm not good at that. You're the expert on psychological manipulation."

"Now, what does that mean?"

Valeriya said nothing.

"Will you at least think about it, not make your decision right away?"

"I'll give it some thought."

The tiny wrinkles around her eyes proclaimed the falsity of her statement. She said it without thinking, placating him for the sake of expediency. Mark spent considerable time pondering what else he could do. *How can you get a woman who doesn't want you? The painful and obvious answer is—you can't.* They continued their journey with small talk that meant nothing at all.

When they arrived, red clouds formed a brilliant sunset that skimmed the horizon, patches of orange cotton candy so bright it seemed like midday. The surveillance house, a single-story brick ranch, was several hundred yards from Lawton's residence. The local realtor had a "Sold" sign in the front yard to prevent people from calling while it was leased to the Bureau. Several FBI agents had stayed there to watch Lawton's infrequent comings and goings, but no one had been at the house since January. Valeriya put on a warm coat, and they carried their belongings through the snow, one suitcase each along with her laptop computer.

The interior was an icebox, and Blackwell raised the thermostat to a tolerable seventy degrees. He would have raised it higher, but Val disliked warmer temperatures. The furnishings were unpretentious, just enough creature comforts for a sustained FBI surveillance. The walls were bare except for a single picture hanging aslant, a child-like painting of a Christmas snowman melting under a blazing sun. Two pairs of binoculars sat on a shelf beside the window facing Lawton's property. Mark inspected the two bedrooms, fantasizing and hoping, but not believing it would happen.

After unpacking and getting settled, Valeriya pulled out her cellphone. She fiddled with the device, turning it on and off several times. "Is your cell working? I want to call Fleming, but I can't get a signal."

"Philip Fleming?"

She nodded.

"Whatever for?"

"He will join us tomorrow morning. He wants to be here when Lawton is taken into custody."

Mark hid his resentment and tried his cell: *Network Unavailable.* "Mine's not working either."

Valeriya opened her laptop computer and crouched over the screen, scowling with revulsion. "This isn't right. There's no broadband at all, not even weak signals. And there's a cellular tower right down the road." More typing. "There's nothing from the commercial satellites. Only the military and NSA systems are working." She turned on the television and tuned in a local Columbus station, finding news commentators discussing another cyberattack. They sat on the sofa and watched the evolving calamity.

Unlike the previous attack on banks, this virus targeted internet and telecommunication systems. AT&T and Verizon issued statements saying over ninety percent of phone and internet service was unavailable in the eastern United States, and the outage was spreading west. A computer virus specialist explained that the malicious code had already infected the besieged systems and was lying dormant until a specified time for activation. This allowed the worm to spread without revealing its existence. The news anchor said Air Force One was transporting President Nightingale back to Washington from her trip to a NATO summit.

Blackwell inquired about food, whereupon Val showed him an assortment of healthy but tiresome ready-to-eat meals. This kiddie snack was not to his taste, not after a day of munching bland protein bars on the road. Mark went to the kitchen in search of something better.

The empty refrigerator hummed like it was still serving a purpose. *Just unplug the damn thing.* He kept looking, smelling something interesting, but not knowing what it was. He opened and closed cupboard after cupboard, rummaging in deep corners and sifting through canned goods: green beans, corn, pickled cauliflower, and lots of pancake mixes. Blackwell stood on his toes and adjusted his eyeglasses: camera on the top shelf, an expensive device with a telephoto lens. He took it down and read the tag: Property of Federal Bureau of Investigation. One of the agents spying on Lawton must have left it. Mark turned the camera on and viewed the display. He clicked through the photos—all the same, magnified close-ups showing Lawton at his roadside mailbox. How boring. He continued looking: same posture, same setting, same ... *Shoes?*

Blackwell pressed the plus key to enlarge the photo. Roy Lawton and Valeriya were wearing the same shoes, the same brand and color, identical in every way. *A coincidence?* He flipped through the previous pictures: same shoes in every shot. *Is this funny or frightening?* He went through the photos again, this time studying every detail. *Holy shit! Lawton is wearing Valeriya's hooded sweatshirt—the same floppy monstrosity she's wearing now.* The date-stamp of the picture was October twelfth of last year. Mark expanded the photo and scrutinized the metal zipper tab, the pull strings, the angle and cut of the pockets, and a slight imperfection in the fabric. He inspected more pictures and found what appeared to be the cheap belt Valeriya had around her waist. Mark struggled with indescribable thoughts. *How? When? Why?*

"Everything is down now," Val called. "No phone service from coast-to-coast. Even the landlines aren't working."

Mark turned off the camera and hid it behind a box of corn flakes on an unreachable shelf. He returned to her, this time sitting in a chair. "No phone service?" he said concernedly. "That will create a mess." Valeriya watched television while he studied her. Those were the shoes all right, the same belt and hoodie in the photos. The slight defect around the collar was there. This wasn't a similar sweatshirt. It was the exact same one! Valeriya never wore a bra or blouse when wearing the damn thing—always naked underneath. What did this mean? Whatever it was, it wasn't good. The food in the house was only stuff Valeriya would eat. Had they been meeting here? The implications were worse than he could have imagined. And what about the investigation? Lovers have no secrets. This was much more than shadowy nastiness. Mark's torrid blood turned to ice.

"What?" Val asked, staring straight at him.

Blackwell focused on the television, pretending to be preoccupied.

"Mark?"

He turned his head attentively, still saying nothing, floundering with awkwardness.

"You look—bothered by something."

He gestured to the news broadcast. "Well, just think of it. Without internet or telephone service the entire country could grind to a halt."

"Nightingale issued a statement assuring everyone that all communication services would be restored in a few days."

Better end this before you hang yourself. "I think I'll turn in early. Tomorrow is a big day."

"I won't be far behind."

He took a lukewarm shower, dressing in soft pajamas, the same velvety material Valeriya liked. He chose the bedroom with the king-size bed, leaving a corner light on but dimmed and the door invitingly open. Val took her shower and crept silently into the other bedroom, closing the squeaking door. *How depressing.* Mark popped two sleeping pills into his mouth, hoping he wouldn't dream.

* * *

A whimsical whiff of something sweet drew him out of a deep and dreary slumber. One sleeping pill would have been enough. Blackwell dressed with some difficulty, his head feeling like it was filled with muddy water. He spied Valeriya whipping creamy-white liquid with a large wooden spoon, adding raw oats and raisins. She ladled the lumpy mush onto a hot griddle, creating six grapefruit-sized pancakes. Soppy pancake batter trickled down the thick spoon handle and was whisked away by an incredibly supple and licentious tongue. Val's favorite Tribal Grounds coffee sat comfortably on the counter.

Mark entered the kitchen, trying to act normal. "Did you sleep well?"

"Not really. Nerves, I guess."

"What's there to be nervous about? We're going to be spectators, and that is all."

She placed four of the golden-brown confections into a dish and set it before him. "There are two kinds of syrup. Sugar-free and genuine maple from Vermont. Which do you want?"

"Vermont maple."

Blackwell tipped the brown jug and smothered the pancakes. Valeriya poured coffee for them. She took the last two cakes and began eating them without syrup.

These were not restaurant pancakes, more like oatmeal flapjacks—thick, chewy, and doubly good when drenched with pungent syrup. Four wasn't enough, and he cajoled her into fixing him two more.

Upon finishing the last cake, a twinge of sugary rush dulled his senses. Blackwell proceeded to his room for his morning insulin, giving himself a larger than normal injection. He put on his coat and stepped outside, believing some frosty air would do him good. Powdery snow blew across the ground, forming miniature dust devils that danced to and fro. The snow wasn't deep, maybe three or four inches, walkable without heavy boots. The homes were spaced far apart, not like the civilized suburbs. This was furrowed farmland, rippling with green corn in the summer but flat and barren in winter. The crisp air cleared his head, and he went back inside. Last night was an overreaction, his irrational fear of Lawton swerving out of control. Valeriya was glued to the television, scowling and shaking her head.

"What's the phone situation?" Mark asked.

"The virus has spread to Canada and Mexico. Most other countries have shut down their Internet as a precaution. Unless you have a government satellite connection, there are no emails or text messages anywhere. They're calling it the Chameleon because it changes its appearance to match the programming code of the host as it moves from one communication system to another. The Secretary of Defense called it the nuclear weapon of cyberspace." She looked up from the television. "And if that wasn't enough, we are at war with Iran."

"You've got to be kidding."

They watched a continuous stream of cruise missile launches from United States ships of war. A banner scrolling across the television said President Nightingale has closed all schools and universities, and only persons holding essential jobs should report for work until phone service is back to normal.

Val checked her computer. "I sent an email via satellite, asking whether the Lawton operation was still on, but they haven't responded."

Mark cringed at the thought—*another delay, another opportunity for something to go wrong.* "They'll probably cancel. I don't see how they can do this without phone service."

Philip Fleming arrived at 9:07 a.m., piloting his knobby-tired Wrangler, the same vehicle he drove in Kentucky. Valeriya let him in through the back door.

Fleming rubbed his quivering hands together. "Baby, it's cold outside. We had such a mild winter, until now."

Val helped Fleming remove his coat. "How are you feeling, Dr. Fleming?"

"Like a rooster at dawn. How much time do we have?"

"Tentatively about two hours, providing Patrick Greene doesn't decide to postpone. Would you like something to eat?"

"You read my mind."

The trembling in Fleming's left hand had spread to the other, and he moved with a spasmodic gait—a noticeable decline since Blackwell saw him last. This was something worse than Parkinson's.

Everyone migrated to the kitchen, where Valeriya mixed up another batch of flapjack batter. Fleming's mood seemed elevated, practically celebratory, nothing like the tranquil psychologist Blackwell had conversed with before. Fleming and Val spoke about the strangest things: the housekeeper who tidied up Fleming's home, the cancellation of credit cards, mail forwarding procedures, and expandable file folders for storing papers. *Expandable folders? Who uses those anymore?* She couldn't stand the sight of Fleming when they were in Kentucky, yet now they were acting like lifelong friends. The psychologist had difficulty cutting his food, and Valeriya mothered him through the meal. Fleming's eyes wandered methodically over her sweatshirt and locked onto her beaming face. No words were spoken.

Everyone retired to the living room and passed the time by watching television. A newsflash said the Iranian Navy sank an oil tanker in the Strait of Hormuz, creating an environmental disaster—Valeriya cursed under her breath. The Iranian President and the Supreme Leader stood hand-in-hand, calling for all of Islam to rise against The Great Satan.

Aerial videos of black muck spewing from the disabled tanker drove Valeriya away from the television. She ambled to the big picture window, folding her arms across the wide windowsill. She perked up, losing her downcast frown while grabbing a pair of binoculars, raising them to her eyes and rotating the focus dial.

"What are you looking at?" Mark asked.

"You gotta see this."

He took the other pair of binoculars, catching sight of a kid playing ball with a white dog. "Is that the girl we saw in the surveillance video several months ago?"

"Yep. That's Cecilia Logan. No doubt celebrating the cancellation of school."

Blackwell chuckled. "Back in my time we had snow days where everyone got to play hooky. Now we have computer virus days. This freezing weather won't spoil her fun." He continued watching. Cecilia kicked a soccer ball, bouncing it from foot to foot and knee to knee. The little dog ran around her, prancing and dancing, barking and jumping in time with the ball. She popped the ball to the dog, and he hit it back to her with his nose. They went back and forth: knee to nose—nose to knee, foot to nose—nose to foot, on and on without the ball ever touching the ground. "That's amazing. They could go on television with an act like that."

Val smiled. "Can you envision the time she spends with that dog?"

"Must be considerable. I'll bet Cecilia plays a mean game of soccer."

A rabbit darted across the road, and the dog chased it in a grand circle, coming close to catching it several times. Cecilia ran after him and vanished behind a house.

Valeriya lowered the binoculars and sighed. "I guess the show is over."

Blackwell sensed the need to recycle some coffee. He went to the bathroom, feeling better now that his blood sugar had stabilized. Upon finishing up and washing his hands, Valeriya called out, "Turn the television off." The newscast went silent, and Mark found her rushing from window to window, binoculars raised and looking.

"What's happening?" Blackwell asked.

"Do you hear that?"

He heard something. "Kids playing?"

Philip Fleming joined them. "I hear it."

Val continued scanning with the binoculars. "Someone is screaming."

The approaching growl of a brawny engine drowned out the distant cries.

Fleming pressed close to the window. "He's here."

A gray pickup truck rumbled past the house. As the driver initiated the right turn signal, a woman darted into the road, both arms waving wildly. The wide-body vehicle skidded to a stop, and she pointed while hopping on frantic feet. The driver accelerated to the left, bouncing across a drainage ditch and driving into an open field, disappearing from view.

"What the hell was that?" Mark asked.

A blast of cold air hit the nape of his neck, and the front door closed with a bang. Valeriya whizzed past the window—no winter coat, nothing but sweatshirt, shoes, and jeans. Blackwell snatched his coat and hurried out the door.

He stumbled through stubby corn stalks, falling twice on the uneven ground. "Val, wait for me." Despite his best effort, the gap between them widened. A split-rail fence came into view, tall enough to keep horses confined. Without breaking her stride, Val planted her hands atop one of the posts and swung to the other side. Intimidating strands of barbed wire appeared at the top of the fence. Mark slowed to a walk and stopped. *Dammit. No gate to the left or right.* He caught sight of Philip Fleming making his way along the road, taking uneasy steps. Knowing he couldn't mimic Valeriya's gymnastic vault, Blackwell climbed. Getting to the top was easy, but then … With one leg on each side, the insidious barbs reminded him of who was in charge. His trousers became entangled, and attempts at freedom made things worse. *Deep breath. Stay calm. Protect the vitals.* He rested in an uncomfortable but painless position. Where was Val? There was no movement at the nearby house and nothing at Lawton's truck. Philip Fleming was nowhere in sight. He finally spotted Valeriya running toward a frozen pond. No, not completely frozen—movement at the center—something thrashing. Mark steadied his gaze: Cecilia Logan down deep in the water.

The woman from the road raced back to the pond, calling Cecilia's name—had to be the girl's mother. Blackwell removed his coat for better access to the barbed wire. Shivering in the fierce wind, he yanked and pulled, freeing himself and dropping to the other side. He put on his coat and ran to the sound of the cries.

Lawton rushed up to a barn and tried to enter. With the doors being locked, he grabbed a trashcan and hurled it through a closed window. He climbed inside and emerged with a rope, untangling the folds as he ran to the pond. He yanked off his shoes and threw off his outer clothing. Valeriya arrived at his side, helping him tie the rope around his waist. She placed her foot in the small of his back and pulled, testing the integrity of the knot.

Lawton got a running start and charged onto the ice, dropping onto his stomach and sliding until he fell through, still short of the girl. One hammer-fist came after the other, sending shards of ice flying as he smashed his way toward Cecilia. Further out in the pond, the little dog had also fallen through, now struggling to keep his nose in the air.

Panting like the fat guy in gym class, Mark tottered up to Valeriya. He bent over, gasping for breath. "What can I do?"

"Stay right here. You can help me pull them out."

"Oh, merciful Jesus," cried Mrs. Logan. "Please help us."

A bearded man wearing a red parka came trotting from the house down the road. He looked at Lawton and Cecilia. "Oh my God." He paused for an instant. "The phones are still out, but I've got ham radio—I'll call for help." The man hurried back to his house.

Mrs. Logan wrung her hands, crying and babbling to herself in fragmented sentences, "—Little Bear chased the rabbit ... fell through—ice is thin over there—geese were there yesterday keeping the water open—Cecilia went to get him—tried to stop her—Roy gave her that dog last year."

A trickle of blood flowed from Lawton's hand, yet the onslaught continued, ice shattering with every blow. Val remained at the edge of the ice, bouncing up and down on her toes, biting her lip, coiling and uncoiling the rope.

Lawton reached the struggling girl—Mrs. Logan dropped to her knees, hands raised to the sky. He grabbed Cecilia, and Blackwell heaved on the rope with Valeriya grunting and tugging behind. They pulled and pulled, but nothing happened—wrong angle of departure and poor traction in the slippery snow. Lawton waved them off and untied the rope. He looped it around Cecilia and placed her on the frozen surface. With her white coat stained with Lawton's blood, the sobbing child glided across the ice and into the waiting arms of her mother. Val coiled the rope in long cowboy-loops, making ready for another throw.

Cecilia lunged at the pond, crying out, *"Little Bear!"*

Mrs. Logan tried to drag the shrieking child toward the house, but she was being overpowered. A neighbor woman came to help, and they carted Cecilia through the snow. Ear-splitting screams shot through the air like flaming arrows in a medieval war.

Resting low in the water, Lawton watched the unruly battle, his heated breath swirling like a steam locomotive. With both hands reaching back, Valeriya flung the rope—the lasso unraveled and landed within grasping distance. Lawton eyed Valeriya, but he never went for the rope. He faced the dog in the water—brow lowered, breathing deep and long.

"You can't do it," Val yelled. "He's too far away."

Lawton's attention never wavered from the dog, its white paws pumping frantically.

The scuffle with Cecilia intensified, the girl shrieking like she was being boiled alive. Teetering from side to side, the women carted her up the steps. With outstretched fingers, Cecilia seized the door frame, making a last stand. She filled her lungs and bellowed a single, desolate wail, a flesh-tearing howl that would have turned the heads of tormented souls in Hell.

Lawton raised his bleeding fist high in the air and brought it crashing down, launching a volcanic plume of ice and water. He pushed forward and struck the ice again, hacking a channel to the dog.

Valeriya dropped the rope and dashed toward the barn, running like she was on fire.

"Where are you going?" Blackwell called.

"To find a hammer."

Mark watched the developing mêlée between ice and man, feeling ripples of admiration and wonder as Lawton rained blow after savage blow with unfading resolve. Fragments of ice dripped with blood. Blackwell looked around, seeing nothing but Lawton, the dog, and blowing snow. Submersion in freezing water will kill a man in about thirty minutes. Mark checked his watch and mentally measured the considerable distance between Lawton and the dog—death was a certainty. This was a good and satisfying thing, hypothermia accomplishing what Alex McCracken could not. It would also put an end to Valeriya's bizarre infatuation.

Val came running from the barn, panic-stricken and empty-handed. She paused at the pond, mouth open and gripping her hair with a devastated glint in her eyes. Mark watched her watching Lawton, deeply distressed at her misery. They had to be lovers—no doubt in his mind. Valeriya picked up Lawton's pants and ran her hands through the pockets, pulling out a key fob. She ran up to Blackwell. "I'm going to take the truck and go for help. There's a fire station just across the county line."

Realizing the pending victory might still slip away, Mark faced her, bold and confident. "That isn't necessary. I called 911, and help is on the way."

Her eyes grew wide. "The phones are working?"

He pulled out his cell from his coat pocket. "The signal was weak, but I got through. *They are coming!*"

Val reached up and kissed him on the lips, a warm and sensuous smooch. She ran back to the ice.

Her open display of affection shocked him, and Mark's stomach shivered with the sick feeling that he had made a horrible blunder, but it was too late now.

Valeriya watched Lawton continue the attack, blood flying with each strike. She called to him, but he didn't answer. The freezing water was taking its toll, and he was slowing down, needing several blows to break the ice.

Mark wrestled with the question of what he would say when no help arrived—all 911 calls are recorded.

Lawton's hemorrhaging grew worse, visibly red in the water. Blackwell gawked in amazement as Val pulled out her gun and wracked the slide.

"Valeriya," Mark yelled. "What are you doing?"

She ran to a different location and aimed at Lawton. Two gunshots echoed off the ice.

Blackwell ran toward her. "Have you gone insane?"

Two more shots came, a crackling thump, and then two more. Mark hastened to get a better view. She wasn't aiming at Lawton—*she was shooting the ice in front of him!*

The gunfire continued with Valeriya firing two shots just before Lawton hit the ice. They developed a rhythm: bang-bang—smash, bang-bang—smash. The ice fractured easily now, and Lawton advanced rapidly. Val inserted another magazine, maintaining her rate of fire. She emptied her third and last magazine.

With labored breathing, Lawton reached the listless dog and lifted him onto the ice. The shaking animal couldn't walk, and Lawton slid him partway to shore. Valeriya crawled onto the ice, spreading her weight across the length of her body to keep from falling through. She grabbed the dog and opened her sweatshirt, shoving him inside and scooting backward until she reached the shore. Lawton nodded to her and rested his head against the ice.

Valeriya bounded back to the house, holding the bulge on her stomach like she was pregnant. She ran up the steps and went inside.

Blackwell ambled around the pond, surveying his wounded adversary: still alive, but not moving, making no attempt to save himself. Hypothermia does that, shuts down the central nervous system. Neighbors were coming from all directions, undoubtedly because of the gunfire.

Flashing blue lights appeared on the road, and a State Patrol car pulled over. Mark shielded his eyes from the morning sun, trying to make out what was happening. Nimble footed Val ran to the officer, swiftly at first, and then she slowed, moving down into a ditch. Blackwell couldn't see, but he wouldn't leave Lawton alone, not when victory was so close. The crowd grew larger, some conversing, others standing idly, coat collars pinched to shut out the frigid wind. Gruesome deaths attract onlookers like kids to an ice cream truck. Mark overheard someone say someone was dead by the road.

Valeriya stood up, pointing in Blackwell's direction. She and the officer jogged across the snow-covered field with Val leading the way. Mark waited for them, knowing nothing could be done to save the dying man.

The trooper surveyed the situation. He unclipped a transceiver from his utility belt and raised it to his mouth. "Jessica, what's the latest on the ice rescue?"

A static-laden female voice replied, "What ice rescue?"

"The one east of Buckeye Lake."

"Ah, let me check."

Mark held his breath. *Here it comes. Act surprised and upset.*

"I've checked all dispatcher alerts," Jessica continued, "and there are no ongoing ice rescues anywhere in Ohio."

Val shot Mark a blistering glance, a mix of panic, puzzlement, and pain. She paused for a moment, wiping both eyes before dashing to the far side of the pond. She moved back and got a running start.

"Valeriya, no!" Mark yelled. He slipped and fell. *"Somebody stop her!"*

With reckless abandon, she hydroplaned across the ice, plunging into the water. She gripped the edge, pulling herself closer to Lawton. With trembling hands, Mark retrieved the rope they used to rescue Cecilia. The State Trooper barked directives at his transceiver, pleas for help and medical assistance. Numerous onlookers followed Blackwell around the pond.

Val reached Lawton and lifted his head, patting both of his cheeks.

"Valeriya," Mark called. "Catch the rope."

Blackwell heaved the rescue line, but she was too far away. It was a symbolic gesture. They needed professional rescuing, firemen with an ice-sled or cold-water suits. He called to her, but she turned her back on him, looking only at Lawton.

The trooper brought the transceiver to his mouth. "Jessica, we got two people trapped in freezing water. What's the story with the ice rescue equipment?"

The transceiver screeched, "The local fire station is engaged on another call. Help is coming, but it may take a while, at least twenty minutes, maybe longer."

Holding Lawton with one arm and gripping the ice with the other, Valeriya sank lower and lower. Mrs. Logan came to the edge of the pond. She stared at the spectacle, a torrent of tears streaming down her face.

Mark shuffled rearward, past the gaping hordes until he could no longer see the agonizing image. The dreadful calm was stifling: mouths ajar, shivers and silent sobs, everyone frozen like ghastly gargoyles. *This is the end.* From the corner of his ill-wiped eye, Mark spied a running man: the bearded guy wearing the red parka. He rested in front of Blackwell, winded and red-faced.

"I reached them on ham radio," the man said. "Air National Guard is sending a chopper with two divers from Rickenbacker."

Mark grabbed the man's shoulders. "How long before they get here?"

"Rickenbacker isn't that far. Gotta be pretty damn soon."

Blackwell glanced around: nobody within hearing distance. "Did you request an ambulance?"

"No. But I would think they would do that automatically."

"We must be sure. Go back and make certain they are sending emergency medical help."

The man nodded and ran back across the field.

Blackwell scanned the southwest skyline and listened for the distinctive chugging of a helicopter's turbo engine, seeing and hearing nothing. A large van with a satellite dish turned into the drive. It parked sideways, displaying WFKZ Channel 17 on its side. Everyone was still watching Valeriya, unaware that they were about to be on television. He searched the sky again, and there, in the distance, through the leafless trees, saw a tiny speck coming this way. *The rescue chopper!*

Mark shucked off his coat and moved into position. *Not yet. They're still unloading the cameras. Okay, two cameramen and a female reporter. Wait until they're halfway here. Hold—hold—now!* Mark dashed onto the ice, bellowing, *"Hang on, Val. I'm coming!"*

The frozen surface cracked under his feet, and Blackwell dove forward, sliding as Lawton had done before. He fell through, still a considerable distance away. Mimicking his archrival, Mark valiantly raised his fist and brought it thundering down, carving a path to the open channel. The reporter and television cameras pushed through the crowd, maneuvering for close-ups. Mark ignored them, keeping his eyes only on Val. He slashed the ice like a storming cavalry officer at *The Charge of the Light Brigade*—people gasped in awe. With his right hand bloody and bent, he swam to Valeriya, lifting her sagging head. She was rigid but seemed conscious, still holding on to Lawton. A pulsating sting spread throughout his arms. His legs grew heavy, and he couldn't kick, but the electrifying atmosphere and roving cameras kept him going. Mark held her up, keeping her face out of the water. Two minutes later, the helicopter appeared above them, and two divers plunged into the icy abyss. The chopper lowered a cabled harness, and Valeriya rose into the air. Lawton was next, and Mark helped the divers maneuver the listless man into the safety harness. Blackwell was rescued last, listening to the shrieks of a cheering crowd.

Waiting ambulance crews removed their clothes and wrapped them in heated blankets. Quietening his chattering teeth, Mark closed his eyes and smiled. *It was a brilliant move. I just might get another chance.*

26 Tilting at Windmills

Suffering only a fractured radius and some minor bruising, Blackwell was discharged from Scioto Medical Center the following day. The cast covering his right forearm was an inconvenience, but he still had full use of his fingers. Mark asked to see Valeriya but was told by the nurse-receptionist that she wasn't receiving visitors. Roy Lawton was in the same hospital, listed in intensive care. Lawton had been in freezing water for an incredibly long time and had somehow survived—an unfortunate medical miracle. With phone and internet service unrestored, the hospital was chaotic, and the hero's welcome Mark anticipated never materialized. Seeing no alternative, he rented a car and drove back to Virginia. He would've boarded a commuter jet if it was available, but all flights out of Columbus were canceled.

Mark spent the next two days in sullen solitude, watching television and passing the time. The viral attack had ground everything to a halt, and only communications technicians and government officials were working. Was Val still in the hospital? Was Lawton still alive? Without phone or internet service there was no way to know.

On the third day, a Bureau courier hand-delivered a message requesting Blackwell's presence in Washington. Mark put on a nice suit and arrived at the J. Edgar Hoover building by late afternoon. He knew something was up when he walked through the doors. People were looking at him, and several stopped to shake his left hand, congratulating him for showing incredible valor in rescuing one of their

304

own. Blackwell still hadn't seen the television footage, but apparently everyone else had.

Patrick Greene also congratulated Mark on a job well done, going above and beyond the call of duty. Blackwell wanted to smile but didn't. He accepted the praise graciously, feeling guilty and nervous about how much Greene knew, sensing a looming calamity. Only now did Mark discover with certainty that Philip Fleming had died, although it was unclear what had happened. Greene wanted details about what transpired, both at the house and the pond. Blackwell gave a mostly factual account, omitting his falsified conversation with Val.

Greene discussed the searches of Lawton's properties in Kentucky and Ohio, telling Mark the FBI found nothing of interest, neither trace of a chemical laboratory, nor anything out of the ordinary. Greene said one of his assistants declared this would go down as the most expensive wild goose chase in Bureau history. It's natural for people to die from cancer, and that's what happened to Scott Jackson and his associates—pure and simple. Greene didn't say he was closing the case, but it sure didn't look good. Still worried about what Valeriya might have said, Blackwell nodded and remained quiet. He did learn that Val was discharged from the hospital and was understandably taking some time off. Mark said he was also in need of some rest and recuperation, and Greene told him to take as much time as necessary. Blackwell left the building unscathed, seemingly everyone's beloved hero. There was only one conclusion—Valeriya had kept her mouth shut.

* * *

Phone and internet service were restored the following week, and experts on the evening news said the disruption to emergency facilities had cost several thousand lives. The military response by the United States left Iran in far worse shape: power plants destroyed, oil refineries decimated, and a total collapse of the Iranian economy. With passionate anxiety, Blackwell sent multiple emails to Valeriya and left three messages on her answering machine, but there was no reply.

The days drifted by, each leaving him more anguished than the last, and the growing dimensions of her unexplained silence weighed heavily upon him. What happened to Val? What was she thinking? She existed within him, stuck to his soul like a barnacle to the side of a ship. She was inside his mind, his blood, and the air he breathed, the shifting shadow in every darkened room. A deeper reflection was sluggish in coming, but it finally arrived. Mark's farcical rescue at the pond fooled everyone—*except for Valeriya!* He sought solace in the fact that she remained silent, allowing him to bask in the light of gallantry.

Six weeks after their last meeting, Patrick Greene called Blackwell at home, saying a biochemical workshop had been discovered. The unbridled enthusiasm in Greene's voice was evident as he explained how Bureau technicians believe the apparatus may have been used to create carcinogenic poison. Mark broke into a prancing dance. *The Stealth Killer case is still alive!* The cast on his arm was gone, and he was ready for a fresh start. He rushed headlong to the meeting, confident that at long last, he was going to see the woman he loved.

During the drive to Quantico, Mark rehearsed what he would say. He rejected an act of expiation, preferring something less damaging. The dropped 911 call was a technical glitch, something to be expected under the unusual circumstances. He honestly believed the fire department was coming. What else could Valeriya be angry about? She couldn't read his mind or know that he knew the helicopter was minutes away.

Blackwell entered the FBI Academy and proceeded to the Behavioral Analysis Unit, looking every which way for Val—she wasn't there. His recently acquired fame preceded him, and he was greeted warmly, being forced to shake everyone's hand. They showed him photographs of what had been found: spiraling tubes of glass, bunsen burners and crucibles, an assortment of beakers and flasks.

"Where was the laboratory found?" Mark asked, believing it had to be in one of the limestone tunnels underneath Lawton's Kentucky farm.

"In Philip Fleming's basement," Special Agent McMurphy replied.

Blackwell blinked. "Where?"

"In the basement of Fleming's home. You know, the psychologist who helped Alex McCracken with the case."

Mark gave a scornful snort, waggling his finger while saying, "Balderdash. *Roy Lawton is the killer!*"

McMurphy laughed and looked around the room, eyeing the other agents. "Yeah, that's what everyone thought. But it just ain't so. The evidence is overwhelming."

Mark was aghast, silent as a student who unexpectedly failed a class. *How could it be?*

McMurphy continued the discussion, showing organic chemistry formulas and compounds that would be needed to create the remarkable poison, all covered with Fleming's fingerprints. Blackwell listened and watched in miserable silence, unable to dispute the Bureau's experts. *This is another disaster!* His mind constantly drifted. *Where is Valeriya? Why isn't she here? Could I rework my three completed research papers about Roy Lawton, focusing on Philip Fleming instead?* It seemed unlikely. Aside from their casual conversations, Fleming was a complete mystery. Mark returned home, plagued with self-doubt and annoyed with the difficult situation.

Early the next day, Blackwell picked up his copy of the *New York Times*, and the smiling image of Philip Fleming leaped off the front page. The bold headline read *Serial Killer Wreaks a Winding Trail of Bloody Havoc*. Details in the accompanying article said a chemical workshop had been found in Fleming's home, and the deceased man was believed to have poisoned Scott Jackson and killed many others. Mark reread the article with dreary discomfort, even more disappointed because Patrick Greene had promised him exclusive rights when dealing with the press.

Upon his arrival at Quantico, Blackwell discovered that the Fleming story had been leaked without authorization. Mimicking the authoritative style of Margaret Marshall, Greene fired off an angry email to a long list of Bureau personnel, reminding them that the Stealth Killer case was ongoing, and having the public aware of what was happening compromised the investigation. Later that afternoon, the Behavioral Analysis Unit was informed of a new discovery, a book appearing to be

Philip Fleming's diary. Agents found it hidden under some floorboards in his laundry room.

Bureau specialists dissected the text, amazed at what they were finding. The handwritten journal chronicled who was killed and why. Fleming claimed the murders were necessary to avenge the mistreatment of animals and to strike back at a society gone mad, a populace lacking compassion and mercy. The thousand-page manifesto gave elaborate details on how the killings were done, including timelines and methods. FBI handwriting experts identified Fleming as the author because the unique slant and distinctively curled letters matched his other writings. A forensic document expert declared the book nothing less than a signed confession. This opinion was corroborated by FBI investigators who said it contained facts only the killer would know.

Much to the chagrin of Patrick Greene, the existence of the diary was leaked to the press, and they besieged him with requests for more information. Reporters seemed infatuated with the tale of a psychologist driven to murder, and their coverage increased day by day. Mark was flabbergasted. *How could I have been so wrong?*

Public pressure steadily increased, and Greene told Blackwell to get ready for a press conference, probably sometime next week. Mark could still use large portions of his research papers when describing Fleming, principally his Freudian analysis of the mindset of a serial killer. Still, he was at a significant disadvantage, lacking the personal insights behind Fleming's private life. Cursing his plight, Blackwell worked at home, developing stratagems that anticipated reporter questions. Patrick Greene would have to approve the disclosures.

Mark tried not to think of Val. He toyed with the pen she used when taking notes on Lawton's hand-written journal, recalling those frustrating yet brighter days. *Why are you hiding from me? I can give you happiness like you've never known. We didn't even get the chance to exchange friendly farewells.*

The day before the scheduled press conference, the panic of yet another disaster arrived. Television news reporters quoted the *Washington Post*, describing some newly discovered papers. Groaning with frustration, Blackwell listened for several minutes before understanding what had happened. The *Post* had somehow acquired Philip Fleming's psychological analysis of Roy Lawton when he was a student at Riverside High. Mark went out and bought the paper, hoping some fresh air would calm him down. Tantalizing excerpts were in the article, along with a website where anyone could download the complete file. Blackwell hurried home and turned on his computer. The website connection was nerve-rackingly slow, but he got the entire file. He began to read, irritated that, once again, he had been left out of the loop.

The digital file was thick, and it would take many days to digest. The early pages suggested a complex and unconventional relationship between therapist and patient, not sexual, but psychological, a titanic battle of opposing minds. The phone rang, and Blackwell was called to Quantico for an important meeting.

Patrick Greene glared at the assembled team, drenched with seething perplexity. He demanded to know what had occurred. Fleming's psychological dossier of Lawton was not leaked because the FBI never had it. With chilled precision, Greene grilled the crew that gathered evidence at Fleming's home, wanting specific details about their methods and chain of custody procedures—who did what, where, and when? The investigating agents said they never logged or tabulated Fleming's vast morass of stored medical papers since they seemed irrelevant to the case. After much discussion and consternation, no one had a clue as to how the *Post* acquired the file. Greene ended the meeting by declaring he would seek an injunction to seize the papers. He spoke to Mark privately, shamelessly having the effrontery to move the goalposts again, postponing the Stealth Killer press conference.

Interest in the voluminous dossier steadily grew. The press may not have had access to Philip Fleming's private diary, but they could now read the actual words of the most notorious serial killer in history. The Bureau refused to confirm or deny the dossier's authenticity, although an anonymous FBI source who saw Fleming's diary said the handwriting and style were the same. The strange tale gathered momentum as prominent psychiatrists chimed in with their own beliefs.

The *Wall Street Journal* printed an excerpt from famed psychoanalytic theorist Gottfried Ziegler of Munich—a man Blackwell knew. Ziegler advanced a punctilious theory that reverse therapy had occurred, a bizarre situation where the patient seems to have pulled the therapist down into a helix of murdering madness. Ziegler's startling conclusion was not distinguished for its sophistication, but rather for a brutal analogy. He said if Philip Fleming is the Frankenstein monster he's made out to be, then Roy Lawton is Baron Victor von Frankenstein. Ziegler interpreted some of the writings, noting their inner harmony and consistency. He also discussed Fleming's gradual but steady metamorphosis into unconventional thinking, yet stopping short of saying Fleming was wrong. Ziegler opined that Fleming was not psychotic and that other explanations for his behavior should be pursued.

Ziegler's controversial article ignited a firestorm of interest in Lawton, and the press stalked him like he was Bobby Fischer. But unlike the reclusive chess champion, Lawton willingly granted extended interviews. He claimed government-sanctioned (or tolerated) animal abuse pushed Fleming over the edge. The media wanted specifics, and Lawton gave them an eyeful of difficult-to-watch videos and photos of animals suffering in factory farms, images he and Philip Fleming had viewed and talked about in therapy.

Lawton appeared on the cable news networks, not defending Fleming's actions, but rather going into fastidious detail about the types of suffering that millions of animals were enduring every day. With mocking hostility, several news commentators tried to lure Lawton into endorsing the murders, but he sidestepped those questions and continued hammering away on the need for humane treatment for factory farm animals—protective legislation was needed. Lawton had a plurality of intriguing abilities: surprisingly witty, not attacking when attacked, yet never retreating. With hair smoothly parted and masterful erudition, he controlled the discussion like a skilled therapist calming a hostile patient—magnetic manipulation at its best.

When hard-nosed reporters challenged Lawton on the anti-American premise that maximizing profits should not be the primary goal of meat production, he showed more photos of organized animal abuse, letting the pictures speak for themselves. Some reporters and cable news commentators (primarily women) turned on their colleagues, kindling a rancorous debate on the morality of minimal-cost factory farms. Videos and pictures of animal abuse began surfacing from other sources, escalating the debate and causing some journalists to go undercover and investigate the actual living conditions of factory farm animals.

Mark scoffed at the media's ghoulish taste for blood, the mechanism driving Lawton's fame. And yet amidst all this turmoil, the FBI had not held a single press conference. Still muzzled by Patrick Greene, Blackwell was relegated to being a passive observer, missing out on one of the most significant psychological debates in history.

Gottfried Ziegler was the big winner, becoming a household name. This frivolous fraudster was quoted in every newspaper every day, magically multiplying his mental meanderings about murky murders and secretive serial killers. Ziegler's seductively deranged creativity stood higher than reality, lower than tasteless inability, and yet everyone seemed captivated by his conjuring thralldom. Mark toyed with the idle urge to break protocol and talk to the press on his own, yet he remained silent.

* * *

Oh, catastrophe! Six weeks after the Lawton fiasco became public, a nauseating portrait of Gottfried Ziegler appeared on the cover of *Time* magazine, posing beside an expandable file—the infamous dossier. The revolting subtitle read *The New Sigmund Freud*. With no brilliant flashes or penetrating insights, Ziegler had permanently engraved his dominating influence across the entire case. He who had done nothing was about to win everything, and that shameless con artist smirk was too much to bear.

Blackwell trudged down an FBI Academy hallway, practically dying of disgust. Patrick Greene had scheduled a press conference for next week, but all the timeliness and thunder were gone. The bumbling ineptitude of the Bureau and ever-present influence of Ziegler was enough to make one go mad. Mark paused at the elevator, battling spontaneous combustion while trying to think of some way to reclaim his intellectual property. Perhaps he could disagree with Ziegler on some of his Freudian theories, maybe provide a detailed exposition of the truth of the case, writing with more exactitude than Ziegler's vague generalities and factual fabrications. *If I ever get another chance, I will not be a good-natured submissive! Fortune favors the fearless, and one must be bold to break the shackling chains of providence.* Someone tapped Blackwell on the shoulder.

"Hey there, Superman," Richard Moore said.

Startled but pleased, Mark shook Richard's hand, folding his *Time* magazine to hide the cover. "Hey there, old buddy. What brings you out this way?"

"A Bureau training session. You know how it is working for Uncle Sam, lots of continuing education."

"I know the feeling. So, how have you been?"

"Doing good." Richard chuckled. "Which means keeping my head above water. I watched the clip of you rescuing Dr. Highland. It's the most amazing thing I've ever seen."

The mere mention of her name tensed Mark's stomach. He swallowed his anguish and pulled Richard away from the elevator doors. "How is Valeriya doing? I haven't seen much of her."

"She's spending a lot of time out of the office. I only see her once or twice a week."

"Really? Any idea what she's been doing?"

Richard shrugged. "Taking vacation time, I guess."

"Does she seem normal? I mean, do you get the impression that she's upset or depressed?"

"No. Business as usual. Most of her work has been transferred to Bridget and Marianne, everything except the complicated searches." Richard perked up. "Oh, that reminds me, do you know a detective named Robert Miller? He called yesterday."

This was more of a minor annoyance than a serious threat, but Blackwell decided to stall. "Let me think." He scratched his chin. "Miller is such a common name."

LESSER EVILS: AN ANIMAL RIGHTS NOVEL

"He works for the Wittgenstein University Police, and since you teach forensic psychology at Wittgenstein, I thought you might know him."

Mark feigned a thoughtful expression. "Miller? Robert Miller? What does he want with me?"

"Not you. He wants to talk to Dr. Highland. I told him she'd be in tomorrow."

A flush of heat trekked up Blackwell's neck. "He … He wants to see—Val?"

Richard nodded.

Don't panic! "Whatever for?"

"He needs a facial recognition scan."

"But why? Police departments do those types of searches every day."

"He wants her to screen airport surveillance footage to find a particular student and see if she was meeting someone."

"Did he say which airport?"

"That's why he needs the DDI databases. All airports, everywhere, going back for two years. He asked the FBI for help, and they referred him to her."

"I see," Blackwell murmured.

"Miller said he believes a Wittgenstein coed was traveling under a false name, meeting someone in some obscure place. If he can find where she went, security camera footage at the airport may have photographed them together." Richard cocked his head to the side. "Is something wrong? You look pale."

"It's nothing serious, just a bit of indigestion. Did Miller identify the student?" Mark asked matter-of-factly. "I might know her."

"He didn't say."

"Did he leave Val a message?"

"No. He wants to personally explain the situation. Something happened to the student, and he has a suspect in mind, hence the need for the search, or maybe two faces to look for now."

Blackwell's head went numb. He tried to appear unflustered. "When did you say Val would be back?"

"She's working a half-day today and will meet Miller tomorrow morning at nine in the above-ground DDI administration building." Richard glanced up at a clock. "I have to go. The training session has already started."

"I hope it's productive."

Mark forced a smile and watched Richard disappear around a corner. He hurried into a restroom and splashed cold water on his face. Once again, providence had entered the fray, asserting her formidable hand. Valeriya would talk to that dim-witted cop in less than twenty-four hours. Would Miller identify Mark as his suspect? Perhaps. But even if he didn't, what would Val find in her search? That damnable trip to Acapulco would do him in. He flew there from Ronald Reagan Airport, and Candy went down the next day, traveling from Miami International under the name of her deceased cousin. *That one kiss in the middle of the airport concourse will be all Miller needs to prove a romantic relationship, and I will be charged with a murder that never occurred!* Blackwell went straight to his car, the one place where he could quietly think.

He got inside and closed the car door. There were additional problems to consider. The hotel bill was paid with Mark's American Express card—Valeriya would find that in a nanosecond. He signed the hotel register as Mr. and Mrs. Mark Blackwell. The hotel would have its own security cameras, covering every hallway, the footage stored away for liability purposes, showing him and Candy entering the same room. *Stupid—stupid—stupid!* His next photo op would be standing before a judge, wearing an orange jumpsuit and handcuffs.

A troublesome fly buzzed around, eventually landing on the dashboard. Blackwell swatted the nasty beast with his *Time* magazine. He flicked the crushed creature off the picture of Ziegler holding the expandable file. *Expandable files—obsolete as buggy whips.* Mark blinked with a feeling of déjà vu. *Expandable folders for storing papers—that's what Valeriya and Philip Fleming were talking about when they were eating pancakes together.* More details from the conversation entered his head. They made no sense, unless ... That's it. Val and Fleming were working together. That's why she was nice to him.

That's why she insisted on him being there. And it must have been Valeriya who leaked Fleming's dossier to the *Washington Post*. Mark ruminated and cogitated, his mind rushing toward the lone light at the end of a dark tunnel. Like finding the missing piece from a giant jigsaw puzzle, everything fell into order. *It was a threesome—Valeriya, Fleming, and Lawton were all working together. It's so obvious. Why didn't I see this before?*

In an expanding wave of lucidity, the clouds of confusion parted, and fresh energy pumped through his veins. Now there was hope—now he had leverage. Blackwell pulled out his cellphone and began punching numbers. *Shit. You can't call her at the DDI because everything is recorded.* He needed to talk with her in private, but where? His home was the only safe place. Mark started again, this time entering Valeriya's home phone number. Her machine picked up, and he waited for the tone to record his message:

"Val, it's Mark. I must see you at once. Please come to my place as soon as you can. It's very important."

Blackwell started the car and left for home. He drove along the highway, analyzing the possibilities. His phone message had the right words, but the strategy was wrong. Val hadn't responded to his previous messages. So why would she do so now? He continued thinking. *I must get her to my house. But what can I say? This is no time for blandish manipulations or begging.* He pondered the dilemma all the way back and bypassed his home, traveling on to the DDI. Mark found her Grand Cherokee parked in its usual spot. He parked in a different location and pulled out a notepad, printing in block letters with gloved hands:

IF YOU VALUE YOUR FREEDOM AND THE LIFE OF YOUR MURDERING LOVER, COME TO MY HOME NOW. TOMORROW WILL BE TOO LATE.

That will get her attention. Mark approached her car and placed the menacing message under her windshield wiper. *All I can do now was wait.*

27 Original Sin

Blackwell parked inside his garage and lowered the door. The last thing he wanted was visitors. He entered his house and paced throughout the rooms, panicky as a fox trapped at the bottom of a well. He cast a quick glance at the clock: 3:23. *The fuse is lit, just eighteen hours before Miller talks to Val.* The narrow column of dust-filled sunlight beaming through the window made it seem later in the day.

A deeper reflection revealed a serious hole in his plan. What he was doing might be misconstrued as blackmail or coercing a federal official. *Forget Robert Miller—blackmail itself is a serious crime!* Valeriya had skewered Alex McCracken with a hidden recorder, digital proof of what was said. Would she do the same to him, especially since he gave her no alternative? Mark pumped the air with his fists. *I must search her, make sure she isn't wired.* He paced throughout the rooms again. *No, that's not enough. I must have my own recording and get her to admit the conspiracy. It's the only way to be sure.*

Blackwell sifted through the cluttered drawers of his desk, slamming them open and closed. *Where is it? I know I brought it.* He went to the master bedroom and continued the search, opening every drawer in the room, tossing things out of his way. He finally found the audio recorder and took it to the living room. The device was small, silent, and voice-activated, only recording when someone talked. He used it at Wittgenstein in conversations with troublesome students. Mark installed a new set of batteries, enough power for twenty-four hours of continuous use. *Now, where should it go?* If he placed it in his shirt pocket, it would definitely record him, but maybe not her, not well enough to be crystal clear. And eagle-eyed Valeriya might see the bulge. After some looking and thinking, he taped the machine beneath the end table next to the sofa. Brimming with his newfound proficiency to alter the path of providence, he gave it a test, speaking naturally from different locations. It worked well. The device had a glowing green LED when activated. Mark sat on the sofa, confirming with vigilance that the light couldn't be seen from that angle, at least not without getting down low on the floor.

Blackwell went back to the bedroom to clean up the mess he made. He picked up a blanket with something rigid inside. *What's this? Oh my God!* The 12 x 16 cherry-framed picture was the last thing Candy had given him—a mental oversight. The glass-covered photo of the beautiful girl was signed *To Mark, with all my love*. He stared into her eyes, mentally replaying those incongruous words. *Deceitful bitch! I teach you about forensics, and then you use it against me.* With a forceful hand, he snatched the picture and carried it to the living room fireplace. He bent one of the tabs holding the picture in place and stopped, turning the photo around. *Think you're pretty smart, don't you? Well my darling, let me show you how it's done.* Blackwell took down a calendar and hung the picture on the wall, delicately tilting the frame so she'd be looking down, witnessing his moment of triumph.

Time drifted along. Mark must have looked at the clock 100 times, asking himself as many questions. *Will she call before coming over? How bad will this be? Must it be a confrontation? The refrigerator is filled with exquisite wine. Could it become just a cozy fireside chat?* He loaded the hearth with wood, deciding to be flexible and see what happened.

The late-day sun sank into the western horizon, and there was still no sign of Val. She was sure taking her time. He hadn't eaten anything since breakfast, but his sullen stomach would not tolerate food. Total darkness fell by nine, and Mark parked himself in his favorite living room chair, lights off, hoping to see those Grand Cherokee halogens washing across the drive. The evening passed slowly, and he wrapped himself in a thick blanket, closing his eyes and listening to the ticking clock.

* * *

Something jarred him awake, like hearing the proverbial bump in the night. But this was a tapping, a steady rap-rap-rap on window glass. Blackwell turned on a lamp and checked the front door: no one there, driveway empty. The clock showed 11:57. He looked out the front and side windows: nothing but tree branches moving slightly in the wind. The knocking intensified. He grabbed his Glock pistol and pursued the clatter, creeping down the unlit hallway. With veins pulsating, he found the light switch. And there she was, waiting on the rear deck, shining palely in the misty moonlight, a disquieting apparition fit for Halloween night. With a sweating hand, he unlatched the sliding glass door and let her in.

"I'm relieved you could make it. We have much to discuss."

Val walked straight past him, not saying a word, not acknowledging his presence, down the hallway and into the living room.

Mark hurried around her and closed the lamp-lit drapes. "Where's your car?"

"I didn't bring it."

"Then how did you get here?"

"I walked."

"All the way from your apartment? That's thirteen miles!"

"I cut straight across, along the railroad tracks and through the woods."

This didn't make sense, and Valeriya never did anything without a reason. Blackwell brandished his pistol, not to threaten, but to let her know he was ready for anything. "You're telling me you came through the forest, at night, like some wild fucking animal?"

"The moon is full. I could see well enough."

Only now did he notice her malevolent apparel: the infamous jogging shoes, tattered jeans, and rumpled hoodie. His already elevated pulse climbed higher.

She shuffled impatiently, eyes fixed on the gun. "Can we get on with this?"

"Sure. We can start. But first, take off your clothes."

Her inclement complexion deepened to cherry-red. "Why?"

He had guessed right. She was hiding something, a firearm or a cunningly contrived recording device. "Because I want to see if you're wired." She didn't move. Having a pistol in hand, a gunfight between them was no contest. "I know everything, Val. I know that you and Lawton and Fleming were partners in crime. I know about the conspiracy." He took a step closer. *"I know, I know!"*

Her lower lip quivered, and hot tears welled up in her eyes. "What do you want?"

"I want you to strip. Then we can talk."

She unzipped the hoodie and took it off: no blouse, bra, firearm, or wire. Next came the shoes, socks, and nylon belt. She dropped her raggedy pants and kicked them aside, wearing nothing but camel-toed undies.

"Come on, take everything off."

Valeriya took a breath and grasped her panties, sliding them down the length of her thighs. Her private parts were shaven clean.

Mark beckoned. "I want to see them."

She kicked her panties toward him with the tips of her toes.

"Shake your head and run your fingers through your hair." She did as he asked. "Pull back your hair so I can see your ears. Show me the bottoms of your feet. Now turnaround and grab your ankles—knees straight—feet apart—wider—wider." The recorder had to be hidden in her clothes.

She faced him, blowing a wisp of dangling hair out of her eyes. "Can I get dressed? I'm cold."

Mark picked up the blanket and tossed it to her. "Use this for now." He pointed to the sofa. "Sit there."

She sat down, wrapping herself in the blanket, edges pulled up to her neck, a short distance from his hidden recorder. Her sphinxlike eyes and unreadable expression gave little away.

He gathered up her clothes and returned to his chair. The pockets were empty. She had no weapons, no wallet, and no keys, nothing but these decrepit garbs. The socks were socks, and the shoes were shoes, except the soles had been ground smooth as glass.

He kept looking, probing like an archaeologist inspecting the wrappings of an ancient Egyptian mummy. "What's the significance of these shoes?"

"Man-made materials. No leather."

"It's that simple?"

She gave an angry nod.

"Same with the belt?"

She nodded again.

He picked up the hooded sweatshirt. "And what about this?"

"You didn't bring me here to talk about clothes. *Just shoot me! Or fuck me! Or do whatever you're gonna do. I want this over with.*"

"You really want it over?"

Her nostrils expanded like those of a furious bull. *"Absolutely!"*

Blackwell went to the fireplace and struck a match, igniting the dry kindling. He picked up her clothes and turned to Valeriya. "I saved your life at the pond, and I'm going to save you now."

"Save me from what?" She sneered.

"Yourself. This sick infatuation with Lawton is killing you!"

Val sat silently observant as Mark threw the sweatshirt into the fire, her face grim as a girl at her mother's funeral. He burned her socks, panties, pants, and belt, watching the rising sparks. Rancid smoke billowed from the nylon belt—he cranked open the chimney flue. Burning the synthetic shoes would be worse, so he set them on the carpet. He turned back to her. She appeared less angry, staring vacuously into the flickering flames, resigned to her helpless condition. The pistol in his hand was an embarrassment now. He needed to secure her complete cooperation.

He sat down. "Don't look so worried."

"I have ample reason to be worried."

Blackwell trailed her gaze to the gun. He held it up and chuckled. "This? You scared the hell out of me, beating on the back door like that. I didn't know who it was." He approached her, arm extended, holding the pistol butt-first in a gesture of conciliation. "Go on. Take it."

Valeriya didn't move. He pulled back the slide to show it was chambered. "See? It's loaded, and I know from that fancy shooting exhibition at the pond that you can shoot much better than me. Take it. I want you to have it. There's nothing to fear." She remained tightly inside the blanket, refusing to touch the deadly weapon. Mark magnanimously laid the pistol next to her. He left the room and returned with socks, boxer shorts, pants with suspenders, and one of his dress shirts. He laid them across a chair. "Now you have clothes and a gun. You can leave whenever you wish." He returned to his chair and waited.

Val stayed in her monk-like shroud, declining to meet his eyes, staring darkly into the fire. Mark suppressed a smile. She couldn't leave, not without knowing what he would do.

He slackened his posture, hoping it would make her relax. "I am truly sorry for what happened here. But I'm under tremendous stress, and I needed to know I was talking to you—you and you alone. Both of us are in serious trouble for different reasons."

A guarded suspicion awakened in her eyes, like a cat spotting a prowling dog.

"This can be a win-win situation, Val. Or we can both go to prison for a long time. It's all up to you."

She arched a quizzical brow. "I'm listening."

"Let's first make a pact to level with each other, the complete truth with no lies of omission. You will tell all, and I'll do the same."

"I don't see where this is going."

Blackwell raised a reassuring hand. "You will. Trust me. Everything will become sparkling clear if you play this my way." He waited, finding Valeriya's elongated pause difficult to bear.

"All right." She pulled back the blanket, exposing her head. "Nothing but the truth."

"Did you leak Fleming's psychiatric analysis of Lawton to the press?"

"It was necessary."

"Why?"

"Philip and Roy formed an alliance. They killed animal abusers to confront the legal system and bring publicity to the plight of suffering animals on factory farms. Philip did the reconnaissance work, taking pictures and observing the comings and goings and personal habits of potential targets. Roy performed the hit and did the forensic alterations. Philip was supposed to confess to the killings and be tried for murder. Roy would be a defense witness, not to deny the slayings, but to explain the circumstances that caused Philip to kill, much like he's doing now. I'm not a lawyer, so I don't understand the legal strategy they planned to use."

"Why would Fleming agree to take the fall?"

"Someone had to be sacrificed, but only Roy had the legal abilities to go toe-to-toe with courtroom prosecutors. Aside from that, Philip was dying from Huntington's disease, so he was the obvious choice. Philip's unexpected death created a serious dilemma. The murderer and the animal rights proponent had to be separate individuals, otherwise there was no chance for success. So the plan had to change, and I released Philip's dossier to a reporter at the *Washington Post*. It wasn't as good as having a televised murder trial, but Roy is still generating significant publicity. He's booked for an appearance on *60 Minutes* next week."

"Why were you helping them?"

Her eyes glazed over as if she was elsewhere. "I was swept up in the cause. His passion is infectious, and I could feel his heated thoughts floating throughout my mind. Light became dark and dark became light, like a photographic negative. I eventually saw myself, the real me, who and what I am." She looked at him. "This is more than societal norms and regulations. It's about justice, a legitimacy that cannot be assailed!"

"What about justice for the victims?"

"The innocent victims or the guilty victims? You can't have it both ways."

Mark stifled a smirk—all of this was being recorded. "You realize that this makes you a terrorist, and even worse, a traitor to your own country."

"One side's terrorism is the other side's fight for freedom." She let out a long sigh. "I wish Roy had found another way to do this, but if such a way exists, I have no idea what it would be. People sit down in restaurants and dine on the flesh of brutalized animals, laughing and smiling as though all is well. It's a travesty, and something had to be done." She looked at him. "Something was done. By Roy. By Philip. By me. I'd do anything to end the torture, anything at all." She glowered at him with ferocious intensity. "Do you understand what I'm telling you?"

He needed more information, details about what was done and why. "When did you discover that Lawton and Fleming were co-conspirators?"

"In Kentucky, when Philip returned my lost sunglasses." She held up her hand. "Don't ask. It's a long story."

Blackwell nodded. "So Fleming was Lawton's inside man. That explains …" It seemed impossible. "Did Lawton kill Franco Larue?"

"I didn't ask."

"But that's what you believe, isn't it?"

She nodded.

Nodding was bad because it couldn't be recorded. He needed articulated answers.

"So Philip Fleming poisoned Franco Larue with botulinum toxin?"

She nodded again, but he dared not press on because she might become suspicious.

"But Larue was following McCracken's orders. Therefore Lawton killed an innocent man."

Valeriya's stony eyes darkened into lumps of black coal. "He killed Larue because of his drug mule operation with dogs."

"Mm-hm." Mark folded his arms. "You know there's a critical flaw in Lawton's scheme, and I'm surprised no one has seen it."

"What flaw?"

"The facts established early on that the killer used a restricted database to identify his victims. It's in your written report."

She nodded.

"Roy Lawton had access to the databases, but Philip Fleming did not. Therefore, Fleming couldn't have acted alone."

"Philip worked as a part-time prison counselor, and that gave him access to the criminal justice databases."

Blackwell shook his head. "It still doesn't work. You did a thorough scan of everyone searching those databases, and Fleming's name didn't appear."

"I made an oversight. Do you remember when we were talking to Sheriff Trimble in Kentucky? His office assistant, Tiny, referred to the crime of voyeurism as a 1730 and video voyeurism as a 1740."

"You mean?"

"That's right. In the beginning I scanned for people searching the databases with queries like 'animal cruelty, animal abuse, or animals killed.' But Philip used State penal code numbers instead of words. No one would do this because that's not how people are trained to search. We use words since words yield better results. What Philip did was considerably more work, but it made his searches invisible to conventional monitoring techniques. Later on I performed a scan to see who was searching penal code numbers related to animal cruelty, and Philip was at the top of the list."

"Of course, you didn't do the search until you wanted the finger pointed at Fleming?"

Val nodded.

Mark mentally tabulated her numerous legal infractions—misuse of government databases, an accessory after the fact, guilty of aiding and abetting, along with a litany of other first-degree felonies—all recorded on his hidden bug. *Now is the time to defuse the threat from Sergeant Miller—gently, if possible.*

"I need a favor from you, a considerable indulgence. And in return, I'll provide an alibi for when you met with Lawton."

"Why do I need an alibi?"

"I overheard Patrick Greene talking on his cell," Mark lied. "He is suspicious of this situation and is secretly investigating your activities. Both you and Lawton are at risk." Blackwell waited for her reply.

"What do you want me to do?"

"Richard has scheduled a meeting tomorrow morning between you and a cop named Robert Miller. He wants you to do a facial recognition scan to find a woman. And after you've found her, he'll want as much information as possible about what she was doing and who she was with."

Valeriya shrugged. "So? I've done countless searches for missing person investigations. It's routine."

"She's not missing. She killed herself, but Sergeant Miller is claiming she was murdered."

"I still don't understand what you want."

"Miller has concocted some hare-brained scheme where I killed the girl. It's true that we started an affair when she was in my forensic investigation class, and it sort of got out of control. After she died, I lied about the relationship because it would cost me my job at Wittgenstein. But I didn't kill her." Mark gestured to Candy's picture on the wall. "There she is, a signed photograph proclaiming her love for me."

Valeriya stared at the picture, not blinking, not moving, frozen in a shaman's trance.

"You know me, Val. I'm not a murderer!" Mark started to rise. "Would you like a closer look?"

She shook her head.

He sat back down. "Look, Val, this can be incredibly easy. You're going to find airport videos of me and this girl in Mexico. Other things can tie us together, credit card receipts, maybe security footage from the hotel where we stayed, enough shit to prove we were involved."

"That's not rocket science. He doesn't need me to locate simple stuff like that."

"Yes, he does. She traveled under a fake name, and Miller doesn't have any idea when or where she went—Europe or Asia, Australia or South America. The FBI referred him to you because of your knack for facial recognition scans in foreign countries."

She gave him a blank stare. "And you want me to ..."

"You must do the search. Otherwise he'll get someone else. Just keep me out of it. I don't want Miller knocking on my door with an arrest warrant." Val sat quietly thinking as a single bead of sweat trickled down Mark's brow. "I want to hear you say you'll do the search and that demented detective will have no reason to contact me." He clasped his hands together. "Say it, Valeriya. *Say it in the name of justice and fair play!*"

Her wandering eyes lurked here and there, eventually resting on the picture of Candy. "I will do the search for Miller, and he will have no reason to contact you, none whatsoever."

"Do you swear? Will you give me your solemn word no matter what you see or find in the search?"

She took a breath and met his eyes. "Yes. I give you my solemn word."

The euphoric rush was overwhelming—Valeriya's word was solid gold. *The crisis is over!* He rushed to her and fell on his knees, taking a jovial breath and wiping a genuine tear. "Tell me what I can do to make amends for my terrible behavior. I'll do anything you ask, anything at all."

She slid her bare foot into his open hands—an astonishing invitation. Mark commenced rubbing her instep with just enough pressure to release the natural tension. With gliding fingers and swirling thumbs, he progressed around the inner ankle, still keeping close to the instep. Each thumb made small circles within the hollow, fingers rubbing back and forth, not too hard, not too soft. He switched to the other foot, flexing the ball and allowing his fingers to move like caterpillars exploring a feast. Val melted into the sofa, moistening her lips with a strawberry tongue, as if her sensual senses were set alight. Her breathing deepened, fingers pressing into the armrest and sofa cushion with mounting zeal. With eyes still closed, she spoke with a toss of her hair.

"Will you let me spend the night?"

In a flash of sudden excitement, Mark rose from his knees. She met him halfway, shedding the blanket and embracing him with fire and passion. She curled her outstretched fingers around his hair and pulled him to her open mouth, kissing him with ardent lips and titillating twists of rapt desire. The flood of arousal was bewitchingly exquisite, far exceeding his wildest dreams. She pressed closer, thrusting her pelvis forward and grinding from side to side, yielding a teasing foretaste of the fabulous feast to come.

He nibbled her earlobe, whispering, "This will be a night you'll remember."

"I know," she whispered back, kissing him again and biting his lips—softly at first, then just a tiny bit harder, and then again with a bold splash of primordial lust. With moistened lips half parted, she shot him a cool and collected smile. "You should take a shower, so I can give you something *really special!*"

Her glowing face emitted a strange radiance, a willful and wanton expression, delirious with a convergence of hidden delights. His heart gyrated with unearthly exhilaration, drenched by what could only be described as a madman's fantasy. With a sharp intake of breath, he seized her mouth in a deep, soul-shattering kiss, capturing her in a possessive embrace. "I'm madly in love with you. I want it all, everything you have."

After another hot-blooded kiss, Valeriya re-cloaked herself in the blanket. "Have you eaten anything? I'm exceedingly hungry."

"Nothing since breakfast." He pulled open the end table drawer and tossed her a phone book. "Romano's thick-crust pizza is the best there is, and they deliver all night long."

"Pizza sounds great." She beamed at him slyly and opened the book, flipping through the pages.

With boundless avidity Blackwell turned the corner into the bathroom, pulling off his clothes.

"What do you want on your pizza?" Val called from the living room.

Mark understood the new rules. "Veggie, of course." He turned the hot water valve and waited for the cold water to purge from the line. "I have Château Lafite in the fridge."

"Sounds wonderful," she called from a greater distance.

He whistled into the shower stall and closed the frosted-glass door—there was room for two. "Do you want to come in with me?" Mark called in a loud voice. No reply—she must be ordering the pizza. With a bar of Irish Spring soap, Blackwell scrubbed away, joyfully dismissing his troubles. *Let gorgeous Gottfried Ziegler keep his ill-gotten fame. Valeriya is finally mine! I'll tell no more lies and work day and night to show her just how much I care.*

"Are you using plenty of shampoo," Valeriya called, "on top and below?"

"Mop degreaser is on the way." Mark took the shampoo bottle and filled his cupped hand, slathering the liquid over his head. As thick suds trickled down his face, the shower door squeaked open, filling him with rapidly rising expectations. "I knew you couldn't resist." A sudden pinch stung his stomach—a prickle of pain mingled with precipitous pleasure. "Hey? What's this, an animalistic love bite?" A stronger nip bit him again. He inhaled sharply, and the shower door closed. "What the ... Val?" He placed his face in the stream of water to flush the shampoo out of his eyes. "Valeriya?" It took another minute to cleanse the soap from his body.

Bleary-eyed and grimacing, Blackwell rolled back the shower door and stepped outside. "Where are you?" He saw and heard nothing. "I don't appreciate your warped sense of humor." He put on his eyeglasses and examined his stomach: no visible mark. Both pains felt like his twice-daily injections, except they were longer and more pronounced. A weird thought gouged him, indescribable yet excruciating. *Ultraviolence from Valeriya? No. That's impossible!* As quickly as flipping a light switch, the room tilted sideways, and a wave of wooziness avalanched from above. *Oh, God.* On wobbly legs, he somehow put on a robe, still looking for Val. His left knee buckled, and then the right, dropping him to the floor. Mark arose, fighting to regain control as he took an involuntary step backward. He fell again and crawled across the carpet, feeling the walls move left and right, like the house was spinning in a tornado. He raised himself to a slumped position against the living room wall, his energy steadily leaching away.

"Just lie down and close your eyes," Valeriya called. She stepped into the room wearing the clothes he had given her, shoeless but wearing socks, backpack hung on her shoulder, latex gloves on both hands.

Out of necessity, Blackwell remained as he was, gasping with panic and eyeing her backpack. "Where did you hide that?"

"Behind the evergreens surrounding the deck."

"How much?" He coughed. "How much did you give me?"

"Two full syringes." Her voice was relaxed, without stress or anger. There were no hot tears like before, just stolid determination.

Taken on an empty stomach, one loaded syringe would cause hypoglycemic coma, but two would be lethal. Insulin overdose was a common method of suicide for healthcare professionals. The thought tore at his insides. He tried to get up but couldn't. He groped for the right words, finally saying, "So this is it?"

She nodded. "It will be easier if you relax and take deep breaths."

He bared his chattering teeth. "May I know why?"

"They get their chance. That's how this goes down. You're a loose cannon, and I'm not taking any unnecessary risks."

He raised himself slightly. "You planned this all along! That's why you walked here instead of driving, so no one would see your car. That's why you shaved yourself clean, to eliminate the chance of a fallen pubic hair if we made love."

Her silence was deafening, lasting for what seemed like an eternity.

From his lower vantage point, Mark spotted his audio recorder—recording light on. He looked for his pistol, but it was nowhere in sight. The phone book she touched burned in the fireplace. "You gave me your word, *your solemn word!*"

"And I shall keep it. I will do the search for Miller, and he will have no reason to talk to you, none whatsoever."

Val went into the kitchen, still visible from where he was. She spread paper towels across the countertop, covering the entire surface. She opened her backpack and deposited two used syringes. She counted his unused syringes (each sealed in a plastic bag) and counted the used syringes in his medical waste jar.

"What are you doing?" Blackwell called. She ignored him. The taped conversation would convict her of first-degree murder, providing she didn't find the recorder. *Make her talk! Get her to give the gory details!* "Answer me, goddammit!"

"I'm making sure the number of used and unused syringes total 100, the number marked on the box. Otherwise it would raise questions."

"Where did you get the extras, the two you dropped in your bag?"

"You stashed some in my glove compartment when we made the trip to Ohio."

With rubber-tipped tweezers and a lighted loupe, Valeriya scrutinized the syringes from his medical waste jar, holding up each hypo like a jeweler inspecting a precious stone. With an unerring eye and rock-steady hands, she went through eight before finding the two she wanted. Gripping his insulin bottle with gloved fingers, Val loaded both syringes and squirted the medication into the sink. She opened the faucet and flushed the residue down the drain.

"What was all that?" Mark wheezed.

"They'll find your fingerprints on the syringes, and chemical tests will show they've been filled with fresh insulin." She carefully placed the modified syringes back in the medical waste jar and closed the lid.

"Couldn't you just roll my dead fingers across them? That's what your murderous lover would do."

"You've just taken a shower, so your hands are free of natural oils. Perspiration alone will not yield good prints."

The toxic degradation continued—he hadn't much time. "There's no suicide note. They'll know you killed me."

"It won't be a suicide. Accidental insulin overdoses happen all the time. You gave yourself an injection and got distracted, forgetting the first and giving yourself a second dose—an unfortunate mishap. There will be no other explanation."

Blackwell marshaled all his remaining strength to speak. *"You're no Roy Lawton!"* he jeered with agonized emphasis. "You'll make a mistake, some small oversight—a strand of hair, a flake of dandruff, something to prove you were at the scene of the crime."

"You left me a phone message saying I must come to this house at once. I'll be back tomorrow and find the door unlocked and your body where it is now. I'll make a call for help and cooperate with the investigation. No one would even suspect me because of your heroic *'rescue'* at the pond." She held his gaze. *"You are my iron-clad alibi!"* With icy vividness, Valeriya walked into the living room and peeled the taped audio recorder from under the end table.

Mark stared in amazement. "How ... How did you know?"

"I noticed a glowing light in the reflective glass image of the girl on the wall." She held up the recorder. "That's when I knew there was no turning back, that you could never be trusted."

His throat jerked with a convulsive spasm. "Murder is a burdensome cross to bear. It will plague you for the rest of your life."

"I'm feeling the weight of it now."

Mark tried to reply but couldn't. Enshadowed in the boundaries between the living and the dead, time slowed to a crawl. He could move his eyes, but that was all. He surrendered to the inevitable, progressively pulled into deeper and darker torrents. Taking his final breath, he languidly gazed up at the smiling picture of Candy Rowan, clearly hearing her cackling laugh. Thick darkness approached from the walls, and Mark sank into the appalling blackness.

* * *

With heavy feet and a downtrodden heart, Sergeant Robert Miller trudged to the top of the stairs. Dr. Valeriya Highland approached from the other direction. She seemed slimmer than the last time they met, and her lovely brown hair was longer, parted in the middle with Indian braids. Miller shook her hand, and they entered a conference room.

"Would you like coffee?" she asked.

"Yes, please. Just a little cream."

She poured coffee, added cream, and passed him a flash drive. "Here's what you asked for."

Miller stared at the tiny device, no bigger than his little finger. "What does it show?"

"It's video footage from the main terminal at Cancún International Airport. It shows Mark Blackwell kissing Candace Rowan on the cheek."

"On the cheek? Nothing more?"

"On the cheek, the same as dozens of other travelers were doing as they greeted their friends and family. You can request the original footage from Cancún Port Authority. Should be here in a week or two."

Miller showed her a newspaper photo from the *Boston Globe*. "Is this you, the woman trapped in the frozen pond?"

She nodded.

"Is it true what the newspapers said, that Mark Blackwell held you up in that freezing water?"

"Two of us were on the verge of drowning, and he held both of us up until rescue divers could enter the water. Otherwise, we would both be dead."

Miller looked down and rubbed his face. "I must be getting old."

"Why do you say that?"

"I was so sure it all fit together."

"That what fit together? I know Miss Rowan died, but you never did say what this was about."

"I had this theory that Professor Blackwell was dating one of his students and got her pregnant. And when she refused to get an abortion, he killed her rather than owning up to the distressing situation, which would have cost him his prestigious position."

"Was Miss Rowan pregnant?"

Miller tilted rearward, exhaling a long breath. "I don't know. There was no autopsy at the request of the family. However, she bought a book for expectant mothers and a pregnancy test kit."

"Go on."

"I wish I could. It was a circumstantial case with disputable evidence, but I believed it—at that time." He held up the flash drive. "I was hoping this would break things loose."

"You could go to Cancún and investigate. I can direct you to the right people."

Miller shook his head. "What's the point? The man is dead, and I have no desire to trample upon the grave of a hero without conclusive proof."

"Is there anything else I can do for you?"

Miller drained his cup of coffee and stood up. "Not for now. But it's nice to know that people like you exist." He smiled and gave the flash drive back to Valeriya. "Thank you for your time."

* * *

Valeriya escorted Miller out of the building. After saying their final goodbyes, they walked in different directions. She paused at a newsstand and bought a copy of the *New York Times*. She carried the paper to a park bench and sat down to read, looking for the article she wanted. Inconspicuously buried at the bottom of page seventeen was a small-print notice of Roy Lawton's intention to run for Congress. Two months ago, that would've been page-one news. Now the press was fixated on Anthony Naples' defection. A Russian submarine picked him up off the coast of Canada. He was alive and well in Moscow, spilling his guts in exchange for the protection of Russian citizenship. Valeriya's cellphone chimed, announcing a text message:

Everything's ready. This is so exciting. I hope you are bringing Shingles and Toni. Silver Bells needs someone to play with. Miss you and head over heels in love. Lisa.

Valeriya typed her reply:

Of course they are coming. Looking forward to a long, relaxing visit—especially those warm and cozy nights. We'll be there next Tuesday afternoon.

Valeriya reread the article about Roy Lawton. *Everyone's watching you, but nobody's looking at me. I'll give you some time—and if you need it, some serious help.*

The End.

Made in United States
Orlando, FL
08 September 2022